FROM THIS MOMENT ON

FROM THIS MOMENT ON

COLETTE CADDLE

ISIS

LARGE PRINT

Oxford

First published in Great Britain 2013
by
Simon & Schuster UK Ltd.

Published in Large Print 2014 by ISIS Publishing Ltd.,
7 Centremead, Osney Mead, Oxford OX2 0ES
by arrangement with
Simon & Schuster UK Ltd.
A CBS COMPANY

CIP data is available for this title from the British Library

ISBN 978-0-7531-9274-0 (hb)
ISBN 978-0-7531-9275-7 (pb)

Printed and bound in Great Britain by
T. J. International Ltd., Padstow, Cornwall

In memory of Maeve Binchy.
The lady who paved the way
in commercial fiction for
Irish female authors.

Acknowledgements

My gratitude, as always, goes to the team of people that enabled this book to make it as far as the bookshelf. Suzanne Baboneau and the wonderful team at Simon & Schuster. Sheila Crowley, my agent and friend. Declan, Helen and Simon at Gill Hess. The booksellers who, despite these difficult times, remain supportive, encouraging and kind.

And my thanks to you, dear reader, for choosing *From This Moment On*; I hope you enjoy it.

CHAPTER
ONE

Lynn could see his shape through the mottled glass and hear his slow, steady footsteps coming down the corridor. She edged backwards until she was flat against the wall, her heart pounding so hard she felt he might hear it. She moved slowly, and as silently as possible, towards the door, groping in the darkness with trembling fingers for the handle. It felt like forever before her hand closed around it and she wrenched the door open and started to run. She fled down the corridors and out through the first door she came to and didn't stop running until she was on the street. She clutched her waist at the stitch from her efforts and looked around, trying to get her bearings. She figured she was at the side of the building; if she took the next right it would bring her safely back to her car.

Despite the pain, she kept going but when she rounded the corner she was on a street she didn't recognize. She cursed, realizing that she'd come in the wrong direction. Should she turn back and risk running into him, or keep going, hoping for another turn that would mean a longer but safer route? She looked over her shoulder and decided on the second option. She started running again and finally, gasping, emerged on the right street. Her car stood alone now, the road deserted, and she hurried towards it. And then she saw a figure emerge from the shadows and walk towards her, and she knew that this time there was no escape and started to scream.

"Lynn! Lynn, wake up! It's okay, you're safe, darling."

She dragged herself back to consciousness, aware that her face was wet with tears and her heart was pumping as if she had just run a marathon. Her nightdress clung to her perspiring body as Frank pulled her close.

"Was it the same dream?"

"Yes," she whimpered, nestling into his neck, her heart rate gradually slowing as he cuddled her and kissed her hair.

"There must be some medication the doctor can give you. I can't remember when you last had an unbroken night's sleep."

"He says the therapy will help," Lynn assured him. "That and time."

He kissed her lightly on the forehead. "Try and get some rest, darling."

"Hold me, Frank," she begged.

"Of course I will, darling. Now close your eyes and think nice thoughts. No one's going to hurt you while I'm around."

How lucky she was to have Frank, she thought, relaxing in his arms. They'd known each other for three years and moved in together eighteen months later after his divorce had come through, setting up home in a small house on the outskirts of Rathbourne. They were probably as close as a couple could be. Their values were the same, they shared similar views on most issues and the mutual attraction had been almost instantaneous.

They had met at a race meeting. A gang from Hawthorn Lodge had arranged a day out once the Christmas and New Year celebrations were over. She knew nothing about horse racing but it sounded like fun, and it was a good opportunity to check out staff morale.

She was enjoying her new management role but realized it was important that she didn't distance herself from the staff. Occasions like this — when everyone was relaxed and had had a few drinks — were often times when grievances were aired.

But Lynn hadn't expected the day to be quite as chaotic and busy as this and she soon gave up trying to keep track of her colleagues. She found herself a good, sheltered spot to huddle in near the winning post, where she could enjoy the atmosphere and excitement as the horses thundered home. It was there that she bumped into Gina, a friend from her school-days who'd left Rathbourne many years ago and was now living in Dublin and working in the advertising department of one of the broadsheets. She had a pass for one of the VIP tents and insisted Lynn join her for a drink. She had just nipped back out to watch a race, leaving Lynn to enjoy it in comfort on the large screen, when there was a roar of approval as an outsider passed the winning post. A girl who had obviously backed the

3

winner threw out her arms in delight, knocking the pint in Frank's hand, and most of the contents ended up over Lynn's arm and in her handbag. He was hugely apologetic about the stain on Lynn's suede coat, but she was much more worried about her mobile phone, which was lying in a pool of beer.

"Quickly, give it to me," he said, and sped off in the direction of the toilets. Lynn lost sight of him in the crowd and ended up standing like an eejit outside the gents' loos. She was beginning to wonder if she'd ever see him or her phone again when he emerged smiling. "I think I might have caught it in time. Try it."

Lynn typed in her password, phoned one of the gang and also checked her texts. "It all looks fine, thank you!" She smiled up at him, noting his blue eyes and nice smile.

"Hey, it's the least I could do. Sorry about your coat." He frowned. "I don't even know your name."

"Lynn Stephens." She held out her hand.

It was swallowed in his firm grip. "Frank Hayes. I should pay for the dry-cleaning bill at least."

She felt herself blushing like a schoolgirl. "Don't worry, this coat is ancient. I only wore it because I was warned that I would probably freeze."

"Well, then, at least let me get you a hot whiskey or an Irish coffee to warm you up."

"I should probably get back to Gina," she said, looking around for her friend although she really didn't want to leave.

"Gina Dolan?"

"You know her?"

He laughed. "I do indeed and, trust me, she'll be down at the winning post and it'll be half an hour at least before she fights her way back up here, so you may as well wait in comfort."

"Okay, then," she agreed, only too happy to accept the offer.

They found two stools at the bar and he ordered their drinks. "So, you're a friend of Gina's."

"We were at school together but her family emigrated to Australia when we were sixteen; we were broken-hearted to be parted. We kept in touch for a while but, well . . ." She gave him a rueful grin. "You know what teenagers are like! Today's the first time we've met since. I didn't even know she'd moved back to Ireland."

"How extraordinary."

"How do you know her?"

"We used to work on the same newspaper." He looked confused. "So, are you here alone?"

"No, I'm with a large party from work."

"Won't they miss you?"

She laughed. "I doubt it. I've hardly spent more than twenty minutes with any of them all afternoon. I had no idea there was so much involved in horse racing."

"It's a bit frenetic, but it's fun."

"Yes, I'm having a ball, despite the cold."

"And having beer thrown over you." He grinned. "What do you do?"

"I'm assistant restaurant manager of a hotel in Rathbourne," she said proudly.

She had always wanted to work in the hospitality industry, and, when she'd completed her degree in hospitality management, Charles Boland, the owner of the prestigious, four-star hotel on the outskirts of her home town of Rathbourne, had immediately offered her a job. She had been eager to learn, and, when he'd seen what a hard worker she was and that she was good with both the staff and customers, he had taken her under his wing and she'd quickly moved up the ladder.

"Hawthorn Lodge?" he asked, looking impressed.

"Yes, do you know it?"

"I was at a function there once; it's very fancy. You seem young to hold such a senior position; you must be good."

"I am," she said, her eyes twinkling, "but I think it's easier to do a job when you love it."

"I agree. There's a lot of deadlines and pressure in my job but I thrive on it."

"Are you a journalist?"

"For my sins," he laughed. "Getting invited to these events is one of the few perks of the job. Do you live in Rathbourne?"

"Yes and have done all my life." She pulled a face. "And still with my parents but, in my defence, it didn't make sense to move out: the hotel's just a fifteen-minute walk from our house."

"I don't blame you for staying. It's a lovely spot. The town is a nice size."

"Yes, small enough that you know a lot of the residents but big enough that you can have privacy if and when you want it." She laughed.

"Do you need privacy?" he asked, his eyes teasing.

"In the hotel business you're surrounded all day, so it's nice to be able to get away from time to time."

"And where do you go to get away?"

"There's a nice spot down by the river that not many people know about. My friend Val and I go there a lot. Where do you live?"

"In Dublin."

"Lovely." She sighed; a part of her had always been attracted to living in the buzzing capital.

"Not really. My flat's over a chip shop in a dodgy part of town but it's central and cheap."

She looked at him curiously. He was well dressed and in a good job. Why on earth was he living *there*?

They continued to talk, finding more and more common ground, unconsciously moving closer together and completely unaware of the people around them. The spell was broken only when Frank's mobile rang. He shot her an apologetic look. "Sorry, I need to take this. It's my son."

Her shock must have been apparent. "I'm separated," he said hurriedly before taking the call.

Suddenly his living arrangements made sense and she felt a pang of disappointment. She should have known he was too good to be true. "I have to go, anyway."

"Hey, Philip, hang on a sec, will you?" Frank put down the phone and pulled a card from his breast pocket. "Will you call me, Lynn? I can't remember the last time I've enjoyed an afternoon so much."

She hesitated. She had no wish to get involved with a married man — even if he *was* separated.

"Please?"

She looked into those gorgeous eyes and took his business card.

"Promise you'll call."

"I promise," she said.

He turned her hand and kissed her palm. "I will count the minutes."

Lynn cuddled in closer to him now, comforted by the memory of that magical day. She had been happy, carefree and confident then. As she closed her eyes and finally drifted off to sleep she wondered whether she could ever be that way again.

"Are you doing anything today?" Frank asked, as he buttered a slice of toast.

"I'm seeing Dr Kelly." Lynn dropped a teabag in a mug and added water from the kettle. She felt tired at the thought. Each counselling session seemed to take more out of her than the last. She didn't want to talk about her feelings or relive what she'd been through, but her GP had insisted it was an important part of the recovery process and her solicitor encouraged it, saying it would help their case.

Julian Kelly was based in the next town. The doctor he'd originally recommended was in Rathbourne and Lynn had refused point-blank to see him. At best, she'd be seen coming and going there; at worst, the psychiatrist would be linked in some way to her ex-employer — everyone was.

Frank glanced up at her. "Anything else?"

"I may drop in to see my folks." She took milk from the fridge and added a dash to her tea. Frank was always pushing her to get out more, see people, but, though sometimes she planned to go out or arrange to meet someone for lunch, when the time came she usually chickened out. Val was the only friend that she remained close to.

"Exciting stuff," Frank muttered and went back to reading his paper.

The phone rang and Lynn waited for him to get it; she never answered the phone if she could help it.

He raised his eyes to hers and gestured to his mouthful of toast.

With a sigh, she crossed to the extension by the door and picked it up. "Hello?" She listened in silence.

"Yes, I'm here, sorry," she said after a few moments. "It's just a bit of a shock." She forced herself to concentrate, aware of Frank's curious eyes on her. "Okay, I'll do that. See you, then. Thank you so much for everything."

Frank lowered the *Irish Times*. "Who was that?"

She sank into the seat opposite him, feeling light-headed. "The solicitor. They've settled. Calum got a call last night and the confirmation was just faxed through to him. I have to sign a confidentiality agreement and that's that."

Frank smacked the table in triumph. "I knew Calum Bailey was the man for the job, but I can't believe he's got a result so quickly."

"A good one, too: he got ten grand more than we expected and a reference, though no apology or admission of guilt." She sipped her tea, barely tasting it. It had taken a while for Frank to persuade her to take the constructive-dismissal case against Hawthorn Lodge and the Boland family, and she'd often wondered whether it had been the right thing to do. Now, six months later, it was over. No court case, no confrontation, no admission of liability. Just a cheque.

"We knew that there'd never be an admission of guilt. Congratulations, my love." He reached across to squeeze her hand. "Happy?"

She gave him a weak smile. "I feel a bit stunned, to be honest."

"I'm not surprised, it's quite sudden. I'm delighted for you, Lynn. Now you can put it all behind you and start again."

Start again? Attend job interviews, step back into the business world? The thought terrified her.

"You'll feel better when you're back at work, and with your experience I'm sure it won't be hard to find a job. Any company would be lucky to have a manager with such drive and ambition."

"I'm not sure I have either any more."

"You're still the same person, Lynn. You can be anything you want to be."

She smiled, touched by the concern so clear in his eyes. "Thanks for the vote of confidence."

He glanced at his watch. "I'm sorry, I've got to go." He stood up and pulled her into his arms.

As he kissed her, Lynn clung to him, wishing he didn't have to go to work, not today.

He groaned as she pressed her body against his. "I wish I could take you back to bed and celebrate all day."

She smiled. "I'll be here waiting when you get home."

"And I'll take you out."

"I don't think so, Frank —"

"Why stay in and hide, Lynn? You've been vindicated."

"Don't forget, I have to sign a confidentiality agreement."

He snorted. "It doesn't matter if you take a vow of silence, word will soon filter around the town. And people will know that Charles wouldn't have settled unless he had to. It's almost better that it didn't go to court: it shows that he doesn't want to wash his dirty linen in public — or Vincent's, to be precise."

Lynn winced. Hearing Frank simply saying his name was enough to make her feel sick. It was over a year since Vincent Boland had started to make her life a misery and seven months since she'd walked out of her job, unable to take it any more. She had gone to his uncle first and told him of how she was being harassed and bullied. She was sure that he would stand up for her but she had forgotten one very important fact: Vincent was family, and family always came first with Charles.

"Come on, Lynn," Frank coaxed, "let's have a night out."

"Okay, then," she said, trying to look enthusiastic. How could she tell him that just the thought of going out was enough to bring on a feeling of blind panic? He had been fantastic since the day she had walked out of her job but he couldn't help her break out of this dark place and she knew that frustrated the hell out of him. He urged her to put it down to experience and move on. At forty, twelve years her senior and working in the tough, unforgiving world of journalism, he'd had his share of knocks, but he had got through them all and gone from strength to strength. He was freelance now, unhappy with being tied to one newspaper, and had recently become a regular guest on TV and radio current-affairs programmes. Lynn's heart swelled with pride when he talked objectively and knowledgeably on so many issues, his voice calm and authoritative.

"Oh, damn," Frank groaned. "I forgot. I'll be a bit late: Carrie wants to see me."

Lynn froze at the mention of his ex-wife. "Why?"

"I'm not sure, to be honest. I was in the middle of a meeting yesterday when she phoned."

Lynn said nothing. She didn't want to argue, not today, but she hated that Carrie always seemed to be contacting Frank on some pretext or other. It hadn't escaped her notice that Carrie's calls had increased since he'd become a minor celebrity and, now that her latest fling with a high-flying fashion designer was over, Lynn wondered whether she was looking at the husband she'd abandoned with fresh eyes. It was only if Lynn had consumed a couple of glasses of wine that she had the courage to broach the subject with Frank. He seemed to find it highly amusing.

"We've been divorced for nearly two years and apart for seven. Why on earth would you think she'd want me back and, more importantly, why do you think I'd have her?"

"You loved her once," Lynn would say on these occasions. "You had a life together. I'm the only woman in your life since she left you. You were without a woman for four years!"

"I was too busy earning money to pay the legal and maintenance costs to date a woman, never mind be able to afford to take her out," he'd point out.

"And Philip will always be a bond between you. Someday you will be grandparents together," Lynn would continue, feeling melancholic at the thought.

He was bemused by her insecurities and the conversation usually ended with his taking her to bed to remind her that she was the only woman he was interested in.

But was that still the case? she wondered. The Lynn he had fallen for had been strong and independent and full of confidence. Not this woman who had no interest in going anywhere or seeing anyone. He tried to hide it but she knew that sometimes he resented going to charity dinners, premieres or awards ceremonies without her. He tolerated it because of all she had been through, but, if she couldn't pull herself together now that the case was over, would he still be as understanding?

"It won't take long, I promise," Frank was saying as he shrugged into the jacket of his suit, "and when I get home you'd better be dolled up to the nines. I'm taking you to Dylan's."

"Oh, Frank!" Butterflies filled her stomach at the thought of going to the best restaurant in the county. She was on the point of refusing when a vision of the curvaceous Carrie came to mind and she swallowed her protest.

He tugged her pyjama top off her shoulder and kissed just above her collarbone, making her shiver. "No arguments, darling. Have a wonderful day. Relax and revel in your success. Forget Vincent Boland and his bloody uncle. They can't hurt you any more."

CHAPTER
TWO

Lynn had good reasons for hesitating in taking on her employer. The Boland family was one of the oldest in the area, originally cattle farmers who owned an extensive amount of the luscious land in the county. But Vincent's grandfather had been the one to see that the scenic area had possibilities outside of the agricultural industry and had built Hawthorn Lodge. Charles had been a chip off the old block and the family now owned two hotels, three pubs and four off-licences. Charles also dabbled in the property market, though few knew to what extent.

Hawthorn Lodge was the flagship of the Boland empire and Charles's pride and joy. He had pumped a lot of money into the place and, with its proximity to Dublin, it was a popular spot for society weddings. When his wife had died people had assumed that he'd sell the house he'd built for his bride thirty-five years ago, but Charles continued to live alone in the imposing grey-stone mansion that overlooked the town.

Lynn used to walk past the long driveway of that majestic house and smile. It was impressive and solid, like its owner. She liked and admired Charles and had been proud to work for him and even prouder when she impressed him. These days Lynn gave it a wide berth, in fact she walked nowhere if she could help it and, after she had first left Hawthorn Lodge, she wouldn't drive anywhere, either.

Just getting out of bed and dressing was a big enough ordeal for Lynn back then, so getting behind the wheel of a car was unimaginable. She had finally conquered that fear but she still rarely ventured far, just to her parents' or to meet her best friend, Val. In the early days, they would stay in but now they ventured out to Brannigans, a shabby, old-fashioned pub five miles out of town that wasn't owned by the Bolands. Other than that, Lynn's only outing was to see the psychiatrist.

"So, Lynn, how have you been?" Julian Kelly asked.

She looked away so he wouldn't see the irritation in her eyes. What a bloody stupid question! And he asked it every time. If she was okay she wouldn't be here, wouldn't still be taking antidepressants. "Okay," she said, as she always did.

"Have you been going out much?"

"A little." Lynn still avoided his eyes.

"In Rathbourne?"

She shook her head wondering if he realized that she would prefer to be anywhere other than here. Their sessions were like a dance, he trying to draw her out, she ducking and dodging and avoiding the issues. She knew that it was ridiculous, that it defeated the purpose, that there was a good chance that, if she completely unburdened herself, she might start to feel better but —

"Lynn? You seem agitated. Has something happened?"

She jerked herself back to the man and felt guilty when she saw the concern in his eyes. But her irritation wasn't directed at him. It was the subject of their discussions that she couldn't stand. "I heard this morning that my case has been settled."

"I see. How does that make you feel?"

She shrugged. "Cheated yet relieved. Angry but guilty, too. Frightened but most of all . . . sad." Her eyes filled up as she looked straight at him, letting him see her pain for the first time.

He reached for a box of tissues and placed them on the table beside her.

"You wanted your day in court."

She waved her hand in disgust. "No. I hate that phrase. I suppose I wanted him to feel humiliated and embarrassed. For one day I wanted him to feel as miserable as *I've* felt since this all started fifteen months ago. I was good at my job, really good. I was happy working in Hawthorn Lodge, and while Charles was running the place everything was great. And then he handed the reins over to *him* and my whole life changed, just like that." She reached for a tissue. "When I told Frank and the solicitor it all sounded so lame and I felt like a pathetic whinger. You can understand, if I felt that way telling my partner, how hard it was going to be for me to get into a witness box but I had geared myself up, it was all I was focusing on and now I feel," she shook her head as she struggled for the correct word, "robbed."

Julian smiled. "Pathetic? The fact that you were ready to do that proves the contrary."

"Maybe."

"What kicked the bullying off, do you think?" Julian probed.

The question took her by surprise. "I told you: Vincent's uncle left. I assume the power just went to his head."

"So up until then you got on well?"

"Yes, we made quite a good team. Haven't I told you all this before?" she said feeling weary.

"Perhaps you have; my memory isn't what it used to be," he said with a smile. "Why do you feel guilty?"

She looked down at her hands, twisting the tissue round and round her fingers. "For upsetting everyone. My parents, Frank, my best friend — they've all been so worried about me." He said nothing for a moment, just frowned and made a note. How Lynn would love to get her hands on that file!

"And the sadness?"

"Sorry?"

"You said that most of all you feel sad."

"I had a job that I loved, that I knew I was good at, and I lost that." She felt tears threaten again. "And I'm afraid . . ."

"Yes?" he prompted gently.

She gulped. "I'm afraid I've lost part of myself, too. It's hard to believe, but I used to be so confident. I was able to negotiate, to discipline staff, to make a presentation to a room full of strangers. Now I start to shake if anyone talks to me — even the postman! I'm a mess, a sad, sorry mess."

"You're talking to me," he pointed out, the corners of his mouth lifting in a kind smile. "In fact this is probably the most that you've *ever* talked."

"That's not the same. You're helping me. In Rathbourne everyone wants to know why I left my job, why I never go out. When this news breaks the gossips will have a field day and if I go out I'll be pestered."

He shrugged. "It'll be you today and someone else tomorrow."

"I think it'll last a bit longer than that. Anything to do with the Bolands is always news."

"So what do you plan to do?" he asked.

She looked blank. "Do?"

"Are you going to stay indoors for the foreseeable future?"

"I wish I could but my man insists he's taking me to dinner tonight to celebrate." She gave a wry smile as she thought of Frank's absolute determination to fix her.

Julian sat back in his chair and stared at the ceiling. "Do you think you're afraid of talking to people in general, or are you really just afraid of bumping into Vincent?"

She recoiled at the mention of his name.

He looked over at her. "It's completely understandable, Lynn."

"Tell me what I can do," she begged him.

"Protect yourself. Don't go anywhere alone where you might meet him. But, if it's any comfort, the reality wouldn't be as difficult as the scenario that you've built up in your head."

"Really?"

He smiled. "Really."

"Thank you, Doctor. That helps."

"I'm glad. Well done, Lynn. You've made great progress today."

Lynn had only just got back into the car when she got a text from her friend, Val:

WE NEED TO MEET. I HAVE NEWS.

She frowned. Surely word couldn't be out already about the settlement, not before she'd even signed the documents. It must be about a man. Val fell in love on a regular basis but her relationships rarely lasted more than a few weeks. Lynn replied,

HOW ABOUT COFFEE TOMORROW EVG?

Seconds later Val responded,

NO, TODAY, IT'S IMPORTANT. I FINISH IN 30 MINS. CAN YOU PICK ME UP?

Lynn frowned and quickly typed,

ON MY WAY. SEE YOU AT THE CHURCH.

She turned on the ignition, her own problems forgotten. Val wouldn't send such a message unless it was something serious. She might be a hopeless romantic but she was no drama queen. Could it be her mum? Angie McCabe had been diagnosed with osteoporosis several years ago but had ignored all the advice given to her regarding diet and supplements and it was only last year, when she'd broken her hip at her salsa class, that she had been forced to take her condition seriously. She'd had a hip replacement last month, which had been pronounced successful, and she seemed to be recovering fast, flying around on her crutches.

"I feel like hiding them," Val had grumbled last week. "She thinks she's bloody Wonder Woman."

"Wouldn't it be worse if she just stayed in bed all day complaining? I think she's an amazing woman."

"Don't you dare encourage her," Val warned. "I'm going to have to hide the key to the garden shed or she'll be out mowing the lawn as soon as the weather improves."

Lynn smiled at the memory of the conversation as she drove. Because Val worked for Charles Boland in the local off-licence, Lynn always picked her up around the corner outside the church.

"I don't know why you do that," Val had said time and again.

"I just don't want to run into . . . anyone." Today Lynn definitely didn't want to go near the place. Charles kept a close eye on all his business interests and, if he saw her hanging around one of his premises, he might think she was gloating and deliberately trying to rub his nose in it.

Val was waiting for her, hopping from foot to foot in the chilly spring breeze, her wild mane of auburn locks fanning out around her.

"Hey." Val slid into the passenger seat and barely had her seatbelt on before Lynn pulled away.

"What's wrong?" Lynn asked anxiously.

"Nothing, why?" Val looked at her in surprise.

"I was just wondering what was so urgent that it couldn't wait till tomorrow. Did Jude Law move to Rathbourne and fall madly in love with you when he dropped in to buy his Guinness?"

"If only," Val sighed dramatically. "The closest I got to a proposition today was when Eamonn Reilly asked me if I'd consider joining the church choir. Honestly, how old do I look? There's no one in that bunch under sixty." She pulled down the visor and studied her face in the mirror, then rooted in her bag for her lipstick and eyeliner. "Let's go to Brannigans. I could murder a lager."

"Sure. Now tell me your big news. You're getting married."

"Oh, please." Val threw her a scathing look.

"You're pregnant?" Lynn shot her a look of alarm.

"Considering that I haven't had a man in months, that would be a bloody miracle."

"Oh, come on, please tell me. I need distracting."

Val finished touching up her make-up and then turned to study Lynn. "You do look a bit washed out. What's up?"

"I've just come from a counselling session."

"Ahhhhh." Val gave her arm a sympathetic pat.

"And I heard this morning that my case has been settled."

"You're kidding!" Val's expressive brown eyes widened. "You mean you won?"

"Yes. They're going to pay me eighty-five thousand and give me a glowing reference."

"But that's fantastic news, Lynn."

"Keep it under your hat, I haven't got the money yet and I've to sign a confidentiality agreement."

"I won't tell a soul, but you know word will get out, especially after today."

"That's what Frank said." Lynn glanced over at her. "Why, what happened today?"

"Martha dropped by earlier, dying to tell me, she was."

Martha worked in the kitchens in Hawthorn Lodge and was a terrible gossip altogether. "Tell you what?" Lynn cried. Lord, Val loved to drag out a story.

"Old man Boland called a staff meeting this morning and announced there was to be a restructuring."

"Not redundancies?" Lynn shot her a look of alarm as she thought of her friends in the hotel. Brenda, a waitress, now in her late fifties, would be an obvious candidate for early retirement, but Lynn knew she would be devastated: she had worked there for more than twenty-five years. Then there was Bob, the porter, well past sixty and one of Vincent's least favourite staff members; but, as he and Charles had gone to school together, he'd had to tolerate him. The new young staff, two receptionists and a payroll clerk whom Lynn had brought in, might also be at risk simply because she had hired them, despite the fact that they were smart and damn good at their jobs.

"No redundancies," Val reassured her, "at least not yet. Just a reshuffle of staff. Not everyone's happy; one person in particular is decidedly *un*happy."

"Who?" Lynn parked the car outside Brannigans and turned to look at her.

"Vincent. He's being moved to The Willows!"

"You're kidding." Lynn stared at her. Charles Boland's three-star, old-fashioned hotel in the next county was probably the least successful of the Boland businesses. "But why?"

"Well, now that I've heard your news I assume it's a rap on the knuckles for costing Charles eighty-five grand. Come on, let's get that drink."

As usual, Brannigans was dead except for a couple of regulars at the bar, and, once they were settled in the corner furthest away from them, Val with her lager and Lynn with coffee, they continued the conversation.

"Is anyone else being moved to The Willows?" Lynn asked.

Val shook her head. "All the other changes were relating to rotas and training."

"Then it was an obvious demotion," Lynn said, dismayed. Perhaps she should feel victorious at Vincent's banishment, but it meant that everyone would link the move to her settlement and gossip would be rife.

"Boland told them that he's planning to renovate The Willows and turn it into a spa and he's putting Vincent in to supervise and mastermind the entire operation."

"I suppose that could be true: spas are all the rage these days."

"Would you think so?" Val looked dubious. "It's in a terrible location, way too far off the beaten track, and the hills were the only real scenery. And now they're putting those windmill yokes up all over them. Have you ever heard the noise from those things? Not exactly the tranquillity you'd expect if you forked out a fortune to get away from it all and relax."

"Charles wouldn't invest the money unless he thought it would be a success," Lynn said. Whatever their differences, she still respected the man as a true entrepreneur who had brought prosperity and employment to this county and beyond. "Emer will be glad to see the back of him." Charles's youngest daughter had never liked Vincent. Lynn used to wonder why. Now she realized that the girl was a damn good judge of character.

"I can't believe you've won and rid Hawthorn Lodge of Vincent too. You must be thrilled."

Lynn sipped her coffee. "I'm not sure how I feel to be honest. It seems wrong that no one'll get to hear what he did and said. Uncle writes a cheque and it all goes away."

"You're better off, Lynn. If it had gone to court it would have been very hard on you," Val said, her voice gentle and her eyes full of sympathy. "And everyone will know that he's guilty of something, what with being packed off to The Willows. Move on, sweetie."

"How can I? Even if he's not around, I'm still surrounded by his bloody family, friends, employees. There's no escape."

"Of course there is." Val looked at her. "Move."

Leave Rathbourne? "But what about Mum and Dad?"

"With all the motorways you could be back here in a couple of hours if your folks needed you. You spend so much time cooped up alone in that house, Lynn. Perhaps leaving Rathbourne would be healthier."

"But what would I do without you?" Lynn said with a watery smile.

"Get in the car and come see me, or we could meet halfway."

"Or you could come visit and even stay over." Lynn brightened.

Val grinned. "You see? It's not such a bad idea."

Lynn took another drink of her coffee and looked at her friend with thoughtful eyes. "Maybe not."

CHAPTER
THREE

By the time Frank got home, Lynn was ready. She had showered, taken care doing her hair and applied make-up for the first time in months. The green eyeshadow, mascara and eyeliner made her eyes seem huge; her lips shone with a bright-red, glossy lipstick; and her hair hung in a silky black curtain down her back. She didn't have to think about what to wear. That was the easy bit, and she had just smoothed the tight red dress down over her slim hips and stepped into her high heels when he walked through the door. He stood staring at her for a moment, his eyes raking her from head to foot. "Maybe you're right: maybe we *should* stay in," he muttered.

She smiled as he advanced on her. "After all the trouble I've gone to? No way, mister! You promised me dinner and you're *buying* me dinner." But, if he kept looking at her the way he was doing now, he might just get lucky. The thought of him undressing her later sent shivers down her spine. He knew her and her body so well that it had always been easy for him to get her into the mood. He knew where to touch and how to excite her and was patient and attentive, prolonging her pleasure until she almost begged for release.

There had once been times when they were out and she would catch him looking at her in that certain way and she would know he wanted her, and within minutes they would be making their excuses, rushing home, touching each other all the way there and then tearing off each other's clothes even before they got as far as the bedroom. But, since she'd left Hawthorn Lodge, she seemed to have frozen up inside and he couldn't thaw her, though God knows he'd tried. Less so recently, she realized, worried that he had tired of her. Tonight she was going to put that right.

Frank pulled her close. "It's so good to hear you talking like that. You sound just like the gorgeous, clever girl that took my breath away at the races."

"I don't feel like her. I'm scared stiff. Don't you dare leave me alone," she warned him. "If you need to use the loo I'm coming with you."

"If I get you alone in the loo in that dress you'll never get to finish your dinner," he said, kissing her.

"Come on, then," she laughed. "Let's go before I get cold feet."

"So what did Carrie want?" she asked when they were in the car, trying to keep her voice light. She didn't want to sound like a nag, but she was curious as to what the woman had come up with this time.

"She was doing the garden and some guy stopped the car and started asking questions about the house, said he was moving into the area and looking for a property with a decent-sized garden."

Lynn's eyes widened. "You're kidding!" Frank's family home was a beautiful sprawling cottage in an elite estate in Castleknock and worth a fortune. They'd been trying to sell it since the divorce but without success.

He grinned happily. "I'm not. She gave him her number and said that if he wanted he could bring his wife over to have a look around."

"So why did she want to meet you?" Lynn asked, irked. Carrie could have told him all of this on the phone.

"She was wondering what price we should ask and she's having some problems with the heating and wanted me to take a look."

"Couldn't she have called a plumber?"

"No need: the radiators just needed bleeding." He chuckled. "I love it when you get jealous."

"I'm not jealous."

"You are, but then it's to be expected: I'm a hell of a guy."

She smiled. "And modest."

"So, how did the session with Kelly go?"

"Okay."

He asked no more. They had agreed at the start of her sessions that if she wanted to talk about them she would but, if not, he wouldn't ask. It had actually been the GP's suggestion. He thought it would be just more pressure on Lynn if she felt compelled to discuss them.

"Did you go to your parents'?" he asked when she volunteered nothing further.

"No, I saw Val. She had some news."

"A new man?"

Lynn laughed. "That's what I thought. No, something much more interesting. Charles Boland is moving Vincent to The Willows."

Frank glanced at her. "Really?"

She nodded. "Apparently he's renovating it and turning it into a fancy spa and is putting Vincent in charge of the project."

"Interesting timing," he murmured.

"That's what Val thought. She thinks Charles is punishing him because he had to pay me off."

"She could be right, and getting him out of town before the news of your settlement breaks is probably not a bad move, either. Does it make you feel better?"

"Sure," she said with a smile.

Frank parked the car outside the restaurant and reached for her hand. "You should feel proud of yourself. You've come through a tough time and I promise you there are good times ahead." He kissed her. "Come on, I want to show off my gorgeous woman to the world."

Lynn took a couple of deep breaths and nodded. "Okay. But I'm warning you, Frank —"

"I won't leave your side for a second," he reassured her.

"Frank Hayes, how are you doing?"

They were only studying the menu when Lynn looked up to see the editor of the local newspaper standing over their corner table smiling. She knew it had been a mistake to come here.

Frank immediately got to his feet and shook hands. "Paul, good to see you. It's been a while."

"Ah, sure, now you're a high flyer up above in Dublin you've no time for the likes of us any more." The man smiled down at Lynn, his eyes kind. "And how are you, Lynn?"

"I'm fine, thanks, Paul."

"You certainly look it." He eyed her appreciatively. "It's good to see you out and about again. So, are you planning to rejoin the workforce?"

Lynn stared at him, feeling like a rabbit caught in headlights. "Well, I —"

"It's early days, Paul," Frank cut in smoothly, "but Lynn's much better and that's what's important."

"Indeed it is."

Frank nodded to a group of men standing in the doorway. "I think your party's arrived."

"Right, best go and see if I can sell some advertising. Enjoy your dinner, you two."

"We will," Frank assured him, and sat down again. "Are you okay?" he murmured.

She nodded mutely, though her hands were shaking slightly. This was exactly why she didn't go out. Not only did everyone know everyone in Rathbourne, they didn't think twice about asking personal questions.

"What would you like?"

"I'll have whatever you're having," she said with a strained smile.

Frank caught the waiter's attention and ordered. "Come on, Lynn, don't let that ruin your evening.

Look how easily it was dealt with. You know what? You need to do what I do when I'm on TV or radio."

"What's that?"

"I decide beforehand what I'm going to say and, regardless of the question, I say it."

She grinned. "Clever, but I can't see how that would work in my situation."

"Of course it would. Let me give you an example. If a woman you know walks through those doors, makes a beeline for you and gives you the 'How are you? Are you going back to work?' bit, here are three replies you could use. One, 'I'm fine. Have you lost weight? You're looking marvellous.' Two, 'I'm great, thanks. What a beautiful dress. I badly need to update my wardrobe. You must tell me where you shop — you have such a great eye for clothes.' Three" — he continued ignoring her laughter — "'I'm fine, thanks. I've taken up gardening/cooking/knitting — use as appropriate — you must give me some tips.' See? Simple." Their glasses of wine arrived and he raised his. "To you, darling, and the future."

Lynn touched her glass to his, smiling tenderly into his eyes. "Thank you. I'd never have got through this without you, Frank. I'm sorry if I've been very hard to live with."

"No more than usual." He grinned.

"Seriously, you *have* been wonderful." Their soup was placed in front of them and she watched Frank tuck in. "Val said something today that I can't stop thinking about."

"Oh, yeah? What was that?"

"She asked why we didn't leave Rathbourne."

He set down his spoon. "You always said you didn't want to move too far from your parents."

"I know but, as Val pointed out, nowhere is that far away any more thanks to all the motorways. I mean how long does it take you to drive to Dublin?"

He shrugged. "It depends on the traffic, but usually just over an hour. You want to move to Dublin?"

"I don't know, Frank, but it would be nice to walk down the street without being self-conscious or feeling afraid of bumping into one of the Boland clan."

"It sounds a bit like running away." He went back to his soup.

"He who fights and runs away lives to fight another day," she countered. "How would you feel about it?"

"I wouldn't mind at all: it would mean less commuting."

"And there would be more job opportunities in Dublin."

He smiled.

"What?" She finished her soup and pushed the bowl away.

"It's just good to hear you talk about going back to work."

"Don't get too excited," she joked. "I'll probably be my usual miserable self by morning."

"I don't think so. There's something different about you tonight."

She took a sip of water. "That's because we've managed to come out and have a nice dinner together and, apart from Paul's visit, I've been able to relax and enjoy it."

He glanced over at the door. "Well don't look now but that could be about to change."

Lynn froze. "Who is it?"

"Mick and Josie O'Grady."

"Shit!" Lynn hissed reaching for her glass and downing half of it. Mick ran the local hardware, was a friend of her dad's and a golf buddy of Charles. And his wife could talk for Ireland.

"Remember the lines I gave you," he said through gritted teeth. "She's into gardening, isn't she?"

"Is she?" Lynn breathed, feeling a cold sweat break out on her forehead. "Are they coming over?"

"No, they haven't spotted us yet. They're talking to the people at the first table. Calm down and remember: nobody knows any details about the case. Tonight, if anything, they'll be speculating about Vincent being moved to The Willows."

"What if they ask me about it?"

"You say you've no idea, you're out of touch with what's going on, that you're spending most of your time gardening. Relax, darling. The only thing that's going to make them wonder is if you start behaving like a guilty schoolchild."

"Can't we just go?" she begged.

"Don't be silly!" he said, a trace of impatience in his voice.

She was about to reply when she felt a hand on her shoulder. "Lynn Stephens, it *is* you! Why, I haven't seen you in months." Josie sat down uninvited and studied her with curious eyes. "How are you, dear?"

"Sure, she's grand, can't you see that?" Mick leaned on the back of his wife's chair and smiled at Lynn.

She smiled back. "I'm fine, thanks, how are you, Josie? That's a lovely dress."

"What, this old thing?" Josie dismissed her floral tent with a wave of her hand. "So, have you heard the news?"

"What news is that?" Frank asked, forcing his way into the conversation.

"Charles Boland is turning The Willows into some sort of clinic and he's sending young Vincent over there to run it."

"Really?"

Mick scratched his head. "So he says."

"I doubt the lad is up to the job," Josie said. "What do you think, Lynn? You worked closely with him for a long time, didn't you?"

Lynn looked at Frank, begging him with her eyes to save her but he said nothing. "I'm sure he'll be fine. Sorry, excuse me," she said and fled to the ladies', bolting herself into a cubicle. Before Josie came along she had been in good humour and enjoying herself, and now she was a snivelling wreck again. She forced herself to take deep, slow breaths. She couldn't stay in here all evening; she had to get a grip.

A good ten minutes later she returned to the table. Frank was alone, halfway through his roast lamb. "Well, you handled that really well," he muttered.

She stared at him, stung by his tone. "What did you expect? She completely ambushed me and you sat there and watched."

"I told you what to say. I can't always be around to bail you out, Lynn. You have to learn to cope alone. Anyway, she was just making idle chitchat. I could understand your difficulty if you were confronted by a Boland or someone from Hawthorn Lodge, but you can't go through life being afraid to talk to people."

"But they were talking about *him*, Frank."

"Yes, *him* and *his* situation."

"Oh, please, you heard Josie with her 'What do you think, Lynn? You worked with him.'"

He looked at her in disbelief. "Well, you did! You really are blowing this totally out of proportion."

She stared at him. "So you think I'm just paranoid."

"There you go again." He rolled his eyes in exasperation. "That's not what I said. Stop putting words in my mouth. I'm just trying to help."

"Like you helped when Josie O'Grady started to grill me?"

"She did not grill you. She asked you a question and, as you did work closely with Vincent, it was a logical one."

Lynn reached down and picked up her handbag. "Well, thanks for the support. I'd like to go home now."

"You haven't even touched your food," he protested.

"I've lost my appetite."

"Oh, come on, Lynn, you're being —"

She held up her hand, her eyes full of tears. "Ridiculous, oversensitive, stupid? Yes, I get the

36

message, Frank. Now, I want to go. Either you can take me or I'll get a taxi."

"Fine." He flung down his napkin and stood up.

Lynn stared at her untouched meal as she waited for him to pay the bill.

"Ready?"

She stood up and slipped on her jacket, well aware that Josie was watching them closely. She waved and smiled and, as Frank called goodbye to a few people, she hurried out of the restaurant, keeping her smile in place until she was in the safety of the car.

They drove home in silence and it was only when they were parked that Frank spoke.

"Lynn, you know that I would never do anything to hurt or upset you. You're much too sensitive, darling."

"I think that may be why I'm on antidepressants and seeing a psychiatrist," she said, her voice loaded with sarcasm. She got out of the car and stood at the door, waiting for him to open it. When he did she made straight for the stairs.

"Is that it?" he called after her.

She stopped and turned to face him. "I'm tired and upset. It's been quite a day. If we keep talking we'll just argue, and I don't want that."

"I don't want that either," he said, looking completely fed up.

"Then let's leave it. Goodnight, Frank." She smiled and went quickly upstairs.

"Night," she heard him say before she shut the door and let the tears fall.

She was awake but turned away and almost on the edge of her side of the bed when he finally came into the room. She kept perfectly still as she heard him undress and then slip into bed beside her.

"Lynn? Are you awake?" He moved nearer.

She felt his lips on her shoulder but she didn't respond, nor did she move away. Despite being upset, she was still comforted by the warmth of his body next to hers. He leaned across and kissed her lightly on the forehead. "Goodnight, darling, sweet dreams," he whispered as he slipped a protective arm around her.

Lynn smiled in the darkness at the tenderness of his words and his kiss, realizing that nothing had changed. He may not always understand her but he loved her and that was all that mattered.

CHAPTER
FOUR

When she woke the next morning, Lynn felt refreshed and happier. There had been no nightmares and she smiled at the memory of falling asleep with Frank tight against her. She rolled over with the intention of waking him with a kiss, but he was already gone. She raised her head to check the clock: it wasn't even seven. With a stretch and a yawn she climbed out of bed and padded downstairs to find the kitchen empty. She felt the kettle but it was cold — and then she noticed a note propped against the toaster.

> Breakfast meeting, mad day and on TV tonight so home late, don't wait up. I'll call you when I get a chance, x

Lynn sighed and went to fill the kettle. As she sipped her coffee she reread the note over and over. It didn't seem all that conciliatory, but neither was it curt. She wished she could talk to him; she hated starting the day not knowing how he was feeling. She was sorely tempted to climb back into bed and sleep for the day, but she knew that her parents would have heard of Vincent's transfer and be wondering about it and how she was feeling. She also had to tell them the good news about the settlement. Like Frank, they would expect her to be over the moon, expect her anxiety to disappear overnight. It was a huge responsibility having people care about you sometimes. It was almost easier to pretend she was fine than to see the concern in their eyes. And she would be fine soon, she assured herself. She had been a damn good manager and would be again. Val was right: her future wasn't in Rathbourne. She needed to move to Dublin. Once surrounded by people who knew nothing about her or her past, she would be fine.

She was determined to go into her parents' house wearing a smile, and, throwing the dregs of her coffee into the sink, she ran upstairs to get dressed. She put on a little make-up, brushed her hair till it shone and then decided to go mad altogether and wear a dress.

It was only a few weeks ago that she had told her parents about the bullying and impending court case. Frank had urged her many times to say something, but she didn't see the point in worrying them and couldn't handle the inevitable questions.

"Don't you realize they're worrying anyway?" Frank had said. "Their once successful, happy daughter has been off work for months suffering from depression and is afraid to go outside the door."

"If they knew the reason why I left, it would cause an enormous rift between the families. Dad and Charles Boland have known each other for ever; they've done business together and support and promote each other. They're both members of the local Chamber of

Commerce and the Lions Club. But if Dad knew what Vincent had done he'd be furious, and it could destroy all relations between him and Charles and maybe even have repercussions on his business."

"Darling, they will find out; there's no way to prevent that. I think it's better they hear it from their daughter and not a customer, don't you?"

And so she had finally capitulated and gone with Frank one night to her parents' house to explain, although she had kept the details as sketchy as she could. Jack had got angrier and angrier as she talked.

"I'll kill the bastard," he'd said.

"No, Dad. You'll say nothing and do nothing. It's in the hands of the solicitor now, so just forget about it."

He'd looked at her, incredulous. "How can I do that?"

"Because it's what I want. If you approach Vincent or Charles, then it'll be only a matter of time before it's the talk of the town. And this is my business. And remember, when this is all over you'll still have to live and work with these people. I can fight my own battles, Dad."

"Can you, now? Is that why you're on tablets, seeing a quack and afraid of your own shadow?" he'd demanded, punching his fist into his hand.

"I'm getting better, Dad, but if you stir it all up again, you won't be helping."

She knew that had been hard for him to accept, but he had agreed though he'd been upset that she hadn't come to him sooner. Her mother had sat in silence as she'd talked, her eyes bright with tears, and when they were leaving she had simply folded Lynn in her arms. Her dad had walked to the car with her.

"I know now, so promise that you'll talk to me and come to me if you need help."

She'd put her arms around his neck and hugged him. "I will, Dad."

Her parents had treated her like delicate china since then, so she was glad that she was able to bring them good news. When she let herself in through the back door of her family home her efforts weren't lost on her mother. Nell Stephens was sitting at the kitchen table peeling potatoes, but her expression brightened as soon as she set eyes on her daughter.

"Well, look at you! Don't you look gorgeous today? Are you off out somewhere?"

"No." Lynn bent to kiss her mother's cheek. "I was just in a good mood and felt like making a bit of an effort."

Nell sighed. "Good for you, love. Would it have anything to do with the fact that Vincent Boland is leaving town?"

Lynn smiled. "You heard."

"You know that you only have to stand in our shop for ten minutes and keep your ears open to know what's going on in this town."

"I think he's only leaving the hotel; he'll probably still live here."

"More's the pity," her mother said, her eyes bitter. "Put on the kettle, love. Your dad will be in for his break in a minute. It'll make his day to see you looking so well."

"So what are people saying?" Lynn asked.

"I don't think anyone is swallowing the line about the spa." Nell stood up and emptied the basin of peelings into the bin. "From what people are saying I think they'll be throwing a party to celebrate his departure."

Lynn's ears pricked up. "Oh, why?"

"He's obviously not well liked. But, though there may be mutterings and grumblings about him, people are still careful what they say in public about the Bolands."

"Don't I know it." Lynn took down three mugs and went to the fridge for the milk. The Boland family stuck together and, whatever Charles might think of his nephew, he would take a very dim view of a staff member spreading gossip about him.

"Hello, love, you're looking lovely this morning."

Lynn turned to see Jack entering the kitchen. He planted an affectionate kiss on her cheek, which she returned, and smiled. "Thanks, Dad."

"And smiling, too." He rubbed his chin thoughtfully and peered at her over his glasses. "Now I wonder why *that* is."

She laughed. "Have I been that much of a misery guts?"

"With good reason," he assured her.

"There's more news," Lynn said, carrying the teapot to the table and sitting down. She waited until her parents joined her before continuing. "My case is settled."

"Thank God!" said her mother. "You must be relieved that you don't have to go to court." Nell patted her hand.

"Did he cough up what you asked for?" her dad demanded.

"Ten grand more, thanks to Calum," she told him.

"No more than you deserve," he retorted with a frown.

"But you won't be going back to work there, will you?" Nell asked.

"No way, Mum, and I wouldn't want to."

"Damn right," said Jack. "With your skills you could work anywhere." He winked. "Even a supermarket."

"I'm not sure I fancy the hours." She laughed.

"There's no need to rush into anything," he said.

"There's no need to work at all, is there?" Nell said. "Haven't you got Frank to look after you now?"

Lynn smiled, thinking that in the old days she would have bitten her mother's head off for a remark like that. "I'm an independent woman," she'd have railed, "and don't need any man to take care of me, financially or otherwise." But she couldn't say that now, nor did she feel that way. She was so grateful to have Frank by her side throughout this awful time and couldn't imagine life without him.

"Now the two of you will be able to settle down properly and make plans."

"That's code for 'get married and have a baby'," her father told her.

Nell gave him a dirty look. "And why not? Aren't they happy together? And Frank isn't getting any younger."

Lynn laughed. "You better not say that to him!"

"Will you let the girl alone?" Jack shook his head in resignation. "Lynn, do you have time to have a look at a few invoices?"

"Sure, Dad." Lynn jumped to her feet and, with an apologetic smile at her mum, followed him out of the kitchen and across the courtyard to the small office at the rear of the supermarket.

"Don't mind your mother. She just worries about you."

"I know."

He sat on the edge of the small untidy desk. "Do you feel better now, sweetheart?"

"Yes, I'm fine."

He eyed her over the rims of his glasses.

She sighed. He always could see right through her. "I'm getting there."

"You probably would be better off getting back to work; it would distract you."

"Dad —"

He held up his hand. "It's just a thought. You'll know when you're ready. In the meantime, I'm quite happy to have unpaid help occasionally."

"Speaking of which, where are the invoices that you want to show me?"

"There aren't any. I just thought you could do with a break before your mother started picking out baby names."

She laughed. "Thanks."

"Lynn?"

"Yes?"

"If you ever want to talk, I'm more than happy to listen — and I don't charge."

She hugged him. "Thanks, Dad. I'll bear that in mind."

CHAPTER
FIVE

Instead of going straight home, Lynn headed for Clogher Head. It was a forty-five-minute drive to the coast but she felt restless, and walking the beach always helped calm her nerves. This location in particular held a special place in her heart. It had been the scene of her fourth date with Frank and she remembered it as if it had been yesterday.

She switched off the car engine and gazed absently out at the waves crashing on to the shore.

Meeting Frank Hayes had knocked Lynn for six. She'd had a few boyfriends but no serious relationships. She'd spent so much time studying and then working that she had little time for dates. And then she met Frank.

She held out for four days before sending him a text to say that she had enjoyed meeting him. Immediately he texted back and invited her to lunch. She refused but agreed to an early-morning coffee instead. Lynn had sworn that she'd never get involved with a married man, but she hadn't factored in meeting a tall man with a sexy smile, grey-blue eyes and an ability to make her laugh. But a coffee didn't count as a real date, did it?

They picked up exactly where they'd left off: exchanging histories and talking about their jobs. She was itching to know about his marriage but didn't want to ask, afraid that he'd get the wrong idea. She wasn't interested in a serious relationship, especially as he was only separated. Nor did she want him to think that she was up for a quick fling. Old-fashioned as it may be, Lynn had no interest in sleeping around.

As it turned out, Frank was the one to raise the subject of his marriage, and he did so in such an open and honest way that she warmed to him even more. He'd only just started when he received a call and cursed when he looked at the screen of his phone. "I can't believe it," he said when he had hung up after a brief conversation.

"Is there something wrong?" she'd asked.

"I'm supposed to be interviewing a councillor in Wexford in thirty minutes but I completely lost track of time."

She stared at him. "No! What are you going to do?"

"I don't have to do anything. That was him cancelling; we've rearranged it for later this afternoon."

"That was lucky."

"This has never happened to me before," he said, looking slightly bemused. "I've never forgotten an appointment because I was too busy talking. In fact I can't remember ever talking to anyone the way I talk to you."

"Not even your wife?" she asked, looking at him in disbelief.

"No, we rarely talked."

48

"You must have!"

"No. Really, it's true. We never had much in common. I met Carrie at a friend's twenty-first. We spent most of the evening together — she loved to dance. I asked her out and couldn't believe it when she said yes. She was a couple of years older than me and seemed so gorgeous and sophisticated. I couldn't figure out what she saw in me. We were only together a few months when she got pregnant. I was stunned. I was only twenty-one. We'd always used condoms, but I suppose accidents happen. She said that if she told her father he'd kill her, but I said we'd tell her parents together and get married straightaway — and that's what we did."

"Marriage and a baby at such a young age. That must have been overwhelming."

"You have no idea," he laughed. "But Philip was a good baby and we had lots of help from her mother and mine."

Lynn smiled at the warmth in his voice and the pride in his eyes when he talked about his son.

"Am I boring you?" he asked.

"Not at all," she told him, and it was true. As they parted, he gave her a brief kiss on the cheek but, as he did so, he smoothed his hand down the full length of her hair and it had been more sensual than any kiss on the mouth. She had drifted back to work in a daze.

The third time they met had been in a busy café in a shopping centre, Lynn still trying to convince herself that this couldn't be called a date. It was just two friends meeting for a chat over lunch. Again they were interrupted, this time by a text.

"I'm sorry, I'm afraid it goes with the job," he explained. "Oh, it's not work: Philip's mother wants me to take him for the weekend." He smiled, obviously delighted. "I love that she has such an active social life."

"Do you still get on well?" Lynn asked.

"A hell of a lot better than we did when we were together." He laughed. "But that wouldn't be hard."

"So you're really getting divorced? Oh, I'm sorry, that's a very personal question." She felt her cheeks grow hot.

He looked straight into her eyes. "You can ask me anything you like, and the more personal the better. We separated more than three years ago and the papers have already been filed. It should be finalized by next year."

"Why did you split up?"

"Carrie had been having an affair throughout our marriage with her boss. He was married with two kids and had no intention of leaving his wife. The only reason she married me was because she was pregnant. She didn't even know whose baby it was."

Lynn stared at him in dismay. "Oh Frank, I'm so sorry."

"There's no need to be. I know now that I never really loved her, I was just infatuated and if it wasn't for her I wouldn't have Philip." He saw the look in her eyes. "And, yes, he is definitely my son. His blood type made that clear, and you only have to look at him to know he's mine." He found an image on his phone and showed it to her.

She studied the tall gangly boy with the shock of dark hair and blue eyes and smiled. "There's no doubt about it. How old is he?"

"Fifteen."

That made Frank thirty-seven. He didn't look it. "When did you find out about the affair?"

"On Philip's eleventh birthday. Her boss's marriage had finally broken up and she told me everything and announced that she was going to live with him."

Lynn paused, pushing her long black hair out of her face and staring up at him. "That must have hurt."

He considered this for a moment and then shook his head. "I was shocked but, no, not hurt. We were never meant to be together. Philip was my only concern; there was no way I was going to let her take him away from me. But we finally worked out a schedule where we both had regular access and, surprisingly, it's worked quite well. He's now a well-balanced, happy, if scruffy, teenager."

"Is she going to marry her boss?"

Frank snorted. "Not at all. He dumped her a few months later. So she came home and she lives there with Philip and I ended up over the chip shop!"

"That doesn't seem fair."

"It was the best for Philip. She's at home all day, I'm not, and it meant he got to stay near his friends and stay in the same school. It was important that he had that stability."

"You're a good man, I think Carrie was crazy to ever let you go," Lynn told him when it was time for them to part.

"You're not crazy, are you?" he asked, looking into her eyes.

Lynn had laughed and had given him a quick hug. "Bye, Frank," she'd said, and hurried away but couldn't help looking back, and her pulse had quickened to see that he was still standing where she'd left him, staring after her.

The fourth date had been the turning point in their relationship. It was her morning off but her body clock was such that she woke at six thirty as usual, and so she reached for the novel by the bed. She had just started reading when a text came through on her phone. It was Frank.

IT'S A LOVELY MORNING. FANCY A WALK?

Two hours later they were strolling the deserted beach at Clogher Head, and, when he took her hand, she didn't protest. It felt nice — more than nice.

"Your turn," Frank said.

She looked up at him. "What do you mean?"

"You've heard my life history; now I'd like to hear yours."

"There's not much to tell. I'm an only child and, as I told you, still live at home and I adore my job. I'm a very boring person."

"I don't agree with that," he said, squeezing her hand. "What made you such a workaholic?"

She thought about it for a moment. "I think it was all down to Gina."

He frowned. "Gina Dolan?"

"Yes. Val, our other friend, and I were very upset when her family had to leave Ireland — her father and brothers couldn't get work. We were devastated after she'd gone and spent our time, either in my bedroom or hers, listening to music. And then one day my father pointed out that I was going to be emigrating too if I didn't start to spend more time on my schoolwork and less time feeling sorry for myself. That got through. I had less than two years of school left and it was up to me whether I ended up scrubbing floors or running a company. So I started to work really hard. And, well . . ." She shrugged. "Here I am."

Frank stopped and turned her to face him. "And here you are," he said, and kissed her.

It was the softest kiss, but a beautiful kiss, and Lynn closed her eyes and lost herself in the moment. He pulled away and looked at her. "I've been dying to do that for weeks and now that I've done it I'd like to do it again. Would that be okay?"

She nodded, her eyes not leaving his, and this time when he kissed her he put his arms around her waist and she found her own hands automatically going around his neck. When they finally pulled apart, he looked as startled as she felt.

"Okay, you can say when and where but you and I are going out on a proper date at night-time, understood?"

"Understood," she whispered, and he'd wrapped her in his arms and held her like that for ages.

Lynn smiled now at the memory. She was about to get out of the car when her phone rang. It was Frank.

"I sensed that you were probably missing me terribly, so I thought I'd better call and let you hear my dulcet tones."

She laughed, delighted that there was no rancour in his voice. "That was very magnanimous of you. Guess where I am."

"Having lunch at Hawthorn Lodge?"

"Ha, no, I'm at Clogher Head."

"Ah," he sighed. "I wish I was with you."

"Me too. Remember the first time we came here together?" she asked.

"How could I forget? It was our fourth date and you finally let me hold your hand and kiss you. If I was there now, I wouldn't settle for a kiss: I'd drag you into the sand dunes and ravish you."

"If you were here now I might let you," she admitted, surprised at the thrill that ran through her.

He groaned. "I am so tempted to jump in the car."

"Don't give me that!" She laughed. "You would never drop everything and come over here: you're much too conscientious."

"I like the idea of you dropping everything."

"Will you be home very late?" she asked, longing to feel his arms around her.

"It'll probably be midnight."

"I'll try to stay awake." She heard some commotion in the background and him talking to someone.

"Sorry, darling, I have to go. Now don't go into those dunes with anyone else, do you hear me?"

"I promise." She laughed. "Bye, Frank, I love you."

"I love you too, darling."

CHAPTER
SIX

"I think you're right," Frank announced a few days later.

"About . . .?" Lynn had cooked shepherd's pie for dinner and they were watching a second-rate movie on the wide-screen television. She was lying on Frank's lap and simply enjoying the fact that he was home from work early for a change.

"I think we should move."

She sat up and straddled him so she could look straight into his face. "Really?"

"Yes. It makes sense. I'm spending more and more time in Dublin and it would be nice to be nearer to Philip when he starts university."

"True, but we're tied into the lease for another year. We can't afford two places. I know we could use the settlement money, but what if I don't get a job?"

"When Carrie sells the house we'll have plenty of money. We'll be able to buy a place of our own, Lynn."

"Oh, wouldn't that be lovely?" She sighed. "A place all of our own, not too big. But we'd need two bedrooms, anyway, then Philip could sleep over or my mum and dad or Val could come to stay — Oh, this is

56

silly." She shook her head. "We're just dreaming. It could take months, years, for her to sell that house."

"You think? Did I forget to mention that the couple who viewed it have asked to take another look?"

Lynn punched his arm. "You know you did! Really? Does she think they're serious? When are they coming?"

Frank chuckled. "Slow down. Yes, she said that the wife was definitely smitten. They're coming back on Saturday and Carrie's convinced it's just to measure up. But don't get too excited, darling. They may make a very low offer."

"You're right."

"But, even if it was half what it was worth before the property crash, we could still afford a decent place."

"And if they don't buy it?" Lynn asked, not sure if she wanted to hear the answer.

"If we sublet this place we could still afford a small place, but in one of the less salubrious areas of the city."

"I don't care where we are once we're together," Lynn said, feeling ridiculously happy.

"Do you really mean that?" he asked, searching her eyes. "The age difference doesn't bother you or the fact that I have a son and an ex-wife?"

"The age difference is meaningless, I'm mad about your son, and your wife I can tolerate — at a distance." She kissed the corner of his mouth. "Nothing matters once I have you. I've never felt this close to anyone before. I love you more than I ever thought possible."

He looked at her intently. "Do you, Lynn?"

She stared straight back at him and smiled. "I do."

"Would you be willing to say that in front of witnesses?"

"What do you mean?" she asked, confused, as she thought back on what she'd said; and then she put her hand to her mouth as she realized what he was saying. "Oh, Frank!"

"Well?"

"No way!"

"Really?"

She shook her head and almost laughed at his crestfallen expression. "You are *not* getting away with that, Frank Hayes. Ask me properly."

He smirked. "Do I have to?"

"You most certainly do." She crossed her arms and tried to look serious.

"You're a hard woman to please," he complained, but, taking up the remote control, he switched off the television and proceeded to get down on one knee.

She stared at him and felt a lump form in her throat as he looked up at her, his eyes full of love.

"Lynn Stephens," he said, taking her hand, "I fell in love with you the moment we met and I've kept falling ever since. I love everything about you. Your hair, your beautiful eyes and your lovely voice. I admire your strength and your soft heart and I worship that gorgeous body. You are the love of my life, Lynn. Will you do me the honour of becoming my wife?"

"Oh, Frank!" she whispered, overcome by his words and the sincerity in his voice.

"You're supposed to say yes or no, not, 'Oh, Frank!'" he reminded her.

"Yes," she whispered.

"What?"

She smiled at him. "I said yes."

"Really?"

"Really."

He crushed her in his arms and kissed her. "You won't regret it, darling."

"I know I won't," she said, her arms tight around his neck. "I'm not so sure about you, though. Do you really want to be saddled with me? I'm not the same girl you fell for."

"You *are* the same," he insisted, "and we are about to start a new and exciting chapter of our lives. The best is yet to come."

For the first time in a long time, Lynn felt truly optimistic. Planning a wedding would be quite a distraction and surely, in a new home and a different environment as a married woman, she would regain her confidence? "Had you a date in mind?" she asked.

"The sooner the better," Frank replied. "Why wait?"

"How do you think Philip will react?" Although she and Philip were great friends she wasn't sure how he'd take the news that his father was getting married again less than two years after his divorce.

"He'll be delighted, of course. I was thinking of asking him to be my best man."

She smiled. "That's a lovely idea. So you've been thinking about this for a while and assumed I'd say yes, huh?"

"How could you resist me?"

She sighed happily. "I couldn't. So should we perhaps move to Dublin first and then get married?"

"That's up to you, darling. Do you want a big day with all the trimmings?"

"No." Lynn shuddered at the thought. "I've had enough attention from the people in this town. I want our day to be about us."

"As do I, but I don't see why it should be a second-rate event because of the Bolands."

Hearing the annoyance in Frank's voice, Lynn decided it would be best to change the subject. A full-blown row was not how she wanted to remember the day of her proposal. "And it won't be. Let's concentrate on finding somewhere to live first."

"Okay. So, darling, how would you like to celebrate our engagement?"

The thought of another disastrous evening like the one in Dylan's hung between them. "How about you go get us some food and a nice bottle of wine?" she suggested as she put her hand on his thigh. "And then we could have an early night."

He looked at her, his lips twitching. "Are you feeling tired?"

She smiled. "No, are you?"

"Not at all." He grinned, pulling her into his arms and kissing her hungrily. "What would you like to eat?"

"Surprise me."

He jumped to his feet and grabbed his car keys. "I won't be long."

"I'll be waiting," she promised.

After he was gone, she hurried upstairs, grinning broadly, and changed into the red, silk negligée he'd bought her last Valentine's Day but she hadn't been in the mood to wear. She admired her reflection in the full-length mirror. The gown wasn't very revealing, but it clung to every curve. It did look sexy, and she knew that he would love it. Having brushed her hair, she left it hanging loose around her shoulders, put on lip gloss, sprayed perfume on her wrists and between her breasts, and after slipping into the matching wrap, went downstairs to set the table and light some candles. She was just flicking through CDs, looking for something romantic, when her mobile phone pinged. Her eyes widened in horror as she read the text from Val.

IN PUB. VINCENT HERE, DRUNK AS A SKUNK AND NOT LOOKING AT ALL HAPPY.

Lynn felt sick as she read. She knew that Val had sent the text to make her feel better but it was having the opposite effect. She shuddered at the thought of what Vincent might be saying under the influence of drink and who he might be saying it to. He was a loose cannon when drunk and even more dangerous if he was angry as well. She froze, remembering Frank had gone out for wine. If the off-licence was closed, he'd go to the pub to get it. She picked up the phone. "Val?"

"Hey, calling for a live commentary?" Her friend laughed.

"Please tell me he's not loud. Who is he with?"

"The usual hangers-on. He's loud but he's slurring so much it's hard to make out anything he's saying."

"Is the off-licence closed?"

"No, of course not, it's only eight o'clock."

"Yes, sorry, stupid of me. Listen, Val, I have to run. Text me if anything happens."

"Relax, Lynn. I'm sorry I sent you that message now. I was just trying to cheer you up. It's clear to everyone here that he is most definitely not happy about the move to The Willows."

"I know, and thanks, Val. I'm glad you told me. It's just —" She heard Frank's car pull up outside. "Sorry, must go. I'll call you tomorrow."

Frank went straight through to the kitchen. "Does champagne go with Indian food?"

"Champagne goes with anything," she said absently, relieved that he was back.

"Where are the glasses?"

"In here." She went to the door. "I thought we'd eat in style."

He turned around and stopped dead when he saw her. His eyes travelled from the hair cascading round her shoulders and down the length of her clinging negligee. "Let's take the champagne to bed and eat later." He put the bag down on the table and reached for her.

She dodged him, laughing. "Patience, darling. Eat. It will give you energy."

He grabbed her and kissed her neck. "I look forward to afters."

She opened the cartons of food while he popped the champagne and poured.

"A toast, darling: to us."

"To us." She smiled.

"When will we announce our engagement?"

"We need to tell our parents and Philip first."

"And Carrie, I suppose."

Lynn let that one pass. "I know Mum and Dad will be happy for us, but how do you think your folks will take the news?" Frank's parents had retired to his mother's family home in a small town in Devon, and she had met them only twice. On both occasions she'd felt the atmosphere had been strained. They were lovely people but she'd sensed they feared that, in taking up with someone much younger, Frank was jumping out of the frying pan and into the fire. She could understand their concern: he'd already been humiliated and duped by one woman. But she was philosophical about it. They would find out in time that she would never do anything to hurt Frank, she was mad about him and she had grown very fond of Philip, too.

"They'll be delighted," Frank assured her. "Why don't we go shopping for a ring and go and see them at the weekend?"

"*Next* weekend?" Lynn looked at him, startled.

"Why not?" He shrugged. "Wouldn't it be nice to get away from Rathbourne for a couple of days? It's been a long time since we had a break. We could tell your parents before we go and then announce it to everyone else when we get back."

"Once we tell people we'll be persecuted to name the day. Perhaps we should wait until we find somewhere to live first."

"Are you sure you actually want to get married?" he asked, dipping a piece of naan bread in his sauce.

"I have no doubts on that score, darling, but I've been the centre of attention in this town enough lately, I really could do with a quiet spell. Do you mind?"

"No, of course not." He put down his fork and looked up at her. "Sorry, Lynn. My timing's lousy. The proposal stands but if you want to keep it just between us for the moment then that's fine by me."

She smiled gratefully. He really was the loveliest man. "The answer stands too but, yes, I would prefer that. Right now I'd like to concentrate on finding a place in Dublin. I just know that I will be happier there."

"Let's have a look online and see what's on offer." He reached for his iPad.

She moved around beside him so that she could see the screen.

"Any preferences where, exactly?"

"It would be nice to be near the sea and central. I'd love to be able to walk to work. But I suppose a house fitting those criteria would cost a fortune."

"I'm sure there are bargains to be had. If we concentrate on places like Ringsend, Sandymount or Marino you'd have both and be on the Dart line. Then you could apply to hotels in the city and the ones on the coast."

"True and I like the idea of taking a train rather than driving. I could read my book instead of sitting stressed out in traffic jams. That's one part of city life that doesn't appeal."

"Ah, but think of the restaurants, the theatres, the galleries," he pointed out.

She smiled. "You really like the idea of moving back to Dublin, don't you?"

"I am a city boy at heart, it's true."

Lynn felt a wave of happiness at the thought that they were actually going to make this happen. "What are Carrie's plans?" she asked. The last thing she wanted was to move anywhere near that woman.

Frank laughed, seeing right through her. "She's looking at apartments on the Northside within easy reach of the university in Glasnevin. I take it that means you fancy living on the Southside?"

She grinned. "Now why would you think that? Not that it'll stop her calling you. We need to fix her up with someone."

"Find a rich, married man with kids; that's her type."

Lynn heard the bitterness in his voice and wondered, despite his protestations to the contrary, if he had really loved Carrie. She wouldn't have had the power to hurt him otherwise, would she?

"That looks interesting." Frank pointed at a picture of a small, redbrick, terraced house in Ringsend.

Lynn leaned closer to read the details. The house was in a quiet cul-de-sac, had three bedrooms and was fifty years old. It was clear from the small, well-tended front garden and freshly painted yellow front door that the owners looked after it.

"It's been recently renovated," Frank said, quickly scanning the description, "and only ten minutes' walk to the train station. Of course, it could be in a dodgy area and that's why it's such a reasonable price."

"My mother has a cousin who lives around there." Lynn frowned. "I was there when I was small but all I really remember is that there were pretty tiles in her hall and a long, skinny back garden."

"Does she still live there? Could you ask your mum?"

"It would mean telling her we're thinking of moving."

"You can't put it off for ever," Frank said. "And, remember, it's only an hour's drive."

"Yes, and I suppose I could hint at marriage. That would keep her happy."

He switched off the iPad and swung her round to face him, her legs between his. "Enough. It's too distracting having you leaning across me looking like that."

"So what should we do?" she asked innocently.

He traced a finger from her lips down her neck to between her breasts, and she leaned forward to kiss him. Frank ran his hands over her body and she shivered at his touch through the thin material of the flimsy negligée. Still with his mouth on hers, Frank moved his hands to her waist and loosened the sash of her robe. He pushed it off one shoulder and kissed her bared skin.

66

"You're beautiful," he said, and ran his finger down the silken strap and dipped it into her cleavage before following it with his mouth.

Lynn automatically arched her back and gasped. After a moment, she raised his head to hers and stared into his eyes. "Shall we take this upstairs?"

"That's the best offer I've had all day."

CHAPTER
SEVEN

Lynn went about the housework, humming along to a song on the radio. It was incredible how good she felt, how happy she was. She and Frank were closer than ever. Her mother had taken the news of their planned move much better than she'd expected, and, when Lynn hinted that a wedding might be in the offing, the twinkle in her mother's eye told her she was already imagining grandchildren.

Lynn had never given much thought to being a mother until Frank came along. It was only then that she knew she wanted a child — *his* child. But, despite the fact that she was feeling much stronger, she didn't think she was quite ready for that. For now, she was content to house-hunt and was particularly excited at seeing the house in Ringsend that her mother had assured her was in a nice little estate where several of the houses had been in the families for generations. Their appointment was for one o'clock and Frank was due home within the hour to collect her.

After hurrying upstairs, she put on some make-up and changed her T-shirt for a silky, multicoloured, tight-fitting top that Frank loved. She smiled as she smoothed it down over her hips. The day she'd bought it and modelled it for him, he'd admired it and then proceeded to strip it off her. She was so happy that they were returning to those days. When the phone rang, she threw herself across the bed to grab it before it stopped. "Hello?"

"Hi, Lynn. Problem."

She rolled over onto her back and sighed at the apologetic note in Frank's voice. "Something's come up?"

"Yes, I'm afraid so, darling."

"I'll call the estate agent and reschedule. When do you think you could fit me in, sir?"

"That's a whole other conversation," Frank teased. "Don't cancel, Lynn. Take your mum or Val along to see it and then, if you're impressed, we can organize a second viewing."

Lynn's stomach lurched at the thought of driving to the city and dealing with the estate agent alone. Since she'd left Hawthorn Lodge she'd let Frank handle all their interactions with the outside world until he'd finally twigged what she was up to and started pushing her gently towards being more independent. Was this another such ploy? "But it's going to be our home. We should be looking together."

"I told you: if you love it, I'll go back with you another day. It would be a shame to cancel so late, and your mum would be chuffed if you asked her along. Remember, she knows the area."

Lynn knew he was right. Mum would jump at the chance of a few hours out together. "Okay, I'll ask, but if she's busy I'm going to cancel."

"Fair enough. If I get finished early I'll meet you and take you both out for an early dinner."

"Oh, that would be nice." Eating out in Dublin was a much more attractive prospect than venturing out in Rathbourne. And Lynn was so proud of Frank, but, the more of a media darling he became, the less she saw of him. Another very good reason to move — and quickly: she missed him.

"Great. I'll call you later. Drive carefully. And Lynn?"

"Yes?"

"Have fun."

Nell Stephens craned her neck to read the street name. "I think it's the next turn, but it's so long since I've been here and so much has changed."

"The agent said it was the second turn left after the garage," Lynn said, jumping as the driver behind blew his horn. "Oh, feck off!" she muttered as she crawled along looking for the turn.

"Here!" Nell pointed. "This must be it."

Lynn turned and drove down the narrow street, then took the next left. "It looks like a quiet enough estate."

"Yes, and the houses all seem in good order," her mother said, studying them closely. "You always know the rented properties because the gardens are overgrown and the curtains and paint-work are a mess."

Lynn smiled at the generalization, and then put on her indicator to turn right. "This should be it."

"Yes, there it is!" Nell pointed at the house near the end of the small road with the sign in the garden.

After she'd parked, Lynn took her first proper look at the property. It was much as it had been in the brochure, although smaller than she had expected.

"Well, come on, let's go in," her mother said.

Feeling apprehensive, she followed her mother up the path. You're the client, she reminded herself. This agent will be bending over backwards to impress you.

Nell had already rung the bell and the yellow door swung open almost immediately.

"Miss Stephens?" A jovial, red-faced little man smiled at them. "Joe Stafford."

"I'm Lynn Stephens and this is my mother."

He shook her hand and then Nell's. "Nice to meet you both. Come in."

He stood back and Lynn found herself in a narrow dark hallway that was less than appealing.

"Ugh, how could anyone put a dark red wallpaper in a small hall with no light?" Nell said in her usual blunt manner.

The agent laughed. "There's no accounting for taste but, trust me, in this job I've seen a lot worse. A coat of paint would transform it, and the floor I think is lovely."

Lynn looked down at the tiles. They too were dark but, with cream flecks, pale walls would indeed make the space much more welcoming.

"This is the living room." Joe Stafford threw open the first door. It was brighter in here, thanks to the large bay window, but Lynn was disappointed at how small it was. Still, they didn't need much room.

The agent's mobile rang.

"Excuse me, ladies. Feel free to wander around. I'll be back in a moment." He went out into the front garden to take his call and Lynn looked at her mother. "What do you think?"

"It's okay," Nell said without enthusiasm. "Let's check out the kitchen."

"This is better." Lynn pointed at the arch in the centre of the large bright room. "They obviously merged the dining room and kitchen."

Nell opened some of the mustard-coloured cabinets and peered into the oven. "Ugh! You would need to put in new units."

Lynn walked to the window that looked out over a small paved area and garden, which again looked smaller than in the photograph. Did estate agents use special cameras to make things look bigger than they were? she wondered.

"Let's check out upstairs," her mother said, already halfway down the hall.

Lynn followed her up the creaking stairs and groaned when her mother opened the first door to reveal an olive bathroom suite.

Nell laughed at her expression. "Coloured suites were all the rage in the eighties; it wouldn't cost much to replace that."

"It all adds up, though," Lynn said. The main bedroom was simple enough and looked out onto the street; the second bedroom was smaller and south-facing, and so brighter; but the third —

"You couldn't swing a cat in here," Nell exclaimed. "They have a cheek calling it a bedroom. If you put a bed in here you'd have room for nothing else."

"Well, ladies, what do you think?" Joe said, from the landing. He didn't even attempt to join them in the tiny room.

"It's a bit small," Lynn said.

"But there's plenty of room to extend out the back," he pointed out.

"It's a dark house," Nell chipped in.

"Fresh paint would sort that out."

Lynn doubted it. Her gut told her that this was not the house for them. Were Frank with her, he would have cut short this viewing ten minutes ago. "Could we see the other properties you mentioned?"

"Of course. Let's take my car."

The second property was a few roads away and, though it was larger, the surroundings were not as pleasant and the narrow road was jammed with cars.

"You see what I mean?" Nell nodded at the unkempt gardens as the estate agent locked up. "You can bet most of these houses are rented."

"Yes," Lynn had to agree, taking in the flaking paint and broken gate of the house next door.

"With rentals you never know from one year to the next what kind of people you'll end up living next to."

"But that's true anywhere, Mum," Lynn pointed out.

"It doesn't stop you keeping an eye out for a place where people have lived in the neighbourhood for a long time. It's a sign that they're content and it's a good community."

"Shall we move on, ladies?" Joe led them towards his old Volvo. "I think this last property might be more what you're looking for."

"Have you a brochure?" Lynn asked.

"No, it's only just come on the market. You're the first viewers. It's quite a special property; I expect it to be snapped up."

Nell looked at her daughter and rolled her eyes at the salesman patter. "Is it far?" she asked.

"No, about a mile."

They were heading away from the city and Joe had turned onto the coast road. Lynn stared out across the strand, thinking how nice it would be to live close enough to the beach to go for long rambles; Frank would love that.

The agent turned into a small laneway lined with garages. "Here we are."

Nell shot her daughter a dubious look. "Where?"

He chuckled. "You'll see." He got out and tapped a code into a panel beside the first garage, and the doors swung open, silently revealing a courtyard with enough room for two cars.

"No garden?" Lynn said, disappointed.

"What would you do with a garden?" her mother scoffed.

"Sit in it and read a book," Lynn retorted, with a grin. It was true that neither she nor Frank had green fingers, but they both liked to sit outside on a nice evening, and Frank was a dab hand with a barbecue. Still, the views from this house had to be good, it being right on the coast, and instead of a garden they would have a beach; it was worth looking at.

Joe was standing at a polished black door, going through his bunch of keys.

"Here we are," he said, and opened the door.

"Wow," Lynn said, stepping inside. Like the first house, this had a long narrow hall, but that was where the similarity ended. The tiles were highly polished black marble but, thanks to the clever strip lighting and a skylight that ran almost the length of the ceiling, the space was classy, sophisticated and bright. The walls were the colour of honey and there were photos and prints artfully arranged in groups. Whoever owned this house not only had flair but also knew how to create a homely feel. "I have a feeling we've just stepped into a completely different price bracket."

Joe grinned. "Take a look around and then we'll talk about money."

"He wants you to fall in love with it and then he'll break the bad news," her mother said, but she too was staring around her in admiration.

Chuckling, he led them to the first door. "This house is sort of upside down. There are two bedrooms and a bathroom down here and the kitchen and living area and main bedroom are upstairs." He opened the door on what was obviously a little girl's room.

"Ah, isn't this just gorgeous!" Nell's expression softened at the matching duvet and curtains in mint green with tiny pink flowers, at the abundance of cuddly toys and at the child's artwork that covered the walls. She smiled at her daughter. "It would make a lovely nursery."

Lynn shook her head in resignation and walked to the glass sliding doors that led to a small garden with a swing and a slide and another house, with sliding doors, on the opposite side of the tiny square. Lynn shook her head in confusion. "A shared garden?" She felt so disappointed. This was a definite deal-breaker.

Nell joined her at the window. "Oh, I wouldn't like having a neighbour that close, no matter how well we got on!"

Joe laughed. "Let's move on." The next door led into a small but immaculate bathroom and the next to the second bedroom, decorated as a guest room in neutral colours.

"Come and see," Joe said, walking to the window.

"We're on the other side of the garden," Lynn marvelled. "That's fantastic."

"This place must cost a fortune," her mother said, joining her.

"Clever, isn't it?" he said. "And you don't have to worry if you have little ones: these doors are all fitted with childproof locks. And privacy is not a problem either, these windows allow you to see out, but others can't see in."

"We don't." Lynn ignored her mother's look and imagined Frank and herself sitting in the small courtyard, reading. "Let's go upstairs," she said, eager to see if the living area was as nice.

The stairs were steep and led straight into the kitchen cum living area. Though it wasn't huge it had been well thought out with the glossy white kitchen units at one end of the room and two cosy black sofas and a flat-screen TV at the other.

"Oh, my Lord!"

Lynn turned at her mother's gasp and saw that a window ran the length of the room and outside it was a balcony fitted out with a table and chairs, a barbecue and two recliners. Beyond it, looking beautiful even on this cloudy afternoon was the beach and Dublin Bay. "Crikey!" she breathed.

"That was pretty much my reaction," the agent said, laughing.

"I really wish you hadn't brought me here," Lynn groaned. "There's no way we could afford a place like this."

"Don't be so sure. Let me show you the main bedroom."

This room and *en suite* were small and simple, but Lynn could see herself lying in Frank's arms and staring contentedly out at that view. They went back into the living area and Joe opened the door and led them out onto the balcony. "I expected it to be noisier," she said, surprised given their proximity to the coast road.

The agent beckoned her to join him at the rail. There were three garages separating them from the road and as a result, though you could hear the traffic, it was muted.

"But we came in the first gate," she said, confused. "That's why."

"Access to those garages is from the lane on the other side," he explained.

"And who owns them?" Nell asked, obviously equally confused.

"They belong to the houses opposite."

Lynn sank into a chair at the table. "Go on, then, give us the bad news."

Joe held a chair for Nell before settling himself opposite them. "It is outside your budget —"

"I knew it." Lynn sighed.

"But the vendors want a quick sale. They're leaving the country and have found a house they want to buy, but they can't afford it until they sell this one. Now, you're renting, correct?"

"Yes," Lynn agreed.

"So you would be in a position to move fast. Most people looking at a property in this price range would have a property to sell, and that brings with it all sorts of issues and delays. I think you're in a very strong position. If you're interested, make them an offer."

"What's the asking price?" Lynn asked, and winced when he told her. "I need to talk to my partner."

"You do that. The owners are away this week and I have the keys, so, if you want to show him around, call me any time." He handed over his card.

CHAPTER
EIGHT

"It really is lovely," Nell said again when they were seated in a coffee shop in Sandymount discussing their afternoon.

Lynn had called Frank but his phone was switched off. She'd left a message telling him where they were. "It is, but I think it's out of our league."

"If it's to be, it will be," her mother said, patting her hand. "It would be a lovely place to raise a baby, wouldn't it? Five minutes' walk and you're on the beach."

"Mum, I told you I intend to get a job," Lynn said, regretting she'd told Nell they were getting married.

"Lots of mothers work, and when you were at Hawthorn Lodge you always kept strange hours, so I'm sure you could do both."

Lynn had to laugh. "We're only looking at houses. Slow down, please."

"But you would like a baby, wouldn't you, love?" her mother probed, her eyes anxious.

"At some stage I would," she admitted.

Nell beamed at her. "I'm so glad, darling."

Lynn's phone rang. "That's Frank now," she said. "Hey, how are you?"

"Fine, just finished. Will I pick you up and we'll go into town or do you want to head back towards Rathbourne and we'll stop off somewhere on the way?"

Lynn glanced at her watch. "Come here, Frank, would you? There's a house I'd love you to see and if we're quick we might be able to do it this evening."

"Fine, I'm only in the studios in Donnybrook, so I could be with you in ten minutes."

"Great." Lynn rang off and pulled out Joe's card. "Frank's free. Let's see if Joe can meet us."

"Won't that look too eager?" Nell cautioned.

"I don't care," Lynn said, tapping in the number. "Joe? Hi, Lynn Stephens here. Any chance of seeing that house again?"

"So it's not the house we looked at online?" Frank said as he drove them the short distance back to the house. Nell had elected to wait in the coffee shop.

"No, that was very disappointing. Now turn here."

"Are you sure?"

"Yes! And now, stop at the first set of gates."

Frank parked next to Joe's car and looked at the house before looking at Lynn. "This is . . . different."

She laughed. "It's *very* different. Come on." Leading the way to the door, she smiled at Joe. "Joe, this is my partner, Frank Hayes. Frank, Joe Stafford."

The two men shook hands. "Many thanks for meeting us at such short notice," Frank said.

"My pleasure. I'll leave you to wander around," Joe said, and went back to his car.

Inside, Frank stopped and stared around the hall just as Lynn and Nell had earlier. "Nice."

"Isn't it incredible?" Lynn said.

"The skylight was a clever touch. It would be very dark otherwise."

Lynn led the way to the first door, then turned to watch his face, her hand on the handle. "The second surprise," she said, and threw the door open with a flourish.

"A bedroom." Frank wandered in and smiled at the girly decor. "Cute. Are you getting broody, Ms Stephens?" he asked, squeezing her bum.

"Don't, I've already had all that from Mum. Come and look out the window." Frank crossed the room and she could see the same bewildered expression on his face when he eyed the tiny courtyard and the proximity of the next house.

"If you were into voyeurism this would be a very interesting setup, but I'm not sure I'd fancy it."

"All is not as it seems," Lynn said and led him back out to the hall and showed him the bathroom.

"And now the third surprise," she said, and led him into the second bedroom.

He laughed as he took in the fact that this bedroom was a mirror of the first and that its window was the one he had taken to be the neighbouring house. "Clever."

"Isn't it? And you don't have to worry about the voyeurism. Apparently, the windows are coated in some way that stops people being able to look in."

"This all sounds expensive," Frank said.

"I'll get to that when you've seen everything," Lynn said, and led him up the stairs that led directly into the living area.

"Very impressive," he said, eyeing the flat-screen appreciatively.

"Turn around," Lynn told him.

He did, and his eyes widened when he saw the balcony and the lovely view beyond it. "That is very, very nice."

"I knew you'd love it," Lynn said excitedly. She pulled back the sliding door and they stepped out into the open. "Can you imagine sitting here in the evenings or reading the papers on a Sunday morning?"

He walked around the balcony, looking over the side to inspect what was around and below them. "It's very private," he said, his eyes twinkling. "You could get up to all sorts out here."

"You have a one-track mind," Lynn said, laughing.

"But it's going the right way," he murmured, bending his head to kiss her. "So, are you going to show me the main bedroom?"

"It's a bit of a letdown after all this," she warned him.

"It's fine," he said when he saw it, again drawn to the window, "especially with that view. But darling, can we afford it? It's a small house but so well fitted out it must be out of our price range."

"I'm not sure," she admitted, leading the way back into the kitchen and perching on a high stool.

"How much is it?" He sat beside her.

She told him the figure but quickly went on to tell him what the estate agent had said about the owners being desperate to sell. "I know it would stretch us but, if we did sublet our apartment and we used my settlement, wouldn't we have enough to afford a mortgage?"

"I suppose," he said. "It would be best to put it all in just your name, though."

"Would a bank give me a mortgage when I haven't even got a job?" she asked.

He sighed. "Probably not, but they won't be too keen to give me one, either, until I've got rid of Carrie's place."

"So it's impossible," Lynn said, feeling deflated.

"You really love it?" he asked.

She smiled sadly. "What's not to love? It's got everything we need."

"It does," he agreed, thoughtfully.

"What?" Lynn recognized that look: he'd thought of something.

"Let me talk to a couple of people and take a look at the figures. If we were in a position to put in an offer we'd have to figure out how high we could realistically go. The agent —"

"Joe," Lynn reminded him.

He grinned. "This morning you were going to cancel the viewings because I couldn't come and not only did you do it without me but you are completely relaxed and comfortable with the man you were so terrified of meeting."

She smiled, realizing the truth of his words. Though she had been initially nervous with Joe she'd soon become so absorbed in the house hunt that she'd soon forgotten her fears. "It helped having Mum with me."

"You are so much better when you have a project, darling." Frank stood up and pulled her to her feet. She turned within his arms, rested her head against his chest and together they stared out across the bay. "You really would be happy here, wouldn't you?" He kissed her hair.

"I already told you that I'd be happy anywhere with you but, yes, I love the house. You?"

"It's perfect, and so central. We would have much more time together."

"To walk on the beach," Lynn sighed.

"And test the privacy of our balcony." He turned her around and kissed her. "Now, let's go talk to your pal Joe and see if we can get him to name a figure that he thinks they'd accept."

This part Lynn was happy to leave to Frank, but she picked up on his cues and went along with it when he pointed out some drawbacks of the location. He questioned the area, referring to a dodgy estate nearby well known for troublesome teens, and also the open expanse of green down the road that no doubt was a favourite spot for drinking parties. Lynn looked suitably concerned about these issues. Joe swatted away their concerns like a true pro, reminding Frank that the Garda station was close by and that the security system in the house was the best available.

Frank changed tack and asked Joe about the market in general and house prices in the area. Finally, Joe agreed to call him the following day with his best guess of a figure that the owners would consider, and they left him to go and collect Nell.

Jack Stephens beamed happily as Lynn told him all about the house. "Delighted for you both. I hope it works out," he said, when she paused to draw breath.

"You don't mind me leaving Rathbourne?" she asked.

"I don't mind where you live as long as you're happy," he assured her.

"It's got three bedrooms, so you could come and stay."

Her father yawned. "And who'd look after the shop?"

"Everyone needs a break from time to time, Jack," Frank said.

Nell shook her head in despair. "At our age we should be out enjoying ourselves, but he won't even leave the place for a weekend."

"Would you have me leave Norman in charge?" he retorted.

Lynn smiled. Norman Foley had worked for her father since she was a child and, though he was a hard worker, he was a shy, timid, simple man who got flustered if he was even left to put on the alarm and lock up. Lynn knew her dad would have loved her to join him in the family business, but he had always told her that she must follow her own path and not his. She had felt torn but in her heart she knew that, though they were close, working together would be impossible: they were too much alike.

"You could take Cathy on full-time," Frank suggested.

Lynn shot him a scornful look. "So she could spend more time texting behind the fridge?"

"You've never liked that poor girl," Jack said.

"Because she's good for nothing, Dad, and completely unreliable."

Nell sighed. "He only took her on because she's Norman's niece."

"Jamie would be more use," Lynn retorted.

Frank frowned. "Who's Jamie?"

"Cathy's little brother. He's only sixteen but he's a good head on his shoulders and is a quick learner."

"He's a grand lad," Nell agreed.

"I've managed to run the business more than thirty years without all your advice, thank you very much," Jack grumbled.

"We just don't want you overdoing things, Dad." Lynn gave him an apologetic smile. "You always seem to be tired these days."

"He should sell up," Nell muttered, shooting her husband a reproachful look.

Lynn sighed. She could appreciate her mother's frustration. Dad had suffered a stroke two years before and, though he had made a complete recovery, it had scared the hell out of his wife and daughter. They had begged him to retire then, but Dad wasn't the sort to sit around and Lynn knew that he would miss the banter with his customers. Charles Boland might be the kingpin in town but Stephens's Supermarket was the heartbeat of Rathbourne, and her father a hugely respected part of the community.

A workaholic herself, she could completely understand why he didn't want to walk away and even his doctors had said that it might not be such a great idea. But everyone agreed he should work fewer hours, and, though he'd said he would, Lynn knew he'd never had any intention of handing over the reins.

The atmosphere had grown tense and Jack was glowering. Lynn caught Frank's eye. "I think we'd better get going. Didn't you say you had an early start?"

Frank checked his watch and jumped to his feet. "Hell, yes. I didn't realize it was so late. I'm on the radio at seven and I'll need to be in the studio at six thirty so I have a chance to check what's in the newspapers."

"Go." Nell smiled at him. "And thank you for a lovely dinner."

Lynn bent to kiss her mother's cheek. "Night, Mum. Thanks for coming with me today."

"Oh, it was my pleasure, love, I enjoyed myself."

Jack walked them to the door and Frank said goodbye, knowing he liked a moment alone with Lynn.

"It's good to see you looking more yourself, Lynn." He squeezed her shoulder as they watched Frank drive away. "Or is that just an act for your old ma and da?"

"No, I do feel better and I think this move is exactly what I need; it's like a clean slate."

"Then I'm happy for you," he said, suppressing another yawn.

Lynn laughed. "Go to bed, you're banjaxed."

"I just have a few papers to go through first."

"They'll wait," she told him. "Slow down a bit, Dad. Mum may nag but it's only because she worries about you."

"I know. Okay, I'll leave it till morning. Is it all right if I watch the news before I go to bed?"

She grinned and hugged him. "If you must. Night, Dad."

"Night, sweetheart, I love you."

CHAPTER
NINE

Lynn was sitting with Val at a petrol-station café drinking disgusting coffee. Not an ideal venue but the safest place to meet near the off-licence.

"So what's the news?" Val asked, her eyes alight with curiosity.

"I found the most amazing house in Dublin. You'd want to see it, Val, it's fabulous."

"Wow, that was fast. You only started looking yesterday!"

"I know and I'm probably getting excited over nothing. It's far too expensive. Oh, but Val, it's gorgeous with the most amazing view, and the beach is only five minutes' walk."

Val smiled. "Then I hope you get it. You deserve to. I can't believe you went house-hunting without Frank. I'm so proud of you."

"Mum came."

"That's not the same at all. You've come a long way, girl." Val's expression sobered. "I have some news too. I saw Orla in the post office yesterday."

Lynn's stomach churned at the mention of Vincent Boland's wife. "Did you talk to her?"

"No, when she spotted me she couldn't get out of there fast enough."

It shouldn't be like this, Lynn thought. There was a time when she, Gina and Val had been friends with Orla and if they met it would be straight into the nearest café for a catch-up. Thanks to Vincent, those days were gone. She hated the fact that Orla had lost her friends at such an important time of her life. It was obvious that Orla was overawed to find herself a Boland and, being so timid, would find it hard coping with his forceful mother and intimidating uncle. And now Vincent would spend most of his time in the next county and Orla would just have to cope. Lynn felt guilty for the way her problem had impinged on a good friend. "How did she look?"

"Big!" Val laughed and then was silent for a moment. "She'll make a great mother."

"Yes," Lynn agreed. Would Vincent be the ideal parent? she wondered. She prayed that he was a different man with his wife and that he would look after Orla and their baby.

"So what's going to happen about the house? Are you going to go and see it again?"

"There's no need. It was love at first sight. If it were possible financially, we wouldn't hesitate. The agent's supposed to call Frank today about the lowest offer he thinks they'll accept and then he'll see if it's possible. A lot depends on Carrie managing to sell the house."

Val glanced at her watch. "I should get back to work. I'm leaving early tonight. I've a date!"

90

Lynn smiled at the excited twinkle in her friend's eye. "How come you're only telling me this now? Who is he? Where are you going? Details, woman. What's he like? How did you meet him? And how come you never mentioned him before?"

"He moved into the flat downstairs. I didn't pay much attention to him. He's not my type at all: very quiet and studious and, well, boring."

"Well, that sounds promising," Lynn said with a smirk.

Val laughed. "He looks like a skinny teenager but he says he's thirty-one. He's a little taller than me and has brown hair and eyes."

"So how did he come to ask you out and when?"

"You won't believe it. Yesterday I was watering my pot plants on the window ledge and I knocked one over and I heard this cry and I looked out and he was flat out in the garden."

Lynn stared at her in shock. "Oh, my God!"

"I know! I was almost afraid to go down and check in case I'd killed him. But by the time I got there he was sitting up, rubbing his head and just looking confused. I wanted to take him to casualty but he said no way, he was fine, but if it made me feel any better that I could ask him questions to check if he was concussed. That was it, really. The questions turned into a chat and then as an apology I offered to make him some dinner."

"You don't waste time," Lynn teased.

Val giggled. "It was the least I could do for the poor man."

"The very least," Lynn agreed. "Go on."

Val sighed. "We stayed up till eleven talking and when he was finally leaving he asked me would I like to go to an art exhibition this evening?"

"That's an interesting first date," Lynn said, thinking that this relationship wouldn't last a week.

Val laughed. "I know, but it's a friend of his, so he says he has to show his face and then we can go for a drink."

"Oh, well, then, that should be fun."

"I hope so."

"Did he kiss you?"

"Just on the cheek." Val sighed, a dreamy look in her eyes.

"Ah, nice. Have a great time, darling. I look forward to a full report."

Val hugged her. "Thanks, I'll text you."

Lynn was almost asleep when her phone beeped.

"Who the hell is sending you texts at this hour?" Frank grumbled, sticking his head under the pillow.

Lynn moved from under his arm to the edge of the bed and groped around on the floor for her phone. She peered sleepily at the screen and then with a chuckle dropped it and rolled back over to Frank, slipping her arm around his waist. "Val. She's in love."

"Again?" he mumbled.

She snuggled up against him. "Again."

Another ring woke them. Lynn struggled into consciousness, clocked that it was daylight, and nudged Frank. "There's someone at the door."

Frank grunted and pulled the duvet up around his ears.

Lynn yanked it down again. "Frank!" She looked at the alarm clock. Who the hell was visiting at eight o'clock on a Saturday morning? As he slept on, she climbed out of bed, reached for her robe, and, tying it tightly around her, went downstairs and opened the door a crack.

"Hey, Lynn."

She blinked at the sight of Frank's son standing before her, resplendent in luminous cycling gear. With his unruly locks, bright blue eyes and long tanned limbs he looked the picture of health. "Philip, hi."

"Is he ready?" He strode past her and through to the kitchen.

"Ready?" She followed him, yawning and rubbing her eyes.

"The charity cycle?"

Lynn's eyes widened. "That's today?"

"Dad's forgotten?" Philip said, looking incredulous.

"Given he's out cold, I think that's a safe bet. I'll go wake him. Why don't you make some coffee?"

"I didn't get a chance to have breakfast —"

"Help yourself," she called over her shoulder, and then hurried upstairs. "Frank, wake up. Philip's here."

Frank opened one eye. "He is, why?"

"Nothing important," she said with a casual shrug, "but you had better get up. Your charity cycle starts in two hours."

"*What?*"

"Breakfast in ten minutes," she said and went back downstairs.

Philip had already raided the fridge and eggs, bacon and sausages were lined up on the counter.

"You said help yourself," he said with a cheeky grin.

"Sit down, I'll do it." She laughed. "How's life? Are you looking forward to college?"

"Yeah, it should be great. From what I'm told there's more time off than there are classes."

"Somehow I doubt that." She put the rashers and sausages under the grill and broke eggs into the pan.

He stretched his lanky legs out and linked his hands behind his head. "Honestly, it's the truth. I don't know how anyone is supposed to learn anything. On the upside, I hear the social life is good."

"Well that's all that matters, isn't it?"

Frank appeared in the doorway in tracksuit bottoms and a T-shirt and cuffed his son across the head. "Why didn't you call me yesterday and remind me?"

"Morning, Dad. Good to see you, too."

Frank went to stand behind Lynn, wrapped his arms around her waist and kissed her neck. "Smells gorgeous. So does breakfast," he murmured. "How long is the cycle?" he asked Philip as he sat down and reached for the juice.

"Fifty miles." Philip smiled.

Frank coughed. "What? Are you trying to kill me?"

"You'll be grand."

"I haven't cycled more than five miles in years."

Lynn divided the food onto two plates and set it down in front of them. "That'll give you the energy."

"Or finish me off," he retorted. "Have you two taken out a life-insurance policy on me or something?"

Philip pulled a face at Lynn. "Damn, we've been sussed."

She laughed, pouring tea for them all. "What is the charity?"

"My rugby club."

"What?" Frank yelled. "Why, you cheeky little — That's not a charity!"

"Sure it is," Philip said, slathering two slices of bread with butter. "You're helping young lads stay healthy."

"It's a nice day for it." Lynn nodded towards the window at the sun breaking through the clouds.

"So come with us," Frank challenged.

"I've a house to clean."

"That's just an excuse."

"It is." She smiled sweetly. "And I'll be seeing Val later."

Frank groaned at the memory of the late-night text. "Please ask her to stop sending messages in the middle of the night, will you?"

"No point. After she's had a couple of glasses of wine she doesn't notice time."

"Mad idea, but why not just switch off your phone?" Philip suggested, before taking a bite of his carefully constructed sandwich.

"Maybe," Lynn murmured, knowing she never would. Her phone had been switched off the night her mother had called to tell her about her father's stroke and she'd never left it off since.

Frank gave her a reassuring smile and she sighed, wishing they were spending the day together. Between Frank's long hours and commuting, they seemed to snatch only moments together.

"Has your mother heard any more about the house?" Frank asked Philip as if reading her thoughts.

"Oh, yeah, she got an offer."

Frank and Lynn exchanged looks.

"Didn't you think of mentioning that sooner?" Frank asked. "How much?"

Philip scrunched up his face, chewing thoughtfully. "Can't remember."

Frank sighed in exasperation. "Was your mother awake when you left?"

"She dropped me off. She's spending the day with a friend in Tullamore."

Frank looked up at Lynn. "I'll phone her after I've eaten, but I wouldn't get my hopes up, darling. If it had been good news she would have called in."

Lynn sighed. That was true. Carrie couldn't accept an offer without agreeing it with Frank first. But she was still wondering an hour later when Frank and Philip headed off, bikes strapped to the back of the car.

Frank said as he kissed her goodbye, "I left Carrie a message. I'll let you know as soon as I hear from her."

"Okay." She stood on the doorstep to wave them off, arms wrapped tightly around herself. "Break a leg! Oh, no, don't! Good luck!"

"If he has a heart attack I'll call you," Philip said with a grin.

96

Lynn went upstairs to the bathroom, turned on the shower and pulled off her nightdress. As she waited for the water to heat she studied herself in the mirror, trying to be objective. She had dismissed their concern but Frank and her mother were right: she had lost weight and it didn't suit her. Her neck seemed scrawny, her face shrunken and her eyes huge against the cloud of hair. Her breasts were smaller and her legs and arms looked thin and fragile, yet her stomach, typically, was still round. She needed to eat more healthily and exercise. Sitting around the house had taken its toll and, if she was going to go back to work, she would need to get fit.

She stepped into the shower and turned her face up, the flow of hot water calming the feeling of panic that always threatened to overwhelm her when she considered the prospect. As she shampooed her hair and soaped her body she reminded herself of how normal she'd felt that day in Dublin viewing properties. Her curiosity and eagerness to find a home had quickly made her forget her fears and she had actually enjoyed herself in the end. It would be even better when she was doing something that challenged and engrossed her, and she looked forward to coming off medication. Now for the next step. This morning, she decided she would write a Curriculum Vitae.

Fired up, she dressed quickly, dried her hair and was about to curl up on the sofa with her laptop and a mug of coffee when she realized there was no milk. She hesitated for only a moment. She usually avoided going to the corner shop but it was early and she was unlikely to bump into anyone.

Her pulse quickened as she left the house; it always did when she went out alone. Thankfully, the roads were deserted and she reached the shop without incident. Before going inside she put her phone to her ear, pretending she was on a call so Mags, the nosy owner, wouldn't engage her in conversation. The woman's face lit up when she saw her but that was quickly followed by a flash of irritation when Lynn continued to nod and talk and mouth "sorry" as she handed over the money. She was congratulating herself on her ingenuity when, in her hurry to escape, she crashed into someone in the doorway and her phone went flying across the pavement outside.

"Oh, I'm so sorry!" The other girl bent with some difficulty to retrieve it and turned to hand it over. "I hope it's okay — Oh, Lynn!"

Lynn's stomach did a somersault as she looked up into the startled, embarrassed eyes of Vincent Boland's wife. "Hi, Orla." She closed the door, acutely aware of Mags craning her head to watch them. She checked her phone. "It's okay, it's still working," she reassured her old friend.

"Great." Orla made no move to go inside. "Lynn —"

"Orla —"

They exchanged nervous smiles.

"Sorry about . . . everything," Orla said.

"Thanks. How are you feeling?" Lynn nodded towards the girl's enormous bump.

"Like a beached whale, but I'm fine." Orla patted it. "Only six weeks to go."

"That's good. Where are you going to have it?"

"I was going to the maternity hospital in Dublin, but Vincent's mum found me this great midwife, so I'm having it at home."

"That will be nice." Lynn tried to hide her alarm. She could think of nothing more terrifying than having a first baby outside the security of a hospital, but Aideen Boland was a force of nature and she could understand why her quiet friend would cave under the woman's pressure.

"Yes," Orla agreed, though it was clear from her expression that she was nervous. She swayed slightly, her eyes fluttering closed.

Lynn's arm shot out to steady her. "Are you okay?"

"My blood pressure is up — one of the joys of late pregnancy," she joked.

Lynn frowned at her pallor and the beads of sweat on her forehead. "You need to sit down."

"I'll be fine."

"My place is only around the corner. Come and have a cup of tea and a rest."

"I shouldn't —"

"Orla, please, think of the baby."

"Yes, okay, then."

Orla allowed Lynn to take her arm and lead her slowly back down the road.

CHAPTER
TEN

"Feeling better?" Lynn asked, glad to see that the colour had returned to the girl's cheeks.

Orla finished the last bite of her Kit Kat and nodded. "Much. Thanks."

"Does that happen often?" Lynn poured her a second cup of tea.

"Not often, and only in the last few weeks," Orla assured her. "I've been fine otherwise."

"You shouldn't really be out on your own, should you?"

"Probably not, but I hate being in the house. It's so quiet without Vincent."

"Sorry."

"It's not your fault, Lynn," Orla insisted.

"Maybe not, but it seems wrong that you are the one suffering . . ." Lynn trailed off. She had no idea what Orla knew or didn't know, and she didn't want to say anything to upset her.

"How are you doing?" Orla asked.

"Not so bad."

"Are you working?"

Lynn figured Orla already knew the answer to that. "No, but I hope to soon. Frank and I are thinking of moving to Dublin."

"Really?"

"There are more jobs to be had and Frank spends most of his time there anyway."

"He's got quite famous, hasn't he?"

Lynn laughed. "I suppose he has."

"I'm glad you have him."

There was an awkward silence, and Lynn struggled for something to say. "Are you looking forward to being a mother?"

Orla's face lit up. "Yes, I can't wait, although I'm a bit terrified."

"Of the birth?"

"That and the thought of dropping the poor child. Imagine a baby having to depend on me!"

"You'll be great," Lynn assured her. "You were always looking after the girls in school. If anyone felt sick or miserable in school you were always the one to comfort them; you're a natural."

Orla rubbed her bump and smiled. "I hope so."

"Have you thought of names?"

Orla pulled a face. "I have but Vincent isn't keen on them. He wants to stick with family names."

Typical, feckin' Boland, Lynn thought. "Oh, well, perhaps it's best to wait until the baby's born. My mum always said that she was planning to call me Angela but that when she saw me she decided I looked like a Lynn."

"Didn't your dad have a say in the matter?" Orla smiled.

"No, of course not. You know my mother!"

Orla glanced at her watch. "I'd better go. Aideen is dropping in with samples of wallpaper and curtain material."

Again, Lynn thought that was surely something Orla would want to do with Vincent, but kept her opinion to herself. "Will your mother come up for the birth?" she asked instead. Orla's mother was a widow and lived in Limerick and suffered badly with agoraphobia.

"I don't think so. She would never travel alone and it's unlikely Vincent will get time off to go and get her."

Lynn squeezed her hand. "That's a pity."

"It can't be helped." Orla stood up, her smile strained. "Thanks for the tea, Lynn. It was nice to see you again."

"And you. Will I walk you back?"

"No, that's probably not a good idea."

"I suppose not." Lynn opened the door. "Take care, and best of luck."

"Thanks." Orla gave her a quick hug and hurried down the path as fast as her bump would allow.

Alone now, Lynn sat staring into space and wondered if Orla was happy with Vincent. When the couple had started dating, Vincent had drawn Orla away from her friends and they'd seen less and less of her. Lynn hadn't really noticed at the time. Lots of girls drifted away from their friends when they fell in love. It was only in retrospect that Lynn realized Orla hadn't as much drifted as been completely cut off. It was probably Aideen's doing. Once she realized the relationship was serious, Vincent's mother would have set about grooming her to become a worthy member of the Boland clan. While her girlfriends' skirts got shorter, their shoes higher and their tops tighter, Orla took to wearing more conservative clothes, lost a stone, and her curly, blonde hair that distinguished her from the crowd was tamed and straightened to within an inch of its life.

With pregnancy, though, Lynn noticed, some of the old Orla had returned. She had been wearing a simple loose top and leggings, her cheeks were plumper and bare of make-up, and the natural kink in her hair had returned. Perhaps motherhood would give her the confidence to step out of the Bolands' shadow. Strange, Lynn mused, how they had both changed so much because of Vincent, but for very different reasons.

"But, to hell with you, Vincent Boland, I'm going to change back," she said aloud as she flipped open her laptop. She was going to put together a slick, impressive CV that would knock hoteliers' socks off. She smiled as she imagined Frank's face when she showed it to him. She didn't dwell on the interview process. "One step at a time, Lynn," she told herself and got down to work.

Vincent Boland threw down his pen. He sat back in the squeaking chair and looked around the drab, musty office. He couldn't believe that he was in this dump and couldn't wait to get out of it.

"It's not for long," his uncle had said when he broke the news.

"But you are as much as telling the world that I'm guilty," Vincent had protested, pacing the floor of Charles Boland's study.

The older man had raised his eyes from the papers in front of him to give Vincent a sharp look. "I'm saving your skin. Considering what you could have cost the business in terms of money and reputation, count yourself lucky."

That bitch was to blame for everything. He swung his chair around and gave the ancient filing cabinet a vicious kick. He should have taken care of this problem himself, quickly and quietly. Still, he'd learned a valuable lesson, and he'd never let a woman pull a stunt like this on him again. He bent to take the well-thumbed file from his briefcase that held her statement and read it again with mounting anger. All this bullshit about depression and agoraphobia as a result of his bullying her — it made his blood boil. Charles had settled out of court so that none of the details of the case were in the public domain, but, since the news broke, Rathbourne was full of whispers. Of course, it had all been down to that fucking boyfriend of hers. Lynn would never have had the nerve to take that case alone.

When Charles had first called him in to tell him the news, he'd felt sick, but, once he had heard the content of the action, he had relaxed a little. As time went on and the case progressed he became more confident about his position. Lynn hadn't been entirely forthcoming and her claims seemed pathetic and flimsy. Vincent had prepared his own statement, a stinging attack on her incompetence and unreliability, and had claimed he had been very tolerant with an employee who had turned out to be a liability. When Charles announced that he was settling the case Vincent had been both stunned and furious.

"But this is ridiculous, you can't settle."

"I've no choice," Charles had snapped, and told him of his expulsion to The Willows. "You got away lightly this time, Vincent, but, so help me, if anyone else comes forward with complaints about you then you'll be looking for another job."

It was no idle threat, Vincent knew. The good name of the family was everything to Charles and, though he'd assured his brother Desmond on his deathbed that he would always look after his wife and son, his uncle would not think twice about cutting him loose if it came down to a choice between him and the business.

Again Vincent cursed Lynn as he thought of the damage she had done to his relationship with Charles. His only son, Andy, had inherited none of his father's business acumen and, though he had obediently followed him into the business, it didn't take long for Charles to realize that his son would never be able to step into his shoes. When Andy had declared he was taking his guitar and moving to Ibiza to work the pubs, there had been a general sense of relief. Of Charles's three daughters, only Emer worked in the family business, part-time, as an accountant. She had a family of her own, though, and had no ambition to become a full-time career woman. Therese and Anne-Marie were non-executive directors but showed little interest in the business once the money rolled in. The scene was set and all Vincent had to do was wait patiently in the wings until Charles realized he was a worthy successor, and he had.

But, though Charles had stood by his nephew through the case and allowed him to remain as manager, there had been a distinct change in his demeanour and Vincent knew that he was on very shaky ground.

"Make a success of The Willows," his mother, Aideen, had urged during one of their breakfasts at the hotel. Despite being married to Orla for three years he still came to her to talk about the business. She had a quick brain, was ambitious for him and understood, in a way that Orla never would, how Charles operated. "Show him that you're above all of this, that you're mature enough to accept the situation, and move on."

He knew she was right and so had cleared out his desk and moved his belongings down to this hovel without further complaint. Charles had commissioned him to produce a report on the best way to turn The Willows around and, though they both knew it was just an excuse to get him out of Rathbourne, Vincent was determined to come up with a viable plan for the hotel and prove himself to his uncle. More importantly he wanted to do it fast. He would show the residents of Rathbourne that he was still very much in control. Since many of the local residents were employed by his family, that would soon put a stop to their gossiping. He knew he didn't have to worry about Lynn Stephens. From what he'd seen and heard she had turned into a recluse. His mother was right: he had to stay calm and ride out this small storm. Then he could return to

Rathbourne and take up his rightful place by his uncle's side.

Vincent picked up the phone and dialled the manager's extension. "I want a tour of the hotel and grounds, and then I want to see the staff. Meet me in reception in ten minutes."

CHAPTER
ELEVEN

Lynn was alone in her father's office working her way through a pile of bills, but her mind wasn't really on the job. All she could think of was the meeting that Frank and Carrie were having right now about the house sale. There had been an offer and, no, it wasn't at all what they had hoped for, but Frank predicted the market would get much worse before it got better and that they should snap it up. Carrie wasn't convinced, or so she said. Lynn thought it was more a case that she enjoyed these sessions with her ex-husband and was being deliberately obtuse to prolong them.

"I hope you didn't say that to Frank," Val had said when Lynn had voiced her feelings the other night. Frank was out and her friend had come over to keep her company.

"Of course I didn't."

"Good because he'll get tired of you being so jealous."

"I'm not jealous," Lynn protested. "She just annoys me."

"Yeah, sure." Val laughed. Her pink mobile phone chirruped on the coffee table and she lunged at it and read the message, smiling.

"Lover boy?" Lynn asked.

"Yes." Val gave a happy sigh.

"Is it serious?" Lynn asked.

"I think so. He's invited me to a family dinner on Saturday night."

Lynn pulled a face. "Yikes! How do you feel about that?"

"I'm a bit nervous," Val admitted, tugging on the red curls that framed her face. "There seems to be lots of them."

"Is there an occasion or are they just there to meet you?"

"It's his parents' thirtieth wedding anniversary." She looked at Lynn with worried eyes. "I'll have to buy a present. What should I get them?"

"Nothing, you don't even know them," Lynn protested, laughing. "Just bring wine and chocolates or flowers."

"Yes, right, okay." Val pulled even more frantically on her hair.

"I've never seen you so het up," Lynn marvelled.

Val smiled, her eyes shining. "I think he might be the one, Lynn."

"You always say that."

"I know I do, but John is different."

Lynn poured Val more wine. "So, when do I get to meet him?"

"Whenever you like."

"You could bring him to dinner."

"Are you sure?"

Lynn saw the surprise in her friend's eyes. It was true: it had been a long time since she'd entertained, but she felt stronger now, she would be fine. "Yeah, why not? I'll just do a lasagne and salad, nothing fancy. It'll be fun."

"I would like you and Frank to meet him; I know you'll love him."

"I'm sure we will."

Lynn's daydreaming was interrupted by her phone ringing. "Frank?"

"Hi, darling, how are things?"

"Okay. Any news?"

"Yes. I've just put down the phone to the estate agent; Carrie and I accepted the offer."

Lynn let out a little whoop of delight. "That's fantastic news." She wondered if the wonderful house in Ringsend was still on the market.

"I'll call Joe Stafford," Frank said as if reading her mind. "We can't put in an offer yet but there's no harm in letting him know where things are at."

"He said the owners wanted to move fast," she reminded him anxiously.

"And we could. Once the deposit's paid I'm happy to go ahead with it if you are."

"I can't believe it, Frank. I'd given up hope and thought we'd have to rent."

"No way," Frank said. "Even if we can't get that house, Lynn, I think we should keep looking. This is definitely a good time to buy."

110

"Okay," she said happily. "What time do you expect to be home?"

"About seven. Will I bring some dinner?"

"Sounds good." Lynn said goodbye and went back to work on the accounts.

"Someone sounds happy."

Lynn looked up and smiled at her dad. She hadn't even realized she was humming. "I'm making great progress," she told him as he pulled up a chair beside her. She checked through some queries with him and recommended a few ways of cutting costs. "Have you thought of having a 'local produce' corner, Dad?" she asked.

"Shoppers aren't interested in supporting local businesses. They just want the best deal they can get and, if they don't find it in my shop, they go to one of the bigger supermarkets."

"It might be cheaper given there's no middle man or transport costs," Lynn argued. "You should talk to local farmers and bakeries; it can't hurt to ask."

"I'll think about it."

"Thinking about it won't get you far, Dad," she argued. "You need to act."

"Don't nag," he said, but gave her a quick, tight hug.

She looked at him in surprise. "What's that for?"

He smiled at her. "It's nice to have the old Lynn back."

"Even if I *am* telling you how to run the place?" She laughed.

"Even then."

"So, will you look into the local produce idea?"

He sighed. "I've a better idea. You do it."

111

She stared at him. "Oh, I don't know —"

"It would just be a few phone calls, and you are going to have to get used to dealing with strangers again if you plan to return to work."

"I suppose."

"You'd be doing me a favour."

She scowled at him. "That's emotional blackmail."

He looked all innocence. "It was your idea, but I'm too busy to take it on. And you're always offering to help."

"Okay, okay, I'll check it out," she said with a sigh of resignation.

Lynn finished up in the office and went across to the house in search of her mother. Nell was in the living room going through old photographs.

She smiled and held out a photograph to Lynn. "Remember that?"

Lynn peered down at the picture of her and Gina dressed in ball gowns. "Yes, that was when the school put on *My Fair Lady*; we were in fourth year." They had thought they looked so grown-up in the dresses but they had been only babies.

"Do you ever hear from Gina now?"

"I haven't seen her for over three years. We exchange texts and emails from time to time and talk about getting together — she lives in Dublin — but we haven't managed it yet. But then she has three little girls to keep her busy."

"Perhaps you'll see more of each other when you move to Dublin. Look at this one." Nell handed her a photo.

112

It was of Lynn and her dad struggling to get a Christmas tree in the door. Jack had been calling for his wife's help but instead she'd grabbed the camera. "This must be ten years ago," she said. How much younger and stronger her dad looked.

"Two thousand and four," her mother told her. "That was a great Christmas. Your Aunty Brenda was over from Florida, remember?"

"Oh, yes." Lynn had been mesmerized to meet her three cousins, who were all golden limbs, white teeth and American accents, though their mother was still a Dubliner through and through. Lynn had taken them out clubbing with her friends but they were more captivated when she took them to a traditional music session in the local pub. All the girls had fallen for her tall, dark cousin, Matt. There had been a lot of laughter in the house that Christmas. "Weren't we supposed to go and visit them?"

"We were, but as usual your father wouldn't leave the shop and I wouldn't go without him."

Lynn said nothing. She knew that her dad would take her mother on any holiday she wanted if Lynn offered to look after the business, but she couldn't bring herself to do that. The prospect of being the subject of curious glances and plagued by questions was terrifying. "I better go," she said abruptly, and stood up.

Nell looked up at her. "You only just got here. Is everything all right?"

"Yes, sorry, I just hadn't realized how late it was. I need to make a start on dinner. Frank will be home soon."

"Okay, then, love. Pop your head in and say goodbye to your dad before you go."

"I will. Bye, Mum." As she'd hoped, her father was busy with a customer when she stopped in the doorway, so she waved, smiled and hurried out to her car.

Lynn drove straight to Clogher Head to clear her mind. She was excited that Frank was finally able to sell the family home and that they could realistically plan to buy a place together, but looking at the old photographs had triggered feelings of guilt. She couldn't help feeling that she had let her parents down by not joining the family business. But the fact remained that, had she and her father worked together, they'd have been at loggerheads all the time. She'd want to adopt some marketing strategies, but her father didn't like change and argued that if his customers felt they were being conned they'd take their business elsewhere.

"I'm not suggesting you con them, Dad," she had argued several times, "but it's a business and you need to make a profit."

"How on earth have I survived this far at all without your words of wisdom?" he'd retorted once, his voice scathing but his eyes hurt. Of course she should have used more diplomatic language but, once she started arguing with her father, diplomacy was inclined to go out the window; he was so incredibly stubborn.

"How do you *expect* him to react?" Frank had said after such an exchange. "You're as much as saying that he's making a botch of it."

114

"But I'm only trying to help," she'd protested, horrified.

But of course Frank had been right and she wouldn't have the relationship she had now with her father if they were working together. Feeling better, she decided to go home and start researching local suppliers. If she couldn't work with him she could still help out in these small ways and she was convinced her idea had some merit.

She was still bent over her laptop, notebook and pen at her side, when Frank arrived home with food. She looked up in surprise and then sniffed appreciatively, realizing that she was ravenous.

"You look busy," he said, carrying their dinner through to the kitchen.

"I'm doing some research for Dad," she said, joining him.

"Oh, yeah?"

She took down two plates and turned at his distracted tone. "What's up?"

He took the fish and chips out of the bags and portioned them out before meeting her eyes. "You're sure you like that house?"

"The one in Ringsend? I love it."

"Good because I just made an offer on it."

"You *what?*" she screeched and threw her arms around him, laughing as he pretended he was choking. "I don't understand. How on earth did all this come about? When we talked you were just going to talk to Joe."

"I didn't want to get your hopes up but it really seems that our timing is spot on. First when I was with Carrie she got another call from her estate agent. He'd been talking to the prospective buyer and immediately she thought he was upping the offer because she hadn't come back to him. He wasn't," Frank added quickly when he saw her hopeful expression. "But the news was nearly as good as far as we are concerned. He's starting a job in the pharmaceutical company down the road in a couple of weeks. His kids have already started in the local primary school and they're staying with friends, so he wants to move in as quickly as possible."

"That's great news." Lynn lowered herself into a chair and stared at him over the steaming plates of food, her hunger forgotten.

"I know. Apparently he'd been looking for months but this was the first house to come on the market that really suited them. So I called Stafford and put in the offer. I gambled a bit," he admitted.

"Oh?"

"I offered twenty grand less than Stafford had suggested but told him we could exchange contracts straightaway."

"Can we?" She looked at him in surprise.

"Yes, it's unlikely Carrie's buyer's going to pull out if he has accepted the job nearby and the kids are in school," he pointed out. "Now we just have to sit tight and wait."

"I can't believe it," Lynn said, already imagining them in their new home.

116

"They haven't accepted yet, darling," he warned. "Now, eat your dinner that I paid good money for. You'll be living on bread and water if they accept and Carrie's deal falls through."

Lynn cut into her fish and took a mouthful. "How was Joe with you? Did you get any sense of what he thought of the offer?"

"He reacted like an estate agent, darling. They never show their hand. So what's this research you're doing?"

"I was suggesting to Dad that he should consider stocking local produce. He said he was too busy to check it out and that if I thought it was such a good idea I should look into it."

Frank laughed. "You walked yourself into that one."

"I did!" She smiled. "But I'm going to have fun telling him 'I told you so'. You wouldn't believe the number of farms within a thirty-mile radius that could supply us with fresh eggs, vegetables, even cheese. And I haven't even started on jams, marmalades or pâtés."

"I'm not surprised they exist, but will their prices be competitive, and will the quality be up to the standard required and expected?"

She pulled a face. "That's why I need to call them and check."

"You are going to have to go and see them and examine the produce and the setup, to be sure," he said, watching her thoughtfully.

The chip in Lynn's mouth suddenly seemed too large to swallow and she reached for her glass. Could she go and visit these suppliers? Was she up to it?

"You'll be fine," Frank said.

She looked at him doubtfully. "You think?"

"Absolutely. It's just like the house-hunting: once you're interested you'll soon forget your nerves."

"But I'm not so sure about negotiating deals. I've never done anything quite like that before."

"You're getting ahead of yourself, Lynn. If you get that far with a supplier and your dad agrees, he'll take it from there. You really think it's possible to do it and make a profit?" Frank asked.

"I really do."

"Then trust your gut and prove to him that the idea's worthy of his consideration."

She nodded. He was right. And also she knew that the fact that the outcome might benefit her dad would help steady her nerves and keep her focused.

"You can do this Lynn," Frank said and squeezed her hand.

"Yes. I think I can."

CHAPTER
TWELVE

Orla was dozing on the sofa when the door banged. She sat up and felt the baby react to her sudden movement. She put a protective hand over her bump and then smiled with relief when her husband appeared in the doorway. "Vincent! I wasn't expecting you, you startled me."

"What the hell did you think you were doing?"

She took in his thunderous expression and stopped smiling. "What do you mean?"

"What were you doing talking to *her*?"

From the way he almost spat out the word she suddenly realized what he was talking about. It had been days since she'd bumped into Lynn Stephens. She'd thought she'd got away with it but she should have known better. Mags had obviously been talking. "You mean Lynn? We just ran into each other." She gave a nervous giggle. "Literally."

"You went back to her house," he said, his expression furious.

My God, how the hell did he know that? This bloody town — you couldn't scratch yourself but everyone knew about it. Orla picked up a cushion and hugged it to her. "Yes, I did. Sorry, but it was only because I almost fainted."

"Mags would have looked after you but no, you went with *her*. Are you trying to make me look like a complete idiot?"

"No, of course not —"

"Because of her I've lost my job and everyone knows it, and as soon as I'm out of the way you decide to become buddies?"

"No, darling, I wouldn't have gone but I was caught by surprise and then I felt dizzy and sick and I was afraid for the baby. I'm sorry, sweetheart," she said. "I'm sorry."

He flopped down onto the sofa beside her and put his arm around her. "Me too, love."

She nestled in against his chest with a sigh of relief. She hated it when Vincent lost his temper.

"What did you talk about?"

He was rubbing her back, but she could hear the tension in his voice. She kept her face pressed against him. "The baby."

"Just the baby?"

"Yes."

"How long did you stay with her?"

"Just until I felt well enough to walk. About half an hour."

"And she didn't say anything about me?"

"No. Oh, but . . ." Orla sat up and looked at him. "She did say she might be moving to Dublin."

"Did she, now?"

120

"Yes." Orla thought back on Lynn's exact words. "She said there were more jobs there and that Frank is up there most of the time anyway."

Vincent smiled and kissed the tip of her nose. "Now that *is* good news."

"Is it?" Orla yawned, wishing she'd had a longer nap. She seemed to be constantly tired these days. Her back ached and her ankles were like balloons. The sooner this baby came into the world the better.

"Of course it is. As soon as she's gone I'll be able to come back to Hawthorn Lodge."

"Oh, my God, I hadn't thought of that. Do you really think Charles would allow you to?" Orla was half afraid to get her hopes up, but having Vincent nearby as her due date approached would make her feel so much better. Yes, Aideen was very good and checked in on her every day, but Orla found her to be a very cold woman and, if anything, it emphasized how much she missed her own mum.

"I don't see why not. He only sent me to The Willows to give things time to settle down. If she's gone I don't see any reason for me to stay there. Apart from which Charles needs me here."

Orla smiled happily. "He's not the only one."

Vincent kissed her. "I know, darling. I'm sorry I shouted."

"It's okay, I understand. But honestly, Vincent, I would never have gone back with her, only I felt really dreadful."

He glanced at his watch. "I have to get back. Enjoy your nap. I'll try to get home a bit earlier tonight. Don't worry about dinner. I'll nick something from the kitchen."

Orla smiled, touched by his thoughtfulness. "Thanks, that would be great." When he was gone, she stretched out once more, relieved that he had left in better form than he'd arrived. Vincent didn't often lose his temper with her but, when he did, he frightened her. She was glad she didn't work for him.

Her thoughts immediately went to Lynn. What had made her confident, bubbly friend turn into the nervous, thin shadow that she'd met the other day? Was it all down to Vincent? Had his protestations that she was bad at her job and couldn't handle criticism been true or had he really bullied her? She didn't know any of the details surrounding Lynn's departure from Hawthorn Lodge. Any time she had tried to raise the subject with Vincent he said it was hard enough dealing with the fallout at work without being interrogated at home too. When she'd asked Aideen, her mother-in-law told her that it was a business matter and nothing for her to worry about. Orla knew that the town was humming with gossip but her friends said nothing in front of her and she couldn't ask. That would be disloyal. This whole business had really highlighted how isolated she had become. She was no longer Orla Cassidy, she was Orla Boland, and, from the moment Vincent had slid the ring on her finger, people had treated her differently.

Her eyelids started to droop and she pushed Lynn to the back of her mind and instead thought about how wonderful it would be to have her husband back

122

working in town, able to nip in and out and see her and the baby at any time. She drifted into sleep smiling.

Lynn tried to concentrate on the screen in front of her but had found herself constantly looking from the clock to the phone. She'd even picked it up a couple of times to check that it was working. How had they not heard about the house yet? Joe Stafford had told Frank he'd call as soon as he got word and he had both their mobile numbers. She thought about phoning him and instead decided to text Frank first. She never rang in case he was in the middle of a meeting or an interview.

"Any news?" she typed, and waited. There was no reply. He must be tied up. Feeling frustrated, she closed down her laptop and decided to have a hot bath and read her book. She needed some distraction.

She was immersed in bubbles and the story when she heard the front door close. "Frank?" she called out, surprised. He wasn't due home until this evening. She sat up and was reaching for a towel when the door opened.

"That was good timing," he said, eyeing her up appraisingly.

"What are you doing here?" She dropped the towel and settled back in the water. He sat down on the edge of the bath and cleared the bubbles from around one nipple with his fingers. "Mmm, that feels very nice."

He moved his attention to her other breast. "You look good enough to eat."

She smiled. "Is that why you came home, Mr Hayes? Are you feeling randy?"

He leaned over and kissed the breast nearest to him, making her shiver. "Always, but there was another reason."

She looked at him expectantly. "Tell me."

His fingers slid down over her stomach and disappeared under the bubbles, making her moan.

"We just bought a house," he said, his voice ragged as his fingers continued to explore.

Lynn shot up in the bath with a squeal. "Really? Are you serious?"

"I'm serious." He stood up and pulled her to her feet and then took a step back so he could look at her.

Lynn licked her lips as his eyes travelled down her wet body and then finally came back to meet hers. "Let's celebrate," he said and lifted her out of the bath.

"Let's," she murmured, wrapping her wet arms around his neck and turning her mouth up to his.

They made love fast and furiously, and afterwards Lynn lay staring into his eyes, her breath still uneven. "That was wonderful."

"It was," he agreed, smiling.

She propped up the pillows and pulled the duvet up around them both. "So tell me what happened."

"There's not much to tell. Joe just phoned and said that our offer had been accepted and I gave him our solicitor's number. Then I called Matt to tell him to expect the call and he said that he was about to phone me to let me know that the deposit has been paid on Carrie's house."

"No, really?" She gaped at him.

124

He smiled. "Really."

"I can't believe this is all going so smoothly."

"No reason why it shouldn't: it's a straightforward deal. We should be able to move in within the month."

"We have so much to do before then, Frank. We have to buy furniture."

"We don't need much."

"I suppose you're right." Lynn smiled, remembering the beautiful fitted kitchen.

"All we have to move are our belongings and we should be able to do that with a few trips in the car. Or perhaps your dad would loan me the van."

"Of course he will."

"Happy?"

She met Frank's eyes and smiled. "Deliriously."

"Then I am too." He glanced down at his watch. "I suppose I should do some work."

"Are you going out?"

"No, I have an article to write."

"Then you get started and I'll make us a sandwich." She leaned over to kiss him. "I seem to have worked up an appetite."

"You certainly did. You know, when we move I'll be able to drop in and out any time."

"So you will." She grinned. "And on sunny days we can check out the privacy of our balcony."

"The neighbours may not be able to see you but, based on this morning's performance, they'll definitely be able to hear you!"

She raised her eyebrows. "Is that a complaint?"

"Not at all." He kissed her neck. "Perhaps that article can wait."

"What about the sandwich?" she said, groaning as his mouth moved lower.

"It can wait."

She closed her eyes and surrendered herself to the glorious feeling of his mouth and hands on her body. "It can."

They ended up spending the rest of the day in bed, Lynn curling up with her book as he worked on his laptop. As she listened to him tapping away, his bare arm brushing against hers, Lynn thought that she had never felt so content. The thought of moving into their wonderful new home and becoming this man's wife filled her with happiness. She twisted her head around and kissed his arm.

"What was that for?" he asked still tapping.

"I'm just happy."

He stroked her thigh. "Good. Let's keep it that way."

As twilight descended and the room darkened, they drank wine and watched a black-and-white movie. Then they put on some music and talked about the things they would do and the places they would go of an evening when they were living in Dublin. They made love again, gently and quietly, and, as Lynn started to fall asleep, she felt his arms tighten around her. "I love you, Lynn."

She pressed her lips to his chest. "I love you too."

★   ★   ★

126

She was in a garden, it was summer, the scent of roses hung in the air and she could feel the heat of the sun on the top of her head. Frank and her father were kneeling on the ground concentrating hard. She went over to see what they were doing. They were making daisy chains and when she asked why her dad looked at her in surprise and said, "To sell in the shop of course!"

The dream came back to her the next morning. She couldn't remember the last time she'd had a happy one. She turned to tell Frank about it but he wasn't beside her. She glanced at the alarm clock. It was nine o'clock. She rubbed her eyes unable to believe it. She had been asleep for almost ten hours. Rolling over, she stretched, luxuriating in the memory of the previous day. Paper crinkled beneath her. She pulled out the note and laughed.

Hey, Sleeping Beauty, the wedding's off — you snore!! I didn't want to disturb you. In RTÉ most of the day so the phone will be off. I'll call you when I get a chance. Have a good day, x

"I will," she murmured, "and I do not snore!" She stretched again and reached for the phone and sent a text to her friend. She was dying to tell Val her news and to hear how her friend's evening with John's family had gone. She was up, dressed and halfway through a bowl of Rice Krispies before Val replied.

LOTS TO TELL YOU!! I HAVE A BREAK AT FOUR, WILL YOU PICK ME UP?

Lynn sent back a message saying she would collect her in the usual place, finished her breakfast, made a pot of tea and then settled down with her notepad and the house phone.

CHAPTER
THIRTEEN

When she pulled up at the church to collect Val, her friend was waiting, a broad smile on her face. Lynn laughed. "No need to ask how you got on," she said as Val climbed in beside her. She glanced over when Val didn't answer to find her friend staring at her, wide-eyed. "What?" she said, self-consciously.

"You're gorgeous!"

"Oh, don't be silly." Lynn shrugged off the compliment although she had put a lot of thought into what to wear today.

Her heart had been thumping in her chest when she'd called six local businesses and she'd been stunned when three of them suggested she should come over and see the operation for herself. She had wavered over what to wear. She wanted to look businesslike but at the same time she had to be practical. She finally decided on black jeans, a white shirt and a tailored jacket. She wound a silk scarf around her throat to add a dash of colour. She put on pumps but put her wellies in the boot just in case. She took time over her make-up and carefully gathered her hair into a long plait to hang over one shoulder. She had been pleased with the effect and Val's reaction was reassuring. "I was checking out some suppliers for Dad, so I thought I'd better make an effort."

Val looked at her in surprise as she grappled with the seat-belt. "You went to see them? On your own?"

Lynn couldn't suppress a grin. She was proud of herself and amazed at how much she'd enjoyed the day. "Yes, on my own."

"Good for you!"

"Tell me, how did you get on with John's family?"

"It was fine. They were quiet but all very nice, and they seemed to like me."

Lynn listened to her talk as she drove them to Brannigans, where they ordered coffee and biscuits. "This is serious, isn't it?" she said studying her friend.

Val took a sip of coffee and then met Lynn's eyes. "Yes, it is. He seems to really care about me and wants to be with me all of the time."

"I'm glad you're happy."

"Sorry, I've been droning on and on. Any word on the house?"

"Yes, we made an offer and it's been accepted."

"Oh, my God, that's wonderful news! I'm so happy for you. But what about Carrie's house?"

"She's sold it too."

"Wow, you have been lucky. So much for the housing market being at a standstill."

"I know. I can't wait for you to see it, Val, it's so gorgeous."

"It sounds it. So when do you expect to move in?"

"In a matter of weeks. Frank's trying to sublet our place but we can just about afford to move whether he's successful or not."

"I'm so happy for you. It's about time you had some good luck and I think you're going to blossom once you're away from Rathbourne."

"I've put together a CV, too," Lynn confided.

Val leaned over and gave her an impulsive hug. "I'm so proud of you."

"Don't get too excited. I haven't sent it to anyone yet," Lynn said, laughing.

"You will. Your dad must be thrilled that you're getting so involved with the shop."

"I'm not really. I suggested that he source some local produce but he said it would be much too expensive. I think the only reason I followed it up was to prove him wrong."

"Still, it's great that you did. I think it's really important that you get out more and see people."

"Oh! Speaking of seeing people, I forgot to tell you. I ran into Orla."

Val's eyes were round. "Really? Where?"

Lynn groaned. "It was just outside Mags's shop. The woman nearly turned herself inside out to get a look at us. It was a bit awkward at first but then Orla had a weak spell and I took her home with me for a rest."

"And she agreed?" Val marvelled.

"I didn't give her much choice," Lynn told her. "She was deathly pale, she gave me quite a scare. But she was fine after a few minutes. She says it's blood pressure."

"So what did you talk about?"

"Not Vincent or the case," Lynn assured her. "We talked about the baby, mainly. I feel sorry for her, Val. She seems lonely. I get the feeling that Aideen Boland has her completely under the thumb

"Do you think Orla knows?"

Lynn met her eyes. "Knows what?"

"What he put you through."

"No, and I'm glad. What good would it do? He's her husband and she seems happy with him. I would hate if that changed because of me. I wish her nothing but the best."

"And Vincent?" Val probed.

"As long as he stays away from me I don't care about him. I just hope he turns out to be a better husband and father than he is a boss. I can't help wondering . . ."

"What?" Valerie eyed her curiously.

"Do you think it was just me or do you think he's harassed other women?"

"Why do you insist on dwelling in the past?" Val berated her. "You're moving house, helping your dad, looking for a job. They're the things you should be focusing on now."

"I am, really I am, it was just seeing Orla got me thinking about it again. Anyway, I can't exactly forget what happened when I'm going to a counsellor whose sole aim is to get me to talk about it."

"Perhaps Frank's right. Maybe you'd be better off giving that up."

"Not yet," Lynn said quickly.

"You know you can talk to me about anything, Lynn, and I'd never tell anyone."

"I know that." Lynn felt bad when she saw the almost reproachful look in Val's eyes. "I don't really talk about it," she tried to explain. "He sort of drags things out of me in bits and pieces. I can't say that I enjoy it but I think it's helping."

"You certainly seem in better form and I think you've put on a little weight."

"A little," Lynn agreed, nodding happily. "I think it's because he put me on a lower dosage of antidepressants."

"You'll be back to yourself in no time. So," — Val's smile grew coy — "you and Frank buying a home together. Any other developments I should know about?"

"Just one," Lynn said casually. "Frank asked me to marry him."

Val let out a screech of delight and jammed a hand over her mouth as other customers turned to see what the fuss was about. "That's fantastic news, Lynn. Oh, I'm so happy for you!"

"Hang on, I didn't say that I'd said yes."

Val raised an eyebrow. "I know you're getting counselling but you're not completely bonkers. Of course you said yes."

Lynn beamed. "Of course I did."

"So when's the big day?"

"We've made no plans at all. We haven't even bought a ring yet. I don't want to announce it until we've moved."

"Oh, this is so exciting." Val's eyes twinkled. "I wonder which of us will make it to the altar first."

Lynn stared at her, stunned. "Are you saying what I think you're saying?"

"No, but we've decided to move in together. And I know what you're thinking; I can see it in your eyes: She's doing it again, rushing into things."

"I never said that," Lynn protested lamely.

"You didn't rush to congratulate me, either," Val retorted.

"Congratulations!" Lynn leaned over to hug her. "Sorry. I just don't want you to get hurt."

"John would never hurt me." Val was emphatic. "Really, Lynn, he's a great guy."

"I believe you, but do you have to move so fast? He's only downstairs. Isn't that close enough for now?" Lynn couldn't believe her ears. Val had always been impulsive but this took the biscuit. And what was John playing at? Weren't teachers supposed to be sensible?

"It just feels right," Val said with a dreamy smile.

"Then I suppose that's all that matters," Lynn said, knowing there was no point in arguing. "I can't wait to meet him. How about Friday night?"

"You just want to check him out," her friend accused.

"Of course I do." Lynn laughed. "I'm dying to meet the man who's swept you off your feet. And, remember, I had already invited you. We just hadn't agreed a date."

"That's true." Val gave her a shy smile. "Okay, then, I'll ask John how he's fixed and let you know."

"Great!" Lynn smiled brightly. "I can't wait!"

134

"You are kidding me." Frank stared at her in dismay. "You've given up our Friday night to entertain Val and her latest love, who'll probably be gone by the following Friday?"

Lynn splashed soy sauce into the wok and stirred vigorously. "Sorry, but I'm worried about her. She really seems to have it bad. He only lives in the flat below her and she says they're planning on moving in together."

"Ah, well, that will be it, then. He's probably broke and wants to save money on renting."

"Cynic." Lynn added peppers and onion to the pan and hoped Frank was wrong.

"I bet I'm right."

Lynn sighed. "I was hoping the fact that they just met by accident and not in some club full of desperate, drunken people was a good sign — but I am beginning to wonder. Why rush into things? She can't know that much about him."

"At least he took her to meet his relations." Frank looked up. "Is he Irish?"

She turned, frowning. "I assume so. She didn't say otherwise. Why?"

"I just wondered was it someone desperate to stay in the country. What did she say about the family? Where did she meet them?"

"In his parents' home in Drogheda. She said they were very nice."

"I suppose it's a good sign that he took her to the family home," Frank allowed. "What do they make of all of this?"

"I don't think they know yet." Lynn took out two plates as Frank checked to see if the rice was ready.

"Her mother will not be impressed," he smirked, sitting down at the table.

"I know." Angie had less patience with her daughter's love life than Lynn did. "Val always seems to rush into things without thinking them through. I do hope we're wrong. I hope he really is nice and that it works out for her."

He smiled. "We'll find out on Friday. It's not going to be a late night, is it? I want us to head up to Dublin first thing."

"Oh, why?"

"I'll have the keys to the house and we can measure up and then go shopping for furniture and" — he slid an arm around her waist as she placed his dinner in front of him — "a ring."

She lowered herself into his lap, put her arms around his neck and smiled at him. "Really?"

He kissed her. "Oh, yes."

"We're not spending big money. We need every penny —"

He silenced her with another kiss. "I want to get you a nice ring, something you'll love."

"You're putting it on my finger. I'll love it no matter what it costs."

"In that case, grab the Argos catalogue."

"No chance!" She laughed and stood up to fetch her own plate. "Has Carrie found a new place yet?" That's how happy Lynn was feeling, that she was able to make such an enquiry. Though Frank didn't mention it,

136

knowing it irritated her, she knew Carrie still called him on the smallest of pretexts. He glanced up at her and she could see him trying to gauge her mood. "It's okay, I'm not going to bite your head off."

He grinned. "She has a shortlist of apartments she wants to view."

"In Glasnevin?" Lynn asked, hoping.

"I'm not sure."

"So, now that Philip is over eighteen and once the house is sold, does that mean that you have no further obligations to her?"

He took a drink, watching her steadily. "It does."

She sighed. "Good."

"Why does it matter?"

"I'm not sure," she admitted. "I suppose I just get jealous."

"You have nothing to be jealous about, you know that."

"I know," Lynn said but she would still feel better when there were fewer ties between Frank and his ex. She was still convinced that Carrie wasn't ready to let him go. Despite her now long list of men, she always seemed to come back to Frank for advice. Lynn stood up to wash her plate and smiled when he came to stand behind her and pulled her back against him. "You have no reason to be jealous," he repeated, lifting her hair and kissing the nape of her neck.

Lynn closed her eyes and moaned softly as he pressed himself against her. She turned in his arms and turned her mouth up to his. When they pulled apart she saw surprise and excitement in his eyes at the intensity and hunger of her kiss.

"I want you," he said.

"I want you too," she said and led him towards the stairs.

CHAPTER
FOURTEEN

"Mum?" Lynn called from the kitchen doorway but there was no answer. She went back outside and crossed over to the office but that too was deserted. She hated going into the shop itself but she could hardly stand around here all day, so, taking a deep breath, she went through the storeroom and opened the door into the supermarket. All she had to do was let her dad know that she was here and duck out again, nothing to it. She hovered in the doorway and then walked swiftly down the cleaning-products aisle towards the checkout. There was no sign of her father, only Norman looking flustered as he tried to process a credit-card transaction while four impatient customers waited. She was about to turn on her heel when Niall Dorgan, an old friend of her dad's, spotted her. "Hey, Lynn, I'm parked on a double-yellow. Can you take this?" He thrust a litre of milk at her.

She stared at him, speechless. Norman looked up in relief. "Would you, Lynn? I can't get this bloody machine to work."

Before she had a chance to reply the queue had moved over to the other checkout and she had no option but to go behind the counter and key in her code. She scanned Mr Dorgan's carton and accepted the money with a shaking hand. He smiled broadly at her.

"Thanks, love. Good to see you again."

"And you."

Next was Mrs Lawlor with a full trolley. She eyed Lynn with relish; all she was short of doing was rubbing her hands together.

"Hello, love," she said, her voice full of false sympathy. "How are you?"

"Fine, thanks." Lynn quickly scanned the items, bagging them as she went. "Where's Dad and Cathy?" she called over to Norman.

"Your dad's at the bank and Cathy's out sick."

"You must be relieved that all that business with Hawthorn Lodge is sorted, love," said Mrs Lawlor.

Well aware that the other customers had fallen silent and were waiting for her answer, Lynn kept her head bent over, a tight smile on her face, her mind blank.

"Lynn, there you are!" Her father materialized at her side, smiling. "Your mother's looking everywhere for you. Go on, I'll look after Mrs Lawlor."

"Thanks, Dad," she muttered and, squeezing past him, she hurried down the shop and fled across the yard to the safety of the house.

Her mother, at the cooker frying bacon, looked up in surprise. "Hello, love, this is a surprise."

Lynn couldn't even answer. She just stood leaning against the door trying to breathe.

Nell was immediately at her side, an arm around her. "Take it easy, love, it's okay."

140

As Lynn tried to get her breathing under control she remembered a similar scene almost a year ago. It was shortly after she had taken the case and the Bolands' solicitor had demanded that she visit a psychiatrist appointed by them. The man had been gentle and kind but had asked her questions that had made her feel sick, humiliated and vaguely dirty. Frank was in London and her father had driven her, and when he saw the state she was in afterwards he had refused point-blank to drop her home to an empty house. Once she'd walked in the kitchen door and met her mother's eyes, Lynn had slumped into a chair and dissolved into tears. Her parents had held her between them, comforting her and rocking her as if she were a baby, and then, when she was spent, they had taken her upstairs and tucked her into her old bed.

"Feeling better?" Nell asked now, her eyes searching Lynn's face.

She nodded. "Yes. Sorry."

Nell led her to a chair and went to put on the kettle. "What brought this on?"

"I went into the shop and Norman roped me into helping out and Mrs Lawlor cornered me about the case. I was just struck dumb."

"Evie Lawlor has that effect on everyone," her mother said drily. "You were caught unawares, love. Don't worry about it. It'll get easier."

"Will it?" Lynn said, her voice hoarse. She had come out this morning feeling optimistic and confident and a simple question had been enough to reduce her to a quivering wreck.

Her mother patted her hand. "Forget about it."

"Yes, sorry." Lynn took a grateful sip from the mug of tea her mother had put in front of her and smiled. "By the way, we got the house."

"Go away!" Her mother stared at her. "Are you serious?"

"I know. I can't believe it either."

"That's wonderful news. Your father's going mad because I keep saying how different it is, but I won't tell him why. Are you sure you can afford it, love? You're not putting yourself under pressure buying it, I hope."

"No," Lynn promised. "The sale's going through on Carrie's house at the moment, so we're fine. We put in a very low offer but they were desperate to move quickly, so they accepted."

Nell beamed at her. "I'm thrilled for you. Does this mean I can start shopping for a hat?"

Lynn, relieved that she hadn't said cot, laughed. "You can look but there's no rush. Moving is the priority, and then I'll be job-hunting." Lynn's stomach churned at the thought. If she couldn't cope with an old-age pensioner, how was she going to handle the stress of a job in the tourism industry, where dealing with people was ninety per cent of the job?

"Are you sure you're ready to go back to work?" Nell said, looking worried.

"No," Lynn admitted. She tried to hide her anxieties from her parents as much as possible but today she wasn't up to putting on an act. "I suppose it'll be easier if it's somewhere where no one knows me or anything about me."

"What will?"

She looked up and smiled as her father walked into the kitchen. "Going back to work. Sorry about Mrs Lawlor."

"Nothing to be sorry for," he said and went to the sink to scrub his hands.

"I was just telling mum that we got the house we wanted."

"That's great news. I'm delighted for you both."

"Thanks, Dad."

"When do you move?" He sat down at the table as Nell bustled around preparing his lunch.

"In a couple of weeks I think."

He looked at her in surprise. "That's very fast."

"I know. Can we borrow the van to move our things up?"

"Of course. If you do it on a Sunday or Monday I can leave Norman in charge for a few hours and help."

"That would be great. I can't wait for you to see it."

"Neither can I. Your mother's turned it into this huge mystery."

"You're bound to be disappointed, then." Lynn shared a conspiratorial grin with her mother. She couldn't imagine anyone not loving her new home.

Her spirits started to lift again. It would be hard to feel down looking out on the view or walking the beach whenever she wanted. But being able to spend more time with Frank was the best part. She had found his increasingly frequent late nights in Dublin hard to

143

handle. It crossed her mind that she and Orla had a lot in common at the moment.

"I suppose you won't have time to investigate this local-produce idea," he said with a sly grin.

Lynn bent to pick up the binder she had brought with her and slid it across the table. "Already done, Father dear."

He leafed through it, his eyes widening in surprise. "Did you get all of that off the computer?"

"I got some of it on the Internet and then I phoned around a few places. It's all in there, plus the contact details of the people I met with yesterday."

He sat back, a slight smile playing around his lips. "You *have* been busy. And what did you think?"

"I was quite impressed. I had no idea that there was so much going on in Meath. Sadly, most of them rely on the export market to survive."

"That is sad," Nell said from her position at the sink. "We should be supporting our own in these difficult times."

"They're not competitive enough for the Irish market." Jack said irritably.

"They're better than they were," Lynn told him, deliberately keeping her voice low and even. If she pushed it he would push back. That was just the way it was, had always been. "Times are hard, and I found the three that I met were very flexible and ready to make deals."

Jack grunted. "What products did you check out?"

"Fruit and vegetables — the basics: cabbage, potatoes, onions, tomatoes."

"I've never understood why we import tomatoes. Anyone can grow tomatoes," Nell said, going to the oven to take out an apple tart.

"Take a look through the binder when you get a chance, Dad. It's quite interesting." Lynn stood up.

"You're off already?" He looked surprised.

"Yeah, I have to get started on the packing."

"Stay and have some apple tart," her mother protested.

It looked gorgeous and she was tempted, but Lynn knew that if she wanted her dad to take notice it was better to leave now rather than keep talking. "No, I'll get on. See you."

Nell walked with her to the car. "Are you okay to drive, Lynn?"

"I'm fine now, Mum, don't worry." She hugged her. "I'll call you later in the week."

As Lynn pulled up at the lights, she spotted Mrs Lawlor talking to two other women. The woman saw her and immediately bent her head close to the other two before the three of them turned to stare. Lynn gripped the steering wheel tighter and, keeping her eyes on the road ahead, pulled away at speed. As she drove home she could hear Frank's voice in her head: "Fuck them. They're just gossips and not worth worrying about."

But that was easy for him to say. He wasn't the subject of the gossip. If people turned to look at him it was because they recognized him as a successful and familiar public figure. If they looked at her they were thinking, There's the one who took that action against the Bolands, the one who had the breakdown. Their looks were pitying, curious or suspicious.

"Snap out of it," she said aloud, angry with herself for letting it get to her. What did she care what they thought of her? What did it matter? The fact was that Vincent Boland had made her life miserable and now he was paying for it.

She could still see his expression when she'd put her letter of resignation on the desk in front of him. He had been surprised but he had quickly recovered his composure, sitting back in his chair with his feet on his desk.

"You won't get far without a reference," he said with a smug smile.

"I don't care." She stood her ground, her hands clenched so tight there were marks in her palms for days.

"You're being ridiculous, childish."

"Call me what you want, it doesn't matter any more."

"What's your beloved Frank going to say?" he taunted.

"He'll say well done for standing up to you."

Vincent's expression had darkened at that. "What have you told him?"

"That's none of your concern. You're not my boss any more. I don't owe you any explanations."

"You owe me everything," he said, his face puce. "My uncle would never have promoted you if I hadn't put in a good word for you."

146

For the first time she met Vincent's eyes. "I was promoted because I'm good at what I do."

He laughed. "You're kidding yourself and you're making a big mistake."

She'd looked back down at her shoes and shrugged. "I'll take that chance."

And she had. And it had finally paid off. She was free, leaving Rathbourne, moving into a fabulous new home and marrying the love of her life. She had won! Smiling, Lynn turned up the music, lowered the window and let the cool spring air invade the car and whip her hair into a frenzy. Frank was right, this was her chance to make a fresh start and she would, from this moment on, put Vincent and Hawthorn Lodge firmly behind her.

CHAPTER
FIFTEEN

Jack Stephens took off his glasses and massaged his temples. Stocktaking was always the least favourite part of his job, but this evening Norman was being particularly obtuse and irritating and also whingeing at having to stay back when he should have been at home with his cocoa watching the Chelsea match. Jack opened his eyes and they settled on the binder Lynn had left. He hadn't had a chance to go through it and he wasn't sure there was any point. Still, it might give her a lift if he went along with one of her recommendations, and that would be worth it. Watching her change from his bubbly, outgoing little girl into the frightened, trembling figure he'd walked in on in the shop today was heartbreaking. Sometimes he had to fight the urge to go round to Hawthorn Lodge and break Vincent Boland's neck. What the hell had he said or done to cause Lynn to fall apart the way she had?

Jack reached for his cigarettes and went outside for a smoke. Damn the laws that meant he had to stand shivering outside his own premises to enjoy a cigarette! The world had gone mad. He glanced over at the house; he wasn't allowed to smoke there, either. Nell said it turned the walls yellow and made the curtains smell. He didn't notice it but he took her word for it and didn't argue. He never smoked in anyone else's house, so why should he treat his wife with any less respect? He saw her silhouette at the kitchen window. She seemed to be ironing; the woman never stopped. Nell was a good wife and mother and had been worrying herself sick about Lynn. She had relaxed more lately as their daughter was obviously stronger, but the panic attack in the shop today had taken them both by surprise. He was almost glad that she was leaving town, although he would miss her popping in and out. Nell was doing a great job of hiding her feelings from Lynn, but he knew that she was dreading their daughter's move and he'd heard her crying softly many a night.

"Boss, I think we're out of beans."

Jack took a last drag and ground the butt with the heel of his shoe. "Why? Are they not on the list?" he asked going back inside. Lynn had set up a simple system of tracking stock. All Norman had to do was cross items off the list taped to the warehouse door whenever he was moving stuff into the shop and, when they got down to the last pallet, they would order more. It couldn't be easier, but Norman couldn't seem to get his head around it. Either he forgot to update the list, and so they ran out of the product, or he ordered more of something without checking. Finally, Jack had banned him from ordering anything. It was easier to do the job himself and leave Norman to serve and keep the shop neat and clean.

"Do you have the list?" he asked, looking at the bare door.

"I thought you had it." Norman stood, a blank look on his face.

"I'll check the office," Jack said and, right enough, there was the list on his desk; he was losing his marbles. He took it back into the warehouse. "I've found it. Right, let's get back to work and with a bit of luck we'll be out in an hour."

Norman gave a snort of disbelief.

Jack laughed. "Okay, that's unlikely, but I'll try and get you out of here in time to watch the second half. Fair enough?"

"Grand." Norman smiled happily.

Once they were done, Jack let Norman out of the front door and locked it before going back to the office. Sitting down, he pulled Lynn's binder towards him and opened it. It was laid out in her usual professional manner, sectioned into products, then suppliers, a covering note on each with her own impressions and thoughts. She would be a great asset to any business, he thought sadly. It was such a pity that she had no interest in this one. He started to read her notes on the local egg producers and was surprised at some of the figures she'd jotted down and the farmers' client lists: there were some big names there. Perhaps he had been too hasty in dismissing her idea, he thought, turning the page.

Vincent was engrossed in football when the phone rang. He ignored it. It had to be for Orla. None of his family or friends would call in the middle of a game. Orla lumbered in from the kitchen and handed him the phone. "It's for you."

"Yes?" he barked into it irritably and reached for the remote control to turn down the commentary.

"Hi, Vincent, it's Gareth."

"Gareth, what's up? Don't you know there's a bloody match on?" Vincent laughed. The estate agent was a mad Chelsea fan and never missed a game.

"I have it on here but I had a bit of information I thought you'd be interested in."

"Oh, yeah?"

"Frank Hayes is subletting his house."

"Is he, now? That is interesting." Vincent now muted the sound on the TV completely.

"It gets better. He says it'll be available by the end of the month."

"That's only a couple of weeks away."

"I know. He's bought a place up in Dublin."

"Is she going with him?" There was no need to mention Lynn by name: Gareth knew whom he meant.

"She's going," Gareth assured him, "no doubt about it."

Yes! Vincent let out a sigh of relief. "Thanks, Gareth. I appreciate the call."

"No problem, mate. Goodnight."

Vincent put down the phone and stared blindly at the silent football match. He thought of phoning Charles but his uncle didn't like being disturbed in the evenings and would probably let the call go to the answering service. He decided to pay him a visit instead. Vincent ran upstairs to tidy himself up and put on a decent jacket and then came down to tell Orla where he was going.

She looked up from her book in surprise. "Now? Isn't there a match on?"

"Yeah, but I need to talk to Charles and you know how he hates late callers."

"Is everything okay, darling?" she asked, looking up at him with worried eyes.

He bent to kiss her. "Everything's fine, Orla. I shouldn't be long."

She yawned. "I was going to bed anyway. I can't seem to find a chair that's comfortable these days."

He patted her bump. "Not long to go now. Will I bring you up a hot chocolate when I get back?"

She beamed at him. "Thanks, darling, that would be lovely; you are thoughtful."

When Vincent buzzed the gate it was a while before he got an answer, and then he heard Charles's voice, curt and gruff. "Yes?"

"Charles, it's Vincent."

"Yes?"

Vincent sat stunned. Did he plan to keep him standing there? The old bastard was getting more contrary as the years passed. "Sorry to drop by so late but there's something I need to discuss with you." He was careful to keep his voice even and deferential. There was no response, but the gates started to open. Vincent drove up the gravelled driveway towards the imposing residence. He quite liked the idea of inheriting this house along with the business, but with four cousins he knew that was a pipe dream. He would have to be content with the power, and he'd build his own mansion, even more palatial.

He parked next to his uncle's large Mercedes, the sight of it making him glower. Another thing that irked him was the strict limit Charles put on his car allowance and the fact that he was allowed to replace it only every three years, while Charles drove a top-of-the-range car and changed it every two. That would be different when he was in control, Vincent vowed. But for now he would have to continue with the penitent act until he had his feet well and truly back under the table.

The polished mahogany door was open but Charles was nowhere in sight. He didn't even bother waiting to greet him now. Vincent felt another flash of irritation at the blatant rudeness of the man; he seemed to enjoy humiliating him at every opportunity, and it was all thanks to Lynn bloody Stephens. He walked down the hall in the direction of his uncle's study. As he'd expected, Charles was sitting behind his desk waiting for him, his hands linked across his stomach. There was a time when he would have brought him into the library and poured them two large brandies, but Vincent wasn't even offered a glass of water these days.

"Well?" Charles said.

Vincent bristled at his dismissive tone. He gave a tight smile. "I got some news that I thought you would like to hear first-hand. Lynn Stephens is leaving Rathbourne."

Charles didn't move, but there was a flicker of interest in his eyes. "And you know this how?"

"Gareth Mooney, the estate agent, called me. Her partner Frank Hayes is subletting their house from the end of the month."

There was a long silence while Charles absorbed the information, and, used to his ways, Vincent said nothing.

"Do we know if it's a temporary move or a permanent one?" he asked finally.

"It seems they've bought a house in Dublin, so it doesn't look like they're planning to come back in the near future," Vincent replied, his tone neutral.

Charles pondered this for a moment. "We know Hayes is putting the house up for rent and a house has been purchased, but do we know if it's a joint investment? Just because her partner is leaving Rathbourne doesn't necessarily mean she's going with him."

"I don't know, but Gareth seemed confident she was going, and Orla bumped into her recently and she mentioned that she and Hayes were thinking of moving to Dublin."

Charles frowned. "Orla's in touch with her?"

"No, not at all," Vincent said quickly. "They merely bumped into each other in the street and exchanged pleasantries."

"Of course Jack and Nell aren't going anywhere," Charles mused. "She will be back regularly to visit."

Vincent was prepared for this. He had put himself in Charles's position and thought about what attitude he would expect from a worthy successor. "I see that as a bonus," he said and saw the surprise in Charles's eyes.

154

"It's been a difficult time and I can't pretend I've enjoyed being held up as some sort of monster, but it's over now and I wish her well. If she's coming and going and it's clear that she's happy, I think we will all be able to move on."

"That makes sense," Charles admitted. The words were reserved but, for the first time in a long time, Vincent saw respect in the old man's eyes. He felt like punching the air, but instead he sat silent, his face grave. "On a completely different subject, Charles, I've got some ideas on how best to move forward with The Willows. I won't go into them now. I've eaten into your evening enough. I expect to have a report for you in the next couple of days."

"I'll look forward to reading it. I hadn't expected anything quite so soon."

Vincent glowed at the praise in his voice, but he didn't show it. "I'll be perfectly honest with you, Charles, I wasn't happy to leave Hawthorn Lodge but I've become quite excited at the thought of turning things around in The Willows. Having said that, I think I could continue to do that from Rathbourne and, given that Orla's so close to her time and Lynn Stephens will be out of the picture —"

"You want to come back." Charles's voice was blunt and Vincent could hear a trace of suspicion in it.

He sighed heavily and then looked up into his uncle's eyes. "She needs me, Charles. She is scared and lonely and I feel I've let her and my son down."

Charles's eyes widened. "It's a boy?"

Bingo! Vincent decided he deserved a fucking Oscar. He put a hand to his head. "Damn, that was supposed to be a secret; Orla didn't want anyone to know."

"I can assure you it will go no further."

He gave a brief smile. "Thank you, I appreciate that."

There was another pause and Vincent waited patiently, feeling like a puppeteer. He hadn't realized before how easy it was to control his uncle. The thought of the power that gave him was heady. This old man would never be able to dismiss him again.

At last Charles spoke, stroking his chin as he did so, his eyes thoughtful, the coldness gone.

"Let me know when you have that report and we'll discuss it over lunch in Hawthorn Lodge. If you have come up with a plan to make The Willows profitable I don't see any reason why you shouldn't return to your old job. It would suit me, as it happens: I need to go away for a short while."

Vincent's ears pricked up and he watched his uncle closely. "Oh?"

"The damn GP wants me to go in for some tests. Bloody waste of time," Charles said dismissively, obviously uncomfortable talking about such a personal matter.

"Charles, what is it? Is there something wrong?"

His uncle gave a disgusted wave of his hand. "He's overreacting. I've been having some stomach trouble and he ran some blood tests and he wasn't happy with the results, so he's insisting I go into hospital for further tests."

156

Vincent struggled hard to suppress a grin. He was sick? Could it get any better? Now he looked at him he realized that Charles had lost weight and looked quite washed out. "I'm sure there's nothing to worry about, but it's best to get it checked out. I'll be glad to hold the fort."

"Emer will be working full-time while I'm gone," Charles told him, "but I would feel happier having you back in Hawthorn Lodge."

Vincent managed to hide his dismay at the news that Charles's youngest daughter would be a permanent fixture at the hotel. An accountant, Emer worked mostly from home, only occasionally dropping into the hotel. She was sharp as a tack, Charles's golden-haired girl and his closest confidante. Vincent knew that she didn't trust him. She'd been delighted when he was banished to The Willows. He needed to work hard to change her opinion or she could be dangerous. "It's good to know that Emer will be on site," he said smoothly.

"Well, she'll be keeping an eye on all the businesses, so she will need back-up."

"I'll do everything I can to help her keep things ticking over in your absence," he promised, and was pleased to see Charles visibly relax; he was home and dry. "If there's nothing more, I should get home to Orla." He got to his feet, smiling. "I've promised her supper in bed."

Charles stood too and nodded his approval. "You have your priorities right, son. Look after your family. It wasn't fair of me to send you away at a time like this —"

Vincent held up a hand to silence him. "In your position I'd have done the same thing. Goodnight, Charles, and thank you."

Vincent drove away positively euphoric. He felt like getting drunk and he was horny as hell, but he headed straight home. He had managed to get himself out of the tightest corner he'd been in yet and he wasn't going to do anything to blot his copy book. For the next few months he would be an attentive husband, a doting father and the ideal boss.

At home, Vincent went straight to the kitchen and made creamy hot chocolate and took it upstairs. Orla was reading the baby book. She was always reading that damn thing. Her face lit up when she saw him and she put the book down and struggled to sit up. "Hello, sweetheart," he said and set down the treat on the bedside table. "Here, let me help you."

"Thanks, darling. Oh, you are good to me!"

"It's easy being good to you." He sat up on the bed beside her and stroked her leg as she sipped the hot drink.

"How was your meeting?" she asked.

He sank back into the pillow beside her and closed his eyes. "Damn good. I hope you know that you're married to a genius. I have convinced my beloved uncle that the prodigal son should return."

She set down her mug and turned to him, her eyes wide. "Really?"

158

"I have to jump through a few hoops, but I think that it's a safe bet that I'll be back behind my desk in Hawthorn Lodge before the month is out."

She set down her mug and threw her arms around him. "Vincent, that's wonderful! I'm so happy."

He kissed her on the mouth and massaged one full breast. God, pregnancy had made her so voluptuous and sexy. "Are you, darling?"

"Oh, yes."

"Are you grateful, Orla?" He kissed her again.

She drew back, looked at him and then smiled. "I'm very grateful, sweetheart."

He settled back on the bed, loosened his belt and closed his eyes. "Show me, darling."

CHAPTER
SIXTEEN

Seated in the comfortable armchair in Julian Kelly's office waiting for him, Lynn marvelled at how much her attitude had changed towards him and their sessions. The first day, he had got very little information from her and she'd spent most of the time crying. He had asked her about her sleeping patterns and her thoughts and her fears, and then he had very gently suggested the course of antidepressants that he felt would help her cope better. And she had no doubt that they had got her through that terrible time, although she felt her last session with him and her impending move to Dublin had more to do with her growing confidence. Yes there were still hiccups, like the day in Dad's shop, but they were becoming fewer and she recovered from them more quickly than she used to.

"Sorry for keeping you." The psychiatrist breezed in, smiled and settled himself in the chair at right angles to hers. "How are things, Lynn?" He opened her file and scanned his notes from their last session before giving her his full attention.

"Pretty good," she said. "A lot has happened since I was here last."

"Oh?"

She filled him in briefly on the events of the past fortnight and he made some notes as she talked.

"You have been busy," he chuckled. "Congratulations on your engagement."

She smiled. "Thank you."

"Tell me, any plans to tell him the full story?"

She shook her head furiously and wrapped her arms tightly around her chest. "No, I could never do that."

"Why not?"

She gulped. "I don't think that our relationship would survive it. You don't know what he's like. He couldn't handle knowing all of the details. It would eat him up inside and it would come between us at some stage." Lynn wiped her eyes. "I'm still in shock that I told you," she joked.

"Did it help?"

"Yes, it did, although it's also brought back other memories," she admitted.

"Tell me." Julian reached for the box of tissues.

"There was one time that I had to miss Frank collecting an award. I bought a gorgeous dress for the occasion and I couldn't wait to walk in there as his partner. I felt so proud of him. I finished work early and got my hair done and I was just going back to the house to change when Vincent phoned me. He said that I had screwed up, that there was a double-booking for our function room the following day and that I had to sort it out. I told him that I had nothing to do with the booking and that I was on my way out but he said that he was in Cork, I was on call and that if I wanted to keep my job then I'd better get off the phone and go and sort it out."

"So what happened?"

"It was a setup. He'd told two different couples that there had been a mistake and that both their weddings were booked in for the same day. I arrived into the hotel to find two hysterical girls waiting for me. It took me ages to calm them down and convince them that everything was okay."

"And you missed the awards ceremony?"

"No, I got there but not in time for Frank's presentation." She leaned over to take a tissue.

"He put the hotel's reputation on the line just to mess up your evening?"

She nodded.

"Did you confront him about it?" Julian asked.

"Yes but he just shrugged it off and blamed my illegible handwriting."

"Maybe you're a lot more important to him than you think. Perhaps he's jealous of Frank."

Lynn shook her head, smiling. "No, it's all about control and power with Vincent. I don't care why he did it, any more. It doesn't matter."

He looked at her. "Really? That's a huge step forward, Lynn. Tell me about before the harassment started."

"What do you want to know?" she asked, frowning.

He shrugged. "A picture of your working relationship before it turned sour."

"I've told you this before," she protested lightly.

"And as I've told you before, I've a terrible memory."

Her smile was sad. "I was very happy. When I started in Hawthorn Lodge, Charles, Vincent's uncle, was running it then. I didn't expect to see him from one end of the week to the next but he took an interest in my progress and seemed delighted that I was enjoying it so much." She smiled at Julian. "I was very focused and serious then, and every so often he would take me aside and talk to me or show me the way he did things. To be honest, I think it was that none of his children were that interested in the hospitality business and I became a sort of surrogate daughter."

"Do you think Vincent might have seen you as a threat?"

She laughed. "No, not at all. I was three years younger and straight out of college and he was a Boland. He was also good at what he did. He was fully behind my first promotion to assistant restaurant manager and I was very grateful for the opportunity. I couldn't believe my luck. It's only in hindsight I realize that Vincent's action was self-serving. I worked so hard. I couldn't get enough and so he was able to skive off whenever he wanted. The more that I learned, the easier his life became. We made a great team. The restaurant got some amazing reviews at that time though. Then Charles promoted Vincent to assistant hotel manager."

"And you were still getting on well?"

Lynn pulled a face. "Yes, although the more I worked with him and watched the way that he did business and the way he treated staff, the less I liked or respected him."

Julian's eyes were sharp. "Do you think that he realized that?"

Lynn thought back on the arguments and her frosty behaviour around him when she saw him upbraid a staff member or treat his pals to free drinks after hours. "Yes, he knew," she admitted. "And yet that night . . ." She shook her head and sighed.

"Did you ever tell anyone what happened?"

"No, of course not, who could I tell?" she exclaimed. "My dad, Charles's friend for years? He'd have gone berserk. My best friend, Val? She would have tried to do something about it and she works for the Bolands. She'd be out of a job."

"And Frank?"

"Frank would want to kill him then or now," she said simply and met his eyes. "So tell me, please. Who could I possibly tell?"

Julian's eyes were so full of pity that she felt the tears threatening yet again, and she grabbed a tissue.

"How did the harassment start?" he asked.

"Very subtly. I could feel his anger. When we were in a room together it was almost tangible. And then he changed tack. He's so much cleverer than people realize, than *I* realized. He didn't really do anything that I could object to without seeming childish or a silly, oversensitive woman. He would stand too close or stare at my breasts. Or he would deliberately knock something over so I had to bend down to pick it up. I wasn't allowed to wear trousers; all the women front of house had to wear skirt suits. It meant I was always waiting for him to do something and always trying to

164

avoid situations where we would be alone together. I took to leaving the door of my office open but, if he wanted to talk to me, he came in and closed it and sat on the edge of my desk. And of course no one thought anything of that: he was the manager. But what I really couldn't handle was when he started to exclude me from meetings or criticize me in front of others, especially those who reported to me. It just chipped away at my confidence."

"I'm not surprised." He glanced at the clock.

"Time's up?" Lynn looked up in surprise.

He smiled. "The first few times you came to me you never took your eyes off the clock."

"Sorry."

"It's all right. It's a natural reaction. Are you okay?"

"Yes, fine." She gave him a shaky smile and stood up. She felt exhausted for some reason. Who knew talking could be so tiring?

"You're doing so well, Lynn. I think we could probably leave the next session for four weeks and you can cut back to one tablet every other day."

"Really? That's great." Although the thought of not seeing the counsellor for so long made her feel as if she were jumping out of a plane without a parachute. Kelly obviously noticed her anxiety.

"You have my number. Call me any time if you feel you're in trouble," he said.

She took the hand he held out to her and shook it, grateful that he was so empathetic, though it had taken her a while to appreciate it. "Thank you."

Frank glanced up from his laptop as Lynn whirled around him, plumping up cushions, rearranging magazines and examining the cutlery and glasses for the third time.

"Are you okay?"

"Fine!" Her voice came out as a tiny squeak, her smile brittle. She went back into the kitchen and peered into the oven at the bubbling lasagne. It looked and smelled good. She turned down the temperature and glanced at the clock. Val and John were twenty minutes late. Still, she reminded herself, she had told her friend that it was going to be a relaxed and informal evening and twenty minutes was nothing by Irish standards. She took the wine into the other room and put it down on the table, and then, on impulse, splashed some into a glass. She took a gulp, pausing when she saw Frank watching her, eyebrows raised. "What?"

He shrugged. "Nothing?"

"Want some?"

"Please." He closed the laptop, put it down on the floor and stood up.

She handed him a glass and he smiled down at her. "It'll be fine, Lynn."

"I know."

He reached past her and helped himself to a breadstick. "Val's probably more nervous than you."

"Why would she be?" Lynn shot him a look of disbelief.

"Because she's introducing her fella to her best friend. Weren't you nervous when you introduced me to her?"

166

Lynn smiled at the memory and put a hand up to touch his cheek. "No, I knew she would love you."

He turned his head to kiss her fingers. "Flattery will get you everywhere."

The doorbell rang. "Showtime!" Frank grinned and went to answer it.

Lynn took another quick sip of wine, set down her glass and hurried out to the hall. "Hi!" Her smile faltered when she saw that Val seemed to be alone.

"Hi, Lynn. Sorry we're a bit late but John needed to stop off at the library." Val turned to gesture at her boyfriend and Lynn did a double-take at the figure behind her. Val hadn't been kidding when she said John looked like a teenager. He was shorter than she'd expected and stick thin and wore thick, round glasses that looked enormous on his small face. Remembering her manners, she went forward, hugged Val and held out her hand to John, giving him a warm smile.

"Welcome, John, lovely to meet you."

"How do you do?"

His hand felt limp and clammy in hers and Lynn was happy to release it. "Come in!" She waved the couple in past her and pulled a face at Frank.

"Weirdo," he mouthed.

She sighed and followed them in.

"Wine?" Frank picked up the bottle.

"Lovely." Val gave him a nervous smile.

"Not for me," John said.

"There's lager, and I think we have a bottle of Bacardi somewhere if you'd prefer it."

"Any sherry?" John asked.

Lynn grinned and then realized he wasn't joking. "Sorry, no."

"Then I'll have the wine and some milk, please."

"Together?" Frank joked.

John looked at him as if were stupid. "No, separately, please."

"Er, yes, of course," Lynn said, and went through to the kitchen to get a glass of milk as Frank poured the wine. When she returned Val and John were on the sofa and Frank was leaning on the mantelpiece, remarking on what an excellent library Rathbourne had.

"We're lucky. Are you doing research. John?" she asked, handing him the glass.

"No, I just borrow books. I refuse to buy them and pay those extortionate prices."

"John's an avid reader," Val said proudly.

"Oh, really?" Frank perked up. "What are you into, John? Thrillers, mysteries or do you prefer the classics?"

"Paranormal horror's my passion." John's face lit up like a little boy's.

Frank frowned. "Do you mean vampires?"

"That's an example but I prefer the darker end of the market."

"Nice," Frank said.

"It's a fascinating genre and when I'm not reading I'm writing it."

"You write? How interesting." Lynn tried to inject some enthusiasm into her voice for her friend's sake.

"He's written a novel," Val said.

"Two," John corrected her.

"Are you published?" Frank asked.

168

John gave a long-suffering sigh. "Not yet. I've sent them off to a few publishers but my plots are very complex and my style is quite literary and these days editors are only interested in light, fluffy, commercial reads." He cast the John Grisham novel Frank was reading a scathing look.

"That's probably because they're in business to make money," Frank pointed out.

Lynn shot him a warning glance and went to fetch the food. "Let's eat. I hope you're hungry. I've made a huge lasagne."

"John has an enormous appetite. I don't know where he puts it all." Val laughed.

"I have a very high rate of metabolism," he said, sitting down at the table and helping himself to a breadstick.

"Val tells us you're a teacher. Do you enjoy it?" Lynn asked as she served.

"Not particularly."

"What made you go into teaching?" Frank asked.

"My parents are both teachers, so I suppose you could say that I just joined the family business, but I must admit it doesn't stimulate me at all. In fact sometimes I could cry with boredom."

Lynn felt a moment's pity for the poor children in his care. She wondered, did their parents realize what a cold, dispassionate man was teaching their children? The more that he talked the more her heart sank. She'd really hoped that Val had found a good man, but John was as egotistical and self-obsessed as his predecessors but without their looks or charm.

"Once I sign a publishing contract I'll be out of there damn quick, I can tell you."

"I'll just get some water," Lynn said and escaped into the kitchen. Poor Val really could pick them. She sobered at the thought that her friend was seriously thinking of moving in with this man.

"I'll get more wine," she heard Frank say and turned as he walked in, rolled his eyes and tapped the side of his head. "That guy is barking," he whispered.

Lynn muffled her giggles in a tea towel. "What on earth does she see in him?"

"Maybe he's good in bed." Frank winked.

"I doubt it." Leaving him to open the wine, she carried the jug of water in to the table. It struck Lynn that Val had hardly opened her mouth since she'd arrived other than to praise John, and that he had directed all his conversation at her and Frank rather than his own girlfriend. Despite her jollity, Val seemed ill at ease. Lynn hoped she hadn't realized that she and Frank were laughing at him. She resolved to make more of an effort with him. Perhaps he was just nervous, although, as she watched him help himself to more lasagne, she thought he seemed to have made himself at home. "How's your mum doing, Val?" she asked.

"She's sick of the restrictions placed on her although she doesn't need the crutches now. She doesn't seem to be in much pain, but, then, she'd never say if she was."

"I don't think I've ever seen her in bad form," said Lynn. She was very fond of Angie and full of admiration for her indomitable character.

170

"She saves her grumpiness for the doctor and physiotherapist." Val laughed.

"Have you met Angie, John?" Lynn asked.

"Not yet, no," he said with a pointed look at Val.

"I wanted to wait until she was well on the road to recovery before introducing them," Val said hurriedly. "You know how vain she is, Lynn, she hates anyone seeing her if she's not at her best."

"As if I'd even notice," John said, holding out his glass for a refill as Frank walked in with a new bottle.

"You'll meet her soon enough," Val promised.

Perhaps she was already having second thoughts; Lynn certainly hoped so. She could only imagine what Angie's reaction would be when she met John: she'd be horrified. It suddenly struck Lynn that all her nerves had disappeared when she started to worry about Val and what she was getting herself into. She glanced up and caught Frank watching her, his eyes tender, and realized he was thinking along the same lines. She smiled.

"Any more progress on the new house?" Val asked. "Lynn and Frank are moving to Dublin," she told John.

"Yes, you told me." He looked bored.

"It's all going very smoothly," Lynn said. "We're going up there first thing in the morning to measure up."

"You must be so excited," Val enthused.

"She is," Frank assured her.

"You are, too," Lynn retorted.

"I'm looking forward to spending less time commuting."

"What do you do?" John asked.

Lynn looked at him. Was he serious? Anyone who tuned into current-affairs programmes knew Frank.

"I'm a journalist."

"Don't you recognize him, John?" Val flushed. "Frank's always on TV."

"Can't say I do."

"Not surprised," Frank drawled. "It takes hours and a ton of make-up to make me presentable for the nation."

Lynn smiled gratefully at him. He was the perfect host but, that said, his good manners were showing up John's bad ones. As if to confirm her poor opinion, the man topped up his glass again and didn't offer anyone else more wine. "Coffee and cheesecake?" she said, flashing Val a warm smile.

Val looked up at her. "Are you sure? Don't you have an early start?"

"Not *that* early."

"I love cheesecake," John said.

Lynn gave him a bright smile. "Great!"

As she departed for the kitchen she shot Frank a desperate look and immediately he launched into a story about a politician who had fallen asleep during an interview. As she made the coffee, Lynn was relieved to hear both John and Val laughing. Where would she be without Frank? He was a natural entertainer. She was taking the cheesecake out of the box when Val joined her. "Just something I prepared earlier," she joked.

Val smiled. "Well, what do you think?"

Lynn was surprised by the eagerness and anticipation in her eyes. Hadn't she been in that room? Couldn't she feel how uncomfortable and awkward it was? "Well I've only just met him but he seems nice."

"He really is, Lynn," Val gushed. "I know he's a bit quiet but it's just because he's shy. He's great fun when you get to know him."

"I'm sure he is." Lynn smiled. Shy and fun were not words she would associate with John. Boorish and rude, perhaps. "But Val . . ." Lynn racked her brains for the right words to use. "Don't rush things. Getting to know someone and falling in love is such a special time. Relax and enjoy it. Do things together, go on a holiday, have fun."

Val's expression softened. "Oh, that would be lovely."

"Wouldn't it? Go. You deserve one and to be spoiled and cosseted."

Val hugged her. "Do you know that you're the best friend in the world?"

Lynn held her tight, feeling a bit ashamed of her duplicity, but she was just trying to protect her. "No, I think you hold that award, Val. You've been a true friend to me these last few months."

"Where's that cheesecake?" Frank yelled from the next room. "There are two men starving to death in here."

The girls looked at each other and laughed, and, taking the coffee and cake, went back to join their men.

"What an idiot," Frank muttered as the couple walked down the road.

Val turned to wave, and Lynn waved back. "He's awful, isn't he?" she said, going back inside to clear the table.

"I don't think I've ever met someone with such an enormous chip on his shoulder and I've met a lot of idiots in my time." Frank carried the glasses out to the kitchen and turned on the hot tap.

"He definitely knew who you were." Lynn followed him with the last of the dirty dishes and started to stack the dishwasher. "He just didn't want to acknowledge it. Val seems completely blind to his faults. How am I going to make her see that she's worth ten of him?"

"You can't. It's nothing to do with you."

Lynn closed the dishwasher and stood up. "But how can I pretend to like him?"

"You must if you want to keep her as a friend."

She flopped into a chair and watched as he polished the clean glasses with a cloth. "She knows me too well to be fooled."

"It's one thing her knowing it and another thing entirely you putting it into words. Look, Lynn, John is no different to the other guys. I'm sure she will soon realize that."

"She never talked about moving in with any of the others," Lynn pointed out. She knew that her friend was intoxicated at the thought of living with a man, probably to the point that she would deliberately close her eyes to the fact that John was the wrong one. Still, it would be a good idea to encourage Val to go on holiday with him. Two weeks alone together might make her see sense.

174

Frank put the glasses away and pulled Lynn to her feet. "There's nothing you can do."

She smiled. "Don't bet on it."

Frank's eyes narrowed. "Lynn —"

"Don't worry, I won't say anything. You're right: it would send her running into his arms. But" — her eyes twinkled — "there are ways."

He linked his arms around her. "What's going on in that head of yours?"

She laughed. "Nothing much. Just thinking of more subtle ways to stop her making a huge mistake."

CHAPTER
SEVENTEEN

Frank opened the steaming pack and they were enveloped in the mouthwatering aroma of chips covered in salt and vinegar. "When I said I'd take you out to lunch, this isn't exactly what I had in mind."

Lynn laughed and stretched out on the balcony of their new home, gesturing at the panoramic view before them. "This is better than any restaurant."

He lay down next to her and popped a chip into her mouth. "It's not half bad, is it? Although I'll be glad when the furniture's delivered." He moved around, trying to find a more comfortable position.

"There's the man who said he wanted to indulge in some outdoor rumpy-pumpy," she teased.

"The man didn't say he'd do it without a mattress. Mind you, the garden furniture we bought looks very comfortable." He fed her another chip and she licked his fingers.

"We spent more money than we should have," she said, although she was thrilled with the table and chairs and large sofa.

"It'll get good use. We'll spend a lot of time out here."

"We will," Lynn agreed, gazing out to sea. To the left was the south wall stretching out, the Poolbeg Lighthouse on the end of it, and to the right Sandymount beach shone gold in the afternoon sunshine. She held up her left hand and admired the diamond glistening there. "We spent too much on this, too."

"Rubbish! That's a fraction of the money Carrie spent on jewellery."

Lynn's smile faded. She hated to think that Frank had put a ring on another woman's finger, that he had walked up the aisle with her and that she had borne his child.

"Are you sure you like it?" he asked, searching her face.

She leaned over to kiss him, tasting the salt on his lips. "I love it. It's going to be hard putting it back in its box."

"Not for long. As soon as we've settled in we should make an announcement."

"We agreed to wait," she reminded him.

"I don't like waiting." He balled up the chip wrappers, tossed them over his shoulder and moved closer to her.

"I've noticed," she smiled.

"I would love to lie here all day with you, but if I don't stand up soon you're going to have to get a crane to get me into an upright position."

"What am I doing marrying such a wreck?" She laughed.

"No idea, but it's not too late to change your mind," he retorted.

She cupped his face in her hands and looked into his eyes. "Sorry, darling, you're stuck with me."

"I'm glad to hear it. He pulled her close, moulding her body against his and kissing her hungrily.

"What about your aches and pains?" she murmured against his lips.

"What about them?" he said, and slipped his hand into the back of her jeans.

It was almost seven when they drove into Rathbourne. Lynn was tired and a little sore from their alfresco frolics but very relaxed and contented. She admired her lovely engagement ring one last time before taking it off and putting it in its little box.

Frank put his hand on her thigh. "You don't have to take it off yet."

"No, I don't, do I?" She smiled and put it back on before covering his hand with hers. "Thank you, Frank. I love it and I love you."

"Happy?" he asked as they pulled up outside the house.

"Deliriously."

Inside the hall door she kicked off her shoes and dropped her bag on the floor. "I think I'll have a bath."

He kissed her. "Mmm, that sounds like a good idea. Let me check my email and then I'll join you."

As she turned to go upstairs the phone started to ring and she groaned. "Tell whoever it is to go away!"

"Will do."

She went straight into the bathroom, put the plug in the bath and turned on the taps. After pouring a

178

generous amount of bath oil into it she went into the bedroom, opening her blouse. She laughed when she heard Frank bounding up the stairs. "You are so incredibly randy today."

"Lynn!"

She looked up at him and the smile died on her face when she saw his expression.

"I'm sorry, darling. Your dad's on his way to casualty. He's had another stroke."

The journey to the hospital in Dublin seemed interminable. She dug her fingers into the seat as she replayed the stroke TV advertisements in her head. Speed of action was critical. "How long was it before he got help?" she asked.

Frank glanced over at her. "I don't know. Norman found him on the floor of his office."

"But how long before that was it since anyone had seen him?" she said, irritated.

He put his hand down to take hers. "I don't know, darling. I didn't ask questions. I thought it was more important to get you to the hospital."

She nodded, visualizing her father lying on the floor, helpless and unable to call for help. "Was he conscious?"

Frank sighed in frustration. "I'm sorry, Lynn, I didn't ask that either. Do you want me to phone Norman and ask?"

"Yes." She sighed. "No." Norman was probably in a right state at being left with the full responsibility of the shop. "Did he close up?" She closed her eyes. "No, I know, you didn't ask. Sorry."

"Jack will be fine, Lynn. Look how quickly he bounced back the last time."

"Yes. I'm sure you're right." But she wasn't. She had a very bad feeling about this. "Why hasn't Mum called?"

"They've probably only just got to the hospital and she'll be tied up filling out forms. And, remember, she won't be allowed to use a mobile phone in the hospital and she wouldn't leave him until she was sure . . ."

Lynn's stomach turned at the unsaid words hanging between them. She stared blindly out of the window and said nothing for the remainder of the drive to Dublin, though there were moments when they were stuck behind a tractor or a learner driver and she could have cursed and screamed with frustration. When he sensed her distress, Frank would put his hand on her leg in a gesture of sympathy and solidarity, but he remained silent and for that she was grateful.

Frank dropped her at the door of A&E and went in search of parking. Lynn went to the reception desk, dismayed to see that there were three people ahead of her.

"Excuse me." She tried to catch the eye of the woman behind the counter, but was studiously ignored.

The burly man in front of her turned and glared. "There's a queue."

"Sorry, I'm just trying to find my dad," she said. "He was brought in by ambulance."

180

A passing nurse stopped in her tracks and came over to her. "Who are you looking for?"

"Jack Stephens." The nurse's expression softened and Lynn's heart sank.

"Come with me. I'll take you to your mother."

"Is my dad . . ." She couldn't bring herself to finish the sentence.

"Your father's being well looked after. A doctor will come and talk to you soon." She opened the door to a small examination room to reveal Nell sitting on a plastic chair looking small and lost.

"Lynn!" She jumped to her feet and hugged her daughter.

"How is he? Have you seen him?"

"I don't know anything. They whisked him away as soon as we got here and stuck me in this damn room."

Lynn turned to the nurse. "Can we see him?"

"Someone will come and see you as soon as there's news. If you want tea or coffee there's a machine at the end of the corridor." She gave them a kind smile and left.

Lynn guided her mother back to the chair and pulled up another for herself. "What happened, Mum?"

Nell clutched her hand and shook her head. "I don't really know, love. Norman came running into the kitchen saying Jack was on the floor of his office, unconscious. I told him to call an ambulance and I ran over. He was breathing and he opened his eyes a few times, but he didn't seem to see or hear me."

"Have you any idea how long he might have been lying there?"

"Not long. Norman said he'd gone to get something for a customer and when he didn't come back Norman went looking for him."

"That's good, then."

"I suppose so."

Lynn looked worriedly at her mother. She was white as a sheet and trembling. "I'll get you some tea."

Nell didn't seem to hear her. "What will I do if this time he doesn't get better, Lynn? How could I carry on without him?"

"Of course he's going to get better. You mustn't think like that."

"That bloody shop. I've begged him time and again to sell it before it killed him, and now it looks like it might have."

"He's not dead, Mum. We wouldn't be left waiting if he was."

"He got a warning two years ago," her mother continued, "and he ignored it."

There was a knock at the door and they both swung around anxiously, but it was only Frank.

"Here you are! I've been wandering up and down corridors looking for you. Any news?"

Lynn shook her head. "We're waiting for a doctor to come and talk to us."

He sat on the edge of the day bed and looked at Nell. "I'm sure he'll be fine. He's a strong man."

Nell didn't look up, just gave a helpless shrug. "I don't know. It's been ages and no one's told me anything, and they don't give you a room to yourself in a hospital unless things are really serious. The last time it happened to me a doctor came and told me that my mother had died."

Lynn hopped to her feet. "I'll go and get tea."

"No." Her mother stood up. "I'll go. I need to get out of here for a bit."

"I'll come with you," Lynn said.

"No, love, stay with Frank," Nell insisted.

After she'd gone, Frank opened his arms and Lynn fell into them and started to cry. "She's convinced he's going to die," she said between sobs.

"He won't."

She nestled into his chest, hoping that he was right. They stood like that for several moments. "If he does come out of this in one piece he'll have to retire," Lynn said eventually. "If he doesn't, Mum will divorce him."

He chuckled. "Not a chance. She's nearly as mad about him as you are about me."

"Bighead!" She pulled away and wiped her eyes on her sleeve. "Mum's been gone a while. Should I go and find her?"

"It's only been a few minutes. Leave her."

There was a sharp rap on the door and a large man with bushy hair and round glasses walked in.

"You're Mr Stephens's relatives?"

Lynn got to her feet slowly. "I'm his daughter. My mother just went to get tea."

"I'll go and find her," Frank said and squeezed around the man.

"I'm Dr Hanrahan." He glanced after Frank, frowning before extending his hand to Lynn.

Lynn shook it. "How is he, Doctor?"

183

"Not good," he said flatly, "but he has stabilized."

"Thank God."

"He's not out of the woods, though," he cautioned. "The next few hours are critical. Can you tell me what happened?"

"Not really. He was found on the floor of his office. Is it another stroke?"

The door opened again and Nell arrived back with Frank. "This is my mother. Mum, this is Dr Hanrahan. And this is my fiancé, Frank Hayes."

He shook hands with Nell and then with Frank. "I thought you looked familiar. I liked your piece on the Stability Treaty."

"Thank you."

"Doctor, how is my husband?" Nell cut in.

"Ah, yes, sorry, Mrs Stephens. I was just telling your daughter that he's stable but critical."

"Will he live?" Nell asked baldly.

"It's too early to tell," he said gently. "It would help if we knew more about the injury."

"Injury?" Nell stared at him. "I thought he'd had another stroke."

"No. Your husband has had an acute subdural haematoma. That's a bleed in the brain that was caused by either a blow to the head or a fall."

"What?" Nell shook her head in confusion. "But he was alone in his office."

"The injury may not have happened immediately beforehand. Sometimes people can be fine for several hours after an accident and then collapse."

184

"He hasn't had any injury," Nell said, "or if he did he never mentioned it."

"Will I call Norman and see if he can shed any light on the subject?" Frank offered.

"Would you, please?" Lynn said gratefully, and Frank left the room again. "What happens now, Doctor?"

"I've referred him to our neurosurgical team. They'll assess him but I suspect that they'll want to perform a craniotomy."

"What's that?"

"They'll go in and remove the blood clot to relieve the pressure on his brain."

Nell put a hand to her mouth and stared at him in horror. "Brain surgery? Is that really necessary?"

"They won't do it if it isn't," he assured her.

Lynn sat down and put a hand over her mother's. "If they remove the clot, will he be okay?"

He held out his hands and shrugged. "I'm very sorry but there are no guarantees. Anyway, we're getting ahead of ourselves. Let's await the verdict from the neurosurgeon and hope for the best."

Nell wiped a tear from her cheek. "Can I see him?"

"Briefly. I should warn you that he's on a ventilator and there are tubes going into his mouth, but it's nothing to worry about. We just need to keep him stable until we get to the root of the problem."

"He opened his eyes a few times on the way here. Surely that's a good sign," Nell said.

"Perhaps," was the doctor's noncommittal reply. "I'll check if you can go in and see him now."

"Thank you." When they were alone, Lynn put her arm around her mother. "He's going to be okay, Mum."

"Hope for the best but expect the worst," her mother said, her voice flat. "That's what the saying is. That's what he meant."

"So let's hope for the best," Lynn replied. "Come on, Mum, we have to be strong. He needs us." She looked up as Frank returned. "Well?"

He nodded. "Mystery solved. Norman says that the ladder in the storeroom was on its side and there were tins on the ground that had been on the top shelf."

"But he made it as far as the office. That's a good sign," Lynn said knowing that she was clutching at straws. "He must have felt dizzy and went in to have a sit-down till he felt better."

The doctor returned and Frank told him about the suspected fall. He nodded. "That would make sense. You can come in and see him now, but just for a moment."

Lynn gasped at the sight of her father in the bed.

Frank kept a tight hold of her hand as Nell moved forward and touched her husband's cheek.

"Oh, Jack, how many times did I tell you that ladder was a death trap? Come on, now, you need to wake up. You're taking up these people's time. Lynn's here too."

Lynn stepped forward. His chest rose and fell in an unnatural, exaggerated fashion as the ventilator breathed for him and his face was like a mask. "Hi, Dad."

There was a flurry of activity behind them and Dr Hanrahan put his hand on Nell's arm. "I'm afraid

186

you'll have to go. The team from neurosurgery are here."

Lynn turned around to the three people behind them. Her father's life was in their hands. "Please make him better."

The man nearest her nodded; his dark eyes kind. "We'll try."

They had been back in the room for nearly an hour before Dr Hanrahan arrived with the other man in tow. "This is Mr Khan. He's the head of the hospital's neurosurgical department."

It was the man with the kind eyes. Lynn moved closer to her mother.

"Mrs Stephens, your husband has a very large clot pressing on his brain. We must go in and remove it," Mr Khan told her.

"Can you make him better?" Nell asked.

"I don't know, but I am going to try. It is a dangerous surgery and your husband's age doesn't help. There is a possibility of him not surviving the operation. If he does, there is still a risk that he could end up in a vegetative state and, even if he regains consciousness, we have no way of knowing how he will have been affected by the haematoma or what his chances of recovery are. Also, with any operation there are risks of infection."

Lynn was conscious of Frank's firm grip on her shoulder. Without it she thought she might well fall over. "Is there any good news?"

He smiled slightly. "Yes. He is stable and apart from the stroke he suffered . . ." — he looked down at his notes — "nearly two years ago, he is in good health. He's a smoker but not an excessive one, I understand, so I don't see that as an issue. Also, this hospital has the best neurosurgical unit in the country, so he couldn't be in better hands." He looked from Lynn to Nell to Frank. "Any questions?"

"How long will the operation take?" Frank asked.

He shrugged. "I can't give you a definite answer on that. Much depends on the size of the bleed and any complications we may have to deal with when we get in there. At least two hours, but perhaps as much as five. We will be moving him up to the operating theatre within the hour. If you wish, there is a room nearby where you may wait and one of my team will come out regularly and let you know how things are going."

"We'd like that," Lynn said, grateful that the man was so direct. "If the operation *is* successful, how long will it be before you know if he'll make a full recovery?"

"We won't have any clear understanding of that until he is conscious." He looked down at a silent Nell. "Mrs Stephens, have you any queries?"

She looked up at him. "Will you tell me honestly, what are the odds are of him surviving this surgery?"

He held her gaze. "If it is straightforward he has probably an eighty per cent chance of survival. With complications the chances are about fifty-fifty."

"And the chances of a complete recovery?" Lynn asked.

"Every patient is different. There could be two people with very similar case histories and with the same type of haematoma and yet they could have completely different outcomes, and we have no idea why." He glanced at his watch. "Now, unless there is anything else, I should get ready for surgery."

CHAPTER
EIGHTEEN

The next couple of hours were like a dream, or perhaps nightmare was a better description. Her mother had to sign a consent form and then they were taken up to the waiting room next to the operating theatres and handed over to a girl around Lynn's age. Her name was Niamh and she was kind and considerate and diligent. She had suggested they go home, but both Lynn and her mother were aghast at the suggestion. She didn't seem surprised. She told them about the hospital restaurant and, jokingly, what food to avoid.

"Go and get something now," she suggested. "There will be no news for at least an hour, and it could be a very long night. You need to keep your strength up."

The food tasted like cardboard to Lynn, and she had to coax her mother every few minutes to lift the fork to her mouth. When they finished, Frank went to the car to make some calls. He joined them in the waiting room with his laptop under his arm. "I have some work to do," he told Nell, apologetically.

"Don't worry, love. I'm jealous. I wish *I* had something to distract me."

"I have a book," Lynn offered.

Nell shook her head. "I couldn't concentrate."

Lynn sighed. "Me neither."

They looked at each other as they heard footsteps coming down the corridor and pausing at the door. Niamh came in, smiling. "How are you?"

"Fine. What's happening?" Nell asked.

"The operation's just starting now."

"I thought it started ages ago." Lynn stared at her in dismay.

"There was an emergency that had to be dealt with first."

"I thought Jack was an emergency."

"Your husband's stable and a man came in with a gunshot wound, so that took priority. I'm sorry. I know it's frustrating, but that's the way these things work. I'll tell you as soon as I have any news."

"This is so nerve-wrecking," Lynn said. "I feel so helpless."

"At least Jack is in a good enough state to have been jumped on the list," Frank pointed out.

"You're right," Nell said, and stood up. "I think I'll go down to the chapel and say a prayer. If there's any news —"

"I will come and get you straightaway," Lynn promised.

Frank looked over at her when they were alone. "Are you all right?"

"No, I'm scared stiff. Even if he does make it through the surgery, what if he doesn't wake up or has serious brain damage? I think I'd prefer it if he died." She looked at him, feeling guilty and ashamed. "Is that a terrible thing to say?"

He shook his head. "I'd imagine Jack would agree."

"Mum wouldn't. She would want him to live regardless of his quality of life. I think she'd happily become a carer and devote her life to nursing him rather than lose him." Tears welled up in her eyes and she pulled out a tissue. "It's so unfair. The one thing that she's been looking forward to is his retirement so that they could finally travel together; there were so many places she wanted to go and now . . ."

"He could make a full recovery, darling, and if he does I think he will have a very different attitude towards work."

"I suppose so." But Lynn wasn't optimistic; she was afraid to be. What was that saying again? Hope for the best but prepare for the worst. "I think I'll stretch my legs."

"Want me to come with you?" he asked.

"No, you get that article written. I'll just be outside. I'm cracking up sitting around doing nothing."

Lynn was still pacing the corridor an hour later when Nell stepped out of the lift. "Are you okay, Mum? Do you want some tea?"

"No, love."

The two of them went back to join Frank.

He looked up. "Any news?"

"Nothing." Lynn slumped into a chair.

"We should have heard something by now," Nell fretted.

"He said two to five hours," Lynn said irritably, "and we don't know exactly when the operation began. Stop worrying until you have something to worry about."

192

Nell sighed but didn't say anything.

Lynn came to crouch in front of her. "I'm sorry, Mum."

Nell touched her face and smiled. "It's okay, love. We're all worried and tired."

Lynn took her hand and kissed it. Nell gasped. "What?" Lynn asked and then saw that her mother was staring at the ring on the third finger of her left hand. She looked over and smiled at Frank. "You see? I knew I should have taken it off in the car."

"I'm delighted for you both. Congratulations!" Nell smiled at Frank and hugged Lynn. "Your dad will be thrilled."

If he lives to hear the news, Lynn thought, and knew that Frank and her mother were thinking the same thing.

"Do you like it?" Lynn stretched out her hand.

"It's beautiful."

"You weren't supposed to find out like this," Frank said. "I was planning to do the whole thing properly and ask Jack for her hand."

Nell laughed. "Oh, he'd love that. He'd probably say no just for the craic."

There was a tap on the door and Niamh came in.

"How is he?" Lynn asked.

"He's doing really well." Niamh smiled. "So far everything's gone exactly as planned. They're getting ready to close up now."

"Thank God." Nell crossed herself.

"Mr Khan will come and talk to you as soon as the surgery's over and he'll be able to tell you more."

"Well, that's the first hurdle behind him," Frank said when the nurse left them.

Lynn saw the spark of hope in her mother's eyes. "But he's not out of the woods yet," she cautioned.

"That's true." Her mother nodded.

Frank shook his head. "You two take this 'prepare for the worst' business too far. It has to be a good sign that the operation was successful and relatively short."

Lynn grinned. "Yes, of course you're right. I suppose I'm just afraid of getting my hopes up."

"Whatever happens, we'll cope," Nell said, her voice firm. "Whatever he has to face, we'll be at his side and he'll get better."

"If determination and strength of will has anything to do with it, he'll get through it; he's a fighter," Frank told them.

Nell looked up at the clock. "I wish I'd asked her how long it would be before the surgeon came out to talk to us."

Frank stood up. "I'll go and see if I can find out."

"Thanks, love." Nell stood up and started to pace the room. "I can't wait to have him home. This place drives me mad. I can't bear sitting around doing nothing."

Lynn looked at her in alarm. Did she really think that this was like tonsillitis: a couple of days and Dad would be home? "You'd better bring in your knitting or sewing from now on, Mum. Dad won't come home for a long time."

"You don't know that." Nell said, looking cross.

Lynn was about to argue the point but bit her lip. The last thing she should be doing was upsetting her

194

mother. Let the surgeon tell her and perhaps it would be good news. She took her hand and held it tightly between her own. "No, you're right, I don't."

They sat in silence like that until the door opened and Frank walked in followed by the surgeon. Lynn searched Mr Khan's face, but couldn't read it, so she looked at Frank and, though he gave her a slight smile, she could see that the expression in his eyes was grave. Feeling sick, she held on tight to her mother's hand.

CHAPTER
NINETEEN

"How is he, Doctor?" Nell asked, a slight tremor in her voice.

He sat down opposite her. "He is stable, Mrs Stephens. He came through the operation without incident. The bleed was serious, we were right to operate, but it wasn't as bad as we had feared, and also the location could have been much worse."

"So he is going to be okay?"

"That is much too early to predict. We have put him into a drug-induced coma to give him time to recover. That is standard procedure," he added when Nell put a hand to her mouth. "We will monitor him closely. The next forty-eight hours are crucial."

"What could go wrong at this stage?" asked Frank.

Lynn glanced up at him, sensing he was trying to prepare them. But, then, being a journalist, he had probably been online researching subdural haematomas when he had told them he was working.

"The main risks are a blood clot forming where we operated. Also, he could have a seizure. He is also vulnerable to infection. His age means his chances of a full recovery are less than that of a younger person. But in his favour is" — the surgeon counted off the points on his fingers — "we operated very quickly following the accident; he was lucid enough to make it into the other room; and the bleed is in a relatively benign location."

"How long will you keep him in the coma?" Lynn asked. Somehow, the thought bothered her. It was like the life-support machine. Until she saw her father breathing without these alien, cold, medical aids she would not feel comfortable, she would not feel safe.

"Probably twenty-four hours, perhaps less."

"You said he's less likely to make a full recovery." Frank said. "What sort of problems could he have?"

"The bleed happened in the right hemisphere, which controls the movement of the left side of the body. It also controls analytical and perceptual tasks, such as judging distance or position and seeing how parts are connected to wholes. As a result, he may experience some paralysis or lose the ability to judge distance. There's also a possibility of personality changes or loss of short-term memory."

"But those would be temporary problems, wouldn't they?" Lynn asked, willing him to give the answer they all wanted to hear.

"The effects and the rate of recovery differ for each patient. Some people return to exactly as they were before but others never recover some of these brain functions."

"He's strong. He'll recover." Nell's tone made it clear that she wouldn't tolerate opinions to the contrary. "Can I see him?"

"Not yet. He is still in the recovery room but shortly we will be moving him to intensive care and you can see him then — but just one at a time and only for a few minutes." He stood up. "I will be in to check on him first thing in the morning."

Nell looked at him in alarm. "You're leaving? But what if he has a bleed or a seizure?"

"Dr O'Keefe will be on duty through the night and he will be keeping a very close eye on your husband. If any problems arise he is more than capable of dealing with them, I assure you."

Left alone, Nell looked at Frank and Lynn in disbelief. "He's leaving Jack in the care of some feckin student?"

"Don't worry," Frank reassured her. "I met O'Keefe outside. He's no student. He must be nearly as old as me."

Nell sighed and looked from him to Lynn. "I'm not sure what to think. I couldn't tell if he was optimistic or not."

"I think he gave it to us straight. Everyone's different and I don't think there's much they can tell until Jack wakes up. We just have to wait and see."

Lynn said nothing. This was the easy part, she felt. Asleep, Dad would still be the man she knew. Once he was awake, there was no telling how he would be.

"Are you okay?" Frank asked after Nell had left them to go and see her husband.

She looked into his worried eyes and nodded. "Just tired."

198

"I think we should go home. Your mother's dead on her feet."

"She won't leave him, and neither will I. If anything happened and I wasn't here I'd never forgive myself." He put his arms around her and she laid her head on his shoulder.

"You both need rest. The next few days and weeks aren't going to be easy. You'll need to decide what to do about the shop."

Lynn raised her head and looked at him. "What do you mean?"

"You're always saying that Norman isn't up to running it alone and your mother is going to have her hands full with your dad."

Of course, Frank was right, but it hadn't occurred to Lynn. It was as if they had been living in a bubble these last few hours; real life seemed far away and irrelevant. "I'll talk to Mum. You're the one that needs to get some rest. Don't you have to be in RTÉ in a few hours?"

"I cancelled."

"Oh, Frank, you shouldn't have," she protested.

"There is no way I'd leave you."

"It's such a pity that we can't stay over in our new house. It would be wonderful to be so close," she said.

"It'll be ours in a week or so. If your dad does have to stay in hospital then your mum can stay with us and we'll be able to take it in turns to visit."

Lynn didn't want to even consider the possibility that her father could remain in hospital for quite some time. She didn't want to let her mind go down the path of what the future held for him, for them all. Frank was right about the business, though. They would have to come to a decision as to what to do.

Nell returned, crying. "He looks so helpless," she said between sobs.

Lynn led her to a chair. "He's bound to: he's just come through major surgery, Mum."

"You go and see your dad; I'll stay here."

Frank took her place and put an arm around Nell's shoulders.

Lynn left them and went down to the ICU. When the nurse drew back the curtain of Jack's cubicle, she stood staring at him. It could have been anyone. There was a large dressing on his head and, with no expression or life in his face, he seemed like a stranger. But, as she pulled the chair nearer to the bed and sat down, she could see the tiny scar on his neck where a dog had nipped him when he was a little boy. She looked down at his hands and felt better. They were unmistakably her father's. Tentatively, she took his left hand, careful not to disturb the line going into it. It was gnarled and rough and told its own story of how hard its owner worked. "Oh, Dad." Lynn bent her head and kissed it. She searched his face for some glimmer of a reaction, but there was none.

Why did he have to push himself so hard? He was always tired. She had no doubt that the accident had occurred because he hadn't taken the time to make sure the ladder was secure. "No more ladders for you. You need to hire someone young and strong to do all the donkey work, you hear me?" she scolded him as her tears fell on his hand. "Or better still retire. Think

200

about all the things you could do. You could come up to shows in Dublin and stay the night with us. You could take trips down the country at the drop of a hat. You could even take Mum to see Aunty Brenda in Florida. You know that she's always wanted to go." She looked up and stared into his face. Could he hear her? Was he okay? Would they ever have a proper conversation again or would he become a vegetable or, worse, be conscious but unable to communicate? For such a vital, clever man to be trapped inside a useless body would be cruel, and she knew he would hate it.

She stroked his fingers. "Come on, Dad, don't give in. Mum needs you." She gulped. "I need you. I'm getting married, Dad, and I need you by my side when I walk up that aisle so don't let me down, okay?"

The curtain moved and the nurse came in. "Sorry to interrupt. I just need to check him."

"Of course." Lynn glanced at her name badge. "Do you want me to go, Una?"

"You can have another few minutes. Talking to him can't do him any harm and may do some good."

"Do you think he can hear me?" Lynn asked as the nurse leaned over him and shone a torch in his eyes.

"Some patients have said they were aware of people around them when they were unconscious. It certainly can't hurt. If you were frightened or confused wouldn't it soothe you to hear a familiar voice?"

"Yes." Lynn nodded. "Thanks."

"I couldn't help overhearing, by the way." Una glanced up and smiled before checking the drip going into his hand. "Congratulations!"

"Thanks." Lynn smiled and looked down at her hand.

"It's a gorgeous ring."

"We only bought it this morning." Her eyes flew to the clock. "Or should I say *yesterday* morning? We weren't going to announce it for a few weeks but I was wearing it when we got the call about Dad and I forgot to take it off."

"Keep talking to him about walking you up that aisle. If he can hear you it'll give him a goal to aim for."

Lynn watched as she jotted down some notes on her father's chart. "Can I ask you something?"

"Sure."

"You must have seen many people after a craniotomy. On a scale of one to ten, how do you think he's doing?"

The nurse glanced down at the chart. "I'm no neurosurgeon but if there aren't any problems in the next four hours I'd put him at a seven right now."

"Thank God!" Lynn said.

"But let's keep that between us. I would hate to get your Mum's hopes up."

Lynn nodded her agreement. "Can she come in again? I'll tell her to talk to him."

"Of course."

There was no sign of Nell or Frank when Lynn came outside, so she headed back to the waiting room, knocking tentatively in case there was another family there now. But, inside, Frank was sprawled in a chair,

202

asleep, while her mother sat at the window staring out into the darkness. "Mum?"

Nell whirled around. "Is he okay?"

"Fine," Lynn assured her. "You can go back in if you want."

Her mother stood up and lost her balance. Lynn put a hand out to steady her. "You're exhausted, Mum. Why don't you try to sleep? There's nothing you can do for Dad at the moment, but he'll need you when he wakes up."

"I'll just go down to him for five minutes and then I'll have a rest," Nell promised.

She was at the door when Lynn remembered the nurse's words. "Oh, Mum, talk to him. The nurse said he may be able to hear."

Her mother looked at her in some surprise. "Of course he can hear," she said as she slipped out into the corridor, closing the door softly behind her.

Lynn snuggled in close to Frank. Her eyelids felt heavy, but she fought to keep them open, not happy to rest until her mother returned.

She was barely conscious by the time Nell crept back into the room with pillows and blankets.

Nell covered Frank and Lynn and dropped a kiss on her daughter's forehead. "Get some sleep."

"He's going to be okay, Mum," Lynn mumbled.

"I know he is." Nell wrapped herself in a blanket and settled a pillow behind her head. "Goodnight, darling."

CHAPTER
TWENTY

Jack was having the strangest dream. It was as if he was in a swamp — or quicksand? Either way, he knew that he was in trouble. There was a rock about a yard to the left in front of him and if he could just reach that he'd be able to pull himself to safety. Yet, no matter how hard he tried, he couldn't get to it. Something was dragging him down, holding him back. He started to panic and tried to call out for help, but he couldn't speak. In his head he was shouting, screaming, roaring at the top of his voice, but he could see people ambling along in the distance oblivious to him and the danger he was in. Feeling frightened and alone, he cried out again like a little boy crying for his mammy.

"Steady now, Jack. Steady. It's okay."

The man's voice was strong and reassuring, but for some reason Jack couldn't see him. He struggled to open his eyes but couldn't. He tried to raise his hands to rub them, but they seemed to be weighted down and he cried out again in frustration.

"Relax, Jack." The man's voice, level and calm was soothing and Jack stopped fighting. He felt tired. Maybe he'd just sleep and let the Voice look after him.

Lynn opened her eyes. It took her a moment to remember where she was. Frank was gone but her mother was still sleeping, a pillow clutched in her arms. She pulled up her sleeve to look at her watch. It was almost seven. It had to be a good sign that they hadn't been woken. She clung to the thought. Her mobile phone vibrated in her pocket and she pulled it out and checked her texts. There was one from Frank.

IN THE CAR, MAKING CALLS. SPOKE TO NORMAN.
HE'S ASKED HIS NEPHEW TO HELP IN THE SHOP.
X

She smiled. She was so grateful that Frank was here to take control. It hadn't occurred to her to phone Norman, and he would have been anxious had Frank not checked in. It was wonderful that Jamie was in a position to help out today. Between Norman, him and Cathy, they should manage fine for the few hours the supermarket was open on a Sunday.

She stood and stretched and, taking her bag with her, headed for the loos. She splashed water on her face and gargled; how she longed to brush her teeth. She pulled her hair into a ponytail and headed back to ICU.

"Hi, how's my Dad?" she asked Una.

"Good. Dr O'Keefe was with him an hour or so ago and he's happy with him."

Lynn stared at her. "Did he move? Did he open his eyes?"

"Not really. He seemed to be dreaming, but that's all good."

"Can I go and sit with him?"

"Go ahead. I'm going off duty now." The nurse smiled. "Good luck."

"Thanks for everything," Lynn said sincerely, and went into her dad's cubicle. She pulled the chair close to the bed. "Hey, Dad. Are you ready to wake up yet?" She touched his hand and searched his face for any sign of a reaction. "Mum's getting some sleep but no doubt she'll be in soon. Norman's roped in Jamie to help in the shop today so you don't have to worry, they'll be fine." She stroked his fingers and chuckled. "Do you know, this is probably the longest you've spent in bed in years? But there was no need to go to such extremes to get a rest. Is that why you fell off the ladder, Dad? Were you tired? Do you remember what I was like before exams? I used to stay up till all hours and you would get really cross with me, saying that all my revision would be wasted if I fell asleep at the desk. Well, now it's my turn. It's time that you got sense. Mind you, you're not going to be given a choice: Mum will make your life hell if you don't slow down."

The curtain was pulled back and she looked up to see Mr Khan and Dr O'Keefe standing there, a gang of students behind them.

"Your father has had a good night I hear, Miss Stephens." The surgeon smiled. "Could you give us a few minutes to examine him? Then I will come and talk to you and your mother after my rounds." He waved a hand at the students. "Do you mind if my doctors stay?"

"Not at all."

"You should go and grab something to eat," the day nurse suggested. "It'll be an hour at least before he'll get a moment to talk to you."

"I am hungry. I'll go and wake my mother. If there's any change —"

The nurse pointed at a Post-it. "Una left your number right here; I'll text you."

"Thanks."

Nell was sitting up straight, pulling a comb through her hair, when Lynn came back with the news.

"How is he?" she asked anxiously.

"The same. Mr Khan's with him right now. He's going to come and talk to us after his rounds."

Nell stood up, massaging her neck. "I should call Norman."

"Frank already did. Everything's fine."

"What would we do without him? He's been so kind. I'm so glad that you've found yourself a good man, Lynn. Where is he?"

"In the car on the phone. I'll text him and tell him to meet us in the restaurant."

They were halfway through breakfast when Frank joined them, his plate piled high with rashers, sausages and eggs and toast on the side.

Nell smiled. "I like to see a man eat a good breakfast."

"I usually try. In this job you never know when you'll get a chance to eat again. How's Jack?"

"They say he had a good night," Lynn said. "Mr Khan was just with him and he's going to come and talk to us later."

Nell glanced up at the clock before taking another tiny mouthful of scrambled egg. Lynn saw the look. "We have plenty of time, Mum."

"I hope they wake him soon. I won't relax until I see him awake."

"We need to think about accommodation," Frank said between mouthfuls.

"Accommodation?" Nell looked at him.

"You can't spend every night in a chair, Nell," he said, "and I know I'd be wasting my breath suggesting that you go home."

"You would," she agreed.

"I'd love a shower and a change of clothes," Lynn said.

"I'm tied up most of the day but you could take the car and go home, pick up some clothes, and I'll book us a couple of rooms in a hotel."

Lynn's mind raced. If she went to her parents' house she would be surrounded in minutes by neighbours and customers anxious for news of Dad. She'd have to go into the shop to talk to Norman and there was no doubt he would have a lot to say and take all day to say it. "I don't feel comfortable driving your car."

"You can take it slowly," Frank said, too busy with his breakfast to notice her discomfort.

208

"It would be great if you could pick up some things for me, love, and your dad will be dying to get out of that hospital gown and into his own pyjamas."

"I'd rather stay here and you might need the car." Lynn willed Frank to look up at her. "We can drive down tonight. We'll have a better idea of how things stand by then."

He looked up at her and finally got the message. "Yes, okay, that makes sense."

Lynn gave him a grateful smile.

Frank had just put down his knife and fork when Nell was on her feet. "We should get back."

The doctors hadn't returned but the nurse let the two of them into the intensive-care unit. They sat across the bed from each other, holding Jack's hands and chatting. Lynn watched her father's face for signs of any recognition or awareness and when she glanced at her mother she could see that she was doing the same.

When Mr Khan arrived back with Dr O'Keefe, he asked them to move away from the bed while they examined him once more. Then he turned and smiled at Nell. "I think it is time for Jack to wake up, Mrs Stephens. He has been stable all night and I am very pleased with him."

"I'm so glad," Nell said, smiling.

"How do you waken him," Lynn asked.

"We reduce the medication gradually and allow him to regain consciousness."

"How long will it take?" Nell asked.

"It could be as early as this evening. But remember" — Mr Khan's expression was grave — "he may be disoriented or not even know you."

"I don't care; he's alive, and that is enough," Nell assured him.

Lynn watched the two doctors exchange glances and felt a twinge of unease about what lay ahead. Khan went back over the sorts of problems her father might face but Lynn tuned out, her eyes trained on her father. She hoped he couldn't hear. She didn't want him to wake with the sense that he had a battle to fight or, worse, feeling that there was no point. That wasn't the man who had reared her but, then, if his mind was all scrambled, perhaps they would need to get to know a new man, a stranger. She could see huge frustrations ahead for all of them and wondered, would her mother be able to handle it? On the face of it Nell was very capable but, while Mum ruled the home, Dad had looked after everything else. Would she be able to cope if she had to make all the decisions from now on and look after her sick husband? Lynn sighed. What a time for her to be leaving Rathbourne.

There were more voices, different ones, women. He tried to make out what they were saying but it sounded like a different language. Where the hell was he now? He tried to open his eyes but couldn't and, feeling tired, he gave up. He let the voices wash over him. The sound was comforting and he felt himself relax. Then he became aware of a hand in his and he no longer felt frightened or lonely. He was safe.

210

"He squeezed my hand!" Nell exclaimed.

The nurse went around the other side of the bed, took out her torch and, lifting one eyelid, examined the pupil. "Are you coming back to us, Jack?" she asked in a loud cheerful voice. "I'm looking forward to meeting you. Nell and Lynn have been telling me all about you."

Nell smiled as Jack's fingers tightened around hers once more. "He did it again. So he's not paralysed."

Lynn arrived back from the loo. "What is it?" she said.

Nell beamed up at her. "He's waking, love."

Her father's eyelids fluttered open for a moment and her mother's face lit up with delight and relief. Lynn felt her own face almost split in two with her smile.

"I'll page the doctors," the nurse said, and left them.

"Has he said anything?"

Her mother shook her head. "Not a word yet, just some groans and grimaces."

Lynn sat down and took her father's hand. "Hey, how are you, Dad?" she said, with forced cheerfulness. "Come on, wake up. If you were looking for sympathy, you've got it, okay?" She heard a sound, muffled and incomprehensible, and she wondered, had she imagined it? She glanced across at her mother. "Did he say something?"

Her mother laughed, tears in her eyes. "I think he said, 'Stop nagging.'"

Dr O'Keefe pulled back the curtain and Lynn dragged her eyes from her father's face. "He's waking and he spoke and it made sense. And he squeezed Mum's hand so he's not paralysed; he's going to be okay."

They went out into the corridor while the doctor examined him. "He's going to be fine, Mum." Lynn hugged her mother in relief. It felt as if a great weight had been lifted off her shoulders. She had imagined so many different scenarios in her head, but his waking up just fine had not been one of them.

Nell was more cautious. "He could still have problems."

"I know that, but the one that scared me most was the thought that he might not know us or not be able to communicate and here he is, barely awake, and he's done both!"

"It's wonderful." Nell agreed.

They were left kicking their heels for a while longer before Dr O'Keefe emerged.

Nell looked at him, anxiously. "Well?"

"I can't tell how severely Jack's been affected until he's completely lucid. I don't know him so you'll have to tell me if you observe any change in his manner or personality. I asked him some basic things: who's the president, what year is it, family names, that sort of thing. He was able to answer but his speech is quite slurred and talking seems to be an effort. I think he knew what he wanted to say but was having trouble forming the words. Other than that, the only other obvious problem is paralysis in his left arm and leg."

"Is that temporary?" Lynn asked.

He shrugged. "Perhaps. It could improve over the next few days or over time with therapy."

"Or may not at all?" Nell said.

"He's alive, he's conscious and he knows us, Mum. That's pretty good going for now."

"Yes." Nell nodded. "Yes, of course it is."

"What happens now?" Lynn asked.

"In the morning we'll move him into a ward and continue to assess him and take it day by day." His pager went and he pulled it out and looked at it. "You'll have to excuse me."

It was all good news, Lynn told herself as she followed her mother back into ICU. It would have been incredible if he had come through unscathed and, in the scheme of things, he'd got off lightly.

CHAPTER
TWENTY-ONE

Jack grunted as Nell put the straw between his lips. He found it hard to concentrate and he seemed to be drifting in and out of sleep. One minute Lynn was beside him and the next she was gone and then it was Nell and then that loud nurse. Why did she have to yell like that? Did she think he was deaf? He'd told her he wasn't . . . hadn't he?

"Lynn and Frank are gone to check on the shop," Nell said.

He thought about that for a moment and then frowned. The shop? Had something happened? "The alarm?" he said, but it didn't come out like that. He tried again but his words sounded like gibberish. He'd write it down. He gestured to Nell for a pen. Thank God he was right-handed: he couldn't lift his left.

"A pen! Good idea, love." Nell rummaged in her bag and dug around till she found a biro, rummaged again and found an old shopping list and put the blank side up on the tray in front of him. "Let me help you sit up a bit. There."

The pen felt strange in his fingers. He felt as if he were back in school, learning how to form his letters.

214

Slowly and carefully he wrote "alarm?" and turned the page to her.

Nell screwed up her eyes as she tried to decipher the scrawl and he sighed in frustration, letting his head fall back on the pillow. Lord, he was tired.

"Alarm. Is that it?"

He opened his eyes and grunted his assent.

"No, love, the alarm didn't go off. Is that what you mean?"

He managed a nod.

"No, it's just that you know what Norman's like about locking up, so Lynn said she'd check to make sure that he'd done it properly."

Jack grunted again. Norman. A good man, loyal, and a hard if slow worker, but not the sharpest tool in the box. How many times had Nell begged him to get someone more capable to stand in for him from time to time but of course he hadn't listened. It suited him to have Norman and his nephew and niece do their jobs and leave him to do the thinking; he preferred it that way. He hadn't the time or patience to teach someone how he liked things done and it would take a lot before he would feel able to trust a stranger with his livelihood. How many people had he heard of through the years who had been fleeced by employees or accountants or the like?

"They'll be back soon. Mind you, I'm sure they'll be plagued by people wanting to know how you are. You caused a bit of a stir being carted off in an ambulance."

Jack could imagine. He'd given them all something to gossip about. Lynn would be pestered; she'd hate that. Why was she so nervous these days, he wondered? She never used to be like that.

"Frank's booking us into a hotel tonight. It's a pity the house hasn't changed hands: we could have stayed there."

"House?" He looked at her, feeling confused.

"Lynn and Frank's house," she said. "Remember, love, they're moving to Dublin."

He searched through the fog of his brain but could find nothing. Lynn and Frank lived on the other side of town and Lynn had a great job in Boland's fancy hotel. Why would she be moving to Dublin? He reached for the pen and slowly wrote "Why?" and turned the pad to her and watched her face.

She read it and then looked up at him in dismay. "You don't remember?"

He shook his head and picked up the pen again and wrote, "Lynn. Job???"

Nell stared at the pad and said nothing. He nudged her impatiently and said, "Come on," but it came out like something the Elephant Man would say. Still, he could see that she understood him.

She had started slowly, carefully, asking him did he not remember Lynn leaving Hawthorn Lodge — yes that was the name of the place — and probing his memory. He was taken-aback at the news. Lynn had been doing so well there; why would she leave? He couldn't remember the details, but he didn't have a good feeling about it. Nell was looking at him worriedly, but he nodded for her to continue.

216

"Jack? Are you okay?" She leaned over him when she'd finished and dabbed his eyes with a handkerchief. He patted her hand. "Tired."

"Sleep, love."

"Yes." He closed his eyes, an image of Lynn on her twenty-first birthday in his head. Ironically, it was in Hawthorn Lodge and she was leading a conga line, singing, laughing and pulling people up to dance. His poor little girl.

Val had been in the pub when the ambulance sailed past and everyone had stopped talking and looked at each other. In a town with fewer than two thousand inhabitants, the chances were strong that one of them knew the person in it. Val had immediately phoned her mother to check that she was okay.

Angie was less than impressed to have her Saturday poker game interrupted. "Some old wrinkly has snuffed it, don't worry about it."

Val had to laugh. Everyone over sixty-five that Angie considered boring or grumpy was a wrinkly. She wasn't, of course, as she didn't fall into either category and, in fairness, she was seventy-two going on forty. Val hoped she'd inherited her mother's spirit.

It didn't take long for the word to filter round the pub that Jack Stephens had been the reason for the siren and the loud, raucous chat was replaced with hushed, speculative gossip.

Val was beside herself with worry.

"Will you relax," John said. "You've left her three text messages. What more can you do?"

Nothing, Valerie thought miserably, but she was disappointed by his detached response. He'd met Lynn, after all, and his lack of concern seemed hard. There were a few little things lately that bothered her about John, but there was one in particular: he seemed careful, a little too careful, with his money. Val's salary was modest and she had always been hopeless at making it last, but why have money if not to spend it? John was the opposite. He brought sandwiches to school every day and had only moved to Rathbourne so that he could sell his car and walk everywhere. As for his wardrobe, well, at times, it was embarrassing. Val had been most conscious of his thriftiness last night when they had gone to Lynn's. He had brought nothing, not even a bottle of the €5 wine he'd discovered in Lidl and declared to be just as good as the expensive brands she sold in the off-licence. On top of that, next to Frank, handsome in Jasper Conran jeans and a blue linen shirt, he looked as if he'd just tumbled out of bed in his ancient, threadbare jeans and faded, grubby sweatshirt.

"Want another one?" John nodded at her empty water glass. She shook her head. "I should get back to work. Are you going home?"

"No, I'll finish this and maybe watch the football," he said, swilling the last of his Guinness round the bottom of his glass.

"Okay. See you later." Val leaned over to kiss him but as he continued to watch the screen she had to make do with his cheek.

As she wandered back to work she told herself off. This was what she always did: found a nice guy and then started to look for faults. "As if *you're* so perfect," she muttered to herself, and promised herself not to be so critical. John was a lovely guy and he seemed to really care about her. She still couldn't believe that he wanted them to move in together or, rather, that he was going to move in with her.

"Your place is bigger and brighter," he'd pointed out, and she'd happily agreed.

"You're a lucky girl," she said as she pushed open the door of the off-licence and went behind the counter.

"What was that?" Lorcan looked up and smiled.

"Nothing."

Technically, Lorcan O'Brien was her boss but he never threw his weight around and they made a good team. She'd been working for him for nearly two years now and they were comfortable together. Rhona, the other staff member, was a total pain. She was Therese Boland's daughter, Charles's eldest grandchild, and she clearly saw working here as beneath her and something that simply interfered with her social life. Tolerating her high-handed attitude brought Val and Lorcan even closer and they had a few laughs at the girl's expense.

"Were we that annoying when we were teenagers?" she'd asked Lorcan.

"No, but then we didn't have everything handed to us on a plate."

Lorcan was still single, though Val could never really fathom why. He was twenty-six, quite attractive in a low-key sort of way. He was funny, too, and when they were on duty together they had a lot of laughs, but also he was just a damn nice guy. Yet, in all the time she'd known him, he'd never dated a girl for more than a few weeks.

"Did you hear the news?" she asked him as she started setting up a display of French wines in the window.

"About Jack Stephens, yeah, isn't it terrible? Have you talked to Lynn?"

Val shook her head. "She's not answering her calls."

"I'm sure she'll be in touch when she gets a chance."

"Yes, that's what John said." She climbed up on the step and reached in for the bottles at the back of the shelf but they were still just out of her reach.

"Here, let me do that, you'll break your neck." Lorcan hurried over and leaned past her to get the wine.

On the step, Val was almost on a level with him and she breathed in appreciatively the scent of his cologne. "Nice aftershave. Do you have a new woman?" He blushed and she giggled in delight. "You do, don't you?"

"If you must know, my dear sister bought me that for Christmas. I told her it's wasted on me." He frowned. "Perhaps she's trying to tell me something."

Val stepped down and took the wine from him. "Don't worry, Boss. One of these days Miss Right will walk through those doors though she'll have to leave her guide dog outside."

"Funny." He glowered at her and went back behind the counter.

Val watched him from under her lashes. She wasn't imagining it. Lorcan was definitely making more of an effort with his appearance lately. He'd got his hair cut and the tight crop made him look younger, as did the black skinny jeans. She couldn't help thinking of John's shapeless, unfashionable pair. Perhaps she should suggest they go shopping together. You didn't have to spend big money these days to look stylish. "They're nice jeans. Where did you buy them?"

Lorcan looked up, suspicious. "Go on, what's wrong with them?"

"Nothing, honest, they're great. It's just, er, John was saying he wanted to get some new gear," she fibbed.

"Topman," he told her, before going back to the accounts.

"Great, thanks, I'll tell him." She finished her display and stepped back to admire it. "There! We should open a couple of bottles and have a tasting. You could nip into the supermarket and get some cheese to go with it while you're on your break."

Lorcan didn't raise his head. "I'm not taking one. The boss is coming in first thing to go through the books and I don't want to give him anything to complain about."

"As if you ever do. You're the golden-haired boy." Val laughed, but it was true: Lorcan was a conscientious worker. He ran the off-licence as if it were his own business, with care and precision. Though Charles Boland was not the effusive type, it was clear that he liked and valued Lorcan.

221

Lorcan didn't even reply now, his concentration completely on his work. "Will I go and get some cheese, then?"

He glanced up and smiled. "Yeah, go on. You might find out more about Jack."

Which of course was what she was hoping. "Thanks, Lorcan. I'll bring you back a sandwich and coffee."

"Cheers."

She hurried down the road and wasn't surprised to see quite a few people in the shop, a flustered Norman in their midst. The good and bad side of living in a town like this was that you were never left alone with your problems. She grabbed the bacon roll for Lorcan and hurried to the till, where Norman was serving. It was pointless asking Cathy what was going on. She probably hadn't even noticed Jack was missing. "How is he?" she asked as soon as it was her turn. "I've been trying to get hold of Lynn but her phone's switched off."

"I haven't heard yet," the man said, looking weary and tense.

"Was he" — she struggled for a diplomatic word — "awake when they took him away?"

"He was drifting in and out of consciousness."

"That's good, then, isn't it?" She searched his face.

"I've no idea, love." He nodded at the queue forming behind her. "I'd better get on."

"The shop seems so strange without him and Norman looks completely lost." As she chopped up cheese and

222

stuck it on cocktail sticks, Val told Lorcan the tiny bit of information she'd gleaned.

"It's good that he was conscious," he said before biting into his roll.

"Yes, I thought that." Lynn took tiny plastic glasses out of a box and lined them up on the barrel in the centre of the shop.

"I wonder, will he sell up? God, it's hard to imagine anyone else running the supermarket."

Val stopped and looked at him. "It won't come to that."

He shrugged. "If Jack's had another stroke and it's more serious, what choices are left to him? When is Lynn off to Dublin?"

"In a couple of weeks I think," she said as it dawned on her exactly the way his mind was working. If Jack was laid up for a long time and the business was to remain in the family, someone was going to have to take his place and only one person came to mind. Lynn. Val couldn't begin to imagine how horrified Lynn would be at the thought of working in the shop. It could set her recovery right back.

"She couldn't handle it, could she?" Lorcan said, as usual reading her like a book.

She shook her head. "I don't think so."

"Poor girl. Still, at least Vincent Boland isn't around any more. Anyway, I'm sure Jack will be fine." He gave her a reassuring smile. "He's a strong man."

"He is," Val agreed, and prayed, for many reasons, that Jack Stephens would have a speedy recovery.

CHAPTER
TWENTY-TWO

It took all of Vincent's self-control not to smile triumphantly as he strode back into Hawthorn Lodge. The icing on the cake was that Charles was standing in reception waiting for him and came forward to shake his hand.

"Good to see you," he said, and, putting his hand on his nephew's shoulder, guided him into the busy dining room.

Vincent nodded formally at the faces he knew, enjoying the looks of surprise and the lull in conversation.

"You'll have a glass of wine."

It wasn't a question but yet another sign that he was officially back in the fold. Charles ordered a bottle of Cabernet Sauvignon, not the house wine, Vincent noted, and two fillet steaks with all the trimmings. "You heard about Jack Stephens," he said when they were alone.

Of course he had. The town was buzzing with the news that he had collapsed and been rushed to hospital. "I did. Is it serious, do you know?"

"I haven't heard." Charles frowned. "He's a good man."

"He is." Vincent felt a flicker of impatience. He hadn't come here to talk about bloody Stephens but he knew better than to move his uncle on before he was good and ready. Charles seemed lost in thought for a moment, but then he leaned forward, took off his glasses and reached for his wine. "You have some ideas for me?"

Vincent needed no further encouragement and started to outline his plans. Some of his facts were closer to fiction, but he was confident, given the family's contacts and influence in the region, that they would stand up. The Willows was a dive, anyway, and deeply in debt; things couldn't really get worse and he felt, with this strategy, there was a strong chance they would get better.

"A conference centre," Charles mused when he had finished, pushing his plate aside and wiping his mouth with the napkin.

"Not just a conference centre. It would be more like a club. A place to entertain clients with rooms available for interviews and free Internet throughout, the works."

"And all the function rooms would be available free?" Charles frowned.

"Yes. Let's face it, Charles, it's the only way to get business these days and it would make it the most attractive venue within a thirty-mile radius. The money would be made, as always, on food and beverages. We could offer special residential packages and organize bus tours or golf outings for partners. We could even set up a small spa. All that's needed is a hot tub, a sauna, soft music, good towels and some attractive young girls." He smiled.

Charles's lips barely twitched but Vincent knew that he was pleased. As their plates were cleared away, he handed his uncle a slim file. "The costs and projections are all there."

Charles opened it and ran his eye quickly over the figures. "These look a little optimistic, but there is merit in your idea." He closed the file and put it down on the table. "I'll take a closer look at it later."

"Great." Vincent took a sip of his wine, absolutely convinced now that Charles was impressed. He was longing to raise the subject of his return to Rathbourne but he knew that it was better to let his uncle do so. He could be patient. Charles couldn't hold out for that long. He was under pressure given he was going into hospital. Vincent was confident that once again he was holding all the aces. "How are you feeling?" he asked, his voice suitably low and concerned.

"Fine." Charles's tone was dismissive and he glanced at his watch. "I must get on."

Vincent sprang to his feet. "Of course. Thank you for lunch, Uncle, I appreciate your time and if you have any questions on my proposal, just pick up the phone."

They walked out into the reception area and Charles hesitated.

"Therese is organizing a family lunch at my place next Sunday if you and Orla want to join us."

"Sounds great."

"Excellent. Well, I'll see you then." Charles clapped him on the back. "Good work, Vincent."

"Thank you." Vincent smiled, delighted at the gracious and very public farewell. "Have a good day, Charles."

"He's like putty in my hand," he told Orla later that evening, euphoric at the way the meeting had gone. He poured himself a large glass of wine. "I'll be back behind my old desk before you know it. A small drop?" He held up the bottle of wine.

"No, I won't." She shifted around on the sofa, adjusting the cushions to try to get comfortable. She smiled up at him. "I'm so glad, Vincent. I know it means a lot to you and I'll feel happier knowing you're nearby. But . . ."

He saw the shadow cross her face. "What?"

She pulled nervously on the tassels of the cushion. "I just wondered if Lynn's dad being sick would change things."

"Why on earth would it?" he said impatiently, taking a long drink from his glass.

She stared at him. "If it's serious, and everyone's saying it is, Lynn won't leave."

Vincent had a flashback of the troubled look on Charles's face when he'd commented on Jack's health. Oh, shit, this girl could not screw up his life again. But Orla was right: if Jack couldn't return to work, who else would run the supermarket? Nell Stephens had only ever helped out at the till and Norman was a simpleton. The only person Jack would trust to run his business was his daughter.

★ ★ ★

Lynn lay awake in Frank's arms, staring into the darkness and willing herself to stay calm. When she had sat down to dinner earlier that evening in the hotel with her mother and Frank she had thought the worst was over. She had been wrong.

While they ate, Nell brought them up to date on Dad's condition and the last chat she'd had with Dr O'Keefe. Nell looked up and saw her expression. "He's going to be fine, love, I'm sure of it. He just needs physiotherapy and our support."

Lynn pulled herself together and nodded. If her mother could be optimistic, then so could she. "When we move I'll be able to drop in and out to see him all the time," she said, and took a bite of her chicken Kiev.

"I think you can help in a more constructive way," Frank said.

She looked up and intercepted the grateful look her mother gave him. "Of course. I'll do anything I can to help."

Frank was looking at her, his eyes apologetic.

Nell's face broke into a wide smile. "I knew we could rely on you."

"What is it?" she asked.

"You'll have to look after the supermarket until he's able to return to work," Frank said.

Lynn stared at him, stunned. "I couldn't."

"You have to," Nell insisted.

Lynn had dragged her eyes from Frank's and looked at her mother. "I can't, Mum, please don't ask me," she'd begged.

"The only other option is to close and that would break your father's heart."

Lynn lifted Frank's arm and moved away, turning her back on him, feeling betrayed. She wondered when he and Nell had planned their ambush. And, though she understood their logic, she still felt press-ganged. She had sat in silence while Nell had said how well Dad was doing and she was sure that he'd be back on his feet in no time. Lynn felt sickened by the lie. Who were they trying to kid, her or themselves? Dad's left arm and leg were still practically useless. Even if he made a miraculous recovery it would be a long time before he could return to work.

"What about the house?" she'd asked Frank when finally their forced cheerful patter had dried up.

"Nothing changes, darling, other than we won't be able to move into it properly for a while."

Nothing changes. At least, she thought now, when Frank said those words he'd had the grace to look away. He knew as well as she did that it was a lie. She shuffled further from him to the edge of the hotel bed, chilled by the coldness of the stiff cotton sheets. Had they talked to Dad? she wondered. No. She dismissed the idea. He wouldn't ask her to do this. He had always been adamant that she should follow her own path and he had supported her move to Dublin. She felt a flicker of hope. Perhaps when he heard the proposition he would veto it. In fact, given the scare he'd just had, maybe he would want to close the shop, sell up, retire and finally take it easy. She clung to the hope as she huddled, shivering, under the covers. She longed to roll into Frank's warmth and feel the length of his body pressed against hers, but she couldn't get the feeling out of her head that he had let her down. He was so close to her physically but, mentally, he'd never seemed further away.

Lynn had a fitful night with unsettling, frightening dreams that for once didn't involve Vincent Boland. Frank was gone when she woke and there was a note on the pillow beside her. He had taken her mother to the hospital and ordered breakfast in bed for Lynn. Rather than feeling grateful, yet again, she felt outmanoeuvred. They were going to talk to Dad before she did. She picked up her phone and dialled Val. She had replied to her texts but so far hadn't had a chance to call her friend. How she wished she could jump in the car and go and see her; she could do with an objective opinion.

"Hello?"

"Hi, it's me."

"Lynn!"

She couldn't help but smile at the delight in Val's voice.

"How are things? How's your dad?"

"He's doing okay. Sorry I haven't been able to call but I've spent most of my time in the hospital. I wish we could meet, Val, I could do with your advice."

"When have you ever taken my advice?" Val retorted, but, when Lynn didn't laugh, her tone changed completely. "What is it, pet, what's wrong?"

230

And Lynn explained the situation. "In the cold light of day I understand, Val, but I wish they had let me come round to the idea myself. I feel as if they've ganged up on me." She sighed. This was her mother and her fiancé she was talking about. "I'm being ridiculous."

"Of course you're not. Finally it seemed like your life was back on course and now the rug's been pulled from under you. On top of that, you're worried sick about your dad. That's not at all ridiculous, Lynn."

Lynn drank in her words, grateful for the support. "But there's no alternative, is there?" she asked.

Val sighed. "There's always an alternative, you just have to figure out what it is."

Those words rang in Lynn's ears as Frank drove her to the hospital. She hadn't thought of any solutions to the problem, but Val had made her feel that she hadn't completely lost control.

"Are you okay?" he asked. She had barely talked to him since he'd returned to collect her.

She looked down at Frank's hand on her thigh. She hadn't forgiven him yet, although she knew that she would. But why hadn't he talked to her instead of joining forces with her mother and delivering a *fait accompli?*

"Lynn, I'm sorry. I know this isn't easy for you, but what choice have you?"

"None. Your taking my mother's side made sure of that."

"Taking sides? Oh, that's just rubbish," he protested. "We're not schoolchildren."

She remained silent. She could never win an argument with Frank: he was a professional. Anyway, she didn't have the strength to argue and, though she was upset with him, she couldn't bear a confrontation.

"You know that you won't be alone, Lynn. Your mum and Norman will help. I will too in any way that I can. You can see already from your dad's progress that he will be breathing down your neck in no time and telling you everything that you're doing wrong."

That raised a smile and she covered his hand with hers, but his words didn't comfort her. She still had to stand in that shop, deal with the stares, whispers and, no doubt, some questions. There were several members of the Rathbourne community who wouldn't think twice about asking her outright why she'd left Hawthorn Lodge and how much she'd gotten in the settlement. But, she also knew that after a few days the fuss would settle down. Once she got through that first week, it would get easier.

"I know it's a lot for you to take on but the fear is worse than the reality. Once you've confronted this you'll have conquered it, honestly." Frank glanced over and smiled at her, stroking her thigh. "And if I'm wrong you can come home and beat me up."

"But you won't be there," she complained. "You'll be in Dublin and I'll be coming back to an empty house."

"Of course I won't move in without you." He looked at her, startled. "I wouldn't leave you to go through this

232

alone. I'll come home every night no matter how late it is."

"Promise?" she said.

He lifted her hand to his lips and kissed it. "Promise."

Feeling happier about the situation, Lynn shuffled over in the seat and rested her head on his shoulder. "Thank you."

CHAPTER
TWENTY-THREE

Val bit the bullet. Her mother had been complaining for weeks that she still hadn't met John. She always went to Angie for Sunday lunch and so she finally capitulated and agreed to bring her boyfriend along.

"I'll polish the silver," her mother teased. "I hope he's not a fussy eater."

"He isn't." Thankfully John ate anything put in front of him. "Mum, be nice to him," Val begged.

"I'm nice to everyone! See you at one."

She wasn't sure why she felt so nervous but Val's mood wasn't helped by the sight of John arriving at her door in the same jeans and T-shirt he'd been wearing the night before. Her dismay must have been obvious.

"What?" John looked down at himself.

"Nothing, it's just that Mum is a bit old-fashioned. She likes men to wear a collar and jacket to lunch."

He looked incredulous. "But it'll be just the three of us, won't it?"

"Yes."

"If I'm invited to dinner do I have to wear black tie?"

"Only on New Year's Eve." She grinned.

234

He stood looking at her for a moment. "You really want me to change?" When she said nothing he gave a sigh of exasperation and turned to go back downstairs.

From the moment they arrived, Val knew it was going to be a disaster. Her mother threw open the door and welcomed John, lulling him into a false sense of security by offering him a drink.

She poured white wine for them all and returned the bottle to the fridge. "Please, help yourself when you need a refill, John. We don't stand on ceremony, do we, Val?"

Not much! Val thought after a while, as she watched Angie's eyes narrow when John went to the fridge and did just that — twice. Val could almost see Angie mentally notching up a black mark against him. It was odd: John wasn't really a drinker but Val had noticed that he'd been the same at Lynn's. She did wonder if it had anything to do with the fact that it was free, but quickly pushed the thought to the back of her mind.

"How are you coping without the crutches, Mum?" Val asked.

"Just fine, although I think I'll give this year's marathon a miss." Angie smiled.

"You run in marathons, Mrs McCabe?"

"It was a joke, John," Val said.

As they ate the fresh salmon, baby potatoes and spinach, her mother asked John about his job. She was a firm supporter and great admirer of the teaching profession. "It's a vocation," she always declared. As John waxed lyrical about how bored he was, that he was as much a childminder as a teacher and that his talents were completely underused, Val's heart sank further and further. Angie listened politely but her expression grew stonier with every word he uttered.

"I've always thought that teaching was probably the most important job of all, grooming the future generation who will run our country," she said with a cold smile when he finally stopped to draw breath.

John snorted. "The lot I teach are more likely to be the ones to bleed the country dry."

Angie had positively recoiled at that. Poor John! He really had an incredible knack of saying the wrong thing; he was his own worst enemy. He sounded as if he despised teaching and even hated kids, whereas Val knew that was not the case. He was just a frustrated writer. If he was published — when he was published, she quickly corrected herself — he would be more content and relaxed, she was sure.

John had shown Val his book but she wasn't much of a reader and felt she probably wasn't clever enough to understand or appreciate it; she only liked books that made her laugh or cry and preferably both. But Lynn was an avid reader and Val was sure that she would understand and love John's writing. Yet she held back from suggesting John give her the book in case Lynn was critical — John was incredibly sensitive. Val figured that was why he hated teaching: no matter how hard he worked he seemed to get a very hard time from the parents.

"I will be of more value to society as an author," he summed up now, driving the final nail into the coffin.

Val avoided her mother's eyes; she could imagine the phone call that would follow later.

Angie seemed to be lost for words. Finally, with a baffled smile she stood up and started to clear away the dishes. "Time for dessert!"

"That went well," John said as they walked to the bus stop.

Val glanced at him, looking for a trace of irony, but he was smiling. The three glasses of wine must have dulled his senses. "Yes," she agreed, grateful that he was oblivious to the strained atmosphere.

He put an arm around her shoulders. "I told you it would be fine. I've always been able to charm older women."

Val was irritated by the condescension and smugness in his voice. "Don't be fooled. Mum was on her best behaviour because you've just met."

"You worry too much," he said, taking off his jacket and slinging it over his shoulder. "She loved me."

By the time they got home, John's good mood had started to fade as he grumbled about the pile of homework he had to mark. He refused her offer of coffee and Val went up to her flat, feeling both disappointed and relieved. John hadn't shown much interest in sex lately and she was feeling slightly neglected, but the last few hours had been quite stressful and it would be nice to get into pyjamas, paint her toenails, eat crisps and watch a girly movie, something she could never do with John.

He didn't see the point in watching a film unless you could learn something from it. There had been nights when he'd want to stay up till all hours discussing one when Val would have been happier with a cuddle and a cocoa. When John got all deep and intellectual she felt very thick, and there had been times when she'd had to sneak a look in the dictionary so she could figure out what he was on about. But she loved that he was so clever and flattered that he wanted to be with her. Sex may not be on the menu as often but he seemed as eager for them to live together as ever.

She'd been in the flat only a few minutes when the phone rang. Surprise, surprise! It was Angie. She took a deep breath before answering. "Hey, Mum, thanks for a great lunch, we really enjoyed it."

There was a moment's silence before her mother spoke. "Are you alone?"

Val considered lying but she would just be postponing the inevitable. "Yes, John has a lot of prep to do for school tomorrow; he works incredibly hard."

Her mother snorted. "Sounds like it."

Val pretended she didn't hear her mother's tone. "Isn't he lovely, Mum? You know, I like him a lot." She willed her mother to go along with her.

"Yes, darling, but do you really think he's your type?"

"What do you mean?" Val braced herself.

"He's a bit, well, stuffy, isn't he? You need a man who will make you laugh and take you dancing. I don't know why you don't flutter your eyelashes at that lovely lad you work with. He'd be perfect for you."

"Don't be silly, Mum, I could never think of Lorcan in that way."

"You must be mad, then, and I'd swear he's sweet on you."

"Mum!"

"I'm sure John is a nice man. I just don't think you have anything in common. And, no offence, but he seems more obsessed with that book of his than with you."

That's right, Mum, don't hold back, Val thought. "He loves writing, that's not a crime."

"He certainly loves it more than he does teaching," Angie agreed. "I honestly don't understand why he went for that job. He obviously has no time for children."

Ah, there it was, her Achilles' heel. Val adored children, always had, and couldn't wait to be a mother, and Angie knew it. "They're not his kids, Mum, they're his students."

"You have to love children to be a teacher, I don't care what you say," her mother retorted.

"I'm sorry if you don't approve, Mum, but you'll have to get used to him being around: we're moving in together."

"Once you're happy, sweetheart, so am I."

"Did you hear what I said?" Val asked, unable to believe her ears.

"I heard. I think it's a great idea. Much better to live with someone rather than rush into marriage and regret it afterwards. As they say, 'If you want to know me

come and live with me.' Did you think I'd be shocked?"
Angie laughed.

Val smiled. "I suppose so. Honestly, he is really nice.
Give him a chance."

"Of course I will, darling."

"Thanks, Mum. You're the best."

Jack hadn't believed a word of it. No matter how much
Lynn loved him she would never have volunteered to
look after the supermarket. He'd seen the transforma-
tion that came over her when she was in there. It always
made him long to punch Vincent Boland. No, this was
all Nell's doing. He could almost see her confront their
daughter, that steely look in her eye, and Lynn
wouldn't be able to refuse her. His immediate reaction
had been to close down, to retire. That would make
Nell happy. Yet he couldn't imagine life without the
business he'd started nearly forty years ago. And then
the more he thought about it the more he wondered if
in fact it would be good for Lynn. Perhaps she needed
to confront her demons. Maybe it was the only way she
would be truly free of them. And it wouldn't be for
long: he was getting better every day. So Jack had
pretended not to notice his daughter's strained smile
when he thanked her and convinced himself that the
panic he saw in her eyes was only temporary.

Rescuing Lynn became his goal and spurred him on.
He did the exercises the physio gave him, religiously,
and when Nell visited he pushed her to challenge his
memory, to test him. He still couldn't talk properly, but
his wife was able to understand him most of the time

and there was less need to resort to pen and paper. And, when the nurse took him for a walk up and down a flight of stairs, he'd insist on doing it twice more. It was frustrating and tiring dragging his left leg up each step and he wondered if it would ever improve. His arm wasn't quite as bad, although, being right-handed, perhaps he just didn't notice it as much. He was hungry for information about the business and how Lynn was getting on, but Nell said he had to concentrate on getting better and forget about work, and Frank's visits always seemed to coincide with someone else being around — whether through accident or intention he wasn't sure. Finally, he demanded that Lynn herself come and see him on Sunday evening after early closing, or, he warned Nell, he'd discharge himself. In all honesty he doubted he'd have the strength to make it to the car park but she didn't know that.

Lynn glanced at the clock. Six a.m. on day four — it felt more like *month* four. She had thrown up twice the first morning but it was getting easier. She no longer jumped every time the cash register closed or froze when a customer walked in, but there were still moments. One of them had occurred when a waitress from Hawthorn Lodge had walked in.

Trina and Lynn had never had much to say to each other. Lynn had told her off once over something — she couldn't even remember now what it was — and Trina hadn't taken it well. Lynn went down to the fridges and busied herself rearranging the milk in date order and leaving Norman to deal with her, but of course it was milk that Trina had come in for. Lynn cursed her own stupidity. She should have headed for the dishwasher products; she figured there was little chance of finding Trina there.

"Lynn, great to see you!"

The girl gushed, insincerity oozing from every pore of her orange body, and Lynn realized that's what she'd given out to her for: fake tan coming off on the white tablecloths and napkins. "Hi, Trina." She gave her a brief smile and turned to leave.

"Congratulations! You really landed on your feet, didn't you?"

Lynn stopped. "I'm sorry?"

"Taking old man Boland to the cleaners and now running Daddy's business. Clever!"

In the old days Lynn would have cut her down to size and sent her packing in seconds, her tail between her legs, but right now she couldn't find her voice.

"And yet you're stacking shelves." Trina grinned. "Out of the frying pan, eh?"

"Excuse me," Lynn mumbled and almost ran into the office. She'd flopped into her dad's battered old chair shaking. If Trina could reduce her to this, what would it be like if a Boland came in? What would it be like if she came face to face with Him?

She glanced again now at the clock. She really should get up. Frank stirred and she turned and kissed his shoulder. With a groan of pleasure he reached for her and ran his hand lightly over her breasts, across her

242

navel and down between her thighs; she shivered with pleasure.

He kissed her and went to climb out of bed.

She grabbed his wrist and he looked down at her. "I need something to get me through the day," she whispered.

"You do?" He grinned.

"I do."

"I think I may be able to help," he said and rolled her onto her back.

Lynn arrived at the supermarket still glowing from Frank's lovemaking. Her mother had already switched off the alarm, turned on the lights and taken in the newspapers. She smiled up at her. "Morning, love."

Lynn kissed her cheek. "Morning." She could hear a tremor in her own voice that hadn't been there an hour ago. It was the same every day once she left the safety of her house. "How was Dad last night?"

"Very good. I can see him getting stronger with every day and the doctor says he might be able to come home in a few days."

"Really?" Lynn's heart lifted.

"Yes, they said that he could easily continue his physio as an outpatient or the GP could arrange for someone to come to the house."

"That's wonderful news."

"It is," Nell agreed. "I won't miss that hospital or trekking up and down and I know he'd be happier at home."

Lynn looked at the circles under her mother's eyes and felt guilty. She'd been so busy feeling sorry for herself she hadn't noticed that the situation was taking its toll on her mother too. "You should go back to bed for a few hours. You're going to have your hands full once he gets home."

"Don't I know it! I'll have a tough enough time just keeping him from going over to the shop. He's going mad to know how you're coping without him. He asked if you'd go in and see him after you close on Sunday evening."

"Oh, okay." Lynn nodded slowly.

"Now, you mustn't worry him, love. I know that it hasn't been an easy week, but try to hide your feelings from him."

"Of course I will." Assuring her dad that everything was just hunky-dory would require a serious amount of acting, but if she didn't go he would be even more anxious.

Nell put her arms around her and gave her a tight hug. "I know how hard it was for you to do this and I appreciate it; so does your dad. I think if we'd had to close the shop he might have given up."

Lynn started to open the packs of newspapers and set them out on the stands by the door. "Have they given you any idea when he'll be fit enough to return to work?"

"No. They keep up that it's different for everyone. I'll make you a cuppa before you open."

Lynn glanced at her watch, it was after eight and they opened at half past. "Norman's late today."

244

"Oh, I forgot." Nell turned round. "Norman doesn't come in till twelve on Fridays because he stays late."

Lynn felt the panic bubble up inside her and her mother obviously saw it.

"Don't worry, love. Cathy should be in any minute," she said quickly.

That wasn't much comfort. Lynn would never understand why her dad tolerated the girl; she was a complete waste of space. She saw her mother was hovering and looking anxious, and she summoned a smile. "I'll be fine."

And, remarkably, she was. Most of the regular customers had already been in earlier in the week and had got used to her and accepted her presence. She ignored the few curious glances she received, and, before she knew it, Norman was walking through the door. She glanced in surprise at her watch.

"Everything okay?" he asked.

She smiled. "Everything's fine,"

"Good. That's good," he beamed.

By the time Val dropped in, Lynn was feeling almost comfortable. "Hey!"

"Hiya, Lynn. It's a lovely day. I thought we could have lunch down by the river."

"Great idea!" Lynn still wasn't comfortable going near the pub and so her lunch breaks were spent in either her mother's kitchen or her dad's office. "Give me a sec — I'll grab a sandwich and let Norman know."

"How are things?" Val asked once they were out in the safety of the street.

"Hanging in there. Some days are more difficult than others," Lynn admitted. "Today's been good."

Lynn glanced at her friend as they walked along the luscious banks, towards the most scenic but secluded spot — one that had been their haunt since childhood. Val seemed very subdued. Lynn wondered whether John was the reason. "Is everything okay?" she asked as they sat down on the grass and kicked off their shoes. It was only the beginning of April but felt more like June. Lynn stretched out, enjoying the feel of the springy grass beneath her and the sound of the water babbling past, and began to unwrap her lunch.

"I'm afraid I'm the bearer of bad news."

Lynn turned to look at Val's mournful expression. "Go on."

Val pushed her sunglasses up on top of her head. "Word is that Vincent will be back in Hawthorn Lodge in a week or so."

Lynn paused, her sandwich halfway to her mouth. "You're not serious."

"Would I joke about something like this?"

"I don't understand." Lynn swallowed. Her good humour dissipated and she started to tremble.

"I know. I don't understand it either, but apparently he and Charles are pals again. It doesn't matter, Lynn. Don't let it worry you. At the rate your dad's recovering you'll be up in Dublin in no time."

Lynn couldn't answer. She couldn't process what Val was saying, couldn't rationalise her fear. All she kept imagining was coming face to face with Vincent. She'd only just got used to being in the centre of town again.

246

Was only beginning to come to terms with being around other people. What would she do if he came into the shop? She felt trapped and, just as in her nightmares, she longed to run.

Val took her two hands and stared into her eyes. "You're safer than ever before. Vincent is going to cross the road to avoid you. He won't do anything to jeopardise his future, he's too clever for that."

That got through. "Yes." Lynn nodded. Vincent was much cleverer than people realized.

Val hugged her. "I wish there was something I could do to make things easier."

Lynn held on tight. "So do I."

CHAPTER
TWENTY-FOUR

Vincent was in excellent form; lunch with the family had been a huge success. His cousins hadn't been thrilled to see him, but Charles had made it clear that he was welcome and, as always, everyone bowed to what Charles wanted. He had made a point of sitting next to Emer and had taken the opportunity to talk through some aspects of his proposal for The Willows. She had been surprised and suspicious at first but, when he invited her advice on some of his other ideas and listened attentively to her answers, she'd relaxed. By the time coffee was served, she had thawed completely and his mother, who was sitting opposite her brother-in-law, was gazing at him with warm approval.

"You're very quiet," he said to Orla as she drove them home.

"I'm tired."

He patted her thigh. The sooner the baby was born the better and they could get back to normal. His successful afternoon had left him feeling quite randy, but he knew from the look of Orla he'd get nowhere with her this evening. Perhaps he'd find release elsewhere. He brightened at the thought. "You have an early night, darling. I might slip up to Hawthorn Lodge."

Orla shot him a worried glance. "Do you think that's wise? You've had a lot to drink."

"I'm absolutely fine," Vincent said, irritated. Yes, he'd had a few glasses of wine and then an excellent cognac, but he had also eaten well; he was grand. He saw her into the house and collected his briefcase. He checked the tiny pocket inside and smiled when he saw that he had still had two condoms. Some girl was going to get lucky tonight.

When Vincent walked into the hotel, Alenka was on reception. His pulse quickened. One thing he had to be grateful to Lynn Stephens for was hiring this gorgeous creature. With her smooth sallow skin, heart-shaped face, mesmerizing hazel eyes and full sexy mouth she would tempt any man. She had a slightly haughty manner, which excited him more, and her pert breasts strained against the jacket of her slim-fitting grey suit making him long to rip it off.

"Good evening, Mr Boland," she said formally.

His excitement intensified. He struggled to remain businesslike. "Good evening, Alenka. Is everything okay?"

"Yes. There are no problems."

He looked past her at the floor-to-ceiling shelving, his eyes quickly scanning the top shelf. "I was looking for the registration book for about this time last year. Any idea where it would be?"

"I think so." She turned to the shelving and then bent to pull the small steps from under the desk.

Vincent dug his hands in his pockets as he was treated to an eyeful of bare thigh. He watched, holding his breath as she climbed the steps, and took a quick look around before moving closer and putting his hands on her waist. "Steady, we don't want you having an accident." He felt her stiffen at his touch. "You'll need to go up another step. It's okay, I've got you."

As she climbed onto the top step and then stretched to reach the book, he was rewarded with a glimpse of wispy white pants and he had to muffle a groan.

She handed him the book and climbed down. "Is there anything else I can do for you, Mr Boland?"

Oh, God, yes, he thought, there is plenty that you can do for me. "No, thank you, Alenka. You know you've been doing an excellent job. My uncle and I are very happy with you. Perhaps it's time you had a little more responsibility."

Her face lit up. "I would welcome a challenge, Mr Boland, and work hard."

"I'm sure you would. What time does your shift end?"

"Yvonne relieves me in thirty minutes."

"Excellent, come and see me then. I'll be in my uncle's office." Her smile faltered. "Is there a problem, Alenka?"

She lowered her eyes. "No, Mr Boland."

"Good."

Vincent strode back into town with one condom fewer and was feeling pleasantly sated. As usual, she'd pretended she didn't want to do it, but he liked a little

250

resistance, and the feel of those nails on his back drove him wild. She knew how to play the game and how to be discreet and she was also desperate to earn more money. He was confident that, while Orla recovered from the birth of their child, he would have someone to look after his needs.

He was so lost in thought that he took the direct route home past the supermarket rather than the slightly longer one that circumvented the main street that he had been using since the settlement. No harm, though, the road was deserted except for some teenagers hanging around outside the video shop. He was almost past Stephens's when he heard a cry. He turned around to see Lynn frozen in the doorway staring at him, her eyes wide in shock and a bunch of keys on the ground at her feet. He should have kept walking but his blood was still pumping after his successful lunch and romp with Alenka and he couldn't resist going over. As he approached, he watched her shocked look change to one of fear; this was proving to be a really great day. He came to a halt barely inches from her; he'd forgotten how gorgeous her eyes were. She had her hair pinned back and he itched to touch the soft, white skin of her neck. "Hello, Lynn. Have you missed me?" He smiled, close enough now to smell her scent and see the rapid rise and fall of her chest. How he'd love to drag her down an alley way and make use of that last condom.

"Leave me alone," she whispered, shrinking back against the door.

He crouched down to pick up her keys. "Now, that's no way to talk to an old friend who's come to your aid." He dangled the keys under her nose but, when she reached out a trembling hand to take them, he held them just out of reach. "Hey, what's the rush? Don't you want to catch up?"

"I don't want you anywhere near me," she spat at him, her eyes flashing.

"That's better, Lynn. I like you feisty. This victim act has got quite boring."

"Give me back my keys."

"What's the word?"

"Please," she mumbled.

He moved closer and tilted his head so that his ear was almost touching her mouth. "Sorry, I didn't catch that."

"Please," she repeated, louder.

The tremble in her voice, the feel of her breath on his face and the sight of her chest heaving as if she were running a marathon was really turning him on now. He moved his head very slowly so her full mouth was almost touching his. "As you ask so nicely." He took her hand and pressed the keys into her palm. "Did I tell you that I'm moving back into Hawthorn Lodge?" She stared at him, a mixture of hatred and horror in her eyes, and tried to pull her hand away, but he kept a tight hold on it. "Where are your manners, Lynn? Aren't you going to say welcome back?"

"Welcome back," she said, the words coming out in a hiss.

252

"That's more like it. Oh, Lynn, darling, it could be just like the old days —"

"Get the hell away from her!"

Vincent whirled around to see Val McCabe glaring at him.

All afternoon Val had worried about Lynn. She had seemed so upset and so afraid. The last time Val had seen her like this had been after she'd first left Hawthorn Lodge.

"Have you heard a word I said?"

She looked up to see Lorcan grinning at her. "Sorry, what was that? I was miles away."

"Nothing important. I was just telling you about my plan to take two years off to backpack around Africa and Asia."

She stared at him. "Really?"

"No." He laughed. "I was actually trying to decide whether to have pizza or spaghetti for dinner."

"Oh." She gave him a vague smile.

"Val, you've put the red wine in the fridge."

She looked down and saw that she had indeed put the Chilean Shiraz in the cooler. "Sorry."

"What's up? Tell Uncle Lorcan."

Val leaned against the counter and watched as he moved the red wine up to the Bargain Bottles shelf and replaced it with an Australian Sauvignon Blanc. She wouldn't normally talk about someone else's business but she could trust Lorcan, and he could always be relied on for sound advice. "It's Lynn. I told her that it looks as if Vincent Boland will be back working in

Hawthorn lodge in the next week or so and she went to pieces. I'm really worried about her."

"Poor girl. When old man Boland settled she must have thought her worries were over. Then her dad has that terrible accident and now this."

"Exactly!" Val nodded. "She was only just coming to terms with the idea of working again in Dublin and suddenly she's thrust back into a job where every day she's got to deal with people who know everything about her."

"And either are related to or work for a Boland." Lorcan nodded. "She hasn't had an easy time of it."

"I wish I knew a way to help her," Val said.

"You could have a word with Frank or talk to her mum."

Val shook her head vehemently. "No, she'd never forgive me."

He straightened and shrugged. "Then all you can really do is keep an eye on her."

Which was why, when it was time for her break, Val had decided to slip down to the supermarket and check on Lynn. She had been halfway down the road when she remembered it was Sunday and early closing, and, as it was now after seven, Lynn would probably be gone. Still, it was a nice evening for a stroll, so she carried on. When she came in sight of the shop and saw a man standing pressed up against the closed door she started to feel in her pocket for her phone, convinced she'd stumbled on a break-in. Then the man stepped to one side and she saw Lynn's pink skirt and half a second later realized who the man was. Filled with rage she stormed towards him. "Get the hell away from her!"

Vincent turned round slowly and, though he was smiling, she could see a flash of fear in his eyes. "Val, hi. Just saying to Lynn what a lovely evening it is."

She met Lynn's eyes. "Are you okay?"

Lynn nodded mutely but Val could see the terror in her eyes.

"Get away from here," she hissed, "or I'll call the police."

He spread his hands, his eyes wide with innocence. "Why? What exactly have I done?"

For a moment she was at a loss, but another glance at Lynn's petrified expression was enough to inspire her. "Nothing, of course. You're right. I'll just phone your wife and your uncle and let them know you're here in case they were wondering where you'd got to."

"I was just leaving." He glared at her.

"Good! And don't come back!" she yelled after him as he strode away.

"Shush, people will hear you!" Lynn was white-faced and shaking.

"The more the better," Val declared and, taking the keys from Lynn's cold fingers, opened the door and guided her back inside.

Val eyed her friend warily. She was still shaking so much that tea was slopping out of the mug in Lynn's hands. She took it from her and set it on Jack's desk. "You can't go and see your dad in this state."

"I can't not go," Lynn replied.

"Is Frank taking you?"

"No. He's working. I'm going alone."

"You can't possibly drive!" Val protested. "I'll get John to take you — oh, shit, he went out with some mates for a couple of pints."

"Don't worry, I'll be fine." Lynn reached for her tea and spilled half of it on the short journey to her lips.

"You are not getting behind the wheel of a car in this state." Val racked her brain for a solution. Who did she know with a car who wouldn't ask too many questions? She smiled and stretched out her arm to help Lynn to her feet. "Come on, I've got an idea."

Getting Lynn as far as the off-licence was a challenge in itself. She hesitated, passing every shadowed doorway. As they walked, Val reassured her the way one would comfort a child scared that there was a monster under the bed or a ghost in the closet. Once through the door, she parked Lynn in the back room and signalled to Lorcan across a customer's head. He came over as soon as he was finished.

"What's up?"

"I just stumbled on Vincent pestering Lynn outside the supermarket. He scared the living daylights out of her."

Lorcan's face darkened. "The bastard! Do you want me to go round there and sort him out?"

"No, but I was looking for a favour. She's due up at the hospital to see her dad but she's in no condition to drive. Would you take her and I'll do your shift?"

"Of course."

256

Val smiled. If she had asked John there would have been an hour of questions and argument; Lorcan just did as he was asked without query or judgement. "Thank you so much, Lorcan, I owe you a pint."

He smiled down at her. "I'll hold you to that!"

Jack knew the moment she walked in that something was wrong with his daughter. First, she seemed slightly dazed. Second, her whole body was coiled like a spring and she jumped at the slightest noise. And, third, she was prattling on in a way that was completely out of character, her voice shrill and nervous. "What's happened?" he said, cutting into the middle of her chatter.

She stared at him. "Nothing."

He flapped his good hand at her. "Liar. Tell me."

She sat back in her chair, her eyes full of tears. "I just met Vincent."

Jack felt a flicker of anger. "Where did you meet him?"

"Outside the shop."

From the way she averted her gaze he knew there was more to it than that. "He talked to you?" She nodded and the fury built up in him. "What?"

"He's coming back to work in Hawthorn Lodge and he was just gloating, that's all."

That's all, Frank thought, but she was a nervous wreck before him. That simple statement said everything about what this bastard had done to her life and her confidence. Jack's fury grew but he also felt guilty for putting her in this position. He shouldn't have let Nell and Frank persuade him that Lynn was well able to look after the shop when he knew in his heart it would be an ordeal for her. "If you want to leave —"

She shook her head. "It's okay."

He wanted to quiz her further, he wanted to reassure himself that she really was all right, but if he tried to say more than a few words his voice became slurred, and at the end of the day when he was tired his writing became . . . He struggled to think of the word and failed. Frustrated and angry, he brought his hand down hard on the tray in front of him and his beaker of water tipped over. Lynn jumped to rescue it and grabbed a tissue to mop up the drops that had spilt. "Sorry," he said.

"No harm done."

"Isn't there?" He stared at her, and when she met his eyes he was overwhelmed at the bleakness he saw there. And there was something else. What was it? He searched his dull, foggy brain for an answer, but could find none.

"I'll be fine. You just concentrate on getting better so I can get the hell out of there!"

He wasn't fooled by her smile and suddenly he felt old and tired and useless. "Sorry, love. Sorry."

"Stop saying that, Dad." She leaned forward. "It will be okay."

He stroked her hair with his good hand. "It will, love, it will, I promise."

As soon as she left he reached for his mobile phone but the damn thing was so small that it was impossible to search his contacts with just one hand. He couldn't phone: it would be impossible to make himself understood. But he didn't know how on earth he would be able to send a text. He had made several attempts and was getting angrier and more frustrated when a nurse came in.

"Mr Stephens? Are you okay?" She hurried over and put cool fingers on his wrist.

His breathing was heavy and he could feel perspiration on his brow and upper lip; he must look a mess. "Yes. Help me?" He held up the phone to her. "Text?"

She laughed and took it from him. "Sure. What do you want to say?"

CHAPTER
TWENTY-FIVE

"You fool! What were you thinking?"

Vincent stared. Charles's face was incandescent with rage. It was Monday morning and already his uncle had heard about last night. "I said hello and picked up the girl's keys for her; it's hardly a crime."

"I told you to stay away from her, I warned you." Charles shook his head in frustration. "This isn't just about you. Your actions have much wider implications."

Vincent looked at him. "Such as?"

Charles ignored the question. "You can't possibly come back to Hawthorn now, not as long as that girl is living here."

"That's ridiculous," Vincent protested. "What difference does it make? I live here anyway. Am I supposed to stay indoors during daylight hours?"

"I think it would be better all round if you just stayed out of town and spent a bit more time at home with your pregnant wife." His uncle looked at him with disapproving eyes.

"Is that an order?" Vincent jumped to his feet and started to pace in front of Charles's desk. "I have nothing to be ashamed of and you can't make me hide away as if I have."

260

"No, I can't," Charles agreed with him. "I can only suggest that it would probably be better for you in the long term."

Vincent saw the steely determination in his uncle's eyes. "That's blackmail."

Charles gave a weary sigh. "Don't be a drama queen. I'm not sending you to Iraq."

"Why are you willing to take such drastic action because of her? Who's going to run the place while you're in hospital?" Vincent demanded.

"Emer's husband, Tommy, has been made redundant so he will be in a position to stay at home and look after the children while Emer takes over the management of Hawthorn Lodge."

Vincent felt sick. What if Tommy couldn't get another job? What if Emer got a taste for being the boss? Suddenly he could see his entire future dissolve before his eyes. "This isn't fair," he said, though he knew that he sounded like a petulant child. "I've put everything into this business."

"You should have thought of that before harassing the staff," Charles retorted. "You didn't even have the brains to pick a nobody. No, you had to choose Jack Stephens's daughter. You've brought this on yourself; you have no self-discipline and, frankly, I feel little sympathy for you. Now get out of my sight."

Charles swivelled his chair so he had his back to him, effectively ending the meeting and Vincent had no option but to leave. He forced himself to nod and smile at the few people he passed on his way out, walking through reception with his head held high. He drove the short distance home, shaking. He couldn't believe this was happening and all because of a few careless, harmless words to that bitch. She had ruined things yet again.

"Hey, what are you doing here at this hour?" Orla looked up in surprise at Vincent as he came through the door.

"I have a ton of paperwork to do so I thought I'd come home and do it in peace and quiet."

Orla smiled. "Are you getting nervous about leaving us?" She stroked her tummy.

He forced a smile. "Yeah, a little."

She went to stand up. "Let me make you something to eat."

"No, darling, you rest. I'm not hungry yet. I'll get started on this first," he patted his briefcase.

She settled back on the sofa and reached for her magazine. "Okay then. Just shout if you want anything."

He left her, went into the kitchen, took down the bottle of whiskey and a tumbler and went through to the small study, closing the door firmly behind him. He downed the first glass in one go, wincing as the whiskey burned its way down his throat. He pulled off his tie and sank into his chair and poured a second glass. He would have to come up with some story to explain to Orla why he wasn't returning to Hawthorn Lodge after all, but he hadn't a clue what. Still, she usually accepted what he told her. Now his mother . . . He groaned at the thought of breaking the news to her. She seemed to have been living vicariously through him since his father had died and would be furious. She wouldn't take this lying down. He brightened at the thought. Surely Charles would find his sister-in-law's wrath a more terrifying prospect than Jack Stephens. She was tough and independent, unlike Orla's mother, who was a weak, whiney woman. The one good thing about moving to the sticks was that they should be able to afford a bigger house and there would be enough rooms for him to avoid her when she came to visit — although Orla might want her to move in with them to help with the baby. He drained his glass at the thought and refilled it.

He must have dozed off for he woke up and the room was growing dark. He winced at the persistent ringing that had obviously woken him. It took him a moment to realize it was the doorbell. "Orla, someone's at the door," he shouted. It rang another couple of times and he realized she must have gone to bed. He struggled to his feet and grabbed the desk as the room started to spin. "Shit." The bell rang again and he went out into the hall. "Okay, okay, don't get your knickers in a twist," he muttered.

Vincent barely had the door open when he was dragged outside by the lapels and around the side of the house, his feet barely touching the ground. He was shoved up against the wall and an arm held him in place across his throat.

"Jesus, you're pissed!"

Vincent blinked and looked into the disgusted eyes of Frank Hayes. "What the hell do you think you're doing?" He tried to pull Frank's arm from his throat but it was like a vice. "Let me go, you fucking madman."

"I'll let you go after we get something straight. You will not go anywhere near Lynn Stephens again."

"Ah, is that what this is about? Fair enough." Frank looked surprised and loosened his grip slightly. Vincent grinned at him. "Unless of course she asks me. She hasn't always played hard to get, you know."

The arm was back in place and Vincent felt the air squeeze out of his windpipe, but he didn't fucking care. This was his chance to repay Lynn for destroying his life. "Sorry if the truth hurts, mate, but Lynn and I worked very well together for a long time, very well indeed." He smiled knowingly at Frank. "And sometimes we played, too —"

"You're a liar," Frank said, his face contorted with fury.

"Am I? You ask her about the Christmas party last year." Vincent smiled. "I have very fond memories of Room 112."

"You bastard!" Frank took his arm away, drew back his fist and punched him.

Vincent cried out as his head crashed back against the wall. He put a hand to his face as blood pumped from his nose. He could barely see Frank but he still managed a smile. "Ask her," he hissed into Frank's face before pushing him away and staggering back inside.

At nine o'clock on Tuesday morning Lynn sat in the waiting room, fiddling nervously with her mobile. She glanced anxiously at the time, willing the hands forward. She'd once shrunk from baring her feelings to Julian Kelly, but today she couldn't wait to talk to him.

264

She had called him yesterday but the first appointment she could get was this morning. She had taken a sleeping tablet on Sunday night and was asleep when Frank got in and he was gone again when she woke, much to her relief. She knew that she wouldn't be able to hide how upset she was feeling. She had called Norman yesterday to say she had a migraine and sent Frank a text saying the same later in the day. This morning was the first time she'd seen him since it had happened and he'd seemed preoccupied. It was a relief. She felt close to breaking point and it was almost impossible to hide her feelings.

The door opened and the psychiatrist beckoned her in. "Thank you for seeing me at such short notice," she said, taking her usual chair.

"I'm sorry I couldn't manage it yesterday. You sounded upset on the phone."

"Yes," Lynn said and immediately started to cry, gulping sobs that she couldn't seem to control. Unfazed, Julian moved the tissues closer and poured her a glass of water. "I'm sorry," she gasped as she attempted to regain control. They had only an hour and she was wasting it crying like a baby.

"Don't apologize. What's happened?" He looked at her with concerned eyes.

"Vincent Boland cornered me outside the shop."

The psychiatrist listened in silence as she told him what had happened, his expression growing more and more concerned. "Perhaps you should go to the police," he said when she'd finished.

"It would just make things worse."

"Have you told Frank?"

She shook her head. "I'm afraid of what he'd do. He might end up in a cell himself or, even worse, in the papers." She didn't want Frank's good name linked to gossip or scandal because of her.

"Lynn, you have to stop trying to protect everyone. You are the one who needs protecting from this guy; he is still harassing you."

"Not really. He just took advantage of an opportunity. If I hadn't dropped the keys he wouldn't even have noticed me." Lynn clasped her hands in her lap to stop them shaking. "Like you said, I'll just have to do my best to avoid him. My dad's on the mend and once he's well enough to keep an eye on the business I will leave Rathbourne."

Julian looked at her in exasperation. "Did you get any sleep?"

"I took tablets."

"Good. Any nightmares?"

"Yes."

"The same as before?"

She nodded.

He was silent for a moment, going through his notes and then he looked up at her. "I think we should increase the dosage on your antidepressant again. You need help to get through this."

"If you think so." Lynn hated the thought, but she couldn't pretend she didn't need them — she was in trouble.

"I understand why you didn't tell Frank or your family the full truth about Vincent before, Lynn, but from this moment on you should be completely open with them. The strain of all of this secrecy is probably causing you more psychological damage than the man himself. You're putting yourself under enormous pressure."

"I did tell Dad about Sunday," she said.

His eyes widened in surprise. "Well done! That will do him as much good as it will you."

"I doubt that. He's riddled with guilt that it only happened because I'm looking after the shop for him."

"But you've reminded him that he's a parent as well as a patient and given him a reason to fight harder to return to full strength."

"I never thought of that," Lynn smiled, happier that there was some silver lining to the huge cloud above her.

They talked some more and by the time the hour was up, Lynn felt calmer and ready to face the world again.

"Come back and see me in two weeks or sooner if you need to," he said, scribbling in her file. "One last thing. You said your friend shouted at Vincent."

"Yes." Lynn smiled. Val had been like a tigress.

"And you've told your father."

She nodded.

"So there is no way that you can keep this from Frank. He's going to hear about it sooner or later. It should be from you, Lynn."

She closed her eyes but of course he was right. It would be impossible to keep Vincent's latest behaviour under wraps. She sighed. "I'll talk to him."

"Good," he said, his smile kind. "You have a lot of support, Lynn. Use it."

After the session with Julian, Lynn drove to the beach and walked for thirty minutes before she felt she was ready to face going into work. Val had already let her know there was gossip about what went on on Sunday night and so, when she drove into the yard, it was no surprise that her mother came out to meet her. It was clear from her pinched, white face that she had heard the rumours.

"Is it true? Did Vincent Boland attack you?" Nell said as soon as she opened the car door.

"No, of course he didn't. Who told you that?"

"Mrs O'Malley. She said there was screaming and shouting and then that fecker ran off."

"He was talking to me, annoying me, and Val shouted at him to get lost and he did. That's all that happened, Mum."

Nell didn't look convinced. "So where were you yesterday and this morning? And don't give me the migraine line."

Lynn was about to lie when she remembered what Julian had said. "I couldn't face work, I'm sorry, and I went to see the psychiatrist this morning."

"Oh, love, you could have just come and talked to me," Nell said, tears in her eyes.

Lynn hugged her. "I know, Mum, but sometimes it's easier to talk to a stranger."

"There must be some way we can get him to leave you alone," Nell fumed.

268

Lynn smirked. "I think Val's taken care of that."

"Do you want to take some more time off, love? I could stand in for you."

Lynn was sorely tempted but she knew that it would just make coming in tomorrow even harder. "No, it's okay, really, I'll be grand."

Lynn put her head into the shop to let Norman know that she was in. "I have some calls to make but if you need me just shout."

He touched her arm. "Don't you worry about a thing, we'll manage. I told Frank that we could cope for a few days."

She looked up at him in surprise. "What do you mean?"

"When he phoned yesterday, I told him we could manage without you if you needed more time to get over . . ." He trailed off, looking embarrassed.

"Thanks, Norman but I'll be fine."

She went into the office and sat down. So Frank knew. Why hadn't he mentioned it this morning? She felt a vague sense of unease and reaching for her phone, sent him a text.

CAN WE TALK?

There was no reply, but that wasn't unusual in his business, and he seemed very busy lately. But she knew in her heart that he was probably furious that he'd heard about this from Norman and not from her. But he would calm down and get in touch soon enough. He would want to know every last detail.

269

She dreaded telling him, but Julian Kelly had been right: she had to be completely honest from now on. But how she was going to prevent Frank from going round to Vincent's house and beating the hell out of him she had no idea.

CHAPTER
TWENTY-SIX

Lynn took a frozen lasagne home for dinner that evening, bunged it in the oven and was in the bath with a glass of wine when she heard the front door bang. "I'm in the bath," she called. He came up the stairs and stopped in the doorway. She gave him a nervous smile. "Hello, stranger. Are you okay?"

"Yeah. How are you?" He closed down the toilet seat and sat down.

"Not bad. Why didn't you tell me this morning that you knew?"

"How come you never told me yourself?" His voice was dangerously quiet.

"I was a mess on Sunday evening and I was afraid that if you saw me like that you would do something stupid. I wasn't much better yesterday, to be honest, and I couldn't face work. I tried to get an appointment with Julian Kelly but he couldn't see me until this morning. I knew you would be home late so I just took a tablet so I would sleep and forget."

"I sat across from you at breakfast this morning and you never said anything."

"I was still upset and I knew I wouldn't be able to tell you without crying. I didn't want to send you to work knowing I was in such a state. What good would that have done?"

He nodded, his eyes expressionless. "You seem to be okay now."

"I feel better after talking to Kelly. He helped a lot. I'll be fine, Frank, there's nothing to worry about."

"What exactly happened, Lynn?" he asked.

She sank deeper into the water and told him about her run in with Vincent. "The most frustrating thing about all this is that it doesn't sound like much," she said when she had finished her story. "I can understand people going, 'What's she so upset about?' It's hard to explain why he scares me so much."

"Try," he insisted.

She considered the question as memories and images flashed before her eyes. "It's the way he looks at me, the way he invades my space and the things he says. He has a smile on his face but there's something sinister about the way he looks at me and his tone of voice." She sighed, frustrated. "It's so hard to explain."

"And yet it wasn't always like that, was it? There was a time when you two were friends."

She frowned, wondering where he was going with this. "We worked well together in the restaurant but I don't think I would ever have called us friends."

"Oh, come on, that's not true. I remember lots of times that you told me that you had fun together. What about your last Christmas party at Hawthorn Lodge? That was a good night, wasn't it?"

She froze. "I don't remember much of it."

"I spent the night in Dublin," he reminded her.

"Yeah, that's right." She was silent as she thought back on the night that had changed her life. If she had behaved herself she might still be working in Hawthorn Lodge today. Drink was a dangerous thing.

"You stayed over, didn't you?"

"No. I drank too much and went up to one of the rooms to sleep it off, but I couldn't relax there so I decided to go home."

"What room did you stay in?" he asked.

She looked at him in confusion. "Sorry?"

"In Hawthorn Lodge. Do you remember the room number?" He spun the toilet roll round before rolling it carefully back up again.

That was easy to remember. It was the room staff always used. "One one two. Why on earth do you want to know that?"

He sat staring at the toilet roll for a moment before finally turning his head and meeting her eyes. "I just wondered if your memory was as good as Vincent's."

She stared into his cold, angry eyes and felt her whole world shatter into a million pieces around her. "When did you talk to Vincent?" she whispered.

"Yesterday. After I talked to Norman I went over to his house to warn him off, to play the knight in shining armour. I was trying to protect you." His laugh was bitter. "I think that perhaps it's Vincent who needs protecting."

"What the hell does that mean?" she exclaimed.

"Tell me, did you have a thing with him before I came along or did it start afterwards?"

"I never had any 'thing' with him!"

"But he was with you that night in Room 112, wasn't he?"

She stared at him. "Yes, briefly, but nothing happened."

He looked at her as if seeing her for the first time. "You're lying." He got up to go.

She reached for a towel. "Wait, let me explain."

"You've had well over a year to explain but for some reason you didn't," he said, walking into their bedroom.

She climbed out of the bath wrapped the towel around her and ran after him. "I didn't want to hurt you."

He pulled his travel bag down from the top of the wardrobe and started to toss underwear into it. "If nothing happened, how could it have hurt me?"

She put a hand over his to stop him. "Please, let's go and sit down and I'll explain."

"I have to go. I'm due at the studio in ninety minutes. I got the keys of the house today. I'll stay there tonight."

She looked down at his bag. "You don't need all that for one night."

"It's better if I stay away from you for the moment, believe me. I need time to think."

"You're judging me without even hearing my side of the story," she accused him, stunned that he could walk away from her so easily.

He moved around her and took half a dozen shirts from the wardrobe and shoved them in the bag. "I don't trust myself to stay. We'll talk in a few days."

Lynn stood watching as he put three suits into a holder and fetched his toiletries from the bathroom. She wanted to beg him to stay but his readiness to

274

believe the worst of her stopped her. When he went to leave she blocked the doorway and searched his eyes looking for a trace of the man she knew and loved, but his expression was guarded and he seemed like a stranger. "This is wrong," she whispered.

"It is," he agreed before walking around her. She stood rooted to the spot as he went downstairs. She heard him rummaging in the hall cupboard for shoes and then the door closed with a sickening finality. She curled up in a ball on the bed, shaking all over, her silent tears soaking the pillow.

It was the smoke alarm that woke her and then she smelled the burnt lasagne. She roused herself and went downstairs, coughing as the smoke enfolded her. In the kitchen she switched off the cooker and flung open the back door.

"Everything okay, love?" Her next-door neighbour's face appeared over the hedge.

"I went up to have a bath and forgot that I'd left something in the oven." Self-conscious, she tightened the towel around her.

"It happens to us all." The woman laughed. "No damage done I hope."

"I don't think so." Lynn smiled and ventured back inside. She opened the oven and took out the charred remains of dinner. "Good job I wasn't hungry," she muttered. Gingerly, she carried it outside and set it down on the step before going up to her room to swap her towel for jeans and a sweatshirt. Gathering her hair into a knot on the top of her head, she went back downstairs. She tried to open the windows in an attempt to get rid of the stench and the acrid smoke that was causing yet more tears, but they were locked and she had no idea where the keys were. She gave up, dumped her dinner in the bin and poured a large glass of wine to take outside.

Their two deckchairs sat at the very end of the garden positioned so that they could catch the last of the sun's rays as they sat discussing their day. Sitting in Frank's chair, Lynn breathed in the fresh air and wondered if they would ever sit like this again or, indeed, sit on the balcony of their new house together. The hurt and condemnation in his eyes had scared her. On impulse she went in and searched high and low for her mobile phone. When she found it she saw that she had missed a call from her mother and two calls and three texts from Val all wondering if she was okay. "No," she said aloud. There was nothing from Frank, not that she had expected anything. She sent him a text.

HAD AN ACCIDENT, NEED TO OPEN WINDOW TO CLEAR SMOKE. DO U KNOW WHERE KEY IS?

She went back outside to wait. As she'd expected, he called. Apprehensive, she picked up the phone. "Hi."

"What happened? Are you okay?"

She closed her eyes drinking in the concern in his voice. "I just forgot to take the lasagne out of the oven. I have a sore throat and streaming eyes, that's all." She gave a nervous laugh. "If it wasn't for the smoke alarm you might have been rid of me for good."

276

"Don't talk like that. The key is on the shelf above the kettle."

"Okay, thanks."

"Are you sure you're okay?"

"I'm far from okay, Frank," she said quietly, "but it's nothing to do with the smoke."

"I have to go —"

"I understand," she said quickly, "but promise me that we will talk soon. Please, Frank." He was silent for a moment; she could almost hear his brain ticking over.

"I'll call you," he said finally. "Take care."

"You too." She hung up. Maybe all was not lost. Frank was upset and angry but the reporter in him would want all the details, no matter how painful, and he would push her until he was convinced that he had the full truth. And she was sure that he would understand — but could he forget?

"Once you explain, everything will be fine," Val tried to reassure her a few days later when Lynn still hadn't got a call.

They were sitting in Nell's kitchen, while Nell was probably sitting in Lynn's. She was staying the night with Frank and in the morning they would collect Jack and bring him home. Lynn was touched that not only had he continued to drop in to see Jack for a few minutes every day but had immediately offered his services when they were told her father was to be discharged. But he had talked to her parents, not to her. He'd said he'd phone her, but he hadn't.

Lynn had been living like a hermit since Frank left, going into work early and leaving late. There had been no sign of Vincent.

"I'm not so sure," Lynn carried two mugs of coffee to the table.

"Did Frank tell you what Vincent actually said? I heard he hit him" Val sighed. "Oh, I hope that's true."

"I don't know if he hit him, but Vincent told him that we were in one of the bedrooms together the night of the Christmas party."

"The bastard! It's a wonder Frank didn't kill him. Relax, Lynn, once Frank calms down and thinks about it he'll realize it's a pack of lies and come home." Lynn looked at her but said nothing. Val's eyes narrowed. "What?"

"I *was* in that room with Vincent, Val."

Her friend stared at her. "You slept with him?"

Lynn shook her head vehemently. "No!"

"So, what happened?"

"I was on a high that night. I'd got my promotion. Charles had given me a Christmas bonus and told me I was an invaluable part of the team." Lynn shrugged. "Life was good and we were celebrating, seriously celebrating. Vincent had never been in such good form and the drink was flowing."

"You never drink much," Val said, surprised.

"I know. Someone must have been topping up my drink and I was so busy chatting and singing I didn't notice. Anyway, next thing, Vincent drags me up to dance and immediately I felt the room start to spin and I had to get out of there, I felt dreadful. I was going to

278

go into reception but Vincent said it wasn't a good idea for the assistant manager to be seen worse for wear by guests and took me out the back exit into the delivery area. I still felt dizzy and the sensation scared me. He said I would be fine and just chatted and made me laugh, distracting me until I felt better."

Val snorted in disgust. "How long did it take him to get his tongue down your throat?"

Lynn felt herself blush. "I wasn't expecting it. I never thought of him like that at all. He was always either Orla's husband or my boss. I was in the middle of saying something and suddenly, *bam!*, he was kissing me. It took me completely by surprise and I didn't really know what to do. He'd been so nice and it was just a kiss, so I let him get on with it."

Val stared at her, enthralled. "Then what happened?"

Lynn looked away. It seemed that every detail was so clear in a night that was a blur. Perhaps that was because she had felt, even then through the haze of alcohol, that she was letting Frank down. "He started to move me back against the wall and, it was clear he was getting excited." She shuddered. "I didn't want to embarrass him so I said that I thought I was going to be sick and I needed to go home."

"And he suggested you stay," Val guessed.

"Yes." Lynn sighed. "I was very dense, wasn't I?"

"No, chicken, you were tanked and he took advantage of you."

Lynn couldn't agree. She should have drunk more water. She was a senior member of staff and she'd gotten drunk in front of her staff. It had been stupid and irresponsible.

"Did you realize at that stage what Vincent had in mind?"

"I wasn't able to see straight, let alone think straight. He sent me up the back stairs to Room 112 — it's the room staff usually use if they have to stay over — and he went to get the key. I was sitting outside barely conscious by the time he got back. He opened the door and helped me to the bed. I was lapsing in and out of sleep, but I remember him trying to undress me and I pushed him away. I drifted off again and when I woke my dress was up around my waist. I pushed him off me but he acted all shocked and said that he was only making me comfortable and hadn't left as he was afraid that I would be sick. I nearly fell for that until I noticed that his trousers were open.

"That woke me up, I can tell you. I suddenly realized that, whether I wanted to or not, he was planning on having sex. But he was my boss, we had to work together. I couldn't very well knee him in the crotch and run. So I apologized and said that I was feeling sick again and needed the bathroom. I grabbed my bag and went in and locked the door. I wasn't quite sure what to do and then I thought that maybe if I called the hotel and said there was an emergency and asked to speak to him, that he was in Room 112 that perhaps I could avoid upsetting him and protect myself. So I ran the taps on full and called and I was delighted when Bob answered. I knew I could trust him and that he'd help me. Vincent was at the door, calling me, asking me was

280

I coming out. I started to groan and make throwing-up noises until I heard knocking on the bedroom door. Then I heard Bob's voice and then there was silence. As soon as I was sure that I was alone, I dragged myself down to the back entrance and Bob had a car waiting to take me home."

"Dear God, Lynn, you could have been raped! Why didn't you tell me?"

"I really wanted to, Val. I would have loved to confide in someone. But I know you." She smiled affectionately at her friend. "You would have hated him for what he'd tried to do and you're rubbish at hiding your feelings. He was in a real position of power and if he had an inkling that you knew, that I'd told you, I'd be out of a job and he'd have found some way to get rid of you too. No, as soon as I had a clear head I realized that I could never tell anyone. What was the point? I was safe. It would have destroyed everything and, let's face it, I was partly to blame for what happened."

"How do you make that out?"

"I drank too much. I danced with him, I let him kiss me and I agreed to spend the night. Is it any wonder he got the wrong idea?"

"You were drunk and sick and he took advantage!"

Lynn shrugged. That was the obvious reaction of a good friend but she knew that Frank wouldn't see it like that.

"So what happened then?" Val prompted.

"I felt dreadful the next day. I was still quite dizzy and nauseous but I knew I had to go to work and face him. I figured he would be embarrassed too in the cold

281

light of day so I decided the best thing to do was to act as if nothing had happened and carry on as before. But he was having none of that. Bob had told him there was a fight downstairs but, of course, when he went down, no one was there. And poor old Bob isn't a great actor, he was barely civil to him. Vincent was furious. He said that I had led him on and then made him look like some kind of monster and that all the staff would get to hear about it. He was wrong, though. Bob never said a word and most of the staff were so drunk that night that they didn't even notice what was going on. Even if they had they probably wouldn't have remembered anything the next day. Some commented on me disappearing and I admitted that I'd overdone it and told them how Bob had practically poured me into the back of a taxi." She sighed. "And we got away with it. But Vincent couldn't forgive or forget. Looking back, I realize that he spent every day since trying to drive me out."

"You should have told your solicitor all this. He shouldn't get away with something like that. He should have been charged with attempted rape or assault or . . . something!" Val was flushed with anger and frustration.

"It would have been his word against mine, Val, and it would have come between Frank and me. He would always have wondered if there was a grain of truth in Vincent's story." She smiled sadly. "And you see, I've been proven right. He's left me now without even hearing what I had to say. Then there was Orla to consider. She would have been devastated. And what about Dad? He'd have been furious, and, remember, he had only just recovered from his stroke." Lynn sighed. "So many people would have ended up hurt and all because I'd had too much to drink one night. I did the only thing that I could: I kept my mouth shut."

Val reached out a hand and smoothed her hair. "And you destroyed yourself in the process."

Lynn wiped her eyes on the back of her hand and smiled. "I'm still standing and now I've got you to talk to. Oh, Val, you don't know how good that feels."

Val gave her a hug, her eyes watering. "Will you tell Frank everything now?"

"I think I have to."

"Don't worry. It will be fine. Once he calms down and you explain it to him he'll understand."

Lynn wasn't convinced. Frank would still ask himself how she had got into such a situation and how much of her story was true. He might well forgive her, he was a good man, but for the rest of their lives it would always be there, lurking in a recess of his mind.

"Didn't you say he's bringing your father home tomorrow?"

"Yes, that's right."

"Maybe you'll have a chance to talk then."

"Maybe."

"I can't believe your dad's coming home already."

Lynn smiled. "It's fantastic but I'm a bit nervous, and I think Mum is, too. What if we're not able to look after him?"

"Does he need much looking after?"

"More than he lets on. He's fiercely independent but it's the little things that defeat him. Pulling up a zip or closing buttons, that sort of thing, and sometimes it's hard to understand him and he gets so annoyed with us when we don't." Lynn laughed. "But there's nothing wrong with his mind — he's as sharp as ever. I dread the thought of having him looking over my shoulder all the time. There'll be murder!"

"Have you changed things?" Val smiled.

Lynn sobered. "I've done nothing but try to get through each day."

Val squeezed her hand. "You've been great. I thought you were strong before, but after what you've told me I think you're amazing and incredibly selfless if also very dumb."

"Thanks very much!"

Val grinned and glanced at her watch. "I'd better go. John will be wondering where I've got to. Go home and get some sleep, Lynn."

At the door they hugged and Lynn felt tears in her eyes. "Thanks, Val."

"For what?"

Lynn smiled. "For listening without preaching or judging and for not being annoyed with me for keeping the truth from you."

"Why would I be annoyed when all you were trying to do was protect me?" Val smiled. "Get some rest, Lynn, and good luck with Frank in the morning."

It was true. Vincent probably wouldn't bother her any more, Lynn thought as she made her way home, but it was little comfort. He had already hurt her in the worst way possible: he had driven Frank away. Even if he came back to her, how could it ever be the same? She could just imagine how the subject would be dragged up whenever they rowed and she would always feel hurt that he had doubted her.

She let herself into the house and went straight to the phone to check the answering service, but there were no messages, not that she'd really expected any. She had a shower, got into pyjamas and ate cheese on toast in front of the TV news. The programme Frank often appeared on was next and it felt strange not knowing whether he was on tonight. During the break she went out to the kitchen, tidied up and made tea. She froze as she was adding milk to her mug; she knew that voice. She hurried back into the sitting room and there was Frank looking handsome in a dark suit and the yellow tie she'd bought him the week before. There was a close-up of his face. How tired he looked! She longed to put her arms around him and take that frown from his face — the frown that she was responsible for. What had Vincent said? she wondered. What poison had he fed him?

Frank laughed at something someone said. Lynn sighed. How she loved that sound, although it was much more muted in studio. The silence of the house was a sharp reminder of how his voice, laugh and personality filled the place when he was home and how happy he made her. She had probably taken all that for granted lately. On impulse, she picked up her mobile and sent him a text.

PLEASE COME HOME AND LET ME EXPLAIN
EVERYTHING, X.

She glanced at the screen, Frank was talking again. She
gasped as he hesitated, his hand briefly touching his
jacket pocket. Normally, he switched his phone off
when he was on air but it must have vibrated in his
pocket. Was that so she could contact him? The thought
gave her hope. She checked her watch: the show would
be over in twenty minutes. She waited impatiently for it
to end, the phone in her hand.

At 11.45 she accepted the fact that Frank wasn't
going to call. Surprised and upset that he hadn't even
bothered to acknowledge her text, she went to bed.

CHAPTER
TWENTY-SEVEN

Jack felt both elated and nervous to be going home. It would be great to get away from the noise and the smell of the hospital and he certainly wouldn't miss the food, but he'd felt safe here.

Nell had sent a text saying that she and Frank were running late. Immediately, he wondered whether there was a problem with the shop or with Lynn. If Vincent Boland had been bothering her again he would take a whip to him.

He was sitting in reception when they finally arrived. Frank was dishevelled and unshaven and seemed distracted, but Nell beamed when she saw him. She hurried over and bent to kiss him.

"Hello, darling, you look well," she said before turning to thank the nurse.

Frank gave him a tired smile. "Sorry for the delay, Jack."

"It's OK. What's wrong?"

"I've spent the night in casualty with Philip. It looks like he'll be getting his appendix out today."

Jack shook his head. "Poor lad. Sore?"

"Yeah, but when I left him he was complaining that he was starving and also giving out because he's not allowed to use his phone, so I think it's safe to say he'll live."

The nurse said goodbye and Jack looked up at Frank's anxious face. "We can get a taxi."

"I told him but he won't hear of it," Nell said.

"Really, it's fine. Carrie's with him. Let's go before my car is towed." He offered Jack his arm.

Jack was surprised at how frail he felt and how tired he was by the time he was settled in a chair at home, even though all he'd had to do was walk a few steps to and from the car. Still, he felt happy to be here and devoured one of Nell's gorgeous scones with a decent mug of hot tea — those tiny cups in the hospital barely wet your throat.

Frank downed his tea and stood up. "I'd better get back. Welcome home, Jack."

"Thanks for the lift, son."

"Give Philip our love," Nell said.

"I will."

Lynn burst in through the door, almost colliding with Frank. "Sorry! Hi." She stood for a moment, looking at him, and then came over to Jack. "Welcome home, Dad."

When she hugged him he put his right arm around her. "How's my girl?"

"I'm okay."

"I was just leaving," Frank said.

"I'll walk you out," she said. "Back in a minute." She smiled but Jack frowned at the tension in her eyes. "What's going on there?" he asked his wife when they were alone.

"Some tiff or other," Nell said dismissively. "Now you should have a lie-down."

"Just out of a bed. Not getting straight back into one," he protested.

"The doctor said you should take it easy."

"I'm sitting," he pointed out, his eyes going to the window as Lynn and Frank came into view. They stopped by the car talking but they seemed awkward with each other, and when Frank said goodbye there was no kiss and Lynn didn't wait to wave him off. Something was wrong. Lynn came back into the room, her eyes suspiciously bright.

"So, Dad, how does it feel to be home?"

"Grand." Jack finished his tea and stretched up his arm. "Help me. Want to see Norman."

"He can come and see you," Nell protested as she loaded the tray with the tea things.

"It's busy, Dad, and everyone's going to want to talk to you; that's a lot of standing around for your first morning."

He knew that she was right. He was already tired, but he wanted to see the place and thank Norman, and there was more chance he'd find out what was up with his daughter over there. "I'll stay in back."

His wife looked on in disapproval while Lynn helped him to his feet. They made slow progress across the yard and by the time they got to the door of his office he was a little breathless.

Lynn was looking at him. "Okay?"

He nodded and she turned to lead him into the office. He shook his head. "Shop."

"Dad!"

He looked at her. "Shop."

She sighed. "Mum will kill me."

Norman's face broke into a smile when he saw him; Jack figured there was a measure of relief there, too. Poor old Norman wouldn't know what to do with himself if he didn't have the shop to come to every day.

"Good to see you, Boss."

"Okay, Norman? Lynn driving you mad?"

"Not at all, she's grand."

"I've had to do very little, Dad," Lynn said. "Norman's held the place together."

Jack looked on with amusement as the man blushed at the praise.

"Is there any chance of being served or do I have to go to Dublin to buy a litre of milk?"

Jack turned and grinned at one of his neighbours and oldest friends. "Still whingeing, Pascal?" After that there seemed to be one person after another coming up to shake his hand and welcome him back. He sagged back against the counter, realizing that his wife and daughter were right: this was far too much activity for his first few hours out of hospital, but still his heart felt light to be back among friends. Lynn had melted into the background, but he was relieved to see that she seemed more comfortable dealing with people. He had been afraid that the incident on Sunday would have set her back. But there was definitely something up between her and Frank.

★   ★   ★

290

When he was sitting in his office and she'd made them both a cup of tea he asked her what was wrong.

She sat down on the chair opposite. "Frank got to hear about Sunday and he went round to put Vincent right and —" She stopped abruptly.

"What?" Jack prompted.

"Vincent said something — I don't know what — that gave Frank the impression there was something going on between us. Frank's moved up to Dublin."

"He's left you?" Jack stared at her, incredulous and angry.

"Yes, well, no . . . Oh, I don't know, Dad. We haven't talked. He said he needed some time to think."

Jack watched as she swallowed her tears and he was reminded of her as a child crying over the death of their dog, Prince, but trying so hard to be brave. He was able to console her then but he wasn't convinced he could do it now. He'd thought he'd safely handed that mantle to Frank and he felt let down. Jack didn't even ask Lynn if the story was true. He didn't have to. But, then, he was her father, not her fiancé, and he could imagine how jealous he'd feel in Frank's position. It was human nature. "He's upset but he loves you." Jack felt very tired and he could hear his words blending into each other.

"I know. Come on, you need to rest." Lynn stood up and helped him to his feet.

"It will work out," he told her as they walked slowly back to the house. "I promise."

Lynn smiled slightly as she went back to work. How many times had Dad promised her everything would be okay lately? He still saw her as his little girl. But, it was wonderful to see him so sharp. There was an occasional look of confusion in his eyes as his mind tried to make sense of this new world he found himself in, and sometimes he would stare at his left hand with distaste and resentment. She could understand his frustration but things could have been so much worse.

Her thoughts returned to Frank. It had been a relief to find out that there was a genuine reason why he hadn't called last night. He'd been very apologetic. She had immediately offered her help and said that she would go up and see poor Philip later.

"Don't bother tonight," he'd told her. "He'll be out of it, and Carrie and I will be with him."

Lynn felt as if she'd been slapped. She was the outsider. At times like this when Philip needed them, his parents were a team, all recriminations and bitterness forgotten, and she was excluded. It had always hurt her to witness it, but today it hurt more than usual. She tormented herself with scenes of Carrie dropping by their lovely new home to discuss Philip's progress. She could see her lounging on their balcony next to Frank wearing one of her push-up bras and tight tops. Would he look at her and remember what was under that top? When she put her hand on his arm, tossed her silky blonde hair and looked at him through her long lashes, would he think, Better the devil you know? Frank had left without making any arrangement to meet or talk. His only commitment had been a promise to keep her posted about Philip. When he was getting into the car she'd opened her mouth to say

292

something but closed it again. He looked so exhausted and worried that she couldn't add to his burden, so instead she had pasted on a smile and told him to take care.

"Stop it," Val said as a sullen waitress brought Lynn's creamy latte and her glass of lager.

"What?" Lynn looked at her.

"Stop imagining things and don't deny it! Jeez, Lynn, isn't your life tough enough at the moment?"

Lynn had to laugh. "I suppose so."

"Give him a chance. With Philip taking ill, he's probably got a backlog of work to get through. He'll call you as soon as he can. I'm sure he has a list as long as his arm of questions he wants to ask."

Lynn groaned and buried her head in her arms. "Oh, God."

Val stroked her hair. "Just tell him what you told me. He'll understand and then he'll probably kill Vincent."

"Probably." Lynn sighed and raised her head. "Enough. I'm fed up of talking about me; tell me about you. Has John recovered from meeting your mother?"

Val groaned. "God love him, he is convinced that it was a great success and she thought he was the bee's knees."

"Maybe he'll grow on her," Lynn suggested, although she thought it was unlikely; she couldn't imagine John and Angie agreeing on much.

"If she does she does." Val gave a resigned shrug.

"So when is he moving in with you?"

"I don't know. I need to make some space for him first and I've been so busy in work I haven't had time."

Lynn studied her in silence. Val was having doubts, she was sure of it.

"What?" Val's eyes were defensive.

"A couple of weeks ago you couldn't wait to live with him and now you can't find time to clear some space for him?"

"Yeah, well, it's one thing dreaming of it and quite another thing doing it. John has so much stuff, so many books, and he says that he needs an area to write." Val looked at her in dismay. "He wants to divide the sitting room down the middle so he would have a window."

Lynn struggled to hide her incredulity; the nerve of the man. She wanted to say that Val should tell John where to go but she knew that she must tread carefully. "I see his point," she said instead.

Val looked crestfallen. "You do?"

"Sure. A nice view and good light must be important to a writer."

"I suppose."

"Still, it would be a shame to break up that room. It's so bright and airy."

"It is."

"Maybe you should look for a bigger place," Lynn said. "One of the apartments overlooking the river would be nice."

"Oh, that's a great idea," Val said, her face lighting up. "Me and mum went to have a look at the apartment on show when they first went on the market. The kitchen is to die for and they are so spacious. And they

294

have balconies; John would have lots of space to get creative."

"Sounds perfect."

"The bedroom's cool, too; I'd like him to get creative in there!" Val grinned. "I'll call the agent first thing in the morning."

"Speaking of first thing, I must get home." Lynn yawned. "I'm sorry it's so early but these mornings are a killer."

"Will you drop me back at the off-licence?" Val asked. "I forgot my keys."

CHAPTER
TWENTY-EIGHT

"Sure you don't want me to wait?" Lynn asked.

Val hopped out of the car. "No, I fancy a walk. Night, Lynn, safe home." Val watched her drive away. Her heart went out to Lynn. She was, as usual, putting on a brave face but it was obvious that she was missing Frank and would be devastated if they split up. Val hoped the man would see sense. If he used the evidence of his own eyes, then he couldn't ignore how affected Lynn had been by Vincent's harassment and that she would never have let him near her if she'd been sober. Val suspected that Vincent had been the one filling up Lynn's glass. It was totally out of character for Lynn to overindulge, especially when out with the crowd from work. She had been so chuffed with her promotion to assistant hotel manager. Val still remembered the night she told her.

"Do you remember, we used to lie on my bed listening to music for hours talking about boys? I never dreamed I'd end up with a job like this."

"You got the job because, unlike me, you stopped dreaming and started working," Val had said, laughing. She wasn't jealous or envious of Lynn's good fortune. She had wondered if their friendship would suffer after

Lynn went to college but she never should have. Lynn had made new friends but she had never forgotten her old ones, and once she started work in Rathbourne they spent more time together than ever. Val would miss her when she left for Dublin, but she knew that they wouldn't allow the distance to be an issue, not the way it had been with Gina. Then they were kids but, now they were grown women, Val knew Lynn would be a friend for life.

Smiling at the thought, Val went into the off-licence. Lorcan was on his own and reading a thriller. "Busy, eh?"

He looked up. "Rushed off my feet. What brings you back here?"

"I forgot my keys."

"Huh. I thought you were taking me for that drink you owe me. I should have known better."

Val looked at him, shrugged and smiled. "Sounds good to me." She had no other plans. She'd told John that she was going out with Lynn and it was still early.

"Really?" His eyes widened in surprise.

"Yeah, why not? Let's lock up."

"There's still five minutes to go, Ms McCabe." He gave her a stern look and tapped his watch.

"Yeah, and it looks like you're about to be swamped." She nodded at the deserted street.

"You've twisted my arm." Lorcan started to flick off the lights and went to put on the alarm.

Val found her keys. "Where shall we go? And don't say Hawthorn Lodge," she warned.

He laughed as he put on his jacket. "I'd say you're barred. How about Cava?"

Val raised an eyebrow. Cava was a small, romantic bistro just a few minutes' walk away. "Are you sure? You won't get a pint there."

"That's okay. I quite fancy a glass of wine."

"Fair enough," she agreed, wondering what John would think of her going to an intimate little restaurant with another man. But it was just Lorcan. She had suggested to John they go there several times but he thought the wine was overpriced and he preferred the pub, so it was just tough if it bothered him.

The restaurant was surprisingly busy but Cynthia, the owner, welcomed them with a friendly smile. "Hello, you two. This is a nice surprise. Now, you can sit at the bar or there's a table, but it's tucked away in the back and it's tiny, I'm afraid."

"The table's fine," Lorcan said immediately, and then gave an embarrassed shrug. "I hurt my back playing rugby at the weekend," he told Val. "I'm not sure I could handle a stool."

"Fine with me," Val said and they followed as Cynthia threaded her way through the tables. She wasn't kidding about the size. "Would you like to see a menu?" she asked.

Lorcan looked at Val. "How about a bottle of white and some bread and cheese?"

"Lovely!" she agreed.

When they were seated their knees were brushing and, because there were so many people in such a small space, it was loud and they had to lean forward to catch

298

what the other was saying. Val looked into his eyes as he talked. She didn't think she'd ever been this close to him before. She certainly had never noticed before that his hazel eyes were flecked with green, that he had a very nice smile and that the curve of his lips was quite distracting.

"Earth calling Val."

"Sorry, what was that?"

He didn't answer until the young waiter had poured their wine and left. "I was just asking, is Lynn okay?"

"Not bad. Her dad came home this morning so I think having him around will make life easier."

"That's great news. I always liked Jack. He's a trooper."

Val nodded. "Thanks again for driving her to Dublin that night. I'd have hated to see her get behind the wheel of a car, the state she was in."

He took a sip of wine and smiled. "Happy to help any time if this is my reward."

Cynthia arrived and placed a platter of different cheeses and a basket of warm, fresh baguette between them. *"Bon appétit!"*

"Thanks, this looks great." Lorcan smiled at the woman.

Val laughed. "You're easily pleased."

"I am. You can keep all your fancy crackers. Nothing tastes as good as fresh, crunchy bread and cheese. Here, try this." He slathered a small piece of baguette with a runny Camembert and held it to her lips.

Val closed her eyes as the explosion of flavour filled her mouth. "Gorgeous!"

He reached out a finger to clean some cheese from the corner of her mouth. "You missed a bit."

It seemed such an intimate gesture that Val was lost for words.

"Are you okay?" His eyes clouded in concern.

She looked into his eyes, mesmerized. "Absolutely fine," she assured him.

He took a piece for himself, holding her gaze. "This is really nice."

"It is," she agreed. Somehow she didn't think they were talking about food any more.

He picked up the bottle and went to pour more wine, but he spilled some. "Sorry."

"No harm done." Val mopped it up with her napkin, startled by the undercurrent that was suddenly between them and acutely conscious of his knees against hers.

He took a mouthful of wine. "Can I ask you a personal question, Val?"

"Sure." She reached for her glass, her heart thumping in her chest.

He looked solemn, his eyes raking her face. "Do you plan to spend your life in Rathbourne serving behind the counter in an off-licence?"

She stared at him. Whatever she was expecting, it wasn't that. "I suppose so. Don't you?" She laughed.

"Absolutely not."

Val's smile faded. "Oh."

"All the years that I travelled, I worked in shops, bars and restaurants and I learned everything I could about the businesses and I saved. When the time is right I'm going to start up on my own."

"Wow, really?" she said, impressed. "Where?"

He shrugged. "I don't mind. I'll go where the business is."

"I'm sure an off-licence would do well in any town."

"An off-licence is only one part of my plan." He looked around appreciatively. "I'd like to run a place like this."

"I had no idea that you were interested in running a restaurant," she marvelled.

"You thought I was a loser with no ambition," he said, cutting a chunk of Cheddar for himself. This time he didn't offer her any.

"No, of course not! I just thought that you were . . . content." She took some more Camembert but somehow it didn't taste as good.

"Are you content?" he asked.

"Sure."

He smiled. "Of course you are: you're in love."

She looked away from his curious eyes. "Huh, yeah, maybe."

"Is there trouble in Paradise?" he teased.

She shook her head, feeling disloyal. "No."

He nudged her head up with one finger so he could look into her eyes. "Does he make you happy, Val?"

She couldn't look away and she knew she should say yes to break this spell he seemed to have cast over her. She should go home. She had no business talking to another man in this way. She was practically engaged, although it occurred to her that John had never mentioned marriage.

"I'm sorry, I'm making you uncomfortable. I always ask too many questions when I've had a couple of drinks."

"I'm not uncomfortable. Does he make me happy?" She cupped her head in her hand as she considered the question. "I suppose he does. It's nice to have someone to come home to every day." Oh, God, now she'd made John sound like some kind of loyal pet.

"I'm sure it is," he said, his lips twitching.

"You're laughing at me."

"No, I'm not." He grinned. "Well, yeah, a bit. You sound as if you're with him because it beats being alone."

"That's not what I meant!" She flushed, knowing in her heart that there was some truth in that. "Don't you get lonely?" she asked, emboldened by the wine.

"How could I be lonely when I'm surrounded by people all day?"

"That's not the same. Wouldn't you like to find one special woman to share your life with?"

He looked her straight in the eyes. "No."

She felt an irrational sense of disappointment. "Shame, I'm sure there's someone out there desperate enough to take you on." She smiled to take the sting out of her words. In truth she thought any woman would be lucky to have him. She had always thought of him as kind and funny and smart and, for a guy, quite sensitive, but she'd never seen him as sexy — until tonight. Perhaps it was just this tiny table they were sharing, but she didn't think so. She was mesmerized by his eyes and distracted by his hands and how expressive they were when he was trying to explain or describe something. She wondered how it would feel to be caressed by those hands. He had a lopsided grin that made her want to smile, but then it always had, and when he talked she found herself leaning closer, not just to hear what he was saying but because he smelled so gorgeous. They had worked side by side for so long but tonight she felt they'd only just met. She could almost hear Lynn's voice: There you go again; you're such a romantic. Except that both her friend and her mother had always been fans of Lorcan. She seemed to be the only one who had been blind to his charm.

He ignored the comment, leaned on the table and rested his chin on his hand. "Well, *are* you going to spend the rest of your life in Rathbourne?" he asked again.

Val felt slightly uncomfortable under his scrutiny. "I honestly hadn't thought about it. There are lots of places I'd like to see but I never thought of living anywhere other than Ireland. Not necessarily in Rathbourne, I suppose, now I think about it."

"So if I asked you to come and work for me would you be tempted?"

The question took the wind out of Val's sails. Any electricity between them had obviously been one-sided. She tried to hide her disappointment behind a bright smile. "If the perks were good I might," she quipped.

"I'll bear that in mind." He grinned. "More wine?" He held up the empty bottle.

"I'd better not," she said, although she didn't want to leave.

"How about a glass of port before we go? It'll go really well with the cheese."

"Oh, go on, then," she said, glad he was in no rush to leave either. "I never realized that you were such a foodie."

He ordered their drinks before he answered. "I wasn't when I left Ireland. Then I was strictly a burger or ham sandwich sort of guy, but when I started to travel I had to try different things or I would have gone hungry. I spent a lot of time in France and Italy and I was fascinated at how different their attitude to food is. Meals aren't just about satisfying a hunger but a social event. I like that." The port was brought and he gestured at the table between them. "This is very simple but it's so much more than a meal, isn't it?"

"Yes." Val looked at him thinking, You have no idea how much more. "But if I ate this every day I'd be as big as a house." She patted her tummy.

"A skinny thing like you would have to eat like this every day for a month to put on an ounce."

"No one's ever called me skinny before," Val laughed. She wasn't exactly fat but she certainly wasn't thin. "I think you need glasses."

"I think you're perfect."

Val shivered as his eyes dropped to her lips. Instinctively she licked them. Perhaps she hadn't been imagining the chemistry after all. "Really?"

"Really. John is a lucky man. He's a schoolteacher?"

Val nodded. She was about to add that he was a writer, but she was getting a bit fed up telling people that when she had never seen him settle down to write as much as a paragraph. All he ever seemed to do was talk about it and yet he expected her to alter her living room to suit him. Lynn's idea about buying a bigger place was a good one and yet . . .

"Penny for your thoughts."

Val shook her head, smiling. "You don't want to know."

"But I do," he assured her.

She looked at him from under her lashes. Perhaps it was no harm to let him know how she was feeling. "I'm having doubts about living with John. I'm not sure that we're really compatible. And Mum doesn't like him at all; I'm not sure Lynn does, either."

"You can't worry about what other people think. It's your decision, your life." Lorcan glanced at his watch. "Crikey, it's after midnight."

"It isn't!" Val said shocked. "I must go."

"Of course."

She followed him to the counter and was touched when he insisted on paying. "But I owed you," she reminded him when they were outside.

"You can pay the next time," he said as they left the restaurant, "if you would like there to be a next time."

"Of course I would. I've had a lovely evening."

He put an arm around her shoulders and gave her a friendly squeeze.

He left it draped loosely around her and she felt both delighted and guilty at how good it felt. They strolled on in silence for a while. "It's a nice night," she said, sad as they neared the crossroads where they would part. "I'd like to keep walking."

His fingers tightened on her arm. "Me too."

They stopped at the intersection and she turned to face him. "Thank you, Lorcan."

He looked down at her and she could see his eyes glistening despite the darkness. "By the way, remember I told you I wasn't looking for that special someone?"

She gazed up at him. "Yes."

"That's because I think I've already found her."

"Oh, well, that's good," she said trying to inject some enthusiasm into her voice.

"Not really. You see, she's involved with someone."

Her heart started to race again. "Oh, I'm sorry. Is it serious, do you think?"

"I'm not sure. I don't think she is, either."

Her eyes locked with his. "What are you going to do?"

"I think I'll wait for her to make up her mind."

"But that could take a while," she pointed out.

He shrugged. "She's worth waiting for."

"What will you do if she chooses him?" she asked, her voice barely a whisper.

"I'm not thinking that far ahead." He grinned. "I'm an optimist."

"Goodnight, Lorcan." Val went up on tiptoe to kiss his cheek but he turned his head slightly and she caught the corner of his mouth. His lips were warm and soft and she wondered what it would be like to kiss him properly. She pulled away reluctantly.

"Sweet dreams, Val."

She walked down the road, conscious of his eyes on her, feeling both excited and confused. She tiptoed up

306

the path to the house, opened the door as softly as she could, took off her shoes outside John's door and climbed the stairs to the safety of her flat. Though it was late, she couldn't sleep, reliving every moment of the evening. Was she really attracted to Lorcan, or was she just freaking out about making such a commitment to John? She thought back on those first few days with John. Had she felt this heady excitement, this awareness, this fascination? She honestly couldn't remember.

CHAPTER
TWENTY-NINE

Nell brought Jack his breakfast in bed only to find him struggling into his clothes. "What on earth are you doing, love? It's only nine."

"Meeting at ten. Help me?" he asked, frustrated at how just getting a bloody shirt on was such a challenge.

Nell looked at him, disapproval etched in every line of her face. "A meeting? Where, with who? It's far too soon for you to be working."

"It's only here. Charles Boland."

Nell, who had been buttoning his shirt, stopped and looked up into his eyes. "What about?"

"Just business." Jack wasn't about to bother Nell with this.

"What business do you have with that man?" Nell frowned. Since Lynn had told them what Vincent had done they had given the Bolands a wide birth — well, as much as you could in a town of this size.

"It's nothing. It won't take long."

Jack was sitting in the front room when the car pulled up outside the window at precisely ten. He heard Nell letting him in and sat up straighter in his chair.

The door opened and Charles stepped into the room and stuck out his hand. "Good to see you, Jack."

Nell hovered in the doorway. "Will I make some tea?"

"Not for me, Nell, thanks." Charles sat down in an armchair.

"Nor me." Jack waited until she left, closing the door behind her. He turned his gaze on Charles. "We had a deal."

"I know that."

"You broke it."

"Things changed, Jack," Charles told him.

"It was simple. No Vincent." The name came out slurred but it didn't worry Jack. They both knew who he was talking about.

"And I moved him."

"But he's back. He taunted her, scared her." Jack spoke slowly so that each word would be clear.

"It wasn't premeditated. He'd had one too many and just happened to bump into her —"

"Outside my *shop?*" Jack brought his fist down on the arm of his chair. *"Bullshit!"*

"It was the drink talking. We've all done stupid things when we're drunk," Charles said impatiently. "Anyway, Frank Hayes gave him a good hiding he won't forget in a hurry."

"Ah, yes, Frank may have hit him," Jack glared, "but Vincent landed the real blow."

Charles frowned. "I don't follow."

"He led Frank to believe that he and Lynn were having an affair." Jack struggled to enunciate each word. "Now Lynn and Frank are separated."

Charles muttered a curse. "I didn't know that. I'm sorry. I'll make sure he doesn't bother either of them again but I need him now as much as you need Lynn. You're not the only person with health problems."

Jack didn't even bother to ask what was wrong. He wasn't interested. He just wanted to protect Lynn and take that sad, bleak look from her eyes. "He is evil. He has to go."

"You're being unreasonable," Charles protested.

Jack looked him straight in the eyes. "He goes or the deal is off. Now I'm tired. Shut the door on your way out."

Immediately the front door banged, Nell was in. "What's going on, Jack?"

"Nothing for you to worry about. I need a nap."

"Sleep, but we will talk about this again," she assured him and went back to the kitchen.

Back in the car Charles's mind worked overtime. He phoned his solicitor. "I'm coming up to see you this afternoon; it's urgent. Dig out the contract I signed with Jack Stephens and see if you can find any loopholes. Also, see what property I have that would be suitable for building a house on."

"I'd need some time to do all of that —"

"You have four hours," Charles snapped and rang off. As he pulled out of Stephens's yard he looked in the mirror to see Lynn standing in the middle of the yard staring after him. "The trouble you've caused," he muttered. But she was incidental now. The important thing was to protect the business and secure its future.

310

His brother had been a partner in Hawthorn Lodge and Aideen had inherited his shares. It wasn't a huge amount now, given how the business had grown, but she could and would make life difficult if her darling son was sidelined. Charles slapped the steering wheel in frustration. He really thought that Vincent was a reliable successor but the man was turning out to be a liability. Charles felt tired and ill but he had to focus, he must concentrate. He had to find a solution that would secure the future of his business and keep Jack Stephens happy, and it wasn't going to be easy.

He drove straight to Hawthorn Lodge. The heavens opened as he got out of the car and he hurried into the hotel immediately aware of the hushed whispers of staff as he passed. He paused at the reception desk and smiled at the Polish girl: Alenka, he thought her name was. "Good morning, Mr Boland, can I help you?" She smiled politely.

"Good morning, Alenka. Is Bob around?" He could see she was pleased that he knew her name.

"No, he comes on duty in an hour but Gary is here if you need help."

"No, it's Bob I need a word with. Will you send him in to me when he gets in?"

"Of course."

Charles was engrossed in paperwork when there was a tap on the door and the porter stuck his head into the room. "You wanted to see me?"

"Yes, come in Bob, take a seat." He glanced at the rain lashing the window. "Do you remember the time we skived off school to go fishing? It was a day just like this."

"We were feckin' soaked and I got some hiding for it when I got home." Bob chuckled at the memory.

"Why didn't we have the sense to leave it to another day?" Charles wondered.

"We were young." Bob settled back in his chair and waited.

"I haven't asked you in here just to reminisce." Charles said.

"I assume it's about retiring."

Charles looked at him in surprise. "You want to retire?"

"No." Bob looked equally surprised. "But your nephew said that there were staff cuts in the offing and that retirement and voluntary redundancy would be the first step."

The little shit, Charles thought, furious, but he hid his feelings from the porter. "He got the wrong end of the stick, Bob. Your job here is safe as long as you want it." Bob's expression didn't change. "What is it?" Charles prompted.

"With respect, can you make that promise? There seems to be a lot of change in the air. You talked to us about redeveloping The Willows and that Vincent was moving there. Now it seems he's coming back and you're going away."

"Who told you that?" Charles asked.

Bob shrugged. "People talk. Word is that you're stepping down and Mr Vincent is taking over the company."

"Well word is wrong, Bob. I'll talk to the staff soon. This conversation, however, I would like to stay strictly between us."

"Of course." Bob looked cross.

"I'm sorry, my friend, but I need to ask you about a very delicate matter, one I hope you can shine some light on. It's important, Bob; there is a lot at stake."

"If I can help I will."

"Lynn Stephens." As soon as he said her name he could see a shadow cross the porter's face. "Tell me what you know."

"I'm not sure I understand," Bob hedged.

"This trouble between her and Vincent started after I moved out of Hawthorn Lodge. They always got on quite well while I was here. Do you have any idea what happened to change that? When it started?" Charles gave a helpless shrug. "*Why* it started?"

"I doubt that I can tell you anything you don't know already."

Charles held his gaze. "Oh, I think you can. She maintained he bullied her and undermined her, but I have a feeling there was more to it than that. If it helps, it's in Lynn's interest if I know the truth."

The porter thought for a moment and then with a heavy sigh started to speak. "The Christmas party last year. That's when it started."

Charles felt shell-shocked as he drove to the solicitor's. He wasn't sure what he had been expecting to hear but it wasn't what Bob had told him. There was no way that Jack knew about this. Charles thought of calling ahead

313

to the solicitor to warn him there was another item on the agenda, but this wasn't a discussion to be held on a mobile phone.

The meeting lasted nearly three hours and even then they hadn't come up with all the answers. The situation required careful handling but Charles was battling against time. This health issue loomed large and it meant he had to take action.

Much depended on his dear sister-in-law, a woman who drove him to distraction but whom he admired and respected for her strength, loyalty and unquestioning support of her son. And, yes, in truth, he had been a little bit in love with her since the day his brother, Desmond, brought her home. Not that he hadn't loved his darling Kathleen and been devastated by her death at only sixty. Desmond had followed within months at only sixty-two. Charles, at sixty-eight, was the longest-living Boland in two generations. The thought brought him little comfort at the moment, and he had a feeling that his demise might not prove to be as quick and painless as those of the other Boland men.

He shook himself out of this maudlin mood. He needed all his wits about him now. He needed facts and then he had to make a decision based on those facts. Then and only then he would talk to Aideen. He'd also have to talk to his daughters, though he didn't foresee any problems there. As for Andy, well, he wouldn't give a damn. When his son had walked away from his inheritance, Charles had been furious. But as he got older his anger receded and he came to accept, respect and even grudgingly admire his son's independence.

Andy loved life and was determined to live it in whatever way he pleased — and good luck to him. In the past Charles had mourned the fact that his son didn't have the drive and ambition of his cousin. Now he was just relieved that his son had turned out to be a good man and a son he could be proud of.

CHAPTER
THIRTY

This was too important and Aideen was too smart for him to beat about the bush, and so Charles gave it to her straight, doing nothing to soften the blow. At first she had refused to believe it and tried to blame Lynn: she was a tease, a gold digger, was trying to sleep her way to the top. But Aideen had lapsed into silence, shrinking in her chair, as he laid out the bare facts before her.

"What are you going to do?"

"I have to get him out of Rathbourne as quickly as possible."

"So back to The Willows." She sighed. "How long for this time?"

"My dear." He looked at her, feeling nothing but pity. She had worked so hard, fought so hard for her son, and for what? "There is no question of Vincent ever returning or taking over from me."

Aideen blanched. "You can't mean that."

"It's out of my hands. If any of this comes to light there's a good chance he'd be arrested, maybe prosecuted. It's in his best interests to leave."

She looked at him in disbelief. "You're exaggerating. The Stephens girl accepted her settlement, that's over,

316

and any other rumours could be easily quashed with money and influence. No one would have the nerve to take you on, Charles."

Charles thought of the steely look in Jack's eye. "You'd be surprised."

"He's your nephew. You promised Desmond that you would look after him; you promised *me*," she cried.

Charles sighed. "And that's exactly what I'm doing. Though where I'm going to put him I've no idea. How can I be sure that he won't get up to the same tricks in The Willows?"

"He won't. I'll talk to him."

Jack's words reverberated around Charles's head: "He is evil." Strong words, but there was definitely a bad streak in his nephew that he feared was irreparable, and he doubted Aideen could control it.

"You must do whatever it takes to make this go away," Aideen was saying, some of her spark returning. "Remember, it's not just Vincent you're protecting but the business. If he goes down the chances are you will too."

There was a veiled threat in those words that Charles didn't like. "I am well aware of that," he said coldly. "This is not something that can be sorted out overnight, but there are some actions that we can take straightaway. I don't know what we should tell Orla. She must have some idea what's been going on." He thought of the bruised face Frank Hayes had left Vincent with and his nephew's drinking. "And when the baby comes she will be inundated with visitors who will be only too happy to pass on titbits of gossip."

Aideen waved away his concern. "Orla will believe whatever we tell her, but it can't be the truth. If she were to leave him it would be disastrous."

She was right about that. It would give rise to gossip and resurrect the whole business again. He felt weary. How could he keep all the balls in the air? "I need to sleep on it. Don't say anything to Vincent for the moment."

"But —"

"You have to trust me to do the best for the whole family, Aideen," he said firmly. "Invite Vincent and Orla to dinner tomorrow evening. I'll have something sorted out by then."

"Call me first, Charles, please. I need to be prepared for what's coming."

He bent to kiss her cheek. "Of course. Try not to worry, Aideen."

Orla stared out of the window as Vincent drove them to his mother's house five miles outside town for dinner. "What's wrong?" he asked, clenching the steering wheel. She shook her head and said nothing and he fought the urge to shout at her. She'd been like this since he told her that he wasn't coming back to Hawthorn Lodge as soon as he'd thought. He had sugar-coated it as much as possible but Orla remained cool. It had been a relief when his mother had invited them over this evening. Being confined to the house with a silent, suspicious wife was driving him round the bend. Though he doubted the atmosphere at his mother's would be much better. She had been furious with him for approaching Lynn and still sounded cold and hostile on the phone.

"You idiot, have you learned nothing?" she'd exclaimed. "I'm glad your father isn't alive to see the way you've behaved. It's time you grew up, Vincent. Don't push Charles too far. He won't tolerate you letting the family name down like this."

Sometimes Vincent was sick to the teeth of the family, and now that he was being banished to the arsehole of nowhere for the foreseeable future the Boland name seemed more of a curse than a blessing. He shot a sidelong glance at Orla. She was stiff and unyielding, her hands protectively cupping her enormous stomach. It was so unlike her. She rarely got cross but if she did it never lasted long. Frank Hayes punching him, leaving an angry bruise on his cheekbone hadn't helped. Vincent had said he'd walked into the archway in the kitchen when he was drunk and she'd accepted that, or seemed to. He wondered could she have heard about the episode with Lynn but it seemed unlikely. These days she kept to the house, nervous of going out alone so near her time. If she'd been out it would have been in the company of his mother or one of his cousins and no one would say a word in front of them; they wouldn't dare.

Vincent turned into the drive of his childhood home and parked beside Aideen's Mercedes. "Here we are!" he said unnecessarily, and hurried around to help her out. Orla took her hand from his almost immediately and walked ahead of him towards the house. He sighed, hoping that his mother would manage to cheer her up.

Aideen welcomed them, looking her usual elegant self in a black dress, her pearls and wedding ring her only jewellery. Her copper curls were drawn back into a chignon. Beside Orla she looked even tinier than usual. She air-kissed her daughter-in-law and offered Vincent a cool cheek.

"I hope you're hungry. I have roast leg of lamb with all the trimmings." She smiled warmly at Orla. "We must keep your strength up."

"You shouldn't have gone to so much trouble," Orla said, her eyes widening as Aideen led them into the dining room.

"When I realized I'd cooked far too much I decided to invite Charles, too, and I thought we would be more comfortable in here. Vincent, get some drinks. I'm going to carve."

"Can I help?" Orla offered as Aideen turned to leave.

"No, dear, everything's under control. You make yourself comfortable. You'll be on your feet enough in a few weeks, believe me!" She laughed.

When they were alone, Orla looked up at Vincent through narrowed eyes. "What's going on?"

"What do you mean? It's just dinner," he mumbled, going to the sideboard and opening two small bottles of sparkling water. He'd kill for a drink, but it would probably be better if he abstained. He poured the water into cut-glass tumblers and added ice and lemon.

"On a week night and with Charles? Something's up. Are we being sent to set up a new Boland hotel in the outback?"

320

He laughed nervously. Where had this hard, suspicious woman come from? He'd never seen her like this before. She had always looked at him with faith and trust and could never do enough to please him. The doorbell rang. "That will be Charles. I'll go and let him in," he said, and hurried out into the hall, glad to escape his wife's mistrustful eyes. "Evening, Uncle."

Charles grunted. "I should be watching the golf but instead I'm here clearing up your mess. It's getting to be a habit."

"I don't understand."

"Just follow my lead. No questions, do you understand?"

Charles was already striding down the hall towards the dining room and Vincent had no choice but to follow him.

"Hello, my dear," Charles greeted Vincent's wife with a broad smile, "how well you look!"

"Thank you." Orla smiled shyly.

She had always been in awe of and a little intimidated by his uncle and Vincent could see her whole demeanour change in his presence. Aideen came in, her cheeks pleasantly flushed from the heat of the kitchen, and embraced her brother-in-law.

"Hello, Charles, glad you could come."

"How could I refuse dinner with two lovely ladies? Isn't Orla positively blooming?"

"She is." Aideen accepted the glass of wine her son had poured for her. "I'm so excited that I'm going to be a grandmother. I can see myself spoiling this baby rotten."

Vincent sat down on the arm of Orla's chair and slipped his arm around her. "I'm going to spoil both of them."

"Why wouldn't you? You're a very lucky man." Charles eyes were as cold as ice.

Dinner passed in conversation about the baby and cots and childminders.

"I'll be looking after my baby," Orla said, and, though her voice was quiet, there was a steely look in her eyes and a determined set to her chin that quite turned Vincent on.

"Well, of course you will," Aideen said smoothly, "but when you need a break or if you get sick you need to be sure that you have someone reliable to fall back on."

"That's true," Orla admitted, looking sheepish.

"Have you enrolled him for school?" Charles asked. "Obviously he'll attend Castleknock."

"But that's miles away!"

"As a boarder." Charles smiled at her. "All the Boland men went there."

Orla gaped at him. "I couldn't send my child away from home."

"Charles, I think you're planning a little too far ahead," Aideen said, with a meaningful look. "The poor girl hasn't even given birth yet. Now, coffee? Orla, I have peppermint tea if you would prefer it."

"Thank you, that would be lovely."

Vincent shot his uncle a look of exasperation. Why the hell did he have to talk about school? Orla was clearly upset. At least he wasn't the one to screw up for

322

a change. He reached for her hand under the table and squeezed it, and was relieved when she didn't pull it away.

Aideen returned with a tray of tea and coffee. "Vincent, get your uncle a cognac."

"Would you like one, Mother?"

"Perhaps just a small one."

Vincent poured three; he'd been an angel all evening and one glass wouldn't hurt. Once she'd served the drinks Aideen shot Charles a conspiratorial smile. "I can't wait any longer, Charles. Can we tell them?"

Vincent looked from his mother to Charles. "Tell us what?"

Charles cleared his throat. "I realized I was asking a lot of you to remain in The Willows, Vincent, especially as you'll be a father soon. But the business will be expanding and it makes more sense for you to be located near where the action will be."

"Action?" Orla looked from Charles to Vincent.

"Yes. It's early days, Orla. I won't bore you both with the details tonight but I did want to do something to make this period easier, to compensate for the inconvenience." He pulled an envelope from his inside breast pocket and handed it to Vincent.

"What's this?" Vincent glanced at his uncle as he opened it in confusion.

"It's the deeds for an acre about five miles the far side of The Willows."

"It's on a hill with the most amazing views, Orla. You'll be able to build the perfect family home." Aideen beamed at them. "Isn't it wonderful?"

"It's incredible." Vincent's mind worked rapidly. Was this a payoff? Expansion into the Midlands was certainly news to him.

"I don't know what to say, Charles," Orla said, looking equally gobsmacked. "Thank you."

"And until it's ready you can both live here," Aideen said. "You can move in straightaway and you won't have to worry about being alone when you go into labour. It will give Vincent peace of mind, knowing you've got someone close by, and, Lord knows, the house is big enough for you to have plenty of privacy, yet I'll be here to help with the baby if you need me."

"That's very kind, Aideen," Orla smiled.

"Not at all, dear. It will be wonderful to have company."

"In the meantime, you can get an architect working on plans for the house," said Charles. "I know a good man in Dublin who'll look after you."

"I'm speechless," Vincent said in all honesty. He felt suspicious and railroaded, but it must be good news or his mother wouldn't be looking so remarkably happy with the entire proposition.

"Thank you." Orla smothered a yawn.

Vincent hopped to his feet. He needed to get away and think about this. "Darling I'm so sorry, it's way past your bedtime, I should take you home."

"It is late. I'm so sorry, Orla," Aideen said. "How thoughtless of us."

"Not at all. It's been a lovely evening but I can't seem to stay awake past ten o'clock these days."

Vincent helped her to her feet, kissed his mother and, looking him straight in the eye, shook Charles's hand. "Thank you."

His uncle took it but there was barely veiled disgust in his eyes. "You're welcome. Look after your lovely wife."

Vincent put an arm around Orla and pulled her tight against him. "I will."

"Did you know anything about this?" Orla said when they were in the car.

Vincent shook his head and put his hand on her thigh. "No, honestly, I hadn't a clue."

"I'm not sure about living with your mum, Vincent. Don't get me wrong, she's been very good to me but sharing a home . . ."

He stiffened and took his hand away. "But if it was *your* mother of *course* it would be fine."

She glanced at him. "That's different."

"Why, because blood is thicker than water? My mother has done nothing but try to help you while yours is caught up in her own obsessive selfish little world."

"Mum's sick, Vincent," Orla protested.

He sighed. "I know, I'm sorry."

"But you're right," she relented and put her hand over his on the gear stick. "It's very good of your mum and I really do appreciate it."

Good! She was back to the soft, yielding girl again. He decided this was the perfect opportunity to dispel any doubts or worries that had been in his wife's head about Lynn. "You know, Orla, that land is a very generous present and an indication of how much Charles thinks of me and appreciates all I've done. He's been very impressed with the ideas I've had about repackaging The Willows."

"But I thought you wanted to get back to Hawthorn Lodge." Orla looked at him in confusion.

"I wanted to get back to you, darling, and it's true that I didn't fancy the idea of being exiled to The Willows. But lately I get the feeling that Charles has bigger plans and Hawthorn Lodge may not be the hub of his empire for much longer. One thing I am sure of, darling, is that he relies heavily on me and that land is his way of showing me that settling that damn claim was nothing more than a PR exercise."

"Really?"

"Really." He smiled over at her. "Now, stop worrying and concentrate on packing and getting ready to welcome our new arrival."

Orla smiled. "Okay, then. I wonder why Charles assumed it would be a boy."

"No idea." Vincent laughed. "Wishful thinking, I assume. There are too many women in his family." It had been a gamble lying to Charles over the sex of his child but there was a fifty-fifty chance he was right, and if it turned out to be a girl he could always blame it on the incompetence of the obstetrician.

"I suppose it'll be nice to raise our child in the country," Orla said.

"Sure it will and we'll still be close enough to towns and schools. Everything's going to be fine," he assured her, although he still had misgivings about exactly what Charles was up to. Whatever was going on, the first chance he got Vincent would be back in town and back in control, with or without Orla.

CHAPTER
THIRTY-ONE

Lynn left the supermarket early and set out on the road to Dublin. True to his word, Frank had kept her informed of Philip's progress, but by text. Any time she tried to phone him back the call went straight to voicemail. It was really getting her down. How had she any hope of convincing him that she hadn't been unfaithful if he wouldn't even take her calls? She was going to the hospital to see Philip and hoped to meet him there, but if not then she would go to the house. She had to try.

Frank's son was alone when she arrived, playing some game on his phone. He didn't see her until she was standing over him.

He grinned and pulled off his headphones. "Hey, Lynn!"

"How are you doing?" She pulled up a chair and handed over the novel and his favourite marshmallows she'd brought him.

"I'm a bit tender but fine." He had a quick look at the blurb on the back cover and popped a sweet in his mouth. "Cool, thanks very much."

"How much longer are you going to be here?" she asked.

"I should be out tomorrow or the day after. I heard your dad's home. How's he doing?"

"He's remarkable. He needs rehabilitation to strengthen his left arm and leg and talking is an effort at times, but he's determined to get back to work as soon as he can. I think it's a plus living beside the shop." She grinned. "The frustration of being able to see but not do is driving him nuts."

"So what's the story with you and my old man?" Philip asked curiously.

She looked at him. "What's he said?"

Philip snorted. "Nothing. He's just going around looking miserable."

"We had a misunderstanding." She sighed. "I want to try and explain but he's avoiding me."

"He's a stubborn sod."

She laughed. "He is. Are you expecting him in this evening?"

"No, sorry. He was here earlier. You'll probably catch him at the house. He's definitely not on TV tonight."

"It's weird. I haven't set foot in that house since we took ownership of the place."

"That's just mental. Go and talk to him, Lynn."

"But I came to Dublin to see you," she protested.

"And you've seen me and I'm fine and, er, a friend is probably going to drop by."

She raised her eyebrows as, despite his casual shrug, colour flooded his cheeks. "Oh, a friend, eh? Someone special?"

"It's early days but I like her," he admitted.

"What's her name?"

"Julia." His face broke into a wide grin.

"That's a gorgeous name."

"She's a gorgeous girl."

"I'm sure she is." Lynn hugged him and stood up. "You take care."

"I will. And Lynn, don't let Dad push you away. He loves you and you're really good for him."

"Oh, Philip, what a lovely thing to say," Lynn said, touched.

"Yeah, well, it's true. Now get out of here before you cramp my style."

She blew him a kiss and hurried out of the ward, feeling more hopeful. Philip was right. Frank loved her and she loved him. She was damned if she was going to let Vincent Boland destroy that.

Her heart felt lighter as she drove along the coast road towards their lovely home. Somehow it seemed a good omen that they should talk here. Frank would listen; she'd make him listen. It was strange keying in the code: this was her home but she still felt like a visitor. She climbed back into the car and waited as the doors swung silently open. A gasp escaped her when she saw Carrie's car parked behind Frank's. What the hell was she doing here? Lynn was about to drive off but cold fury got the better of her. The thought of that woman in her house made her feel violated. How could Frank bring her here? She climbed out of the car and cursed that she didn't have a key. How she would love to walk in and catch them. Oh, God! She shook her head, trying to get a grip. Frank loved her and he was an honourable man. He wouldn't be unfaithful, and certainly not with Carrie of all people. She was being ridiculous. She took a couple of slow, deep breaths, combed her hair with her fingers and rang the doorbell. It took a few minutes to answer but then, she wondered, could the bell be even heard up in the living room or on the balcony? The thought of their sitting together outside on their lovely new furniture and sharing that view made her stomach churn. She heard footsteps come down the hall and then the door was flung open.

"Lynn!"

The look on his face didn't make her feel any better. He looked like a man who had been caught out.

"Bad time?" She glared at him.

He hesitated for a second and she turned to go.

"No! Stay, Lynn. We were just sorting out our finances."

Frank stood back and she preceded him upstairs in silence, yet again feeling like the interloper. There was no sign of Carrie, and she glanced outside but couldn't see her out there, either. She was just turning questioning eyes on Frank when his ex-wife emerged from the bedroom.

"Oh, hi." She smiled at Lynn.

"Hi." Lynn looked back at Frank.

"I don't think there's anything else, Carrie. When I've talked to the solicitor and the bank I'll give you a call." He stayed at the top of the stairs. "I'll see you out."

With a toss of her hair, his ex crossed the room. "Philip's feeling a little better if you're interested," she said as she passed Lynn.

"Carrie!" Frank hissed furiously.

"I've just come from the hospital. He was in great form," Lynn replied. "Excuse me, I think I'll go take a shower."

Carrie glowered. "You're very tidy, Lynn. This place looks like a bachelor pad."

"Not for long." Lynn smiled widely. "The boot is crammed. Bye, Carrie."

When Frank returned she was perched on a stool at the kitchen bar.

"I thought you were having a shower," he said.

"I changed my mind." She looked up at him "That was a very cosy scene."

He shook his head in disbelief. "You can't honestly think that there's anything going on between us."

"You seemed to think that there was something going on between me and Vincent, a guy who resulted in me giving up my job, attending a psychiatrist and taking antidepressants."

He looked slightly shamefaced. "That was different."

"How would you know?" Lynn retorted. "You've never given me a chance to explain. You listened to that bastard and then left me."

"I didn't leave you," Frank protested.

"You're living in our new home alone and I'm in Rathbourne, where we agreed to stay as long as Dad needed me." She looked at him. "You abandoned me."

332

He wandered over to their new leather sofa and sat down. "I'm sorry. I was just so angry. I didn't trust myself to be near you."

She sat down at the other end. "You thought you might punch me too?"

"No, of course not."

"Don't you want to know what I have to say?"

He said nothing.

"No." Tears pricked her eyes. "So that's it? Will I go? Are we finished?"

"No!" He turned tortured eyes to hers. "Tell me."

They continued to sit at opposite ends of the sofa, his eyes fixed on her face as she talked. He didn't react until she told him about the kiss. Then she saw the anger and hurt in his eyes and she hurried to reassure him.

"I didn't respond, honestly, but I thought it would be churlish to make a big deal of a little kiss."

Frank stood up and pulled her into his arms. "How exactly did he kiss you, Lynn? Was it like this?" He gave her a light peck on the mouth. "Or this?" Now he was prising her lips open and his tongue slipped gently inside. "Or like this?" He moulded her body against his, running his hands all over her, his thumbs rubbing her nipples, one leg jammed between hers as he plundered her mouth with his tongue.

She wrenched away from him. "Stop it!" she cried in disgust.

He stood looking at her, and shook his head. "I'm sorry." He walked to the other end of the room, as if he couldn't bear being close to her. "Go on."

She sank back down on the sofa, shaken. "What's the point? It won't help."

"Please. I need to know."

She took a moment and swallowed back her tears. "I told him I was sick and I needed to go home and he suggested that I stay the night. I only agreed because I was afraid of throwing up in the taxi; I felt so dreadful. He said that the staff or guests shouldn't see me in such a bad condition and sent me up the back stairs to Room 112. He said he'd meet me there with the key. To be honest, I felt very embarrassed and I was grateful to him for being so kind." Frank snorted in disbelief and she shrugged. "Yes, I was gullible but you know that I'm not used to drink and I really was a mess. I have no idea how I managed to get up those stairs. Everything was a bit hazy after that." She paused. If he was furious over a kiss, how would he handle the rest of the story?

"Tell me what you remember, Lynn, and don't lie to me," Frank ordered.

And she did. She told him what she had told Val, but it was so much harder telling Frank. He flinched at every word, rage, hurt and disgust in his eyes. He wanted all the details that she didn't want to give, but she knew that, if she didn't, he would assume the worst. Tears rolled down her cheeks as he fired one question after the next. "Did he kiss you again? Did you kiss him back? Did you strip for him?"

She shook her head, sobbing loudly now. "I told you: I think I fell asleep immediately."

"Did he take your clothes off?"

"No, but I woke up at some stage and he was crouched over me and my skirt was pushed up."

"How far up?"

"Frank —"

"How far?"

"To my waist."

"The shit! Which pants were you wearing, the lacy ones? A G-string?"

"A G-string," she cried miserably watching Frank's face flush with anger.

He closed his eyes and clenched his fists. "What was he doing? Where was his mouth? Where were his hands? What about your bra? Did he open your bra?"

"No," she said, crying harder. "I think it was him pushing up my skirt that woke me. It must have only been seconds later."

"How do you know how long you'd been asleep? How do you know what he'd been doing to you, what he'd touched or kissed —"

She wrapped her arms around her chest and started to rock back and forwards like a frightened child. "Please don't say that; please don't."

"He could have screwed you."

"No! I'd have known if he had."

"I hate the thought of him seeing you, let alone touching you."

"I do too, Frank." She wiped her eyes.

"Had he undressed?"

She shook her head. "But his belt and zip were open. When I realized that I got scared so I went to the loo, pretending I was about to throw up and called for help."

"Why didn't you tell me?" he said after several minutes.

"Because you'd have killed him and I figured I'd escaped and it was better for everyone if I just forgot about it. I mean think about it, Frank. If I'd reported him to Charles or the police what good would have come of it? It would have been my word against his; it would have been impossible for me to continue to work there; it would have destroyed his marriage; and it would have come between you and me." She wiped her eyes and looked at him. "What did he say to you?"

"He insinuated that you and he had some sort of relationship and when I said he was lying he said I should ask you about the Christmas party and Room 112." He looked at her. "And I did, and the expression on your face said it all."

"Because I felt dirty and ashamed that I had drunk too much and let it happen. I hated myself for that. But I swear to you that there was never anything between us, Frank, either before or since; you have to believe me."

He flopped onto the sofa beside her, looking beaten.

She reached for his hand, sensing he still doubted her. "I wasn't looking for attention, Frank. I didn't fancy him, I didn't flirt with him and I didn't want him. I was just at a party having fun, nothing more. Think about it. If I willingly went to that bedroom with him, why would I have called Bob for help?"

He didn't answer and she took her hand away, filled with sadness and despair. There seemed to be nothing she could say to convince him. She sensed that he wanted to believe her, but that journalistic brain was sifting through the evidence and trying to put together the pieces of the puzzle, but they didn't fit.

"Did he ever touch you again?"

"No."

"Then why did you fall apart the way you did, Lynn? I could understand if it happened after that night but it was months later before you had your breakdown."

She sighed. "I never wanted you to know, but there was a sexual element to his bullying."

He bristled. "You said he didn't touch you again."

"And he didn't, Frank. He was far too clever for that. Instead he would stand too close, brush past me in a doorway or force me to squeeze by him getting into the lift, stuff like that. He'd comment on my clothes, look me up and down and use suggestive language. He'd tell sexist jokes or ask other guys on the staff what they thought of my hair or my figure in front of me so it seemed innocuous. It was all subtle but constant and it wore me down until I dreaded going into work. Finally, I knew that I couldn't take it any more." She looked up at him. "When I told him I was going, he smiled."

"I want to kill him."

"Please don't go near him. Please, Frank? He's hurt us so much already, don't let him do any more. I love you and I hate him for coming between us but I promise you, I wasn't unfaithful. You're the only man I want, the only man I've ever wanted."

He pulled her into his arms and kissed her hair and her eyelids, wet with tears. When she turned up her face he kissed her mouth, his lips soft and gentle. She clung to him. He lifted her and carried her into the bedroom and made love to her very gently, slowly and quietly. Afterwards, as they lay still entangled, she felt a peace descend. She'd told him everything and it was going to be okay.

Frank turned on his side to face her and looked into her eyes. "I hate that he danced with you, kissed you." He ran the tip of his finger along her bottom lip. He continued to trail a path down her body. "I hate that he's seen you." His hand came to rest between her thighs. "Touched you."

"I do too," she said, tears filling her eyes once more. "But there's nothing I can do about it."

"I know." He kissed her briefly, said goodnight and turned away. She stared, shocked, at his back, realizing that it would always be like this. That every time Frank touched her he would wonder if Vincent had touched her there. He would never be able to forget. Once his breathing was steady and rhythmic she slid out of bed, took her clothes and went into the bathroom to dress. She came out and stood looking at his sleeping form for a moment and then she left the house that she would probably never live in and drove back to Rathbourne.

CHAPTER
THIRTY-TWO

Val was on excellent form, singing along to the radio as she dusted the shelves, watching the clock, her heart beating a little faster as midday approached, when Lorcan's shift would start. It had been like this since their night out. She had been afraid that things would be awkward between them, but they weren't. The hours they worked together they chatted companionably, and when they shared a sandwich they talked about everything from their childhoods to the books they liked and the latest movies they wanted to see.

"I'm in the mood for a good, scary thriller," she'd said last night. "But John hates them."

"Really? I think you need to be scared witless every so often — it's good for you," Lorcan had said cheerfully. "We can go to a late-night show after we lock up some time if you promise not to rob my popcorn the way you do my biscuits."

"I never rob your biscuits." She'd grinned. "Only the chocolate digestives." But, despite the banter, the thought of sitting in a dark cinema next to him was producing all sorts of feelings inside her that she really shouldn't be having.

You're in a serious relationship, Val kept reminding herself, and it struck her that serious really was the word. When did she ever laugh with John? When did they ever go out and have fun? She had settled into his life, a routine of Friday nights in front of the TV with a curry watching a movie of his choice, Saturday mornings when she would go and watch him play football. She'd even attended his writing group a couple of times but that was quite enough. The people who were supposed to be supporting one another seemed more interested in picking holes in each other's work and bemoaning how only commercial rubbish got published while their worthy, serious tomes went unappreciated.

As for John himself, well, the truth was he was getting on her nerves. Little things about him irritated her, things she hadn't noticed before. How he would make himself a coffee or get a beer and never ask if she would like one, silly stuff like that. They rarely went out to dinner, but, if she wheedled and they did, he would insist on going out early so they could take advantage of the early-bird menu. Most other evenings he ate in her flat yet never offered to pay for anything or even bring a bottle of wine or something for dessert.

When he had last talked about moving in and she had suggested looking for a bigger place, it had clearly come as a shock. He had put forward many arguments as to why it was a bad idea, none of them convincing. Val felt relieved. Now if he mentioned it she quickly changed the subject. It was a strange state of affairs and made her wonder greatly about what kind of a person she was. She had been nuts about him a few weeks ago and now she felt almost apathetic towards him. She found herself volunteering to do more hours at the off-licence. She'd also taken to dropping into the library and checking out evening courses and upcoming events advertised there.

Since that night in the bistro, she was conscious of how little she was doing with her life. Not that she saw herself as a future captain of industry, but there was nothing wrong with broadening her horizons. She'd joined a book club — readers, not writers; perish the thought! She had told Angie about it and suggested they go together. Her mother had seemed surprised but, nevertheless, delighted and they had enjoyed a great evening with women of all ages.

The other thing that Lorcan had planted in her head was the thought of travelling. Up to now her only reason to get on a plane had been to get a tan and have a good time, but when Lorcan talked about the far-flung places he'd seen she felt a craving start to build inside her. Suddenly, her life seemed very dull and predictable. She knew that if she said this to him he would shrug and tell her to go and do something about it. And why not? she thought, feeling a stir of excitement. There was nothing to stop her.

When Lynn sent a text asking could they meet, Val was glad of an opportunity to talk. She hadn't told her about the night out with Lorcan and she was dying to get Lynn's reaction. "Is it okay if I grab a bite with Lynn?" she asked him. It was his turn to have an early break, but he smiled and said it was fine. "I'll bring you back something tasty," she told him as she ran out the door.

"You always do," he called after her. She was smiling as she walked round to the church where she and Lynn usually met, thinking of the look on his face when he'd said those words.

"Who put that smile on your face?" Lynn asked curiously as she climbed into the car.

Val laughed. "Oh, Lorcan just told me a joke." She glanced at Lynn as she drove them out of town, noting the pale face and tense set of her shoulders. "What's up?"

"I told Frank."

"You told him what?" Val asked.

Lynn looked at her, slightly shell-shocked. "Everything,"

Val absorbed the enormity of that one word. "How did he take it?" she asked, although she figured she already knew the answer to that question.

Lynn pulled into a spot outside Brannigans and sighed. "Not well. I think he believes me but" — tears filled her eyes — "he can't look at me without imagining me with Vincent."

Val led Lynn into the lounge and ordered tea for them both.

"You're scaring me," she said when they'd been sitting there for some moments and Lynn had just stared into space. "Say something!"

"I honestly thought that we would spend the rest of our lives together but I don't think we can get past this."

"Rubbish, of course you will." Val poured the tea and put a cup in front of her. "He'll come around."

Lynn's eyes were grey-green pools of sadness "Even if he does manage to put this behind him, I'm not sure I can."

"Why not?"

"I don't think I can forgive him for doubting me so easily."

"Oh, come on, it was a perfectly normal and human reaction. Think about how you would feel if Carrie told you that she and Frank were still seeing each other."

"That's different. They have a history."

"And you and Vincent worked closely together and got on so well up until that night. You wouldn't be the first girl to have an affair with her boss."

"But he never asked me. Vincent told him lies and he ups and leaves, just like that. The only reason we finally talked was because I tracked him down and made him. And, by the way, guess who was in the house when I got there."

Val sighed. "Carrie."

"Yes, and she was in the bedroom."

Val lowered her cup and stared at her. "What?"

"I don't think anything was going on. The only bathroom upstairs is through the bedroom, but I hated the fact that she'd been in there."

Val sighed, feeling helpless in the face of Lynn's palpable pain. "What are you going to do?"

Lynn shrugged. "I think I'll move out of the house for a start."

"But where will you go?"

"I might crash with Mum and Dad for now; it would make sense while I'm working in the shop."

"You're welcome to stay with me."

"I'm sure John would just love that," Lynn said with a ghost of a smile.

"It doesn't matter what he thinks; it's my flat."

"I don't want to come between you —" Lynn started.

"You won't be." Val looked at her. "I'm finishing with him."

"You are?"

Val gave a small laugh. "That just kind of came out. But I realized lately that he's not the one for me."

"No, he isn't," Lynn agreed, putting her hand over her friend's. "We're a right pair, aren't we?"

"I think we're great." Val smiled.

Lynn raised an eyebrow. "You do?"

"Yes. You never had a serious relationship before Frank came along and this must be very hard for you, but you feel he's let you down and you won't tolerate that and I say good for you. Me?" She sighed. "I've gone out with anyone who asked me and let them walk all over me, but I'm not going to do that any more. I may not be very clever, I'll never run my own business. Or be famous. I'm no great beauty, but I'm not ugly either. I'm a good person and I never knowingly hurt people. I'm just getting through life as best I can. So, you know what? I don't want to be with someone who doesn't believe that, appreciate it and love me for the person that I am."

344

"I think you're damn right and I agree with all of that, except you *are* clever and very pretty," Lynn said, giving her a hug. "What brought this on?"

"It was something Lorcan said. He was talking about the future, about his plans and his dreams, and he asked me about mine and I realized that I didn't have any. So far I've just stumbled through life. The only goal I seem to have had was getting a man and keeping him without giving much thought as to whether he was good enough for me. I'm still not sure what I want to do with my life but I am sure of one thing: I'm not going to settle. If I can't find the right guy, then I'll do without."

"You're amazing, you know that?" Lynn said affectionately.

"Why? Because I've finally come to my senses? It only took twenty-eight years, I suppose. Why do you think so many women are obsessed with settling down? Yet, when I look at some of the married women I know, they can't wait to have an evening out with their girlfriends."

"The grass is always greener. Don't hit me for saying this, but you know I thought you had met the right guy."

Val's eyes widened. "John?"

"No!" Lynn shook her head a little too vehemently. "Lorcan."

"You sound like my mother now," Val said feeling her cheeks grow hot.

"I don't know the guy that well but I've always liked him. The night he drove me to Dublin I thought it was

345

very telling that you turned to him for help. You seem comfortable together."

"Comfortable." Val wrinkled her nose. "Like a pair of slippers." But in the wine bar and afterwards she hadn't felt comfortable: she'd felt electrified. Her senses had been heightened and she had been acutely aware of every touch. But it was more than a physical thing. She loved that he wanted to know about her, whereas most guys she had dated just wanted to talk about themselves.

Lynn stared at her in delighted surprise. "You like him, don't you?"

"I do, but I'm not rushing headlong into this one, Lynn. He has plans and I doubt he will stay in Rathbourne, and even if he wanted me to, I won't just tag along like an obedient puppy. I have to think of me and what I want."

"Oh, Val, you are a force to be reckoned with; I wish I had half your strength."

"You're kidding me. You've been living in a nightmare for, what, eighteen months and you kept it all to yourself."

"I think my counsellor would call that stupid, not strong."

Val patted her arm. "Whatever. You did it for the right reasons. Do your parents not even know the truth?"

Lynn looked at her in horror. "Are you crazy? They'd freak."

"So, what do you think?" Val smiled at her. "Want to move in with me?"

"If you're sure, then yes. Won't you find life awkward with John still living downstairs?"

"I don't think he'll be that bothered; he'll just go and find some other poor woman to live off. What about Frank? This is going to come as a terrible shock to him."

"Perhaps it will be a relief that I've taken the decision out of his hands. We'll have to sort out what happens about the new house." Her voice broke.

"Are you sure you're doing the right thing?"

Lynn shook her head. "Not at all, but I just know that I can't live with him looking at me like that every day. When are you going to tell John?"

"After work; there's no point in putting it off." She gave Lynn a sad smile. "I suppose this is a red-letter day for us both."

Lynn didn't smile. "I suppose it is."

Something had been niggling Frank, something in the recesses of his brain that he couldn't quite grasp. He left the house and made his way down to the beach. It felt strange walking the strands without Lynn's hand in his, and he clenched his fists and dug them deep in his pockets. After his walk, he bought a newspaper and went into a coffee shop rather than returning to the house. Though Lynn had never lived there, it felt like an empty shell without her. He scanned the pages quickly but paused at a small piece in a side column, so small he could easily have missed it. Taking his coffee and paper, he hurried back to the house and went into the first bedroom, where boxes of books awaited unpacking. He found the one with all of his notebooks — he threw out nothing — searching for the notes he'd taken the day he'd first taken Lynn to meet the solicitor. It took an hour before he found what he was looking for. He phoned Calum immediately.

"I'm not sure," Calum said when he explained what he was looking for.

"Please, Calum, it's important."

With a sigh, the solicitor agreed. "But, Frank, if you're going to write something I want to see it first."

"You have my word," Frank assured him. Writing an article was the very last thing on his mind right now.

He had been surprised and delighted when Eileen Quinlan not only agreed to meet, but suggested he come straight over.

"I remember you!" She smiled when she opened the door.

Frank shook her hand. "I remember you, too. It must have been at the opening of the leisure centre."

"That's it," she agreed. "Just before I retired a year ago."

"If you don't mind my saying so you seem a bit young to have retired."

She threw back her head and laughed. "No woman minds being told things like that! They called it retirement but I was pushed out."

"By?"

"Vincent Boland, who else? He never liked me." She sat down and poured the tea. "Is Lynn still having

348

trouble with that fella? I told her solicitor that I would be happy to speak up for her."

"The case is settled, but I'm afraid Lynn's still suffering from the fallout."

Eileen sighed. "I'm sorry to hear that. She was so good at her job and very well liked."

"I can't help thinking that Lynn probably wasn't the only one who Vincent Boland bullied." He looked at her. "Can I speak confidentially to you, Mrs Quinlan?"

"Of course."

"He didn't just bully Lynn, he sexually harassed her, and I wondered, had he done it before? If he did, the chances are that he will do it again and I don't think he should get away with that, do you?"

"Certainly not." The woman sat back in her chair looking troubled. "I feel terrible now."

Frank sat forward. "Why's that?"

"Everyone knew that Vincent had an eye for the girls. He was always drooling over them, making lewd comments and finding some excuse to get one or other of them alone. I thought the girls were more than willing; I was quite judgemental about some of them," she admitted. "But now that you say it I wonder if they had a choice."

"Are any of these girls still working at Hawthorn Lodge?"

"Perhaps, I'm not sure. It was the kitchen staff or chambermaids he usually went for and they never stayed in the job long. It's hard work and not well paid. At least when you were front of house you got tips."

"Is there anyone still working that you think might know and who would be willing to talk to me?"

"Bob, the porter, has been there for ever. He's no time at all for Vincent but he's loyal to the boss so he probably wouldn't. You could have a word with Martha, although she's quite the gossip and it's hard to separate the truth from fiction." Then Eileen's eyes lit up. "I know: talk to Celia Fagan. She's been waitressing part-time there for donkey's years. Nothing gets past Celia."

"Do you think that she would be willing to meet me?"

"I'll phone her and ask if you like," she offered immediately.

"Yes, please, that would be great."

"It's the least I can do. I feel dreadful that he might have hurt someone simply because I kept my mouth shut."

"We don't know that," Frank cautioned, "and please don't mention our suspicions to Celia: it might affect her memory of events."

"I understand." She stood up and went in search of the waitress's number.

Celia Fagan agreed to meet Frank, but only on her day off and in a pub in Dublin.

"Sorry to be so cloak-and-dagger," she said when she arrived in The Fleet, the pub they'd agree to meet in. "But I need that job and if anyone saw me talking to you —"

350

"I completely understand. Thank you for meeting me. Can I get you a drink?"

"Just orange, please. So this is about Vincent and Lynn?" she said when he'd bought her drink.

Frank even hated their names being coupled like that. "In a way. Were you aware that Vincent was making life difficult for Lynn?"

"Oh, yes, he didn't try to hide it. They got on well, or so it seemed, but then things went very sour after Charles left and he treated her very badly. But, you see, that's Vincent for you. Someone was always on the receiving end of that tongue of his."

"When did Charles leave?"

Celia thought for a moment. "It would have been the November or December the year before last."

"And then Vincent was in charge?" Frank looked at her.

"That's right."

Frank made a note. "Eileen said that he was always a bit of a philanderer."

Celia rolled her eyes. "He's a creep. My heart goes out to his poor wife. If she knew the things he got up to."

"So you think it went further than just chatting up the girls?"

"I don't doubt it. There's no accounting for taste and some girls are drawn to power."

"Do you know if he ever forced himself on anyone?"

Celia said nothing for a moment and then shrugged. "I don't know for a fact. I just have suspicions. There's a lovely Polish girl and it was obvious that he fancied her from the start. But she didn't give him the time of day. She was engaged to a man back in Poland; he was all she ever talked about. And then there was a party one night and she had a lot to drink. It was totally out of character but he'd been ordering bottle after bottle of wine and he stayed close to her all night. Then she passed out and he took her outside. He said he'd got Bob to put her up in one of the bedrooms to sleep it off and made a smart comment about foreigners not being able to hold their drink, and then he left." Celia sighed. "Well, that girl changed completely. Suddenly, there was no more talk of her fiancé or her wedding and she stopped going to any of the staff parties. Something must have happened that night, it must have."

"What's her name?" Frank asked.

Celia shook her head, "I can't tell you that; it wouldn't be right."

"Celia, what if Vincent did force himself on her? Do you honestly think that she's the only girl he's taken advantage of and, because he was the boss, they feared for their jobs and so said nothing? If I'm right, don't you think we should stop him?"

She looked at him for a moment, her eyes full of guilt and remorse. "It's Alenka. She works in reception."

CHAPTER
THIRTY-THREE

Jack felt tired but happy after his physiotherapy session. The therapist had said he was making great progress, but what had really given him a lift was what had happened yesterday. He'd given Nell a right earful about tidying away his glasses so that he could never find them and looked up to see her grinning at him.

"What's so feckin funny?" he'd said, crossly.

"Listen to yourself, Jack? Your speech is almost perfect."

And it was true, he'd realized, as she put her arms around him. "Do you think that I'd be understood on the phone?" he'd asked her.

"I do. Why, who do you want to call?"

"No one especially. It's just nice to know that I can."

Lynn wasn't due at the supermarket till noon and, though she felt like pulling the covers over her head and sleeping, she dragged herself out of bed, made a large pot of coffee and showered. She scraped her damp hair into a ponytail, threw on an old pair of jeans and T-shirt and fetched the suitcases out of the spare room. She flung clothes in, not caring too much about whether they got creased. It was when it came to emptying the drawers and going through papers that it got tough. She was on her third cup of coffee, sitting cross-legged in the front room sorting their CDs, when the doorbell rang. She wouldn't have bothered answering but, with her car in the drive, it was hard to pretend there was no one home.

"About time. Imagine keeping an invalid standing on the doorstep?" Philip grinned and walked past her, looking the picture of health.

"Hey, how are you? Please tell me you didn't cycle over," she said, taking in his shorts and sleeveless T-shirt.

"Nah, just hot; can you believe this weather?"

Lynn glanced out at the sunshine flooding the small garden. She hadn't even noticed the balmy spring weather. How lovely the view must be from the balcony of their home on a day like today.

"Mum dropped me off. She's gone shopping. She wondered if you could let us have some boxes." He stopped when he saw the state of the sitting room. "So we're not the only ones packing. You're moving to Dublin? About time you two came to your senses." Philip's broad grin faded when he saw her expression. "Lynn? What's going on?"

"I'm moving out, Philip, but not to Dublin. Please don't say anything. I haven't told him yet."

"But why, Lynn?" Philip looked at her in shock. "I don't understand. I thought you two were getting married."

"He told you?" She looked at him in surprise.

"Yeah. Don't worry: no one else knows."

Lynn shot him a grateful smile. "No one" meant Carrie. Though Philip got on fine now with his mother he had never quite trusted her. He was thrilled that his dad had finally found happiness and he and Lynn had grown close quite quickly.

Lynn struggled with what to tell him now. "We had a misunderstanding and I think that we both need time to think. For now, though, I'm going to move in with Val. I hate living alone and it means that we'll be able to sublet this place and finance the house in Dublin. And your dad will feel happier if I have company."

Philip looked doubtful. "I think he'd be an awful lot happier if you were together again."

"That's not possible right now. I'm needed here. I'll call him and tell him about Val's as soon as I get a chance."

"Good luck with that. His phone goes straight to voicemail any time I try to call."

"Well, there you go! He's obviously very busy. I'll send him a text asking him to call me. But please — not a word."

"Scout's honour," Philip promised, but he didn't look pleased.

"Now, if you want boxes, tell your mum to meet us at the shop."

Leaving Philip with a coffee and a box of biscuits, Lynn hurried upstairs to get ready for work, but first she sent a text to Frank asking him to contact her. It wasn't going to help matters if he heard from anyone else about her moving out.

Nell was sitting with several other women, a pad and pen in front of her, when Lynn arrived at the house. "Oh, sorry, I didn't mean to interrupt."

"That's okay, love, we're just working out the duty roster for the Rathbourne Rince."

"Gosh, is it that time already?" Lynn shook her head. The dance festival was held the first Sunday in May and had been running for four years now. It was always a huge success. Every business in the town and most of the community were involved in some way or another. Stephens's always supplied water, soft drinks and ice creams and sweets for the kids. Charles Boland laid on a charity buffet that was set out on the main street in the evening after the parade. Frank had even got drawn into it, as, with his many connections, he was able to entice musicians to the event with the promise of a free dinner in Dylan's and bed and breakfast in Hawthorn Lodge.

"You can put me down for the same duties as last year," Lynn told Nell now. Last May Lynn had still been working in Hawthorn Lodge and so very involved in the Rince. But she had managed to slip away once the parade was over and she had sought refuge helping out with the small children and well away from Vincent. It was the perfect hiding place. She assumed that he would play a central role in the festival again this year and she wanted to avoid him at all costs. She prayed that Frank would, too.

"It's going to be even bigger this year," Phoebe, the school principal, told her. "We have such a large Polish community now and they're going to give a demonstration of their own native dances and then teach the rest of us."

"That should be a good laugh."

"The kids can't wait. I've told them they must teach their parents that *rince* is the Irish word for *dance*, and pronounced *rinka*, not *rinse*!"

Lynn laughed. "I'll see if I can get my hands on some Polish treats or drinks."

"That would be a nice touch. Thanks, love." Nell smiled at her.

"Where's Dad?"

"In the shop."

"What?"

"He just won't listen to me," Nell sighed.

"Ah, but he looks grand altogether," Maureen Devlin said. "It's great to see him back where he belongs."

Lynn patted her mother's shoulder. "I'll go and make sure he doesn't overdo it."

She was relieved to find her dad at his desk, writing. She leaned against the door jamb and crossed her arms. "Am I out of a job?"

He looked up and grinned. "Not just yet." He tapped the ledger in front of him. "I've been checking up on you and it all looks fine."

"Have you been here all morning?"

"No, just a couple of hours."

"Good, take it slowly."

"I will. But I'm not going to miss the Rince. There's a committee meeting about it next week."

"Oh, Dad, don't you think it would be better to give that a miss? Those things always seem to drone on for hours."

357

"I'm bored and I want the old buggers to see that Jack Stephens is still alive and kicking. Besides, Charles Boland is chairing and he keeps a tight rein on things."

Pity he can't keep a tight rein on his nephew, Lynn thought.

"I'll make sure that fella won't be hanging around bothering you, don't you worry."

Jack didn't need to explain who "that fella" was.

"There's no need. I'll be helping out with the kids' club and staying out of Vincent's way."

Jack grunted. "I don't care. I won't have him there, swanning around like he owns the place. It's not right."

"Forget him," she said, watching in alarm as his colour rose. "The important thing is that everyone enjoys the day and we make a few bob for charity."

"True. You're a sensible girl. I believe Frank's persuaded some great musicians to come this year but it's all very hush-hush."

"Has he?" Lynn was surprised. From her own experience and after what Philip had said she had gotten the impression that Frank had far too much on to bother with the Rathbourne Rince.

Jack sat back in his chair and looked up at her. "Do you two even talk these days?"

"He's busy."

"Lynn?"

"I don't want to discuss it, Dad."

"Okay, sweetheart, but I'm here if you change your mind."

Lynn smiled broadly. "I can't believe how well you're talking, Dad, it's incredible."

"Well, I can't embarrass you when I'm making my father-of-the-bride speech, now, can I?"

She had to turn away to hide the tears that welled up. "I'd better go and do some work."

"Lynn?"

She paused but didn't look back. "Yeah?"

"It will be fine, I promise."

"You keep saying that, Dad," she said with a soft chuckle. "Who do you think you are, Santa Claus?"

Val was poring over leaflets completely engrossed when Lorcan loomed up behind her.

"Well, well, well, what you got there, then?"

"Lorcan, you scared the hell out of me!" He leaned over her shoulder to read and she stiffened, conscious of his proximity.

"Language classes."

He leaned on the counter and she stared at his hands: square, strong, male hands, hands well capable of fixing things, carrying things, hands that made you feel safe.

"Are you thinking of learning a language. Val?"

She gave a casual shrug. "I thought I might. To be honest, you got me thinking."

He looked up into her face. "I did? About what?"

"About travelling, about what I want in life, where I'm going, and it struck me as pretty sad that I was twenty-eight and had given it little thought."

"Or it may simply mean that you're one of those lucky people completely content with what they've got."

359

"I'm not," she said after a moment.

"So you and John are going to travel?"

His expression had changed but she couldn't be sure if it was disappointment or curiosity. She turned her eyes back to the leaflet. "*I* hope to, but it won't be with John; that's over."

"I know I'm supposed to say, 'Sorry to hear that' but I'd be lying. You deserve better. You need to be with someone who will share your adventures, celebrate your triumphs and comfort you when you're down."

She straightened and looked into his eyes. "Do you know anyone who fits the bill?"

He shook his head and she felt mortified that she had read the situation so wrong.

"But I know someone who would love to learn," he said, caressing her cheek with one finger. "Would you consider giving an eager apprentice a go?"

She suppressed a smirk, her heart thudding in her chest. "That depends. The apprentice would have to be a damn good kisser."

He drew her close. "May I try out for the part?"

"You may," she murmured. He lowered his mouth to hers and kissed her very softly, gentle, teasing, butterfly kisses that promised more. His lips were moist but firm and she couldn't help comparing him with John, whose kisses had always been quite wet and invasive; no preliminaries, his tongue was down the back of her throat before she'd even closed her eyes. But Lorcan was in no rush at all and when he finally slid his tongue between her lips she let out a sigh of pure pleasure.

"I hate to interrupt, but is there any chance of getting a bottle of gin?"

Lorcan took his time disengaging, smiling down at her before turning to the customer. "Sure. Sorry about that but you can't blame me, can you? She is incredibly kissable."

Val flushed with embarrassment but she couldn't but smile.

The old man cackled as he stashed the bottle in with his groceries. "If I was ten years younger and didn't have the wife at home I'd have a go myself," he told Lorcan, and winked at Val.

"How did I do?" Lorcan asked when they were alone again.

Val sighed. "I'm not sure that audition was long enough for me to make a decision."

Lorcan drew her into the back room. "Let's remedy that."

Frank was sitting in a rather noisy coffee shop across from Arnott's department store and watching the door. It transpired the girl didn't know Dublin well and that this well-known shop on Henry Street was one of the few landmarks she was familiar with.

He knew her immediately she walked through the door. She had high cheekbones, almond-shaped eyes, full lips and a poise that set her apart from the other women in the room. Vincent might be a sick pervert but he had good taste. Frank raised his hand to get her attention and stood up, smiling as she weaved through the tables to join him. "Alenka?"

She nodded, her smile nervous. "I am sorry to be late."

"It's fine." He tapped his notebook. "I've been working. Coffee?"

"Please."

He went to the counter and brought back two mugs.

"Celia says you're a journalist. I don't want to be in the newspapers."

"You won't be. I'm not writing an article, I'm just trying to stop Vincent Boland hurting women," he said baldly.

Her eyes widened and she took a sip of coffee before speaking. "You're Lynn's partner."

Frank wondered if Lynn would describe him as that now. "Yes."

"I like her very much. She hired me and was always fair and kind; I was sorry she left."

"She didn't have much choice."

Alenka looked at him with dead eyes. "And I have no choice but to stay."

"Lynn spoke highly of you and you have experience. I'm sure you'd easily find a job."

"He says if I stay he will look after me but if I go or if I . . . say anything, he will give me a bad reference and tell people that he thinks I'm in the country illegally."

"He couldn't do that. It might take time to prove him wrong but you would."

"I do not have time. I am due to start my degree in October and I need the money."

"Celia mentioned that you have a fiancé at home in Poland. Will he be joining you here?"

She lowered her eyes. "That is over now."

"I'm sorry." And he was. He could see this girl was sad. "Do you mind telling me your story, Alenka?"

She wiped her eye with the heel of her hand. "I never liked him. He always made me feel uncomfortable. He has this way of looking at you." She shivered. "It was not a problem at first, as I reported to Lynn, but when she left everything changed. He seemed to be constantly looking over my shoulder. He said inappropriate things that embarrassed me but I did not know what to do; there was no one I could tell. Mr Boland, Charles, had always been a gentleman and might have listened but he was never there. Then there was a party and there was a lot of drinking. I don't usually drink but Vincent bought champagne and I had some of that. One minute I was fine and the next I was unsteady and dizzy and I found it hard to think straight. Vincent took me outside and told Bob to take me up to one of the rooms to sleep it off."

"Room 112?"

She looked at him in surprise. "How did you know?"

"You're not the only woman who ended up there. You said Bob brought you upstairs?"

"Yes and I fell asleep. Everything was hazy after that but I woke up the next morning with my blouse open and" — she gulped back tears — "I was naked from the waist down and there was blood on the sheet."

Frank stared at her in horror. The bastard had raped her! He thought how that could have been Lynn and felt sick. "I'm so sorry, Alenka, and I hate asking you these questions. Stop me if it's too much, okay?"

She nodded.

"Do you remember anything about what happened in that room?"

"I didn't when I woke up but it started to come back to me after a few hours." She stared into her coffee but Frank could see that her eyes were full of tears. "I wish it hadn't. I remember waking and Vincent was sitting on the bed beside me with a glass of water and a tablet that he said would make me feel better. I was so grateful that someone was looking after me." She gave a bitter laugh and pulled a tissue from her bag. "I was a very stupid girl."

"Not at all. He took advantage of you."

"I fell asleep again and the next time I woke he was on top of me. I tried to push him off but I was not strong enough. He kept saying I should relax and enjoy it, that he would teach me how to please my fiancé and that I would be a better wife and lover. He said that I was different from other girls, that I was very special and he was going to look after me. I slept after, and when I woke he was gone. As I said, I didn't remember anything straight away but I knew that I'd had sex and I felt so ashamed. It was still early, so I crept out and went home and scrubbed my body, but it did not help. I was riddled with guilt and I knew that my boyfriend would not want me any more." Her tears flowed freely now. "We had agreed to save ourselves until we were married and I had let him down. I knew then that I would never return to Poland."

"But you weren't unfaithful, Alenka. You were raped."

"It does not matter now, it is too late."

"I'm sure it's not —"

"You don't understand," she cried, and then lowered her voice as two women at the next table looked around. She met Frank's eyes, her own full of pain and shame. "It's still going on."

CHAPTER
THIRTY-FOUR

Frank took a moment to take in what she was saying and even then he figured he must have misunderstood. "What did you say?"

She flushed. "Vincent. He still . . . does it to me, though not as much now that he is in The Willows."

He stared at her, sickened. "But, Alenka, why do you let him? Why haven't you told someone?"

"What difference does it make?" she said, her shoulders slumped in resignation. I have lost Jarek and Vincent says if I make him happy, he will look after me. I hate him. I cry and I curse every time he does it but he does not care; I think he likes it. He promoted me and I have more money. I am, I suppose, a prostitute now," she said, dispassionately. "In September I will leave and go to university. I will work hard and get a good job with good money." She raised her head and looked at him, defiant now. "And I will never let a man use me again."

"I am so sorry," Frank said, thinking how inadequate and empty his words sounded. "Why did you agree to talk to me if you've decided to put up with the situation?"

"It was one thing when I thought that it was just me, but, if it happened to another girl because I said nothing, how could I live with myself?" Her beautiful eyes were now dark and troubled. "But I am afraid we may already be too late."

"You think he's done it again?" he said, incredulous. That Vincent might have attacked another girl while still raping Alenka was beyond belief; the guy was a monster.

"I am not certain. It may not have happened yet but it will. I've seen the way he looks at her."

"Who is she?"

"An Estonian girl, Mareeka. She works in the kitchen; she is only nineteen."

"Are there any parties coming up?"

"Just the Rince." Alenka looked at her watch. "I must go."

"Are you quite sure that you are happy to go public with this?" he asked.

"Yes. I will do it." She stood up and put her bag over her shoulder.

"One last thing, Alenka. Does Mareeka drink?"

"Definitely not. She has some sort of allergy to alcohol; she even has to be careful of food that might contain it. Oh!" She smiled in relief. "She is safe! I am so glad. But, if it is not her, then it is only a matter of time before he finds someone else."

Frank sat over the dregs of his coffee doodling and going back over everything Alenka had said. It was heartbreaking to see a beautiful young girl so empty and broken and the idea that Vincent now had his sights set on a teenager filled him with anger and revulsion. His first inclination was to call Lynn, to meet her and talk to her, but this was too close to the bone for her, for both of them. Instead, he paid the bill, went out to the car and started to make some calls. When he had all the information he could muster, he called an old friend who also happened to be a detective.

"Adrian? It's Frank Hayes. I need your advice. Can I buy you lunch?"

Vincent came into the kitchen to find his mother at the table reading the paper. "Morning."

She lowered the paper and looked him up and down. "Why the suit? Going somewhere special?"

"I'm going to work," he announced.

"Forget work. You need to finish the move. It's important that Orla has all her own things around her. I want her to feel at home."

"She has everything she needs right now and the rest I can move over the next few days. Right now it's more important that I keep an eye on things at The Willows and Hawthorn Lodge too. Emer isn't as clever as Charles likes to think and with him out of action for a while someone needs to look out for our interests."

Aideen took off her glasses and put down the paper. "You know that your uncle doesn't want you in town and he told you under no circumstances to go near Hawthorn Lodge."

"I don't know what all the bloody fuss is about. I was just going drop in for a quick word with Emer —"

"No," Aideen snapped and rose to her feet, her eyes boring into his. "Charles doesn't want you there. In fact I had to fight hard to keep you in The Willows, so you had better bloody behave yourself."

He looked at her in frustration. "Oh, come on, Mother. It's bad enough Charles overreacting but I had expected more sense from you and, incidentally, a bit more support."

"How *dare* you!" Aideen practically spat at him. "I have given over my whole life trying to help you and you threw it away. You could have had it all, you stupid fool."

"I still can, and I will," he told her, irritated at being talked to like a child.

She shook her head in disgust. "You still don't get it, do you? When you are part of a family firm like this you have certain standards to maintain."

"I made one little mistake, the girl settled, it's over."

"That's where you're wrong. It is far from over."

"So what's going to happen?" he asked, feeling the world shift beneath him.

"For the moment you will concentrate on organizing the Rince and I will help Emer out at Hawthorn Lodge."

"You?" He looked at her in disbelief.

"I was doing it long before you came along. I've told you, it's a family business and, when you have to, you step up to the plate. Keep your nose clean, do a good job and perhaps when Charles comes out of hospital he will feel more charitable towards you."

"It'll look strange if I'm involved in the festival and not at work," he argued.

"On the contrary, the Rince is a full-time job. Your wife could go into labour any day, and, with Charles away, it's easily explainable that you're looking after his other business interests."

Vincent felt slightly better. It was true that there was a lot involved in organizing the Rince and so he would be visible around Rathbourne. "What about Jack Stephens? He won't be happy working with me."

"I doubt he'll be up to getting involved this year, but we'll cross that bridge if and when we come to it. Just, whatever you do, keep clear of that girl."

Jack's first reaction when Frank called to say he'd pick him up and drive him to the Rince committee meeting was to tell him where to go. He still couldn't believe that he had left Lynn high and dry. On the other hand, it was a chance to give him a piece of his mind.

Frank seemed just as uncomfortable coming into the house and Nell didn't make it any easier for him. There was no offer of a cup of tea or even a seat. In fact she barely acknowledged him. "Are you sure that you're up to this?" she asked Jack worriedly.

He patted her arm. "Of course."

"If it goes on too long bring him home," she ordered Frank.

"Will do," he promised with a smile that she didn't return.

"Nell doesn't seem happy with me," Frank said when they were in the car.

"Neither of us are. You haven't behaved very well."

"It's complicated, Jack, but you have to let Lynn and me sort this out for ourselves."

"Do you think you will?"

"I hope so."

"Good. Don't leave it too long," Jack warned.

There were eight people round the table at the meeting, one of them Aideen Boland. Jack was aware of Frank stiffening at his side.

She greeted them with a cool smile and called the meeting to order. "I'm afraid that Charles has been called away on business, so you'll have to make do with me. I'd like to welcome back Jack Stephens. Good to see you, Jack."

He gave a brief nod as the others joined in with their own good wishes.

"This is our final meeting before the Rince Festival, but you know the drill, Jack, and, apart from a few small changes, it will be run in much the same way as it has in the past. Hopefully, Charles will be there on the day but if not, Vincent and I will do our best to live up to his high standards."

Furious, Jack opened his mouth to tell her that there was no place for Vincent at the Rince or, indeed, in Rathbourne but Frank placed a firm hand on his arm.

"Please don't object. I'll explain later," he murmured.

Jack sat grim and largely silent as the meeting progressed and, when Aideen brought it to a close, he was first out of the door, Frank following closely behind him. "You had better have a good reason for stopping me."

"I do." Frank offered him his arm and they went back to the car. "Brannigans?" he suggested.

Jack nodded. "I can't believe Charles has pulled this; what the hell is he playing at? I warned him that Vincent was to get out of this town and stay out."

Frank glanced over at him. "But why would he listen to you, Jack?"

Jack waited until they had reached the car before replying. "He has to listen to me," he said, looking up into Frank's face, "because I can pull the rug from under him any time I like."

In the pub, Frank bought a pint of Guinness for Jack and a shandy for himself and they went into the snug. "So, tell me."

Jack shook his head. "No, you first, lad. I'd have thought that you'd be the last person in the world who'd want that bastard hanging around the Rince."

"I am, but I've been asking round about Vincent Boland and I'm building up quite a case against him. It's really important that he's at the festival."

"A case?" Jack looked at him, frowning. "What kind of case? Does this involve Lynn?"

"Indirectly. I really shouldn't say any more at this stage."

"You can't make a statement like that and leave me hanging!" Jack glowered at him.

Frank sighed. He hadn't planned on going into any of this but Jack wouldn't be easily distracted and he was burning with curiosity as to what hold he had over Charles Boland. "Did Lynn tell you why we split up?"

"She said that Vincent gave you some cock-and-bull story that the two of them were involved, which you should have known straightaway was rubbish."

"Yes, I should have," Frank admitted. "And when I calmed down and Lynn and I discussed it, part of what she said just didn't make sense."

"Lynn wouldn't lie," Jack snapped angrily.

"That's not what I'm saying."

"Then stop talking in riddles, man, and spit it out."

"This puts me in a very awkward position, Jack," Frank said, feeling frustrated. He would love to tell Jack but it seemed disloyal. "It's not my place to tell you any of this. That should be up to Lynn."

Jack looked thoughtful for a moment. "I've lived in this town my whole life and there's not much goes on that I don't know or can't find out. If this business were all about Lynn, then I would go to her and ask her, but, if she's only a small part of this case that you're building, then don't you think I might be in a position to help?"

Frank looked at him. "You might," he agreed.

"And then, as Hannibal Lecter said, *quid pro quo*. I'll tell you about Charles Boland."

Frank chuckled. "Ah, you know how to arouse my curiosity, Jack. You're a terrible man."

"I do what I have to do." Jack settled back in the chair, cradling his pint.

"Okay, then, I'll tell you, but on one condition. You must never tell Lynn I told you. She would never forgive me."

"The last thing I want is to upset my daughter. I won't say anything; you have my word."

It was a horrific story, it sickened Jack and he wiped at his eyes with his handkerchief. But at the end there was one question uppermost in his head: "Are you sure that Vincent didn't rape Lynn?"

Frank didn't shrink from his gaze. "No, I'm not. She says he didn't but she might have lied because she knows how I'd react. I'd kill him."

"And I'd help you," Jack said.

"But instead I'm going to make sure he has to answer in a court of law for any girls he's abused."

Jack stared at him. "How many do you think there are?"

"Other than Lynn I only know of one but I suspect there are more. But that's a job for the police. The problem right now is that, in my experience of following assault cases, there has to be solid evidence before the police can prosecute and we don't have it — yet."

"So you're going to try and trap him at the Rince?" Jack surmised. It seemed a dodgy strategy to him. "You're surely not going to put some girl at risk?"

"Of course not. The police will be taking care of it and . . ." Frank shook his head. "I'd prefer not to say anything more, Jack. I don't want to jeopardize this. We have to get that bastard."

"They'd better get him, Frank, because he'll be a lot safer in jail than he will be in this town."

374

"You're right. Now, sir," Frank said, settling back, "*quid pro quo.*"

"It'll cost you a whiskey." Jack told him.

CHAPTER
THIRTY-FIVE

He settled back in his chair as Frank went to the bar and called for the drinks. He felt tired but, like Frank, driven. He had the sense that this was a pivotal moment in his life and that things in this town could change radically. He watched as Frank returned to the table, reluctantly placing the glass in front of him.

"Should you really be drinking this stuff?"

"Don't you start. I've enough people telling me what I should and shouldn't do and, all things considered, I don't think I'm managing too badly."

"You're doing great. Looking at you no one would know that you'd had brain surgery a few weeks ago."

"When I get tired my speech becomes slurred and I do get tired and weak easily, but the physio thinks that time will take care of that. I'm one of the lucky ones." He chuckled as Frank drummed his fingers on the table impatiently. "I suppose I'd better put you out of your misery."

Frank smiled. "I'd appreciate that."

"You know I haven't even told Nell or Lynn what I'm about to tell you. Apart from the legal eagles, it was between me and Charles."

Frank leaned forward in his chair, a captive audience.

"It all came about during the so called Celtic Tiger era when it was easy to make money. Charles in particular was raking it in. Do you know that at one stage he was charging a hundred and twenty euro per person per night at Hawthorn Lodge and getting it? I could have understood it if it was in a city centre — but in Rathbourne?" Jack shook his head as he thought back over those boom times. "He bought all the kids cars and a brand-new Merc for himself and another for Aideen. He bought a holiday home in Kerry and one in Italy."

"He always struck me as the sort of man who enjoyed the good life."

Jack laughed. "He made Hugh Hefner's lifestyle look tame back then. Now I have to admit I lost the run of myself too for a bit," he admitted. "I forked out over a hundred grand for a corporate box in Croke Park. You know how I love Gaelic football and hurling. I even brought a gang to see the Tina Turner and Garth Brooks concerts there." He sighed. "Madness, really. I'm embarrassed at the money I spent, although there's no harm in looking after good business contacts. But, that was my only real indulgence. Other than that, I carried on as normal, and I owed no one a penny.

"But Charles didn't know when to stop. It all seemed to go to his head. He wasn't just spending money on private indulgences, he was expanding his empire. He paid way over the odds for The Willows; had some idea of turning it into a swanky golf resort. He ran into

377

trouble with the planners and it cost him an arm and a leg and in the end he abandoned the idea. But he'd been after land at the back of Hawthorn Lodge for years. He wanted to extend the hotel so that he could build on a function room and a leisure centre, but the farmer, Drummond, would never agree to sell. And then he passed away and, as he was a bachelor, the farm and all the land was put up for sale. At this stage Charles was up to his eyes in debt because of the Willows fiasco, but he was desperate to get his hands on that land. But the banks were nervous and so he came to me."

"He asked you for a loan?" Frank stared at him.

Jack nodded. "I didn't hesitate. Charles is a good businessman. He took a lot more risks than I ever did but they usually paid off. The Willows was just bad luck. The plans he had for Hawthorn Lodge made sense and the hotel was already hugely successful. It couldn't fail. I knew my money was safe. So we got the papers drawn up, agreed an interest rate and that was that."

"And then the bottom fell out of the property market and Ireland went into meltdown," Frank said.

"Indeed. And Charles is up to his neck in it, though I don't think many people know that. He's always played his cards close to his chest. Anyway, in the middle of all this, Lynn had her breakdown." Jack stopped as he remembered the day that Lynn came and told them. Why hadn't he realized that there was more to it than met the eye? Nell had. She'd said he should go and talk to Charles, but Jack had promised Lynn

378

that he would never interfere in her life, and he didn't. "If she had only told me right away what was going on —"

"I know, Jack. But by then she found it very hard to talk about it and I suppose she just had to get through it in her own way."

"She wouldn't have had to go through it at all if she'd come to me. As soon as she told me the truth — well, what we thought was the truth — I called Charles and told him to settle and keep Vincent under control or I would call in the loan."

"I always wondered why he settled," Frank exclaimed. "He'd been so dismissive when we took the case and then, *bam!*, we get a call saying it's all over. It makes sense now why he backed down: you would have ruined him."

"I still might," Jack retorted as he thought of what his poor daughter had been through. "I told him after that night outside the shop that I wanted Vincent out of Rathbourne for good and he hasn't listened. The nerve of having him at the Rince Festival!"

"I think that's down to Aideen, not Charles. What you do about the loan is your business, Jack, but I think that you can rest assured that, after the Rince, Vincent won't be bothering anyone for a while. Even if he's given a light sentence the chances are that he'll end up on the sex offenders register."

"I wish I felt as confident as you, but it seems to me that it'll be hard to prove. How could all this have been going on under Charles's nose?" Jack felt the anger start to build in him all over again. "If it turned out he knew and did nothing I think I'd kill him with my bare hands."

"I don't believe Charles knew. From what I can gather, Vincent behaved himself while Charles was running the hotel. He could of course have been getting his kicks somewhere else. From listening to the various accounts, everyone knew that Vincent had a wandering eye and suspected him of the odd fling, but no one guessed there was anything more to it than that."

Jack sighed. "Like I said, it will be hard to prove him guilty. How much of what you've been told is hearsay?"

"I know. There's one person I would love to talk to who might know more, but I've been told he's too loyal to Charles to ever say a word against the Bolands."

"Who's that?" Jack asked, though he had a good idea whom Frank was referring to.

"The porter, Bob. He was the one who rescued Lynn and who apparently put Alenka to bed. I just wonder what else he knows. He was on duty those nights. He might remember details that the girls can't." Frank's expression darkened. "And if there are any other girls who ended up sleeping off their hangovers in Room 112."

Jack swirled the whiskey around in his glass. He wasn't too sure he wanted to know exactly what had happened to his daughter; he wasn't sure he could handle it. He'd always promised her he would protect her but she'd had no one to defend her that night. Perhaps he could help now. He looked across the table at Frank. "He'd talk to me."

★ ★ ★

380

Frank remembered to switch his phone back on only after he had dropped Jack home. There were several messages, all work-related except for a voicemail from Philip and a text from Lynn. He played Philip's first. "Dad, talk to Lynn, and soon."

Then he read Lynn's text.

NEED TO TALK. GIVE ME A CALL WHEN YOU GET A CHANCE.

It was nearly midnight but Frank decided to swing by the house and see if any lights were on. He wondered what, if anything, he should tell her. Perhaps it would be better to say nothing for now. It would be nice if they could just talk normally, as they used to. He missed that; he missed *her*. He hated waking up every morning and looking out at the view they had dreamed of enjoying together. He had to tell her that. He had to move back to Rathbourne and stay with her until she was in a position to leave. He had to show her that he didn't blame her for what happened with Vincent.

He drew up outside the house and his pulse quickened when he saw the bedroom light on. He could visualize her lying reading, probably wearing those skimpy pyjamas. He jumped out of the car determined to work things out with her. Perhaps within the hour they would be in bed together, without the pyjamas.

Lynn was in the process of packing the contents of her chest of drawers when the doorbell rang. Frowning, she

381

crossed to the window and peeked out. Frank's car was outside. Oh, hell, she hadn't expected him to come down from Dublin, at least not without calling first. Smoothing her hair, she hurried down to let him in.

"I got your text."

She stood gawping at him. Did she really have to do this now? "I thought you'd phone."

"Want to talk on the doorstep or are you going to let me in?" He smiled, his eyes twinkling.

"Oh, sure, sorry. The place is a bit of a mess." She opened the door and stood back.

He walked into the living room and stopped short when he saw the boxes and the stacks of DVDs, books and CDs around the floor. "What's going on?" He spun around to look at her. "Lynn, you're coming to Dublin?" He pulled her into his arms and kissed her. "My darling," he murmured against her lips. "You've made my day."

"No, Frank, sorry." Feeling dreadful, she pushed him away and went to sit down. "I'm going to stay with Val. I can't move in with you and it seems unfair to stay here when you could sublet the place and put the money towards the mortgage. And Val and John have broken up, so she offered to put me up."

"I see. I'm glad Val got rid of that guy. He's not good enough for her. You must be relieved."

"I am," Lynn admitted, but she couldn't return his smile.

"I've just spent the evening with your dad and he's not going to need you for much longer. So, for the sake of a couple of weeks — a month, tops — it's not worth subletting this place. But thank you for being so thoughtful."

Lynn almost groaned aloud. This would be much easier if he wasn't being so damn nice and didn't look so great. "It's not about Dad, Frank."

"Then what *is* it about?" He bent to examine the two stacks of DVDs by his feet. "Ah. One pile for me and one for you." He looked up, his eyes searching her face. "You said you wanted to talk to me. What is it that you want to say, Lynn?"

She swallowed hard before speaking. "I don't believe you will ever be able to look at me or touch me without thinking of me with Vincent. Whenever we row you'll throw it in my face. When we're at a party and you see me talking to another man you'll wonder if you can trust me. I'm sorry, Frank, but I can't live with that."

Frank came to sit on the sofa and took her hand. "You're wrong. It won't be like that."

"It will, and I'm not strong enough to go through that again. I can't marry someone who'll walk out on me every time something goes wrong."

He sighed. "I didn't exactly walk out."

"You did. And you left me at a time in my life when I was at my most vulnerable after promising that you would stay in Rathbourne until Dad didn't need me any more."

He stared at her. "So this isn't temporary? You're saying that we're finished?"

She shook her head in confusion. "I love you, Frank, and I know that I hurt you and —" He opened his mouth to interrupt her but she held up her hand. It

383

would be so easy to fall into his arms but she had to be honest with him. "I'm sorry," she continued. "But I've told you all this already. I can't marry someone who will leave at the first sign of trouble. I can't be with someone who won't fight for me."

He stared at her and she could see a range of emotions cross his face. Finally, he spoke and, when he did, he held on tight to her hand and looked her straight in the eye.

"There are things I can't explain now, things that I think would change how you feel. I'm sorry if I've let you down but . . ." He shook his head in frustration. "Move in with Val, Lynn, that's fine. But don't make any decisions yet. Don't tell me it's over. Take some time, as much time as you want, but don't say it's over. Not yet. Please?"

She looked into his eyes wondering what he was talking about but she knew that it would be a waste of time asking. He wouldn't tell her until he was ready. At least he hadn't just accepted her decision and turned on his heel, for that she was grateful.

He squeezed her hand. "Lynn?"

She nodded. "Okay."

"Thank you." He pressed her palm to his mouth and kissed it, just as he had on the day they had met, and then he stood up. "Goodnight, Lynn."

There was nothing Bob McCarthy enjoyed more on an evening off than to go down to the river and fish. It was a dull, calm evening; perfect. He never went to the popular spots where others would congregate and chat

384

and smoke and might even produce a hip flask and pass it round. Bob spent his whole day around people, and he went fishing to get away from them. He walked further along the bank with his bag and rod slung over his shoulder and his stool under his arm until he reached the spot where trees hid him from view of the others and the fish were drawn to the shade. This was the spot where he came to relax, to think, and sometimes to forget. Tonight he wanted to forget because his thoughts of late were troubling ones and guilt weighed heavily on his mind.

When Charles had packed Vincent off to The Willows he had been relieved, but, now Charles had gone off somewhere, Aideen was throwing her weight around and, unbelievably, it seemed that Vincent would host the Rince. Bob had been so sure that Charles had taken on board what he'd told him, but he obviously hadn't. What troubled Bob even more, though, was the fact that he hadn't taken it upon himself to go and talk to Charles. Everyone knew that Vincent was a philanderer, but it wasn't till the night that Lynn Stephens had called him that Bob had realized Vincent Boland might be something more sinister. And what had he done about it? Nothing.

"I thought I might find you here. You would pick the most difficult part of the bank to get to."

Bob looked up to see Jack Stephens limping towards him. He stood up immediately and helped him the last few steps before lowering him onto the stool. "Stupid bloody eejit! What are you doing down here in your condition?"

Jack waited to get his breath back before answering. "I wanted to have a private word, and there aren't many places in this town where that's possible."

"True for ye." Bob pulled a flask of tea from his bag and offered Jack a cup.

They sat in silence for a moment, but Bob knew in his heart what was coming. He supposed he'd been expecting it for months.

"It's about Vincent Boland." Jack took a sip.

"I thought that it might be."

"I only recently heard what happened at last year's Christmas party."

"I'm sorry, Jack."

"What have you to be sorry about?" Jack glanced up in surprise. "I wanted to thank you. If it wasn't for you . . . I'll always be grateful for that, Bob."

"If I'd spoken out about the bastard before then it might not have happened at all," Bob retorted. Jack's gratitude didn't make him feel any less guilty.

"Did he do it before?"

Bob sighed. "I'm not sure. I saw him messing around with a few young girls and, though I knew that he was taking advantage, I thought it was just a kiss and a cuddle. But one night he did what he did with Lynn. Put a girl up in the bedroom to sleep off the drink and then went home. But I spotted him later on coming in the back entrance and going upstairs. Now again, Jack, I didn't think that much about it. Trust me, when you're a night porter you see a lot of goings-on. He was a grown man, a Boland, and what he got up to was his own business. It was only after the night when Lynn phoned me for help that I got to thinking how many women he had forced himself on and how often he'd succeeded."

Jack looked up at him. "If Vincent was brought to court for an attack, would you be willing to give evidence?"

Bob didn't have to think about it. "Of course I would."

"It could cost you your job."

"It would give me peace of mind to know that I had finally done the right thing. Anyway, it's time I retired."

"Thanks."

Bob waved away his thanks. "Don't, Jack. Don't thank me for being a spineless old bastard who should have said something a long time ago."

CHAPTER
THIRTY-SIX

The day of the Rathbourne Rince Festival dawned bright and warm. A stage had been erected over the preceding days and multicoloured bunting was strung between the lampposts. Now the streets were being swept, stalls were being set up selling cakes, chocolates and ice creams, and a large marquee stood on the green across from the church. The playground of the primary school had been filled with bouncy castles and part of the playing field was cornered off for pony rides. The front office of the community centre was to be a first-aid room and there were posters everywhere detailing what kind of music could be heard and where.

The event would kick off with a parade at midday, then the playground would open and, around five in the afternoon, the main buffet would be served. The real fun would start afterwards. There would be every kind of dancing: tap, jiving, jigs and reels, line and set dancing, and even break dancing. Every venue in town had something going on and already tourists were arriving. The marquee would be cleared after the food and that was where most of the young people would gather when the volume was turned up, the lights were turned down and a DJ took over.

The parade went off without a hitch, and there was a wonderful buzz in the town. As soon as it ended, Lynn slipped away to the school and took up her position at the area set aside for the under-fives. She felt happier now that she was here and there was no chance of bumping into Vincent. She'd been nervous of Frank coming face-to-face with the man but thankfully he also seemed to be keeping a low profile. Vincent was now up on a stage presiding over events — the perfect master of ceremonies. It made Lynn sick that, despite everything, his life seemed to be carrying on as normal, whereas hers was in shreds.

She was leading a crying child with a cut knee towards the first-aid room when she spotted Frank on the other side of the road. Their eyes locked briefly and then he walked off in the direction of the green. She saw a man turn to look at him and got a start when she realized that it was the detective inspector, Adrian O'Sullivan.

He'd contacted her last week and explained that they were preparing a file on Vincent Boland and asked if she'd be willing to make a statement.

"I don't understand," she said when they met. "How can you prosecute him? How do you even know about me?"

"Frank Hayes suspected that you hadn't been the only woman that Vincent attacked and he did a little detective work. He was right. One of your colleagues was raped by Boland."

She looked at him in horror. "Who?"

"Alenka. You know her, I believe."

Shocked, Lynn nodded slowly. "I hired her." She looked at the detective. "Did this happen before or after he attacked me?"

"It's very recent."

He said they would arrest Vincent for Alenka's rape but first they wanted to gather as much evidence as they could and that it would help if she gave a statement about what he had done to her. She hadn't hesitated, but it had been tough. The man had been kind and sensitive but he'd still had to ask the hard questions, and it had taken a lot out of her. He explained that he had asked Frank not to discuss the matter with her before he had taken her statement.

"We don't want to lose this guy because of a slip-up, Lynn. So please, don't discuss it with anyone, not even your fiancé, not until Boland is arrested."

She'd been walking around in a daze since that day. All she could think of was Alenka. If she had gone to the police the girl would never have been raped. Even if she hadn't had the courage to go to the police, she could have put the word out in Hawthorn Lodge that they should avoid being alone with the man, especially if they were drinking.

Her eyes returned now to where Adrian stood with Frank. In frayed jeans and a colourful T-shirt he looked nothing like a detective inspector. Something was going to happen today, she could sense it. Why else would he have travelled down from Dublin? Maybe they were ready to arrest Vincent or maybe they just wanted to keep an eye on him later when the drink started to flow. She prayed, for Alenka's sake and any other woman he'd hurt or was planning to hurt, that they would get him.

Adrian was leaning on a wall and watching a young and very talented guy playing the fiddle, a few children dancing around his feet.

"All organized?" Frank asked keeping his eyes on the performance.

"Yeah." Adrian inclined his head in the direction of the stage. "So that's our man."

Frank's dark glasses hid his scowl. "It is. Have you seen Alenka?"

"Yes. I told her that she didn't have to be here but she insisted that she wanted to be. Celia Fagan sent me a text saying that there would be a few young women off duty tonight, among them Mareeka, so he'll have his pick, but of course we won't allow things to get that far."

"You're not using any *local* Gardaí, I hope. Vincent would know them all."

"No, but of course we've briefed them and if you look around, you'll see some here with their families. They'll be tipping us off if they see anything suspicious. Now go and do whatever you normally do at these things and try to look as if you're enjoying yourself."

"What I usually do is spend time with my fiancée, but she doesn't want anything more to do with me."

Adrian's eyes drifted to the playground. "Sorry to hear that. She's a nice girl."

Frank looked at him in surprise. "You've met her?"

"Of course. I had to take her statement, and Bob's too; they're both on board." Adrian patted his shoulder. "Don't worry. We're going to get this guy."

Frank watched him saunter off and glanced back at the playground. It felt wrong that he didn't know what was going on in Lynn's life. The thought of her going alone to the police station upset him; he should have been with her. He wondered how she felt about his playing amateur sleuth. Did she resent him for interfering and talking to the police about her private business without her permission? Did she understand why? She must be so upset about Alenka and he knew she would be blaming herself. How he'd like to take her in his arms and comfort her, but she'd avoided him like the plague today, so it seemed unlikely he'd get the chance.

Feeling totally fed up, he wandered off, pausing when Val gave him a friendly wave; she was standing in a queue at the ice cream stall. He went over to her. "I wasn't sure if you would be talking to me."

"Why wouldn't I be? You've done nothing wrong."

"Try telling Lynn that," he muttered.

Val stepped forward and ordered two cones. She handed him one.

"Thanks," he said, and they strolled on.

"She's hurt, Frank. She thinks that you don't trust her."

"Of course I trust her." He pushed his sunglasses up onto his forehead. "Yes, I wondered why she wasn't honest with me from the start, but wouldn't any man have been the same? I shouldn't have had to hear that from him."

"You can't believe she encouraged him," Val protested. "If it had been consensual, do you think she'd have given up the job she adored? Do you think she'd have changed so much, become afraid of her own shadow? You should have seen the state of her that evening outside the supermarket. She was shaking like a leaf."

He stopped and looked down at her. "Did he rape her, Val?"

"No!" Val frowned and he watched her as she went back over in her mind her conversations with Lynn. She shook her head slowly. "No, she'd have told me. She kept her secret for so long that I'm sure, when she finally opened up, it all flooded out."

"When did she tell you?" he asked.

"Not until you had the run-in with Vincent and moved out. And do you know why she didn't tell me? Because she knew, hot-head that I am, I wouldn't have been able to keep my mouth shut and she was afraid I'd lose my job. And you must realize why she didn't tell you."

He sighed. "Because I'd probably have broken his neck."

"She was protecting us. She would never have told a soul if Vincent hadn't made every day of her life since a living hell."

"He's not going to get away with it, Val, I promise you that."

"I hope you're right." She looked at her watch. "I'd better get back to work. Don't give up on her, Frank. She loves you but she's very fragile at the moment."

Frank nodded. "I know, Val. Thanks."

She gave him a quick hug. "See you later."

"What's going on?" Nell asked Jack as they settled in chairs to watch an Irish dancing display

"What do you mean?" Jack asked, innocently, his eyes trained on the dancers.

"You well know what I mean: you're keeping something from me. Meetings with Charles and Frank, disappearing off and not telling me where you're going. It's to do with Lynn, isn't it? Is there more trouble, Jack? Please tell me."

"No, love, everything's fine." He patted her knee.

"She was planning on going to live in Dublin, planning to get married, and instead she's moved in with Val. Things are hardly fine."

"Leave them to sort out their own lives, Nell. Lynn's a sensible girl and Frank's a good man."

His wife shook her head sadly. "Every time it looks like she's getting on top of things, something seems to happen to drag her down again. She should never have taken that settlement money. She should have taken Vincent Boland to court. He destroyed her."

"She's stronger than you think and you worrying about her won't change things. As for Boland, he'll get his comeuppance, don't you worry."

"There's something you're not telling me, I know it," she said crossly.

"Just relax and enjoy your day; *I* intend to. A few weeks ago I didn't think I'd be well enough to be here."

394

She smiled and squeezed his hand. "A few weeks ago I wasn't sure I'd still have you."

"Ah, ye thought you were going to be a merry widow with oul' fellas queuing up to dance with ye, is that it?"

"There's only one oul' fella I want to dance with."

He put his arm around her waist and gave her a squeeze. "You'll have to settle for a slow waltz, darling."

She kissed his cheek. "Gladly."

For the third time Lynn refused the offer of a break, despite the fact that she was thirsty and her neck felt burnt. But she was afraid of venturing outside the safety of the playground. She didn't want to bump into Frank. She really couldn't deal with him now. There was her mother to avoid, too. Any time she passed she looked in, her face creased with worry. Then there was that detective that she had to pretend she didn't know. And, of course, there was Vincent and his family. The street was full of bloody Bolands. But the person she feared meeting most was Alenka. If Lynn had been more courageous the girl would probably be married and back in Poland now. Her life was ruined and Lynn felt she was almost as much to blame as Vincent.

"Val thought you looked hot."

She turned and smiled gratefully as Lorcan leaned across the fence and passed her a bottle of cold water. "She's sweet."

His kind eyes looked at her in concern. "Surely you've done your bit for today — you've been here hours."

"I'm happier here. There are too many people around that I'd prefer not to meet." She glanced over at a table outside the nearby coffee shop where Orla, Aideen, Anne-Marie and Therese Boland sat.

"The food is about to be served. Why don't I escort you down to the marquee and get you a table with your folks?"

"I don't know . . ."

"Come on," he wheedled. "You know they'd be happier if you joined them. Angie's around somewhere and Val and I will be finishing up soon, if that troll Rhona turns up in time for her shift."

Lynn laughed. "Okay, then. I'll find someone to take over."

Fifteen minutes later, Lorcan strolled with her down the main street, a casual arm around her shoulders, chatting all the way to discourage anyone stopping them. She was laughing by the time they got inside the tent. "You should go into acting."

"I'm glad you appreciate my talents. Now keep talking and looking at me while I find a nice quiet spot for you to sit, then I'll get you something from the buffet."

A few minutes later she, Angie and her parents and some other close friends were sitting around a table next to a large party of tourists. Lynn had her back to the canvas wall and so there was no chance of anyone creeping up on her unawares. She had a perfect view of everything but at the same time it was easy for her to duck down if necessary. She felt a pang of guilt when she saw Frank in the doorway looking a little lost.

Her mother followed her gaze. "Let's invite him to join us."

"It's really not a good idea, Mum."

"Oh, come on, now. Whatever has happened between you, he's still been a good friend to this family."

She was right and Lynn was about to capitulate when Carrie walked in with Philip and his girlfriend. Putting a possessive arm through Frank's, Carrie pointed to a table on the opposite side of the marquee and the four of them went to sit down. "It looks as if he's got all the company he needs," Lynn murmured, feeling utterly miserable.

The evening dragged on and she was relieved when Val and Lorcan joined them. She exchanged a conspiratorial smile with Angie McCabe: it was clear that the couple were perfect for each other.

Val went to pour her a glass of wine. "No, not for me." If her instincts were right and something was going to happen, Lynn wanted all her wits about her. Currently, Vincent was sitting at a table in the centre of the room, with Orla, his mother and the rest of the Bolands. Where was Charles? she wondered. She couldn't remember his ever having missed a major event in Rathbourne. She searched the room, too, for Alenka, but couldn't spot her. Perhaps she was working.

At around eight everyone was asked to move outside while the tables were rearranged to make room for a dance floor, and the older crowd drifted off to the various events, leaving the young people to enjoy the loud music. "What do you want to do?" Val asked.

"I can't go back in there," Lynn murmured as a group from Hawthorn Lodge passed them on their way in. Alenka was with them and Lynn was surprised when their eyes met and the girl gave her a quick, friendly smile.

"Let's just take a few chairs and sit outside," Lorcan suggested.

"Good idea," Val said. "It's too stuffy in there, anyway."

"You know what?" said Lynn. "I think I'll go to Mum and Dad's and put my feet up for a while. Those kids were exhausting."

"Do you want me to come with you?" Val offered immediately.

"No, stay and enjoy yourself. I'll be fine." As Lynn walked away she caught sight of Frank standing alone. She went over to him. He brightened when he saw her.

"Hi."

"Hi. Philip's girlfriend looks nice."

"Julia? Yes, she is. Do you want to join us?"

"No, thanks, I have some things I need to do. Will you text me if . . ." — Lynn met his eyes — "if anything happens?"

"Of course."

"Thanks."

"Lynn," he said, but she walked away, pretending she hadn't heard.

In her parents' house, she flopped onto the sofa, kicked off her sandals and reached for the TV remote. She needed some distraction.

What the hell was that infernal noise? Lynn opened her eyes. It took a moment to get her bearings. The sound, she realized, was coming from her mobile phone, which had slipped out of her pocket and was wedged down the side of the chair. By the time she dug it out it had stopped ringing, but there was a voicemail. It was Frank.

"Lynn? Get down to the marquee."

She looked at her watch and was amazed to see it was nearly eleven. Having tugged on her sandals, she ran out of the house and down the street. The music emanating from the marquee was loud and it looked packed; the smokers were chatting and dancing outside. She edged her way past them and wondered how she would spot Vincent in this chaos and without his seeing her. But, as she stood there, a hand took hers and she looked up to see Frank.

"This way," he murmured.

He drew Lynn through the crowd and then pulled her into his arms and started to sway with her to the music. "Look over my shoulder at the table directly behind the girl in the red dress."

Distracted by Frank's closeness and the heat of his hands through the thin material of her dress, she had to concentrate to follow his instructions and saw Vincent, as she had seen him on many an occasion, full of chat and smiles and pouring wine liberally.

"Where's Orla?" she asked.

"Gone home. Aideen and the others are in the pub at the jazz session."

Lynn's eyes returned to Vincent and his staff. The table was rowdy and boisterous and most of them seemed more than a little drunk except for Celia, Alenka and another young girl that Lynn didn't recognize. They were chatting with Vincent, and Lynn was amazed at Alenka's composure. She was one hell of a good actress. Vincent reached for a jug of orange juice and topped up the two girls' glasses, bending to whisper something into the younger girl's ear, and then, suddenly, Adrian O'Sullivan was behind him, flanked by three other men. "Look!" She swivelled Frank around to watch.

Adrian flipped out his ID. "Vincent Boland?"

"Yes." Vincent looked up in confusion.

"I'm Detective Inspector Adrian O'Sullivan and I have reason to believe that you are in possession of drugs."

There was a break in the music and his words caused a sudden hush and several heads to turn to see what was going on.

Lynn looked at Frank. "Drugs? What's he talking about?"

Vincent laughed. "That's ridiculous. Of course I'm not."

"If you would step outside, sir . . ."

At this stage a small crowd had gathered to watch, mesmerized and though the DJ had put on another track he'd turned the volume way down, obviously as curious as everyone else.

"That's preposterous," Vincent blustered. "You have no right to treat me like this."

Adrian didn't raise his voice but every word was as clear as crystal. "Under Section 23 of the Misuse of Drugs Act, I have every right to search you. Now we can go outside or you can come down to the station."

His face puce, Vincent left with them, Lynn, Frank and many others hurrying after them.

There was a police car outside and Adrian led him to it and watched as Vincent was frisked by a uniformed officer. Moments later the Garda turned and handed Adrian a bubble pack.

"Read him his rights," Adrian said after examining it and walked over to Frank. "You were spot on. Well done."

Lynn looked from him to Frank just as Alenka pushed her way through the crowd to join them.

"Drugs? I do not understand," she said, her face pale.

Frank took her and Lynn to one side. "You weren't drunk," he told them. "Vincent put Rohypnol in your drinks, more commonly known as the date-rape drug."

Alenka stared at Vincent, her eyes wide with shock. Lynn put an arm around her. "Are you okay?"

She nodded dumbly, her eyes still on Vincent as he was handcuffed and pushed into the back of the car.

After having a word with the other policemen, Adrian came over to join them.

"Good job," Frank said and shook his hand.

"What happens now?" Lynn asked.

"He'll be charged. He'll probably try to get bail but we'll fight that. There are a number of charges against him; Alenka's is the strongest. But what can sometimes happen is that, once someone is charged, other victims and witnesses come forward." Adrian looked at Alenka. "Are you okay? I can arrange for someone to drive you home."

"I'll take her," Frank said.

"I'll come with you," Celia came forward and put her arm through the girl's.

Frank hesitated for a moment and looked at Lynn. "Will you be okay?"

"She'll be fine."

Lynn felt an arm round her shoulders and looked up to see her father was beside her.

"Come on, sweetheart. Let's go home."

CHAPTER
THIRTY-SEVEN

Stunned and frightened, Aideen gathered Charles's three daughters and they went back to Hawthorn Lodge. She left them in a small meeting room on the ground floor and went down the corridor to Charles's office to use the phone.

"Hello?"

"Charles?" Aideen frowned. Had she dialled the wrong number? The voice at the other end sounded weak and frail.

"Yes, Aideen, what is it?"

"It's Vincent, he's been arrested. You must come home."

"Arrested? Really."

Aideen frowned. He didn't seem concerned or very interested. "Charles, are you listening to me? The police arrested him at the Rince, in front of everyone. They said they found drugs on him."

"Ha, drugs as well? Your son is some fucking idiot."

"Charles!" She was as shocked by his language as she was by his lack of concern.

"Aideen, I have done all I can for your son," he said, sounding weary. "You're on your own."

She stared at the phone in her hand. "But you said you'd look after us."

"And I have."

"I can't do this alone, Charles. I need you," she said, feeling the panic rise in her chest. "He's going to need the best legal team."

Charles laughed but it was a weak, feeble sound. "Is Emer there?"

"Yes, the three girls are here with me at the hotel. Please come, Charles."

"Put Emer on."

"Charles —"

"Aideen, I can't talk for long. Please, let me speak to my daughter."

Aideen stormed into the meeting room and held the mobile out to her niece. "Your father wants to talk to you."

"Dad?" Emer looked surprised and, taking the phone, went outside. Aideen paced the room while they waited.

"Come and sit down," Therese said kindly. "Have some tea. I'm sure there's just been a misunderstanding and Vincent will be home soon."

"We should tell Orla," Anne-Marie said.

"No!" Aideen massaged her temples, trying to think of a way out of this mess. She was still reeling from Charles's attitude. "Orla's probably fast asleep. There's no point in disturbing or upsetting her."

"Someone should be with her," Therese pointed out. "She's so near her time."

"You're right." Aideen nodded. "Would you, dear?"

404

"Yes, of course." Therese stood up and kissed her aunt's cheek. "Try not to worry."

As she was walking out, Emer returned.

"I'm going to keep an eye on Orla. Text me if there's any news."

Emer hugged her sister. "I will."

"Well?" Aideen said impatiently.

"Anne-Marie, would you mind?" Emer shot her other sister a meaningful look.

"No, that's fine." She jumped to her feet and kissed her sister and aunt. "Call if you need me."

When they were alone, Emer gestured for her aunt to take a seat and she put the file she'd been holding on the table before her. "Please sit down, Aideen," she said with quiet authority.

"We've no time for sitting around, Emer. We need to get Vincent out of prison."

"Aideen, please," Emer said, with barely concealed patience.

She sat and watched her niece open the file. "What's that?"

"My father has had to make some changes in the company structure."

"Yes, yes I know, but this is hardly the time to discuss that, Emer. We must act quickly —"

"Aideen, you need to listen," Emer insisted.

The girl had a look of her father. Funny, that had never struck her before. "Go on, then."

"These are difficult times in the hospitality industry and we've been struggling to survive them. Vincent's behaviour hasn't helped and may cost us a great deal."

Aideen flushed. It was one thing discussing Vincent's indiscretion with Charles but quite another with her youngest niece. And what was she talking about? The fact that Charles had given Vincent some land? It was a drop in the ocean to Charles. Was this some sort of jealousy or begrudgery?

"The company's in serious debt. Not only do we owe money to the banks but also to Jack Stephens."

Aideen was incredulous. "We owe Jack money? That's nonsensical."

"No, it is fact. Jack loaned Dad the money to buy Drummond's land and finance the extension. As a result of Vincent's behaviour, Jack will probably call in the debt. If he does that, he will bankrupt us."

"You must be wrong. Charles was only telling us recently about his plans to expand into the Midlands."

"It was all lies to get Vincent out of town and so as not to arouse Orla's suspicions. There will be no expansion. If anything, we'll have to sell off some property to keep the company afloat."

"But Charles said he would look after us."

"And he has. Three of the off-licences will be transferred into your name. It's up to you what you do with them. But there is a condition."

"Which is?" Aideen said coldly.

"You sell us your shares in the business."

"You're cutting us off," Aideen said, faintly. "You are cutting me and my son out of the family."

"Yes, Aideen," Emer said bluntly. "It's no reflection on you. Father has only been so generous because of you and, of course, Uncle Desmond. But Vincent is a

406

loose cannon. He could destroy the entire business and we can't allow that."

"But you must help me! We'll need the best legal team to defend Vincent —"

"You're not listening. There is no money. You will have to pay Vincent's legal fees or apply for legal aid."

"This is you speaking, not Charles," Aideen said angrily. "Your father would never let me down like this. When he gets back, I'll tell him exactly how you've treated me, young lady. He's the boss."

"Dad won't be coming back, Aideen," Emer said, her eyes sad. "He's dying. As for the boss, you're talking to her."

"Rape?" Nell stared at him.

"That's what he's been charged with," Frank confirmed, "among other things."

"Unbelievable." Nell shook her head. She poured a mug of tea for her daughter. "Do you want to take this in to Lynn?"

"Would *you?* I just need a word with Jack first," Frank said.

She eyed the pair of them suspiciously but took the tea and closed the door behind her.

"Quite a night," Jack said. "Did you know about the drugs?"

"I guessed. I'm sorry I couldn't say anything; it was just a hunch."

"I understand and I appreciate the lengths you've gone to."

"What will you do about the loan?" Frank asked.

"Nothing. Charles and I had a meeting last week and we made a deal. Vincent has effectively been fired. The off-licences, with the exception of the one in Rathbourne, will be put in Aideen's name and it will be up to her to employ him."

"Well done. If he does walk free it's nice to know he'll have less opportunity to prey on innocent women."

"We agreed on something else, too." Jack looked at him. "Lorcan O'Brien will come in and manage the supermarket for a year but still be on Boland's payroll."

"That's fantastic, Jack. It'll give you a chance to recover properly."

"Yes, I'm happy about it. The lad has a good head on his shoulders." Jack looked at him. "And it means that you can take Lynn to Dublin and start your new life."

Frank shook his head sadly. "She doesn't want me, Jack."

"Of course she does," Jack retorted as Nell walked back in the door.

"Will you stop messing about and get in there and talk to her?" Nell glowered at Frank. "You two have wasted enough time."

Lynn sat huddled on the sofa, the mug of tea in her hands. She couldn't get the image of a pale, shocked Alenka out of her head. Lynn had felt so sorry for her. And then there was Orla. Had she heard what had happened yet? Lynn regretted the timing of the arrest, the girl must be only days away from giving birth. But then, was there a good time to find out that you were married to a monster? For her own part, Lynn felt a burden had lifted. She had been drugged. It wasn't her fault that she'd behaved the way she had and it was a miracle she hadn't ended up in Alenka's position. She was grateful that Frank had kept digging until he found out the truth. She assumed this was the reason he'd asked her to hold off on making a decision about splitting up. But still . . .

There was a tentative knock on the door and she looked up to see the man himself.

"Can I come in?" he asked.

"Sure."

He sat down on the chair facing her. "How are you doing?"

"I'm okay." She was silent for a moment, and then she looked up at him. "Why did you do it?"

"What?"

"Adrian says that you're the one who uncovered this whole business about Alenka. Why?"

"Because, once I got over my stupid jealousy and thought about it, I knew it didn't make sense. You never drink much and on the few occasions that I have seen you overindulge you just got incredibly giggly and wanted to dance all night."

She stared at him. That was true! Why hadn't that occurred to her before?

"And then I read a piece in the paper about a guy who'd been convicted of rape; he'd used the date-rape drug and that's what got me thinking. I remembered Calum asking you for names of staff members that you

409

felt would stand up for you and I went and talked to them and, well, that eventually led me to Alenka."

Lynn searched his face. "How is she?"

He shook his head. "Not good. I think she's in shock. She was shaking so much in the car that we were afraid to leave her alone, so Celia took her back to her place and she was going to call her doctor to give her something."

"And she still has the trial to face."

"You may have to testify, Lynn," he warned.

"I know."

He ran a weary hand through his hair. "I hate the thought of you having to go through that. I was so bloody naïve. I thought you would all be happy once he was arrested but now I'm beginning to think that I've made things worse. Perhaps you would all be better off if I hadn't stirred things up."

"Nonsense, you've probably saved other women from being abused."

"Yes. You're right. But there are no winners here, are there?"

Lynn shook her head. "It's Orla I feel really sorry for. This should be the happiest time in her life."

"She'd be better off leaving him and going to live with her mother. Life with Aideen won't be easy without the darling boy around."

Lynn sank back into the cushions. He was right. There really were no winners. Even if Vincent was prosecuted he might only serve a couple of years, yet he had destroyed so many lives. "Why didn't you tell me

410

that you suspected Vincent had drugged me?" she asked, suddenly curious.

"You forget what I do for a living, darling. I knew that if I said anything it could prejudice a case against him. Believe me, it hasn't been easy keeping this from you. There were so many times I wanted to call you and talk to you but, if I put the idea in your head before you'd given a statement, it could have screwed everything up."

"You could have kept your secrets, Frank, but you didn't have to leave me."

His tortured eyes met hers. "I know. That was wrong of me. I was just so angry. Even when I thought it was the drink I believed you when you said that nothing had happened. I just couldn't get the image out of my head of him undressing you, seeing your body, touching you —"

"Don't you think that upset me too?" she cried. "It was my body! But you didn't think of me and how I felt. You just thought about how he had touched something belonging to *you*."

"That's not fair —"

But Lynn had been silent too long and now that she had started she couldn't stop. "Don't you realize I lay in bed every night wondering exactly what he had done? Don't you understand that I hated myself for drinking and giving him that opportunity? Have you any idea of the guilt I felt, of how hard it's been to look in the mirror since that night? But every day I had to pretend that I was fine and every day he harassed me,

humiliated me and intimidated me. Every day, Frank."
She sobbed. "Every bloody day."

He moved over onto the sofa beside her. "I'm sorry,
Lynn, I'm sorry." He kissed the tears from her eyes. "I
hate what he did to you, how he took advantage of you,
and I hate that you were afraid to tell me and I hate
that I haven't stood by you. I should never have gone to
Dublin. I'm sorry."

But she still couldn't stop. "I don't know how you
could even think I would want him. Haven't I shown
you time and time again with my words, my actions and
my body how much I love you?" She grabbed the lapels
of his jacket and shook him, staring angrily into his
eyes, the tears streaming down her face. "Haven't I?
Haven't I?"

He stroked her hair and looked down at her, his eyes
full of pain. "Yes." He pulled her tight against him.

She was stiff in his arms. She loved him so much but
she was hurt and damaged and tired, so very, very tired.

"Forgive me," he murmured.

She felt him kiss her hair and then her neck and her
shoulder and the anger began to drain away.

"Come home with me, Lynn and from this moment
on I promise never to let you down again."

He kept kissing her and she felt herself weaken, but
how could she be sure she could trust him? She pulled
away and cupped his face in her hands. "Let's say I
come to Dublin with you and we live in that wonderful
house together."

He started to smile at the thought.

412

"And then Vincent's trial begins and he gets up there and starts telling lies about how we were having an affair, that I was mad for him. How will you feel if he starts describing our love-making that night?" She watched Frank flinch. "You see? This is never going to go away."

He was silent for a moment. "I love you and I'm a jealous man. You love me, I know you still do, Lynn, and you understand jealousy. You've always been jealous of Carrie, though in your heart you know that you had no reason to be, don't you?"

She nodded reluctantly.

"We can cut our losses and say goodbye and both be miserable or we can stay together, be together, and take each day as it comes. And if, when the trial comes around, I let you down you can walk away. But, Lynn, I have learned a lot about myself these last few months. I've learned that I have a lot of faults but I've also learnt that I have found the love of my life and I'm not ready to give you up without a fight." He bent his head and kissed her, a tender, sweet, gentle kiss full of love and sorrow and remorse. "Have you learnt anything?" he asked.

She thought about it as she finally relaxed in his arms. The anger was gone. All that was left was a feeling of sorrow and pity for Alenka, Orla and even Aideen and Charles. But, with sudden clarity, she realized, what had got her through these last couple of months was her dad. Seeing him in that hospital bed so close to death had brought home what real pain was and she felt angry with Vincent and with herself for the months she'd spent cloistered away from the world. "I don't think I've learned much but I've been reminded what a great friend Val is. How lucky I am to have such great parents and . . ."

He looked into her eyes. "And?"

"That I love you so much, sometimes it hurts. Sometimes it hurts a lot."

He looked sad. "I don't want to hurt you ever, Lynn."

She hugged him. "I know that but it's inevitable."

"Don't say that, it's depressing!"

"But true. You always hurt the one you love."

He groaned. "You robbed that from a greeting card."

She smiled reluctantly. "I do love you, Frank."

He combed his fingers through her long hair. "You know what I would like to do more than anything right now?"

"Tell me." She looked up into his face and wished there was some way of capturing the expression in his eyes and then she could look at it whenever she had doubts.

"I want to take you back to Dublin. I want to make love to you in our bed."

She swallowed hard and put a hand up to his cheek.

He grasped it and turned his mouth to press a kiss into her palm. "I want to fall asleep with you tight in my arms and I want your face to be the first thing that I see when I open my eyes."

She groaned and went to pull his mouth to hers but he wasn't finished.

414

"I want us to lie like that for hours, not saying a word, just looking out over Dublin Bay together. I want us to stay like that, Lynn, until you believe, until you *know*, that I will never leave you again." He traced his thumb across her lips and searched her face. "What do you say, Lynn?"

"I say," she kissed him gently and smiled into his eyes, "take me home, Frank."